Lan had stopped th......... .... .g., ... all he was doing was *feeling*. It was pure fear, and barely contained rage that consumed him, the ice of panic, the heat of anger, contending for his mind. There wasn't much room left over for thought.

He struggled to hold in the rage; somehow he felt dimly that if he couldn't keep control over it, something terrible and irrevocable would happen. But the part of him that tried to hang onto a little rational thought was also the part that *hurt*. The blinding pain of the worst headache he had ever felt without passing out entirely was slowly eroding his ability to hang onto his anger.

The pain of the lash was worse than anything Lan had ever felt. It cut right through the headache, broke his paralyzing fear, and left him with only instinct.

He *had* to get away! *He had to get away, and now!*

The fear joined the anger, and together they destroyed the last of his rapidly eroding control over that overpowering rage—and the terrible thing that his rage had summoned. . . .

NOVELS BY **MERCEDES LACKEY**
available from DAW Books:

*Forthcoming in hardcover from DAW Books

BRIGHTLY BURNING

BRIGHTLY BURNING

MERCEDES LACKEY

DAW BOOKS, INC.
DONALD A. WOLLHEIM, FOUNDER
375 Hudson Street, New York, NY 10014

ELIZABETH R. WOLLHEIM
SHEILA E. GILBERT
PUBLISHERS
www.dawbooks.com

To all the unsung heroes
who stood by
on the evening of December 31, 1999
to ensure that we crossed into the year 2000
with our safety, security, and peace intact.

OFFICIAL TIMELINE FOR THE

by Mercedes Lackey

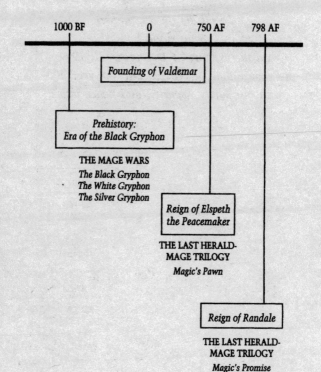

1000 BF   0   750 AF   798 AF

Founding of Valdemar

Prehistory:
Era of the Black Gryphon

THE MAGE WARS

The Black Gryphon
The White Gryphon
The Silver Gryphon

Reign of Elspeth
the Peacemaker

THE LAST HERALD-
MAGE TRILOGY

Magic's Pawn

Reign of Randale

THE LAST HERALD-
MAGE TRILOGY

Magic's Promise
Magic's Price

BF *Before the Founding*
AF *After the Founding*

HERALDS OF VALDEMAR SERIES

Sequence of events by Valdemar reckoning

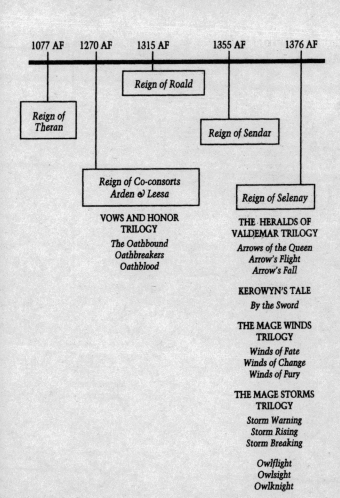

| 1077 AF | 1270 AF | 1315 AF | 1355 AF | 1376 AF |

Reign of Roald

Reign of Theran

Reign of Sendar

Reign of Co-consorts Arden & Leesa

Reign of Selenay

VOWS AND HONOR TRILOGY

The Oathbound
Oathbreakers
Oathblood

THE HERALDS OF VALDEMAR TRILOGY

Arrows of the Queen
Arrow's Flight
Arrow's Fall

KEROWYN'S TALE

By the Sword

THE MAGE WINDS TRILOGY

Winds of Fate
Winds of Change
Winds of Fury

THE MAGE STORMS TRILOGY

Storm Warning
Storm Rising
Storm Breaking

Owlflight
Owlsight
Owlknight

ONE

LAVAN Chitward hated his mother's parties at the best of times, and this one was no exception. When the Guildmaster of the Cloth Merchants' Guild beckoned to him, he unconsciously hunched his shoulders, assuming he was about to receive yet another homily on hard work, his third for this particular party.

"Here you go, lad," the Guildmaster said, shoving a parcel at him.

Lan gaped at the squarish package in the Guildmaster's hands as the babble of partygoers rattled on around him. Words stuck in Lavan's throat, uncomfortable and sharp-edged. *Oh, gods. Now what am I supposed to say?* He was already nervous enough before this guest of his parents singled him out; this only made him more self-conscious. Lavan flushed, forehead sweating, and could only stare at the so-called "present" that middle-aged, red-faced Guildmaster Howell was holding out to him, and tried to think of a response. Any response. Well, maybe not *any* response; if he said what he really thought, his father would skin him.

"Uh—this is—you really shouldn't have gone to so much trouble, Guildmaster," he managed, his stomach churning, as the older man thrust the package at him with hands from which traces of dye would never disappear as long as he lived. The skin was faintly blue, but the nail bed was indigo, giving Lan the unsettling impression he was taking a package from a corpse. The Guildmaster shoved the packet into Lavan's reluctant fingers and let it go, forcing Lan to take it or let it fall. And much as he would have liked to let it fall, he knew that he would never hear the end of it if he did. He fumbled for it and tried not to show how little he wanted it.

His hands closed around it convulsively, and the cloth package fell open, revealing a set of cloth-merchant's tools. There was a lens for examining fabric closely, a rule to determine thread count, a small pair of scissors, other things—exactly what he'd dreaded seeing.

"It was no trouble, no trouble at all!" the Guildmaster said heartily, the corners of his eyes wrinkling as he smiled. "I've outfitted six of my own youngsters for the cloth trade, after all, and I can't think how many others I'm not even related to!" He clapped Lavan heartily on the back, and Lan tried not to wince. "I'll be seeing you in and around the Guildhouse before too long, I'll warrant! Just like your big brother!"

"Ah—" Lavan mumbled something and ducked his head, his hair dampening with nervous perspiration; as he'd hoped, the Guildmaster took his reluctance for shyness, and clapped him on the back again, though a bit gentler this time.

The Guildmaster moved on then, to socialize with the adults, sparing Lavan the task of trying to thank him for a gift the young man didn't in the least want. A quick glance around the crowd in the drawing room showed him that no one was paying any attention to him at the moment, so he hastily rolled up the bundle of tools and shoved it under the cushions on a settle. With any luck, it wouldn't be found until morning, and the servants would assume it belonged to Lan's older brother. He rubbed his damp palms against the legs of his trews and straightened, looking about him. What would Lavan do with a bundle of cloth-merchant's tools, anyway? He didn't know what half of them were used for!

Nothing, that's what. And I don't want to either. I don't want to do anything with cloth but wear it.

In fact, he intended to escape from this gathering as soon as he dared. All of the first-floor rooms of this town house were packed with his parents' guests, all of them important, none of them younger than thirty. It was too hot, too claustrophobic, too loud; the cacophony of voices made his ears ring. The house seemed half its size and it wasn't all that big in the first place, compared with the house Lan thought of as "home," back in Alderscroft. This party wasn't intended to entertain anybody under the age of twenty, anyway, even though the stated reason for it was for the members of the Needleworkers' and Cloth Merchants' Guilds to welcome the whole family to Haven. Lan's mother Nelda and his father Archer were already well known to the members of their Guilds. In spite of living in a village a hundred leagues from Haven, their successes had brought them to the attention of nearly everyone in both Guilds in the capital long before this move. This gathering was supposed to be an opportunity for their children to mix and mingle with the real powers in their parents' Guilds, and hopefully to attract the attention of a potential master to 'prentice to. Samael, Lan's older brother, was already apprenticed to one of their father's colleagues; the other children were of an age to be sent to masters themselves, or so Nelda and Archer kept telling them. No child would be apprenticed to his own parents, of course; a parent couldn't be expected to be objective about teaching him (or her). While an oldest son and heir *might* eventually join his parents in the parents' business, it wouldn't be until he had achieved Mastery or even Journeyman status on his own.

The bare idea of working with his father, even as an equal partner, depressed Lan beyond telling. And this party was just as depressing. He could hardly wait to get out of there. Every passing moment made him feel as if he was smothering.

Sam, Macy, and Feoden could and would more than make up for Lavan's absence. *They* wanted to be here, hovering around the edges of conversations, respectfully adding their own observations when one or another of the adults spoke to them. He only needed to look as if he was circulating long enough for the party to get well underway and the ale to loosen tongues and fog memories—then he could escape.

So to speak. He couldn't get out of the house, but at least he could go somewhere he wouldn't be interrogated by people he didn't know and didn't want to know.

He pretended to busy himself arranging and rearranging the platters of food on the tall buffet near the windows, watching the reflections in the window. His hair clung unpleasantly to his forehead—it really was horribly warm in the room, but it didn't seem to bother anyone else. The many, tiny diamond-shaped panes broke up the reflection into an odd little portrait gallery of the notables of the merchant community of Haven. Lavan didn't know most of their names, and couldn't care less who they were; his attention was on their reactions, their expressions. He was waiting for the time when things were relaxed, and people weren't paying any real attention to anything but having a good time.

As the party continued and mulled wine and ale flowed freely, faces grew flushed and less guarded, voices became a trifle louder, and conversations more

animated. At that point, Lavan figured it was safe for
him to leave.

Just to be certain no one would stop him, he picked
up an almost-empty platter of pastry-wrapped sau-
sages and took it with him, heading in the direction
of the kitchen. If anyone who knew him saw him,
they'd assume he was being helpful.

The kitchen was overly full with all the extra servers
that his parents had hired for the occasion. They
barely had room to move about, edging past each
other with loaded platters held high overhead, and he
simply slipped a long arm just inside the door, left the
platter on a bit of empty counter space, and made a
quick exit up the servants' stair just off the hall that
led to the kitchen. This was quite a "modern" house,
unlike their home in the country, one that wasted
space on hallways rather than having rooms that led
into one another. There was one between the kitchen,
the pantries, the closets, and the rest of the first-floor
rooms. The hallway delineated the boundaries of
"masters' territory" and "servants' territory" and for
some reason that fact brought a tiny smile of satisfaction to his mother's face every time she looked at
the hall.

Lavan was grateful for the hall; it allowed him to
get into the upper stories without anyone at the party
spotting him. He didn't go to his room on the second
floor, though—he'd be far too easy to find there. Instead, he headed for the attics up above the servants'
third-floor rooms.

It wasn't likely that anyone would look for him
here. The previous occupant of this town manor had
taken all of his rubbish with him (or sold it off to rag
pickers), and the current occupants didn't have much
to encumber the space. Lan's mother had seen to it
that the attics had been scrubbed out as thoroughly
as the rest of the house before the family moved in,
so dust was at a minimum. All that was up here was
the stuff that had been too good to leave behind, but

wasn't immediately useful. Here were the few articles
of valuable furniture—as opposed to the country-built
stuff they'd left behind—that didn't (yet) fit anywhere
in the house or which needed repairs that hadn't been
done. The rest was bales and boxes; the heavy woolen
blankets, featherbeds, furs, coats, and clothing packed
in lavender and cedar chips awaiting the cold of winter, and the oddments that had been given to the family by important friends or relatives that were too
hideous to display on a daily basis but no one dared
get rid of.

Lan opened the attic door and stepped softly in; it
was very dark, and he took a moment to let his eyes
adjust to the gloom. At last, he had come to a place
where the air was comfortably cool, and the sweat
quickly dried on his forehead and the back of his neck.
The scent of strong soap mixed with herbs still lingered in the air, and the gable windows glowed with
the light from the party lanterns in the rear and the
streetlamp in the front. The sound of the party was a
dull drone up here, but the hired musicians in the
garden were actually easier to hear than they'd been
in the drawing room.

Avoiding the dim bulk of the stored furnishings,
Lan reached the nearest window without mishap.
Once he opened the window and flung himself down
on a pile of featherbeds and comforters, it was rather
pleasant up in the attic. Or, at least, it wasn't as bad
as it was downstairs.

He could hide out here for as long as it took for
the party to end. Although once the noise began to
ebb, he knew he'd better sneak back downstairs again,
and pretend he'd been there all night.

I wish I could hide out here forever.

He closed his eyes and listened to the music. It
wasn't what he would have chosen himself, of course;
it was rather old-fashioned and played in a manner
that suggested the musicians themselves were well
aware that they were only there to provide a kind of

pleasant background to conversation. Innocuous, that was the best word for it. Lan didn't much care for innocuous music, but he wasn't the one paying the minstrels' fee.

As his father so often repeated, the one who paid the musician had the right to call the tune. However, that old saw was repeated with a sidelong, meaningful glance at his middle son.

Lan's stomach knotted up again. *As if I would ever forget. . . .*

NO one noticed his defection, or he would have heard about it over breakfast. He kept quiet as Sam bolted his food and headed off to his work with Master Iresh, and as his younger sibs chattered excitedly about the important people who'd taken notice of them. Lavan muttered something about the Guildmaster in response to a direct question, but let Macy and Feodor take center stage. They chattered with animation about all the important people who had spoken with them, and Nelda nodded approvingly.

Lan's food was as tasteless as bark and loam. He ate without speaking and left the table almost as quickly as Sam had, retreating to a window seat just off the lesser sitting room where he hoped he would be sufficiently out of the way to be ignored or forgotten. In a few moments after he had settled in, the door to the street opened and closed—that would be Feo, going to join their father. Macy's footsteps faded off in the direction of the workroom, where she would toil diligently and happily on embroidery or lace-making for the rest of the morning. Though she was only fourteen, her work was good enough that she won praise from everyone who saw it.

Now if Mother is just thinking about them and not about me as she gets ready to leave. . . .

No such luck. He heard his mother's footsteps, but didn't turn to look at her, hoping she still might ignore him. "Lan?" she said, and when he didn't respond to her call, she repeated *"Lan?"* in a sharper tone that warned him not to pretend he hadn't heard.

Lavan looked away from the window toward his mother, a dull apprehension making him clench his jaw—not that he'd been really looking outside. There wasn't that much to look at; just the tiny little kitchen garden of their town house, surrounded by a high, stuccoed wall to separate their minuscule yard from the neighbor's equally minuscule yard. But it was better than staring out the window in his room, which opened out to a charming view of the blank wall of the neighbor's town house. And anyway, the servants would be in his room cleaning for another candlemark. He couldn't take refuge up there until they'd gone because they'd just chase him out again with their dusting and sweeping.

"Shouldn't you be doing something?" Lavan's mother asked, her brows knitted with irritation. Her frown deepened when he shrugged, unable to think of an acceptable answer.

Nelda had kept the splendid figure of her youth, and either through luck or artifice her auburn hair showed not a strand of gray. She was dressed for a meeting of the Needleworkers' Guild, in her fine, russet-brown lambswool gown trimmed with intricate bobbin lace of her own making and design, the sash of her office as Guild Representative of five counties so covered with embroidery that there was not a single thread of the original fabric showing. Lavan had taken very little care with his own clothing, in no small part as a kind of act of defiance. Trews and tunic claimed from his older and taller brother had once been black, but had faded to a washed-out gray, and he wouldn't let his mother redye them. He was afraid if she got her hands on them, or any of his clothing, she'd make them . . . cheerful. And cheerful was very far from the way he felt since the move to Haven.

His mother was clearly torn between what she saw as her duty to her son and her duties to her Guild. She hesitated, then solved her dilemma by snapping, "Well, *find* something!" as she hurried out the door, the heels of her scarlet leather boots clicking on the wooden floor.

Lan turned back to his contemplation of the garden, but he pulled his thin legs up onto the window seat and pulled the curtain shut behind him, cutting him off from the rest of the second-best sitting room.

Find something? She wants me to find something? And what is there for me to do around here? Since moving to the town house in Haven, there was nothing to occupy Lan's days. Back home—for no matter what his parents said, this place would never be *home* to him—he'd had friends, places to go, things to do. Riding, hunting, and fishing mostly, or shooting at targets. Just hanging about together and talking was entertaining enough, certainly more entertaining than listening to Sam natter about the exciting doings in the dye vats. Back when he was younger, that same gang of boys had played at being Heralds or Guards, at fighting the Karsites or capturing bandits. The last couple of years they'd abandoned the games, but not each other. Now there were races to be run, game to chase, rivers to swim, and that was enough for them.

Then Mother got made Guild Representative, and Father couldn't get us out of the country fast enough. Lan's lip curled at the recollection. No matter how his children felt about it, Archer Chitward had ambition to be more than a simple country cloth merchant. At least in part that was why he had negotiated the marriage with Nelda Hardcrider, the most skillful needlewoman anyone in their area had ever seen. With her skill, and his materials, he reckoned she could make herself into a walking advertisement for his goods.

Lan knew that was what he'd thought, since he'd

said so often enough. His mother didn't seem to resent being thought of as a sort of commodity, in fact he sometimes wondered if the negotiation and speculation had been as one-sided as his father thought.

He stared out the glass window at the sorry substitute for a forest—a stand of six dwarf fruit trees, an arbor covered with brambles and roses, which would later yield fruit and rose hips, and gooseberry bushes, all neatly confined in wooden boxes with gravel-covered paths between, for a minimum of work. The rest of the garden was equally utilitarian; vegetables in boxes, herbs in boxes, grapevines trained against the wall. The only flowers growing there were those that were also edible.

With an intensity that left a dry, bitter edge around his thoughts, Lan longed for his wild, unconfined woods. In all of Haven he had yet to see a spot of earth that had been left to grow wild; every garden of every house around here was just the same as this one. The only variations were in whether or not the gardens were strictly utilitarian or ornamental. The parks around which each "square" of town houses were built were carefully manicured, with close-cropped lawns, precise ponds or fountains, pruned trees, and mathematically planned flowerbeds.

He wanted his horse. He wanted to saddle up and ride until he found a tree that wasn't pruned, a flower not in a planned planting, even a weed. But that was impossible; his horse had been left back in the country. There was no stable here, and even if there had been, he would not have been allowed his horse. The two carriage horses the family had brought with them were kept in a stable common to the square, and cost (as his father liked to repeat) a small fortune to keep fed and cared for. Only the nobly born could afford to keep a riding horse in the city.

He could have hired a horse to ride—there was a stable with horses for hire and a bigger park to ride them in—but what was the point of that? You weren't allowed to take the beast any faster than a trot, you had to stick to the bridle paths, and the riding park was just a bigger version of the tiny park of their square. Riding in the park was nothing more than a way for girls to show themselves off for young men, and young men to assess the competition. It wasn't even exercise.

Lan hated Haven; he had since he'd arrived, and he hadn't seen anything yet to change his mind. But he was in the minority, because the rest of his family had taken to life in the city with the enthusiasm of otters to a water slide.

His mother was at the Guildhouse every day, her daughter with her at least part of the time. Lan's younger sister Macy took after her mother in every way, and it looked as if Nelda would be handing the reins of her position in the Guild over to her daughter when the time came that she wished to step down. Macy adored every facet of city life, and so did Lan's younger brother, Feodor. Feodor tagged after their father the way Macy trailed behind Nelda, absorbing every aspect of the business of a cloth merchant as easily as a towel soaked up water. Lan's oldest brother Sam wasn't even in the equation—he spent so much time at his Master's that Lan scarcely even saw him.

A proper little copy of Father, he is, Lan thought cynically. *And how nice for him that is. Same for Feodor.* They never got into trouble just for existing; they never got the long looks of disgust or disappointment. Not once. Back home, that hadn't mattered; Lan was out at dawn and not back until dark, and if his parents were disappointed in him, at least he was able to avoid them.

Why can't they just send me back home? he thought longingly. It wasn't as if they couldn't afford it, not with all the silver his father was throwing around lately. They kept saying that it was time he grew up and took on some responsibilities and made something of himself. . . .

Why? Highborns don't have to! There are plenty of people with well-off parents who aren't expected to go out and "make something of themselves."

The only thing he really wanted to do was out of the question, of course. Given a choice, he'd have entered the Guard. He knew he rode well enough to get into the mounted troops; he certainly didn't fancy marching for leagues and leagues on his own two feet. He rather thought he'd look good in the Guard uniform of dark blue and silver, and it was an admitted magnet to attract pretty girls, or at least it had been at home. Even foot soldiers got attention when they passed through Alderscroft.

The one and only time he'd mentioned his ambitions, there had been such an outcry he hadn't dared say anything about it again. And without family support—well, he could pretty much forget about getting into the mounted troops, at least for a long while. If you brought your own horse and passed the riding trials, you went automatically into the cavalry, but if he didn't have family support, he wouldn't have a horse. And he wasn't so desperate that he cared to just run off and join the ground troops.

Definitely not. Without some weapons'-training, real training with a Weaponsmaster, he'd go straight into training with that most basic of front-line weapons, the pike. It would be months before he got his hands on a bow or an edged weapon, and all his time would be spent on grueling marches and drills.

I might as well be a woodcutter, it would be as much work and more interesting.

And anyway, he couldn't even run off to join the Guard for another two years. Even if he lied about his age and identity, his parents would probably find out where he was and drag him home again.

Nobody would believe I was sixteen anyway. Skinny and lanky he might be, but he was also undersized. He didn't even look fourteen. *Feodor* looked older than he did, and was certainly taller.

Of course, as his father pointed out constantly, a lack of height didn't matter to a merchant or a Guildsman.

By this time he had brooded himself into a truly black humor, and the moment he heard the housemaids come giggling into the kitchen for their late breakfast, he bolted up the stairs for his room, now carefully polished and scrubbed, any trace of *him* erased. He took a perverse pleasure in pulling the curtains shut on the morning sunshine and undoing their work by casting himself on the bed, boots and all.

He closed his eyes, nursing his bitterness in silence, wishing that he could will himself back home to Alderscroft.

HE didn't realize that he'd dozed off until he started awake to find his mother shaking him and the curtains pulled wide open again to admit the midday sun.

"Wake up!" she said crossly, the dreaded frown lines making deep creases between her brows. Her face, a perfect oval framed by the braids she wore wrapped around her head, was the very portrait of parental annoyance. Her hazel eyes narrowed with suppressed anger. "When I told you to find something to do, I didn't mean to go take a nap! Here—"

She thrust the same forgotten roll of tools at him that the Guildmaster had forced on him last night, and Lan suppressed a groan. Was he *never* to be rid of the blasted thing?

"Did you hide this in the cushions last night?" she accused.

He blinked and began to dissemble; she cut him off before he'd gotten more than a word or two out. "Don't bother to lie," she said acidly. "You do it very badly. You did. It's just a good thing that the Guildmaster thought Feodor was older than you—he offered to take Feo as his 'prentice, so Feo can use these, and he won't be offended to see that you've given Feo your present."

Relief must have shown on his face, for his mother's lips tightened. "Tidy yourself and get downstairs. Your father and I have something to tell you."

She clattered out of his room, and Lan's relief evaporated, replaced by dread.

Oh, gods, now what? Was he going to be 'prenticed to someone after all? His heart plummeted, and with cold hands he straightened his tunic and swept his hair off his forehead.

Feeling as if he were going to his doom, he plodded down the stairs and into the lesser sitting room where he could hear his mother and father talking.

They both looked up as he entered; his mother still had that tightly closed expression around her mouth, as if her lips were the opening to a miser's purse, but his father looked less grim. Archer had a milder temper to go with his gray-threaded, tidy chestnut hair, but today there was a sense of sadness around his calm, brown eyes, and his square jaw was set in a way that suggested it would not do Lan any good to argue with the fate planned for him.

Lan took deep breaths, but still felt starved for air. "Sir," he said, suppressing the feeling that he ought to bob like a servant, but keeping his eyes down. "Ma'am. You wanted me?"

"Sit down, Lavan." That was his father; Lan took a seat on the nearest chair, a hard, awkward thing that was all angles and a little too tall for his feet to lie flat on the floor. That was the signal for his father to rise and tower over him. Lan's chest tightened, and he truly felt as if he couldn't breathe. "I was hoping for all of my sons to follow in my trade."

"Yes, sir," Lan replied in a subdued tone of voice, going alternately cold and hot, a feeling of nausea in the pit of his stomach. *I'm going to be sick, I know it. . . .*

He looked up through his lashes as his father looked down at him and sighed.

"Well, having two of my offspring take to the trade is more than any man should expect, I suppose." Archer shook his head. "Lan, have you *any* idea what you propose to do with yourself with the rest of your life?"

His feeling of sickness ebbed, but he started to sweat. "Ah—" *Don't say that you want to go into the Guard!* he cautioned himself before he blurted out the truth. That was not what Archer wanted to hear. "I, ah—"

"That's what I thought." Archer looked back at his wife, who grimaced. "You know, in *my* day, you'd have found yourself packed off to whatever master I chose to send you to. You wouldn't have a choice; you'd do what I told you to do, as I did what my father wished for me."

"Yes, sir." A tiny spark of hope rose in him. Did his father have some *other* plan? Whatever it was, could it be better than being sent off to some miserable dyer or fuller? *Unless—he—oh no—not a temple—*

"If you were *lucky,* I'd have sent you to be a priest," his father continued, echoing Lan's unfinished thought. "There's some that would say it's the proper place for you."

"You'd at least be serving your family if we did," Nelda said acerbically. "Which is more than you can claim now, lolling about in bed most of the day and glooming around the house doing nothing the rest of the time!"

"Superfluous" sons and daughters were often sent to one temple or another; the sons of the highborn were the ones that became the priests that were ultimately placed in the best situations. The rest took what they were assigned, normally poor temples in tiny, isolated villages in hardscrabble country or in the worst slums of the cities. Their families were greatly praised, of course, and it was generally thought that they incurred great blessings from the god or goddess of their choice for sending one of their blood to serve.

Lan gulped back alarm and forced himself to keep his eyes up. If he read his mother's words aright, he *wasn't* being sent to a temple either.

"You're luckier than you deserve," she said after a pause, sounding very bitter and resentful of her son's good fortune. "And your father is kinder."

"Now, Nelda, the boy isn't *bad*," Archer admonished. "He's just a bit adrift."

"*You* aren't home enough to see," his mother replied, "or you weren't, back in Alderscroft. Running off with those ne'er-do-well friends of his, never coming back until all hours, and the gods only know what he was up to with them—"

"Nothing that anyone ever complained about," Archer retorted, a sharpness in his tone showing that he was getting weary of his wife's complaints. "No one ever said anything to *me* about Lan getting into mischief."

"Well, they wouldn't, would they?" Nelda muttered, but there wasn't much else she could say beyond that. No one had ever complained to *her* about Lavan's behavior either, as Lan well knew, because no matter what he and his friends got into, they always made sure it wasn't where anyone would see them.

Archer turned back to his son, and rewarded his wary hope with a faint smile. "Times change, more so here in Haven, maybe. We've got another place for you, and you can think the Collegia for it."

"I'm going to the Collegium? But I'm not—"

He wasn't a Bard or a Healer, and he certainly wasn't a Herald! But his father laughed and shook his head.

"Na, na, not to the Collegia—that's for the high-born, not for the likes of you! Or at least, not unless you show some kind of genius, my boy, and since you've not shown anything so far, I rather doubt you're going to start now! But it's the Collegia and the way the highborn send their younger sons and sometimes daughters there for extra learning that made the Haven Guilds think something of the kind was a good place for our younglings." He cocked his head to the side and took in Lan's baffled expression. "You're going to *school,* lad."

"School?" Now he was more confused, not less. He knew how to read, write, and cipher, so what more could he possibly learn? "I've already been to school."

"Not like this, you haven't." Archer settled back on his heels and tucked his thumbs into his belt, looking as proud as if he had thought of the idea of this "school" himself. "This is the school all of the Trade Guilds in Haven put together. You'll be going beyond what the priest at Alderscroft could teach you—history, fancy figuring, oh, I don't know what all else. *And* the schoolmasters will be testing you, seeing what it is you're good at. When they've got you figured, they'll be finding a Master for you to 'prentice to; something you'll fancy more than clothwork, I reckon."

"You'll start tomorrow," Nelda stated, narrowing her eyes, "And you should be thanking your kind father for such a blessed opportunity."

"I am—I mean, thank you sir," Lan replied, still in a daze, and not quite certain if this was something to be glad about, or otherwise. More schooling? He hadn't been particularly brilliant at bookwork before. . . .

But as he continued to stammer his thanks, he evidently sounded sincere enough to satisfy both his mother and father. They dismissed him, and made no objection when he went back to his room.

He stood beside his bed in the open window, staring at the blank wall of the neighbor's house, close enough that if he leaned out, he could touch it. The wall seemed an apt reflection of his state of mind.

Only one thought was at all clear.

Now what am I getting into?

TWO

The School

ONE of the manservants woke Lan at dawn the next morning, gave him barely enough time to dress, and chased him downstairs. While the sullen fellow stood there with his arms crossed, tapping one foot, Lan threw on the first things that came to hand— his tunic and trews from yesterday. His mother waited for him at the foot of the stairs, and eyed him with patent disfavor.

"Get back up there and put on something decent. You don't have to make people think we're too niggardly to clothe our children properly," she ordered sharply. "And get your hair out of your face. You look like a peasant."

He straightened abruptly with resentment, but didn't feel up to a verbal joust that he'd only get the worst of, since most of what he would like to say was likely to bring on some sort of punishment. Instead, he stalked back upstairs with his spine making a statement of irritation and did as he was ordered. He rummaged through his wardrobe, changing into tunic, shirt, and trews of his father's best white linen and indigo-blue wool, and slicking his hair back with a wet brush.

And if something happens that I get this stuff dirty or scuffed up, I'll no doubt hear all about my carelessness.

His mother gave him a brusque nod of approval when he descended again, and allowed him to proceed to the breakfast table. The sun was just at the horizon as the servants placed his food in front of him, for once in company with Sam as well as his father and mother. Samael didn't have much to say this morning, and Nelda ate quickly, leaving the table before any of the male members of the family. Lan had the distinct feeling that once she had made certain that he wasn't going to disgrace her in the way of his appearance, she felt that her duties had been entirely discharged.

Towering over his brother, Sam nodded at Lan as he shoved his empty bowl and plate away, reached for a last hot buttered roll, and stood up. Sam had his father's height, his mother's handsome looks with auburn hair and hazel eyes, and a gentle patience that couldn't have come from either parent. Lan often wished that Sam had more time for him; he had more confidence in Sam's temper than that of his elders. "Good luck today, little brother," he said as he headed for the door himself, giving a quick shake of his head to get his own red-brown hair out of his eyes and a sympathetic grin at his sibling. Sam's clothing was a utilitarian dark gray, so as not to show dye stains, and it was a bit worn at the hems; Lan couldn't help notice that he and Sam had been dressed almost identically before Nelda had made Lan change.

But Mother never says anything about him *looking like a peasant.*

"Get another helping while I finish," Archer ordered, his long face wearing an expression of solemn satisfaction with his meal. "I'll take you to the school myself today; after this, you find your own way."

So Lan took an unwanted roll and slowly picked it to pieces while his father worked his way through por-

ridge and eggs and bacon, hot rolls, and small ale. His
emotions were so mixed at this point that he couldn't
sort them out. They blended into a general tension
that had him ready to spring up like a startled hare
at the least provocation. In contrast, Archer was at
his most stolid and phlegmatic this morning, moving
so slowly and deliberately that Lan wanted to scream.

Finally, at long last, Archer waved away the hovering servant offering yet another helping, and pushed
away from the table. Lan leaped up from his place
causing Archer to make a sound that could have been
a smothered chuckle, perhaps at what he thought was
Lan's eagerness. "Come along," was all he said,
though, and Lan followed his father out the front door
and onto the street.

They walked side-by-side, not talking. Lan was very
much conscious of how much taller his father was than
he, though they were both alike in their loose-jointed
frames, reddish-brown wavy hair, and elongated faces.
Macy, Lan's sister, took after Nelda, she was pretty
rather than beautiful, and square-jawed like her father. And Nelda's features were masculinized in Sam,
to a much better effect. But all three of Archer's sons
resembled their father to a greater or lesser degree,
at least externally. Lan couldn't get over the idea that
his father was disappointed in his short stature and
turned his eyes self-consciously away.

It was earlier than Lan was usually about, but there
were plenty of people on the street, most walking in
the direction of the manufacturing and trade quarters.
There was a general buzz of noise in the background
that never stopped until well after sundown. It was
one of the many things Lan hated about the city, and
after several weeks he still wasn't used to it. The cool,
still air had nothing in the way of what Lan would
have called a scent; most of the autumn flowers growing in and around the houses were scentless, purely
decorative. Fallen leaves got swept up immediately by
servants, and there wasn't so much as a single weed

or blade of grass to be seen. So there weren't any of the aromas that Lan assoociated with fall.

The street was paved with cobblestones; the doorsteps were slabs of stone, and the cobbles went right up to the bases of the houses, for even the fenced front yards were, for the most part, paved over. The town houses themselves were statements of the inhabitants' wealth, with a great deal of attention paid to the street facade. Some were of stone, like a great manor in the country, roofed with slate and ornamented with fantastical animal-shaped spouts at the corner of each gutter. Others were brick, with the brick laid in ornamental patterns, and the roof laid in an imitation of thatch. There were no thatched roofs in this quarter; with the houses so close together, thatch would have been a terrible fire hazard. There were homes with huge, heavy black beams and white plaster between, the plaster painted with fanciful designs. There were wooden manses roofed with tile, and there was even one wooden house completely covered in lacy carvings.

This was nothing at all like Alderscroft, where most of the houses were modest thatched cottages, where there was plenty of room between each house, where everyone had flowers growing at the foundations and little gravel paths led from each cottage, through patchwork gardens, to the fences and gates letting onto the dirt street.

The houses back home were warm and welcoming, giving glimpses of the personality of the people inside. These houses gave away nothing, offering a blank-eyed stare to the passersby, aloof and proud as a wealthy matron.

It's as much as if they're all saying, "I'm rich. Don't you wish you were?" and nothing else.

The occasional horse or donkey and cart came along the street—more merchants, who had farther to go than just a few streets, and preferred not to walk. And once or twice a Guardsman patrolling the neighborhood on horseback paced past them. Lan stared longingly after them, wishing that he could be wearing that uniform, not plodding along beside his father.

They left the street that dead-ended on their own court and traveled eastward, away from the center of town but toward more of the same sort of houses. There were occasional stores here, or rather, "discreet business establishments," mostly dressmakers, milliners, and the like. From the street, except for a gown or a hat prominently on display in a window, it wouldn't be possible to tell these places from an ordinary house.

Archer wasn't disposed to conversation, but finally he made an effort. "You'll be getting in with some lads your age, then," he said heavily. "More like back at the village."

Lan couldn't imagine a situation less like home, but he murmured, "That would be good."

"Aye." That sentence seemed to exhaust Archer's store of conversation, and the rest of the walk continued in silence.

There was a much larger building on the right side of the street they were on, one that towered over its already impressive neighbors and was enclosed by a high wall. Where the town houses were two and three stories tall, this was six; and it occupied a lot that was easily five or six times the size of any of that of the magnificent homes around it. Lan had never been this far on any of his reluctant walks.

"That'll be the school," Archer said with satisfaction as he surveyed the exterior, his expression as pleased as if he owned it himself. "You'll be coming here every morning about this time; lessons start early, but we're going to meet the Master first."

Lan still couldn't comprehend what sort of "lessons" could be taught here, and thought for certain that his father must be mistaken. But the nearer they came to the building, the less certain he became.

His father showed no evidence of hesitation. He led

Lan along the high wall—easily a story tall itself—until they came to the wooden gate. It must not have been locked, for Archer pushed it partly open, and motioned Lan to precede him.

Lan moved hesitantly past his father, and into a mathematically precise courtyard. Most of it was paved. Along the base of the building were pruned evergreen bushes, cone-shaped ones alternating with bushes of three spheres, one atop another. Defining a pathway toward the door were long flower boxes containing neat stands of greenery. Ivy planted in similar boxes climbed the inside of the fence.

"Come along, then. Master's waiting," Archer said, pulling the gate closed behind him. He led Lan to the front door of the building, a surprisingly small door for such an edifice. It appeared no larger than the door of their own home.

Archer pulled open that door without knocking, revealing a long corridor with more wooden doors on either side of it, a corridor far plainer, with ordinary wooden floors and plastered walls, than Lan had expected. There was a hum of voices, a murmur that drifted along the corridor like the murmur inside a major temple during a festival.

Archer immediately turned to the first door on the right and rapped on it. A muffled voice invited them in.

Lan found himself in a small, plain room, furnished only with a brace of chairs and a large desk that faced the door. An older man sat at the desk, a man with close-dropped gray hair and a stern face, all sharp angles, a face made by a mathematician rather than an artist. This gentleman looked up at their entrance, and gave Archer a thin smile.

"Ah, Master Chitward," the man said, his voice no warm-er than his coolly pleasant expression. "I have been expecting you."

"This is the boy," Archer said, putting his hand

squarely in the middle of Lan's back and pushing him forward, so that he was between Archer and the desk.

"Lavan, isn't it?" the man said, making a note on a piece of paper in front of him. "Lavan Chitward. Very good; as soon as I know where to place him, we'll have him settled in no time."

"Aye. I'll be going, then, Master Keileth, I've work to do." Lan turned to look at his father, inarticulate protests freezing on his lips; Archer did not look at him at all. He was perfectly satisfied that he had done his duty, and Master Keileth dismissed him with a nod of thanks.

"Very good, and thank you, Master Chitward. I hope that we will be able to please you with Lavan's accomplishments." Obviously that was what counted with Master Keileth—pleasing Archer Chitward, not his son.

Archer opened the door and left without a backward glance at Lan; Master Keileth motioned impatiently to Lan to take a seat. "Sit down, young man," the Master ordered when Lan did not immediately obey. "I'm not minded to put a crick in my neck looking up at you."

Lan obeyed him, gingerly perching on one of the hard wooden seats, and positioning himself nervously on the very edge of the chair.

Master Keileth gave all his attention to the paper in front of him for a time, then looked up abruptly. His smile was gone, and his eyes held a calculating expression.

"Your father is paying a great deal of money for this opportunity you are enjoying," Master Keileth said abruptly. "I trust that you intend to make his expenditure worth his sacrifice." His mud-colored eyes narrowed a trifle as he waited for a response.

Lan immediately felt a surge of guilt; why hadn't his father told him this? He flushed a little, and Master Keileth's eyes showed that he had noted the flush and found it satisfactory.

Lan dropped his eyes, and Master Keileth did *not* see the flush of anger that had followed the guilt. *Why was Father willing to pay for this, but not to let me go home and live there? Why did he give up the house in Alderscroft where I was happy?*

He only raised his eyes again when he had his feelings under control. Master Keileth was watching him as carefully as a cat at a mouse hole.

"I'm going to ask you some questions, Lavan, so that we know where to place you." Another thin smile that did not reach the cool gray eyes. "You are fortunate in that your family chose to move when they did. Our school term is just beginning; we will not have to place you in a special class and give you extra tutoring to force you to catch up."

Without waiting for Lan to answer, the Master began asking, not a *few* questions, but a great many. Lan was forced to dredge up everything he had learned at the hands of the village priest and quite a bit he thought he had forgotten.

By the time Master Keileth was done with him, he was sweating, and quite sure that the Master had decided he was a complete ignoramus. He sat slumped over slightly, feeling completely drained.

Master Keileth gave no indication how he felt about Lan. He simply made more notes, ignoring Lan altogether. After what seemed like an eternity, the Master finally looked up again.

"Satisfactory, given your limited education," he said. "I believe we can place you in the Third Form."

Lan had no notion what that was supposed to mean, but when Master Keileth beckoned peremptorily, Lan rose and followed him out of the office and into the hall.

They climbed to the third floor, the murmur of voices all around him. Master Keileth brought him into a corridor identical to the one below. This time, they went as far as the middle of the corridor—far enough to see that there were others branching from it—before Master Keileth stopped at a door and opened it without knocking.

The sounds from within the room stopped immediately, and with a scrape of chairs, everyone in the room stood up.

When Lan entered, he saw that there were eight adolescents, six males and two females, at small desks facing a larger one, at which an adult teacher presided. They were all younger than he, about fourteen to his sixteen.

"Herewan, this is a new student, Lavan Chitward," Master Keileth said in his brusque manner. "I have assigned him to the Third Form. Choose someone in this section to take him through his classes."

That said, the Master left as abruptly as he had arrived, leaving Lan to face nine strangers alone.

OWYN, the boy assigned to show him around, was a serious, studious youngster with huge brown eyes, untidy dark brown hair, and an unfinished air like a young owl, who performed his duty with utmost solemnity. As Lan had expected, if he had been ranked with his age group, he should have been in Fourth or Fifth Form, and being ranked with the students his junior was a mark against him. His own classmates regarded him with a certain veiled scorn for his lack of what they considered common knowledge.

Their lives were marked by bells which rang to signify the changing of classes and mealtimes. Pupils remained in their seats; it was the teachers who moved from room to room to impart their specialized knowledge. Lan's set began with Geography, which meant trade routes; routes whose particulars they were expected to have by rote. This knowledge was not only that of finding the way on an unmarked map, but of climate, conditions in each season, dangers on the way, and so forth. They were drilled mercilessly until every person in the class had the current route down perfectly, and only then did the class as a whole move on to the next route. This fascinated Lan; in his mind, he *saw* the conditions the teacher described, and he had no difficulty in memorizing the route, though he wondered if he might start to get routes mixed up when he had to recall more than one.

At the end of the class, the pupils stood up as their teacher left the room—Owyn poking him in the back when he wasn't quick enough—and a new teacher entered.

The next three classes were in language: Hardornen, Rethwellan, and Border dialects. Lan's head was stuffed full before the break came for lunch, and he wondered how he was ever going to keep the languages from running together.

At the sound of the noon bell, the other students jumped up and stampeded for the door. Owyn solemnly took Lan in charge and led him down to the first floor, down a staircase packed full of strange people. Owyn didn't really have to show Lan the refectory where they all took their lunch. Every pupil in the school was headed in that direction, all of them chattering at the tops of their lungs. The two boys just went along, carried on the stream.

When they got to the door of the refectory, though, Owyn deserted him, squirming past students who were younger than either of them, and vanishing.

Lan got out of the traffic to have a look around. This was an enormous room, high-ceilinged and echoing, with the dark timbers of the support beams showing starkly against the white plaster of the ceiling itself. Up above the wainscoting were windows surrounded by handsome carved wood, but from head height on down there were only plain oak panels. There were four long plain oak tables running the length of the room, with chairs, plates, and silverware marking each place. That seemed a little odd to Lan;

he would have expected benches, until he saw how that even with the spacing between each student enforced by the seating they managed to poke and elbow each other. There seemed to be no particular order in which people were seated, although there were obviously seats that were preferred. Those Lan's age and older had taken over the seats at the ends of the tables nearest the kitchen doors; it was obvious why, as they were already being served beef and bread and new peas while the rest were still getting seated. The seats least in favor were farthest from the kitchen, and those near the fireplaces, where stray breezes sent random puffs of smoke out into the room from the fire burning there.

Friends sat together, forming little cliques; sideways glances and whispered comments discouraged approach. Owyn was in one of those, though his group was in a set of the less-favored seats. Lan hesitated, then took an unoccupied chair at the end of one of the tables. By the time he got started on his lukewarm meal, the students at the head of the table were already devouring their second and third portions.

Across from Lan sat a very plain, lumpish girl who kept her head down and didn't look up from her plate. Next to him was a nervous boy much younger than Lan, eleven or twelve, perhaps, who bolted his food so quickly Lan was afraid he was going to choke, and vanished from the table, casting backward glances over his shoulder as he scuttled away.

Shortly Lan found out why he had been in such a hurry to leave. One of the oldest boys, a square-jawed, stereotypically handsome specimen of about eighteen with crisply cut dark-blond hair and indolent dark-blue eyes, strolled down from his exalted seat and surveyed the lesser beings at the lowest end of the table with his hands clasped behind his back, looking for all the world as if he was surveying the offerings at a horse fair.

He took his time about it. Lan decided that discretion was the proper tactic to pursue, and quietly continued to eat, ignoring the young man's arrogant gaze. He could feel eyes burning a hole between his shoulder blades, though, and he didn't like the feeling in the least.

The chattering at this end of the table quieted, and now Lan sensed that there were a great many more eyes on him.

"So, this is the new one." A hand fell on Lan's shoulder, and he restrained the impulse to slap it away. "I hear they put you with the babies, boy. What do you have to say for yourself?"

Lan kept silent, but the arrogant one was joined by three or four of his peers, lesser copies out of the same mold, who rose from their seats and gathered around him. The biggest of them grabbed Lan's chin and wrenched his head around.

"Speak when you're spoken to, country boy," his harasser said in a deceptively pleasant voice. "Sixth Formers are the masters here; the rest of you are scum. The sooner you get that into your head, the better it will be for you."

"Don't argue with him!" the homely girl whispered harshly, and the older boy suddenly turned on her.

"Did you speak out of turn, Froggy?" he asked, with a savage, joyful smile.

The girl shrank down, looking very like a frightened frog. Her olive skin went pale, and she hid her overlarge eyes under the thick, coarse fringe of her dark hair. "He's new, sir," she whispered miserably. "No one's told him the rules, sir. He can't know what to do if he doesn't know the rules, sir."

Lan's first attacker took pity on her. "Quite right, Froggy. We won't have our ladies paint you today. Must tell the new one the rules, *then* we can flog him if he disobeys."

The second one pulled Lan up out of his seat by his collar, then knocked his feet out from under him with a sweep of his leg. The rest of the oldest students had gathered around by then, and they howled with laughter as Lan went to his hands and knees. Lan bit back a yelp of pain, but his eyes watered. Another grabbed a handful of Lan's hair and yanked, forcing his face up so that he looked the leader full in the face.

"Scrawny, undersized," said the leader meditatively. "We've already got one Rabbit, so that's out of the question. But you—you're decidedly scrubby. I believe I will call you Scrub. Now listen well, Scrub."

Lan was red with fury, his insides churning; his knees ached and his head felt as if they'd already torn his hair out. He started to say something, then bit back the words. This was not the time to get into a fight. He was dreadfully outnumbered, and he wouldn't stand a chance.

"The Sixth Formers are the rightful rulers here. You will address us all as 'sir' and 'mistress'—unless you happen to prefer 'my lord' and 'my lady,' in which case you may use those terms instead."

Somebody sniggered, and the leader turned a cold gaze on him; the sniggering stopped immediately.

"You, on the other hand, will be known by the name we have chosen for you—in your case, Scrub— and you will answer to that name, or be flogged, or suffer whatever other punishment we deem appropriate." The handsome Sixth Former was obviously in his element and enjoying himself very much; Lan thought with fury about how much he wanted to blacken those blue eyes and rub mud into that beautiful blond hair. "You will give place to us, give way before us, speak only when you are spoken to, and accomplish whatever task we set you, or be punished. And it is no use complaining to the Master, because if you do, we shall flog you with twice as many strokes. The Master has given Sixth Form the responsibility for maintaining discipline, and he'll assume you are a liar, a slacker, or both if you complain to him. You are nothing; we are everything. Do you understand?"

Lan's throat was so tight with anger that he couldn't

have gotten out a single word, but his second tormentor, hand still firmly buried in his hair, forced his head to nod like a puppet's while the rest laughed like madmen.

"Very well, Scrub," the leader said genially, "You're let off this time. Just make sure you stay properly within the rules from now on."

The one holding Lan's hair suddenly shoved him forward and let go of his head, so that he sprawled at the leader's feet, invoking more peals of laughter. "Now Scrub," the leader said tenderly, "it isn't necessary to kiss my feet, but that was a good thought and the proper attitude."

The Sixth Formers dispersed and went back to their chairs as Lan got slowly and angrily to his feet. He made no move to dust himself off, but dropped down into his seat with his head aching from all the anger he was holding in.

"Just do what they say, 'specially what Tyron and Derwit say," the girl they had called "Froggy" whispered urgently, with a sidelong glance at the retreating backs. "They'll leave you alone, mostly, if you do."

Now they were turning their attention to Owyn and his friends; Tyron addressed Owyn as "Owly" and demanded "the work." A moment later, and Tyron was accepting sheaves of paper from Owyn and his friends. "They have the smart ones do their sums and sometimes other schoolwork for them," Froggy explained, her eyes watering. "But if you aren't smart, they make you do other things for them."

The Sixth Formers had returned to their seats, where they distributed the papers among themselves and sipped small ale poured by the servants, who ignored the rest of the table. Froggy's eyes burned as she gazed on them.

"Just two more years," she said, as if to herself, with the longing of a starving man in her voice. "Just two more years, then it will be *my* turn!"

But Lan, as he looked more closely at the Sixth

Form group, saw that there was a central core of the group who were the true masters of the rest. These numbered about twenty, enough to give them enough muscle to have their way, so long as the less fortunate remained disorganized. The rest hung about the periphery of the group, ignored for the most part, but occasionally tendered an abusive or scornful comment, occasioning much laughter among the rest. When Tyron or one of the others of his clique gave a careless order, it was one of these hangers-on who jumped to execute it just as quickly as if they were not of the Sixth Form themselves.

Somehow, Lan doubted that it would ever be Froggy's "turn" to be one of the select few.

LAN had the sense to finish his now-cold lunch and retreat to his classroom as soon as the Sixth Form turned their attention elsewhere. He did notice that there were several more girls besides the two in his class and poor down-trodden Froggy among the students. There were even some among the ruling elite, and not all of them looked old enough to properly qualify as being in the Sixth Form. All the girls sitting with Tyron and his clique were among the prettiest in the room, which seemed to be their qualification for belonging there. The girls weren't any better than their boyfriends, though; they didn't initiate any cruel "jokes," but they laughed just as hard as any of the boys, and were perfectly willing to participate once something was begun.

The rest of the afternoon passed without incident, much to Lan's relief—four more classes, in mathematics, reading comprehension, writing and calligraphy, and accounting. Once or twice one of the boldest of his class addressed him as "Scrub," but he felt safe in ignoring the insult.

When class was dismissed for the end of the day, however, Lan faced another problem: how to get out without being singled out for more abuse. He felt instinctively that after having been identified by Tyron, others of the Sixth Form would try to impress their superiority on him. When the final bell rang for dismissal, and the rest of the class ran for the door, Lan stayed behind, pretending to read. The teacher said nothing as he left, so Lan supposed such an action was permissible. It would be easier for someone who lived in a large, busy household to study in a quiet room at the school than at home.

So since reading comprehension was clearly one of his weaker points, and it was a great deal easier to feign reading than any other subject, he remained at his desk, slowly turning pages, as the noise from the hall faded and died away. Only then did he rise and move cautiously to the window, which gave a limited view of the courtyard within the school walls.

He saw at once that his guess was correct. As Tyron and his closest friends lounged and watched critically, others of the Sixth Form intercepted selected students and belabored them with insults, shoves, and kicks. Owyn's group was allowed to slip by relatively unmolested except for a chorus of catcalls, but others were not so fortunate.

As the stream of students exiting the building thinned, Tyron laughed and stood up. Lan heard him clearly from the open window where he sheltered, taking care that he couldn't be seen.

"That's enough for today, lads," he said in that deceptively genial voice. "Who's for a game of court tennis? I'll lay two to three that none of you can play a game without being scored against."

Others took up his challenge, and the lot of them moved off and out of the gates in a group. From here, Lan could see the street beyond the gates, and he watched to make certain they actually left the vicinity of the school before he made his own way down the quiet halls and stairways and out the door.

Feeling very much the coward, and angry with himself, he peeked around the gates before he ventured into the street. By this time, it was growing dark, and he was getting uncomfortably hungry. He hadn't had much appetite for his cold meal at lunch, and it had been a very long time since then.

The street held plenty of others hurrying home to their meals, and Lan let out a sigh of relief as he melted into the crowd.

Half of him wanted a confrontation; he kept thinking of all the clever things he should have said, or how he should have stood up for himself. They wouldn't have dared start a fight in the middle of the school, would they? Surely the teachers would have stepped in—

Or would they?

The Sixth Formers seemed very, very confident that no one would stop them. Maybe the teachers already knew about this petty tyranny and didn't care.

After all, they could very well feel that their responsibilities toward the students ended at the classroom door.

That only made Lan angry all over again, and finally he took the only outlet he had for his emotions. He broke into a run, and much to the astonishment of those making their decorous or weary way home, he ran all the way to his own front door.

He paused long enough to catch his breath, then opened the door. One of the servants met him there and took his bag of books; the family was already at dinner, and Lan joined them without a word.

Sam had been in the midst of describing some experiments with new dyes, and took up the thread that Lan's entrance had interrupted. Lan was grateful to Sam for once, for taking all of the family's attention away from him. He concentrated completely on his food, driving all the anger and tension of the day out of his mind. And perhaps that was the only reason why, when he excused himself from the table and his mother asked him how his first day of lessons had been, he was able to look her in the face, and say calmly, "All right."

And before she could continue questioning him, he retreated upstairs to his room. Books had never been his friends, but tonight they were better and safer company than any other alternative.

THREE

L AN wondered if highborn children were as arrogant as Tyron and his coterie. The Sixth Formers certainly couldn't possibly be any *more* arrogant.

Now in the second week of his attendance at the school, Lan's strategy of avoiding his tormentors was having mixed success. By slipping into the Hall behind a clot of taller boys and keeping his head hunched over his food, he had managed to keep from being spotted at meals while the Sixth Form was busy stuffing their own faces. But in order to get out before they got bored and started really looking for amusement, he had to bolt his own lunch like a starving badger, which made for an uneasy stomach during the next class. They *usually* got bored with hanging about and left the entrance before he ventured out to go home, but he couldn't avoid them on coming in, without taking the risk of being seriously late. Tardiness brought its own set of problems, not the least of which was the humiliation and pain of having his hand caned by the teacher.

Lavan had made another major mistake in his first week; he'd tried, shyly, to make up to one of the pretty girls in Fifth Form. How was he to know that she was the girlfriend of one of Tyron's hangers-on?

She'd rejected him quite out of hand, and he'd overreacted by withdrawing from all the girls. Now the Sixth Formers had another name for him.

Shaych.

When he'd found out what it meant, he'd tried to disprove it, but of course by then it was too late. Now there was another reason for Tyron and his friends to bully him.

After being shoved around like a game ball and then thrown sprawling for three mornings in a row, he decided that his best protection was the presence of the other persecuted. So for the past week, he'd waited for a group of the underdogs to arrive for classes, and ducked into their midst. With so many available targets, no one person got excessive abuse.

At least, that was the case so far.

But the whole situation made him so angry he sometimes thought he was going to choke. It didn't help that he always turned a brilliant scarlet with suppressed rage whenever one of the bullies so much as looked at him. They seemed to find that terribly amusing, and went out of their way to put him in that state.

This very morning he had arrived at his desk with his face still flaming, his skin feeling slightly sunburned and tender—and all from his own anger.

"You looked like you were going to have an apoplectic fit this morning, Scr—I mean, Lavan," Owyn whispered as they took their seats for the first class of the morning.

"Is that why you got between me and Loathsome?" he whispered back. Owyn had begun to warm up to him, since he had never once called him by the hated name of "Owly"—and since the one piece of cleverness he *had* managed was to come up with names of his own for their tormentors. "Loathsome" for Loman Strecker, "Tyrant" for Tyron Jelnack (that was really too easy), "Dimwit" for Derwit, and so forth. It gave the younger students a crumb of comfort to have contemptuous titles for their persecutors, though they took care that the Sixth Formers never heard those names.

Owyn nodded solemnly. "You went purple, almost, and your eyes had a funny look to them, like you weren't there anymore."

Lan didn't have to reply to that, because just then the teacher entered the room and all discussion stopped. That was just as well, because he realized that he didn't actually remember Owyn getting between him and his tormentor. He just didn't remember anything from the time that Loathsome had started shoving him repeatedly into the wall, and then to his partner, Dimwit—only that someone had taken his arm and was pulling him out of harm's way while Owyn distracted the Sixth Former with some questions about the work he'd been ordered to do. Between the moment that Loathsome and Dimwit began shoving him back and forth between them and the moment that he found his feet on the stair, there was a blank.

Or, not precisely a blank, but a passage of time filled with such fiery rage that he couldn't even see or hear, much less think. Whatever had come over him, had turned him briefly into something less than an animal, into pure anger and hatred.

Not that it made any difference, except that he suffered for it for half the morning with an aching head and irritated eyes, though the sensitivity of his skin faded as the morning passed.

And for once at lunch the attention of the Sixth Form was off him. One of the Fifth Formers had failed to obtain Golden Beauty apples for Tyron's luncheon pleasure as he'd been ordered; this wasn't a trivial task, as Golden Beauty apples were just going out of season. Tyron wouldn't hear any excuses, nor was he placated by the offer of a basket of Complin apples

instead. Two of his henchmen seized the unfortunate
by his arms and hustled him away.

Lan was now welcome to sit with Owyn and his
friends, and he turned his head just enough that he
could whisper to the younger boy, "Where are they
going with him?"

Owyn's eyes were as big and round as those of his
namesake, and his face was pale. "They're going to
flog him."

Lan felt his own face and hands grow cold. When
Tyron threatened him with flogging that first day, he
hadn't really thought they would actually do such a
thing! It was one thing for the teachers to flog a dis-
obedient pupil, but this!

"They can't do that, can they?" he whispered back
desperately, hoping that something or someone
might intervene.

Owyn just shook his head. "You ought to know by
now they can do anything they want."

Lan lost his appetite, all at once, and as soon as he
thought he could slip away unnoticed, he retreated to
the classroom and buried his nose in his book. He
stared at the same page without bothering to turn it,
since there was no one there to see him.

What he wanted, with the purest desperation he had
ever yet felt, was to be out of this place, to walk out
now and never return. But that was an impossibility
. . . his mother had made it even clearer than Master
Keileth that this year's tuition had cost a very great
deal, and it would be forfeit if he left. *If I were to run
off, I'd better run all the way to Hardorn; if Mother
ever caught up with me, I would be turning a spit in
the kitchen of the worst inn in Haven for the rest of
my life. And that would be if she was feeling generous.*

His head began to throb again, the headache growing worse with every passing heartbeat. And in fact,
by the time the next teacher, a bored, middle-aged,
balding scholar, arrived after lunch for the class, he

felt (and looked) so miserable that even the teacher noticed.

"Lavan," he said sharply, and Lan's head snapped up. That only made the headache worsen, and he winced.

The teacher shook his head, and his bored brown eyes gazed critically at Lan. "You look as if you're sickening with something," the man stated, a combination of irritation and concern on his face.

I certainly am, Lan thought, but said nothing. The teacher studied him a moment more.

"I'm sending you home early. There's no point in having you here if you're too ill to learn."

Lan privately thought that the teacher was more concerned he might catch whatever it was that Lan was allegedly coming down with, but he kept his mouth shut and accepted the hastily scribbled note to give to his parents. All he could think of, other than the pounding pain in his head and an increasing nausea, was that at least today he wouldn't have to run the gantlet of Sixth Formers to get home.

Maybe I am getting sick.

He gathered up his books and plodded out into the empty hall, trying to walk softly so his footsteps didn't echo. As he exited the building and then passed the gates, he felt the relief of temporary escape, at least. He made his way through the uncrowded streets with no more than a single wistful glance at a passing Guardsman. It was chilly today, and overcast; the few ornamental plants in front of houses were evergreens, and wouldn't be touched by frost, but back in Alderscroft, people would be waiting for the first hard frost to turn the leaves to red and gold. Here, the gray sky, gray streets, and the unfriendly houses left an overpowering impression of bleakness.

There was no one home but the servants, who would certainly be surprised and taken aback by his return. He didn't bother to knock, but the housekeeper heard the door open and came running.

"Lavan!" she exclaimed, looking at him in shock, with her frilled cap slightly askew—and there was more than an edge of suspicion in her voice. "What are you doing here?"

"I'm sick," he mumbled. "They sent me home. Here. This is for Mother." He just didn't feel up to making any more of an explanation, he just thrust the note at the housekeeper to give to his mother, and plodded upstairs to the sanctuary of his room, one slow step at a time.

Unfortunately, the relief of escaping from the Sixth Form for a day didn't bring an end to the pounding in his head. He dropped down onto his bed, his head buried in his hands, wishing for an end to the pain.

The housekeeper tapped on his open door, and he looked up. She wiped her hands on her coarse linen apron as she examined him.

"You might as well lie down," she said, and looked at him again with a less critical eye. "You do look puny," she said grudgingly. "I'll send one of the maids up with a hot-bag and willow tea."

He didn't grimace at the idea of the bitter tea; at this point he would drink down oak gall if it would help his head. Evidently the housekeeper considered his ailment serious enough to warrant the household's attention; one of the giggly little maidservants brought him the tea almost immediately, and he drank it down gratefully. It took a bit longer for the hot-bag, a linen pillow filled with buckwheat husks and herbs which had to be put into the bread oven to absorb heat. About the time that the tea took the worst edge off the pounding in his skull, the girl brought him the hot-bag, wrapped in a towel, to put on his forehead. She closed the door after herself, leaving him alone in his room, sprawled still clothed on the coverlet—though he had taken off his boots. His mother would kill him if she caught him on the bed with his boots still on.

With the hot-bag a comforting, warm weight on his

face, he tried not to think at all, just to try and relax
and wait for the pain to go away.

The herbs in the bag gave off a pleasant scent; he
didn't know enough about them to identify them, but
they were nice. The sounds of the servants going about
their business came up to him, muffled by the closed
door. One of the girls sang to herself as she swept, a
simpleminded love song that was very popular just
now. Lan would have preferred something bleaker, to
match his mood, but he wasn't about to get up to
make a request.

Down in the distant kitchen, the cook bellowed and
pots and pans clattered; distant enough not to be irri-
tating. Outside, the occasional horse or mule passing
by was all he heard of the sparse traffic this time of
day. Later, as suppertime neared, there would be more
noise outside; sometimes even a great deal of noise if
one of the neighbors got a large delivery.

His headache responded to the heat; it lessened to
a dull ache just behind his eyes and in the back of his
head. As the pain faded, he wished he could sleep,
but his thoughts were too restless and wouldn't be still.

There was more trouble ahead of him; every day
was colder and shorter. How long would it be before
the Sixty Formers could no longer pursue their after-
school entertainments? He'd heard them speak of
court tennis, of fencing lessons, of riding in the fashionable Leeside Park, before they all went off in a
mob. None of those things would be comfortable or
possible in a bitter rain or with snow on the ground.
And then what would they do for sport?

*As if I need to think about it. They'll go hunting for
sport at school, of course.*

The subject made him feel sick all over again, and
strengthened his headache.

I hate them, I hate them, I hate them! he thought
fiercely, his hands clenching in the coverlet. *If they
keep on coming at me, I'll kill them, I will!*

Really? asked a dry voice in his mind. *You, under-*

*sized and outnumbered, you're no threat to them. You
can't even stop them from pushing you around. How
do you propose even to impress them enough to leave
you alone?*

He couldn't; he knew he couldn't and that frustration was as bad or worse than the anger.

Why *couldn't* they leave him alone? He was nothing
to them; he was less than nothing. He wanted so badly
to batter those smug faces, to pound Tyron until his
fists hurt. Not a chance, not a chance in the world that
it would happen. Even if he could get Tyron alone,
he wouldn't stand a chance against someone so much
bigger and stronger than Lan was. Not someone who
was so fit and athletic. No matter what sort of fighting
Lan learned or practiced, Tyron would always be
ahead of him by virtue of his inches and muscles.

Footsteps outside his door warned him someone
was coming, so when the door opened, he pulled the
hot-bag off his eyes and turned his head to see who
it was.

"Your teacher seems to think that you're ill, or becoming ill," Nelda said, giving him the same critical
glare that the housekeeper had. Today she was
gowned in an amber brown with bands of her own
embroidery around the hems.

"My head hurts," he said simply. "A lot."

His mother came to his bedside and tested his forehead with the inside of her wrist, then tested the hotbag. "You're hotter than the compress; you've got a
fever. There *is* something going around they tell me,"
she admitted with a slight frown. "Your teacher seems
to think you should stay home for a few days and
study on your own."

A few days? It was more of a reprieve than he had
ever thought he would get! *But if I look too eager,
she might send me back tomorrow.*

He closed his eyes as a jolt of pain lanced across
his head from left to right. He certainly didn't have
to feign *that*. "I'll try, Mother," he said truthfully. "If

you think I should stay home—but if you don't want me to, I won't."

That must have been the right thing to say. "You *must* be sick," she said reluctantly. "All right; I'll have your meals brought up on a tray, and we'll keep you home for a while. "There's no point in spreading whatever you've caught to the rest of the family." She pursed her lips as Lan looked up at her. "I'll send to the herbalist for something better than willow tea for your head. Meanwhile, you lie back down." He obeyed, meekly, and she felt his forehead with a surprisingly gentle expression on her face. "Lavan, you've been driving me to distraction since we moved to Haven, but I still love you. It's not been easy for the rest of us here in Haven either."

A pang of conscience penetrated the pain in his head. "I'm sorry," he mumbled, feeling ashamed.

"Just keep on with this school as you have been, and you won't have a reason to feel sorry anymore," she said, spoiling his moment of contrition, as she put the hot-bag back on his forehead.

Just keep on with the school—if the Tyrant will let me! he thought in despair, and the headache returned with a vengeance.

As aromas that should have been savory and only made him feel sick floated up from the kitchen, he fought down nausea and his pain.

When footsteps came up the stairs again, he thought it was the servant with the promised tray, and took off the hot-bag to send her away. But it wasn't; it was the maidservant all right, a vaguely pretty girl with a round face and red cheeks, but she had a bottle and spoon in one hand, and another hot-bag wrapped in a new towel dangling from the other.

"This is from the herbalist for you," the maid said, with a sympathetic smile, holding out the bottle and spoon. "Just take a spoonful; he says it's mortal strong." Lan was surprised and touched by the sympathy. Evidently, now that it was clear he wasn't making his illness up, the servants were less inclined to be critical of him.

She left the hot-bag beside him as he took the medicine from her, leaving him alone in the darkening room. After a moment of thought, he lit his candles at his fireplace, although bending over nearly made him pass out.

Strange. I don't remember anyone coming in to light the fire. It hadn't been lit when he came home, had it?

I—I must have forgotten, my head hurt so much. When the room was full of light, he stripped and got into his nightclothes and got properly into bed, just in case the medicine was as strong as it was supposed to be. He didn't have a great deal of faith in the promises of herbalists, but it might very well be powerful.

His skin felt tender again, that slightly-sunburned feeling. As he stretched out under the bedclothes with the new hot-bag on his head, he was glad he'd gotten out of his clothing. The wool trews had been itchy; the soft linen felt much better. Downstairs, people were starting to arrive home, and the house hummed with conversation and activity. No one else came near him, though; he experienced the odd sensation of eavesdropping on his own family.

As if I were a ghost.

It was . . . interesting. The maid had left his door open, so he heard most of what was going on fairly clearly. No one seemed to notice his absence until dinner, when his mother's brief explanation brought an expression of detached sympathy from Sam, and an exclamation of "Don't let him get near *me!*" from his sister.

But it was just about then that the herbalist's remedy started to take effect, and Lan couldn't have cared if they had all voted to wrap him in a plague banner and chase him out of town.

It began with a dulling of the pain, followed by the oddest sensation of floating. The more the pain left, the more the euphoria took over. At some point, about midway through dinner downstairs, an irrestist-ible tug toward sleep took over where the euphoria ended. He didn't even try to fight it.

When he woke, it was broad daylight, and the head-ache was still with him, although it wasn't nearly as bad as it had been last night. The hot-bag had slipped off his head and onto the floor during the night; he opened his eyes just long enough to tell that it was, indeed, morning. He thought about taking a second dose of medicine, but his stomach rumbled and that decided him against it. He wanted something to eat first; then he'd let the medicine knock him over.

He smelled the frying ham and bacon of breakfast cooking downstairs, and his stomach rumbled again, insistently. *Should I get up and go downstairs?* he won-dered. *But Mother wanted me to stay in bed so I wouldn't spread this to the rest of the family. . . .*

He didn't have to make that decision, for a bump at his door made him open his eyes again. The maid stood there with a tray; she grinned when she saw his eyes open. And now he finally remembered her name. Kelsie.

"Good mornin' sirrah," she said brightly. "I brung up some supper last night, but you couldn't have been budged with a team of horses!"

She brought over her tray and placed it on a stool next to his bed. He sat up, and managed a weak smile. "I guess that medicine was as strong as you said."

"They say he's Healer-trained, is Master Veth, so I suppose he knows his medicines." Kelsie dismissed the herbalist and his remedies with a shrug. "I brought a bell on the tray there; you need something, you ring it and I'll come up."

"Thank you," was all he had a chance to say. She just grinned again, and was gone. Then again, given the housekeeper's firm hand on the household reins, lingering might get her in trouble.

On the tray was typical invalid fare: tea and but-tered toast, soft-boiled eggs. No ham, no bacon, no jam or jelly. He sighed, but tackled the food anyway. Hungry as he was, it all tasted good.

Only then did he take a second dose—slightly smaller this time—of the medicine, and it wasn't long before he was dreaming again.

This time he woke, it was some time in the afternoon, and his headache was measurably better, though still with him. More persistent was his hunger.

He rang the bell, and within moments, Kelsie was at his door with another tray, brown eyes dancing merrily at him from beneath her frilled cap. "Cook's figured you'd be ready for this," she said, putting it down beside him.

He eyed the contents. Bread and broth, more tea. "I am, but I could eat a whole loaf of bread, not just a couple of slices," he said ruefully. His stomach made an audible growl, and he blushed as she laughed.

"Well, the sayin' is to feed a fever, and you got a fever. You eat that up, I'll run down and tell Cook and see what she figures is good for you." She turned in a swirl of gray-and-cream woolen skirts and linen apron, and vanished, while he made short work of the invalid's lunch they'd given him.

It only just took the edge off his hunger. When Kelsie labored back to his door under the weight of a heavier tray, he'd already eaten every crumb.

"Here," she laughed, setting down the heavier tray, then tucking a stray curl of brown hair back under her cap. " 'Fever, Cook,' I told her. 'Not stomach troubles. I should think you could hear his stomach grumbling down here.' So she laughs, and fixes you this." Kelsie dusted off her hands. "Now, I got sweeping to do, so I'll hear you if you need aught else."

"I'll be fine," he replied, but she was already gone.

This is more like it! he thought; it was real food, not invalid's food, and not the leftovers from everyone else's lunch, either. It was twice what he normally ate, but he devoured every bite before he finally felt satisfied.

As he turned away from the tray, his eye fell on his book bag. He weighed the ache in his head against the promise to study.

If I keep up, maybe I can get a bad headache again. No one would be angry at him for being sick, and Tyron and his gang of bullies couldn't touch him here. He didn't know what had caused the headache and fever, but it could happen again.

And if it happens often enough, maybe they'll think there's something at school that's making me sick, he thought, with a tinge of hope.

In a sense, perhaps that *was* the cause. *I didn't get that headache until I got so angry. . . .*

If rage was the cause, he'd be getting headaches and fevers as long as he went to school.

Well, the only way I'll be able to stay home is to prove I can keep up without actually being in the classes. With a sigh, he pulled his book bag onto the bed, and took out the textbook for his first class of the day.

Without the distraction of knowing that the Sixth Form was waiting for him at lunch, he got through the work for the first four classes in half the time it usually took him. He got out of bed a time or two to feed his fire and take care of necessary things. He was very pleased that this house had indoor facilities; it was the one improvement over the home in Alderscroft. It was still early afternoon when he finished, and heartened by his progress, he tackled the next four subjects. By the time Kelsie appeared with his supper, he was able to put his last book aside with a feeling that he had accomplished something.

"Bringing your supper early, or Cook says you're like to be forgot in the bustle," the maid told him brightly. She whisked off, and Lan got up to stretch and light his candles, replacing the stubs in his candlesticks.

Once again, the increasing traffic sounds outside and the smells and noise of cooking told him that sup-

pertime for the family was nearing. He took a third
dose of the medicine, and went back to bed, this time
with the euphoria of having spent a peaceful and pro-
ductive day added to the euphoria of the medicine.

Last night he had slept dreamlessly; this night was
the same. Given that he fought the Sixth Formers virtually every night in his dreams, this, too, was a welcome relief.

His second day as a "patient" was similar to the
first, although a different servant brought him meals,
but his third night was different. His headache was
almost gone, so he hadn't bothered to take the
medicine.

In the middle of the night, he woke, unable to
move, feeling that there was something, some heavy
weight, sitting on his chest and smothering him, and
something else standing at the foot of his bed, watching him with amusement. He didn't so much think as
feel—and his feeling of helpless anger made him label
the presence at his feet as his worst enemy.

Tyron!

Terror and rage drove out any coherent thought,
filling Lan's mind with an explosion of white heat. He
tried to scream, but nothing came out; tried to flail
at the unseen weight, but couldn't move so much as
a finger.

Then, suddenly, the fire in his fireplace flared up
with a roar.

The room lit up, as if the noon sun shone at midnight; a flare of heat washed over him, snapping the
paralysis hold-ing him.

The weight left his chest; he sat bolt upright as the
flames died down to mere flickers and coals again. He
took a shocked breath—and the headache knocked
him flat on his back, spasming in pain and near-
blindness.

For a very long time he couldn't even move, and
hardly dared breathe. Where a moment before, his
entire universe had been terror and rage, now it was

filled with pain. A solid bar of agony ran between his temples and, from the base of his neck to his eyes, his head throbbed.

Finally, between one breath and another, it ebbed just enough that he could grope his hand to the bedside table. He didn't trust himself enough to reach for the spoon; he pulled the cork from the bottle and took a full mouthful, gagging down the thick, bittersweet liquid and putting the bottle back on the table before the pain washed over him again.

Then, after what felt like a hundred, thousand years, came oblivion.

When he woke again in mid-morning, it was the pain that woke him, but this time it was more like the level of headache that had sent him home from school. He reached for the bottle and took a measured half-dose, which relieved enough of the anguish that he could eat, drink, and take care of himself. Then he took a second half-dose, and retreated into slumber.

He missed lunch altogether, and evidently even sleeping he had looked as miserable as he felt, for when he woke at last, one of the scruffy little kitchen boys was sitting on a stool at his bedside.

When he opened his eyes and started to sit up, the boy leaped to his feet and ran off down the hall and the stairs. It was Nelda who brought up his supper tray herself, as he slowly levered himself up into a sitting position.

"Your fever came back," his mother stated, as she set the tray down and sat on the edge of the bed. "Cook came to check on you herself this morning, and sent me a message that you were asleep and as hot as an oven." She measured his temperature with her wrist, which felt pleasantly cool on his forehead.

"It came back last night, I guess," he replied, speaking slowly and carefully to keep from jarring his head. "I took some medicine right away." This time, the medicine had worked its magic more quickly, but there was still an ache throbbing in both temples and the back of his head. He eyed the bottle with misgivings; there was just about a quarter of the stuff remaining; what if he needed more?

"Whatever it is, I certainly hope for all our sakes that no one else catches it," his mother replied in a controlled tone, but with a gentle touch of her hand on his forehead. "Your teachers sent to say they're satisfied with the work you've done, so I suppose it will do no harm for you to miss a few more days until we're certain this fever won't come back a third time."

All he could feel was relief in spite of the pain. *More days! This is—almost worth having my head try to fly apart—*

"Are you hungry?" his mother asked, and to his mild surprise, he realized that he was ravenous.

"I . . . think so," he said haltingly, with the feeling that it wouldn't do to look too healthy.

"Well, Cook informed me that 'feed a fever' is the rule, and the herbalist agreed, so I want you to eat," she told him as she stood up. "He also told me that drinking as much as you can is more important than eating, so we'll be keeping a pitcher of water beside your bed. I've sent for another bottle of this unpleasant concoction since it does seem to have done you some good, and it should be ready in a candlemark or two. He'd have had it ready sooner, but it started raining last night, and it seems everyone in the city is coming down with a cold or the grippe." She looked at the window, though nothing could have been visible but the reflection, and sighed. "It's a nasty, filthy, cold rain, and it's just pouring down. I won't let you go back as long as it lasts, even if it lasts a week."

He sighed, and felt another measure of relief. "Mother—"

Nelda paused and turned back at the door.

"What if this doesn't go away?" he ventured. "What if I stay sick for a month?" *I could live with that.*

At that, she laughed, much to his surprise. "Lavan, we're in *Haven,* not back in Alderscroft. The Healer's

Collegium is on the other side of the city. If this mysterious illness of yours doesn't pass on its own in a few more days, have no fear, I'll have one of the Collegium Healers in to see you. The only reason I haven't had one here before is that this fever doesn't seem to be doing you any harm."

With that, she left, not pausing long enough to see Lan's face plummet with his heart.

His appetite had vanished, but he dutifully pulled the tray to him and ate anyway.

I should have known better than to hope that this was anything more than a reprieve, he sighed to himself. Chewing was an ordeal; every movement of his jaw increased the ache, and he was glad when he'd finished enough that his mother and Cook would be satisfied. He poured himself another generous dose of his medicine, wanting to sleep as long as possible. Sleep seemed to be the one certain cure, and he wanted sleep and relief from pain more than he wanted anything else at that moment.

But sleep seemed long in coming this time; he tried to soothe himself by reminding himself that he had a few more days of peace, if nothing else. For a few more days, he need not even think of Tyron.

At least when sleep did come, it brought no dreams.

FOUR

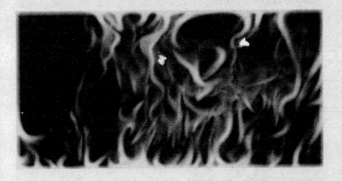

WRAPPED in a heavy, brown wool cloak, a sheepskin hat jammed down on his head, Lan plodded unhappily down the gray, cheerless streets under a leaden sky to his first class since his illness. Cold air numbed his nose, and even through his woolen gloves, his fingers were getting chilled. It wasn't quite cold enough for snow; icy rain had been falling for the last three days, and the skies threatened to make it four days in a row.

The headache had not returned for a third time, perhaps because the herbalist had suggested the use of an ongoing sleeping aid. It was a much, much milder potion than the medicine he'd sent to cure the headache. There had been no more night horrors, at any rate, and when Lan had no more symptoms for a week, his mother had ordered him out of bed and back to school.

He knew, he just knew, that his worst fears were about to be confirmed. By this time, the rotten weather had kept the Sixth Formers from their after-school pleasures for at least a week, and they were surely exercising their wits at the expense of their schoolmates by now.

He saw ample evidence of that as soon as he entered the gate and stepped into the front court of the school.

The Sixth Formers had gathered in a group around some hapless victim, while the other possible targets took advantage of their preoccupation to slink past them and into the front door. Lan did the same, but couldn't help glancing at the group as he slipped past, when a burst of laughter followed Loman's command of, "Jump, Froggy!"

In the middle of the circle stood the unfortunate Froggy, her eyes bulging more than ever, her face smeared with a bright green cosmetic that almost matched her woolen cloak.

Lan averted his eyes before she could catch his gaze, and scuttled for the safety of the door. If the others saw her looking imploringly at someone, they would probably turn to see who she was looking at, and seize on him as a fresh source of amusement.

Another evidence that the Sixth Formers had gotten bored enough to increase their persecution sat in the desk right in front of Lan. Owyn sported a sour expression and a pair of feathers in his curly hair, one over each ear. They did, indeed resemble the false ear-tufts on an owl. Lan resolved to take no notice of the unorthodox ornaments.

Their teachers certainly seemed oblivious. The lessons went on as normal, with perhaps a little more attention paid to Lan, to make certain that he had kept up with the rest of the class. No one commented on Owyn's feathers.

Lan not only proved he had kept up to the satisfaction of the teachers, he was actually able to relax a little, as he had read a trifle ahead of the rest. Confined to bed as he'd been, with the only possible amusement being his books, he'd begun to find them more interesting than he'd thought. He *still* would rather be roaming the woods around Alderscroft, but reading was better than doing nothing.

"Well, if this is the effect of your little fever, Lavan, I could wish that the entire class would catch it," one of the teachers said dryly. As a nervous chuckle ghosted up from another part of the room, the teacher glared in that direction and added, "Perhaps some of you might consider following your classmate's example and actually *study* when you are at home."

But as the lunch hour neared, Lan felt more and more nervous. The Sixth Formers had surely noticed that he'd been gone—had someone told them why? What had they been planning for him? How could he possibly anticipate what Tyron would demand?

He might not demand anything. He might actually feel sorry for me. I have been sick. He might be afraid he'll catch whatever I have. Or maybe the Schoolmaster told him to leave me alone until they know I'm well. . . .

There was nothing for it. When the bell rang for lunch, he left with the rest, and did his best to slip in unobtrusively. He avoided Froggy's company as if she had plague, but so did everyone else. The girl sat all by herself with a ring of empty seats around her, her bright green face hidden by her hair as she kept her head bowed.

Lan could only feel relief that it was Froggy sitting there alone, and not him.

He embedded himself in a group of Fifth and Fourth Formers and ate quietly, with one ear on the Sixth Form table. *I'm not here,* he thought fiercely at them. *Don't even think of me. I don't exist.*

He tried to eat at the same rate as the others, though tension made it difficult to swallow. He wanted to leave when they did, in the crowd, to put off the moment when Tyron noticed he was back as long as possible.

But sudden silence at his end of the table, the stares of those across from him, and a heavy hand on his shoulder told him that all his subterfuge was in vain.

"Come along, Scrub," said Loman, clamping his hand on Lan's shoulder hard enough to bruise, and lifting him up out of his seat. "Tyron wants a word with you."

The Sixth Former shoved him roughly up the aisle between the tables, until they arrived at Tyron's seat. Tyron had turned his chair about and was waiting, watching them down his nose, for all the world like he thought he was the King himself on his throne. Then again—here, he might just as well have been.

Lan stumbled to a halt, managing not to fall when Loman gave him a final push. "So, Scrub, you've been gone a while," Tyron said, with a glittering, false smile.

"I've been sick . . . sir." It was hard to choke out the last word, but he did, anger smoldering, but not yet burning. He dropped his eyes to the wooden floor, determined not to let Tyron see anything in his face that he could use.

"So I've been told. And do you know, I don't believe it. I think you're lying, Scrub. I think you're a slacker, and a liar."

Lan gritted his teeth and said nothing.

Tyron raised his voice so that the whole room could hear—easy enough, now that every other voice had been silenced. "I think you were feigning. You just wanted to slack off, wanted a little holiday for yourself. You might have fooled your mummy, but you can't fool me. Now what have you got to say for yourself?"

"No one fools my mother, least of all me . . . sir. Especially not when it costs her money for the services of the herbalist." He managed not to throw Tyron's accusation back in his teeth, and to keep his tone level, though every muscle in his body strained. And—thank the gods!—Tyron laughed at that. "And when I wasn't drinking the herbalist's wretched medicines, she saw to it I got no holiday from books."

"Owly!" Tyron called. "Is that true?"

"He's ahead of the rest of us, sir," Owly replied sullenly.

Tyron laughed again. "And that's one in your eye, isn't it, little bookworm? That's one in your eye!"

Lan thought for a moment that he might escape, that he'd provided Tyron with enough amusement for the moment.

"Still, you've not been *here,* have you? You've not been here to have, oh, any number of tasks set you." Tyron's voice took on that cloyingly pleasant tone it always did when he was about to do something appalling. "So I believe I'll have to set you something that will make up for your absence. Your father is a cloth merchant, is he not?"

Lan couldn't imagine what his father would have to do with this, but he nodded, rather than trust his tone not to betray him.

"Good. I need a new wardrobe for Midwinter, and my parents are being stubborn about expenses. Bring me a tunic length of scarlet velvet tomorrow. Silk velvet, mind, not wool plush. I have appearances to keep up."

At that, Lan's head snapped up as his mouth dropped open. "How am I supposed to do *that?*" he squeaked incredulously. Silk velvet was worth a gold piece an ell—and scarlet was worth twice that! He couldn't just waltz up to his father and ask for two ells of the stuff!

"You've pocket money, don't you?" Tyron asked, his eyes sparkling maliciously.

"No! I *don't!* My parents—" he choked on the words, blushing as scarlet as the coveted velvet at having to confess in public that he was not given the pocket money that every other student seemed to have.

"Well, then, I suppose you'll just have to find some other way, won't you?" Tyron lounged back in his chair and waved his hand idly. "I'm sure you'll think of something. Remember, two ells of scarlet silk velvet, by tomorrow. I'm sure you know what will happen—" the greedy eyes gloated at him, "—if you were to fail to get it for me."

He stumbled back down the aisle, now as much of a pariah as Froggy; people actually drew back from him, as if afraid his misfortune would contaminate them. He didn't even try to take his seat; he had no more appetite anyway. Instead, he went straight to the classroom, waiting in a dull fog for the rest to return. As he sat there, hands clenched in a knot in front of him, the others filed in, wordlessly, casting odd glances at him. He still felt hot, and that smoldering anger had made such a red-hot coal in his chest he didn't feel able to speak. Not that any of them said a word to him.

Maybe his expression warned them away.

But when the teacher came in, *he* didn't nook as if Lan appeared any different. The teacher looked over the whole class, then rested his gaze on Lan, and said only, "Lavan. Can you recite yesterday's lesson for us?" as if Lan hadn't been away at all. "I hope you've been as diligent for this class as you seem to have been for the others."

Lan stood up with some difficulty, for there was a sort of roaring in his ears and his knees felt wobbly. He opened his mouth to speak—

And the next thing he knew, he was lying on the floor, with Owyn's anxious face leaning over him and the teacher saying sharply, "Clear back, all of you!" As he tried to sit up, he gasped with pain and fell back again. The headache was back, with a vengeance.

And he could have wept with relief instead of pain. He welcomed the agony, every throb, every lancing blow through the temples, as the teacher assisted him to his feet and helped him out of the classroom. The gods had granted him a reprieve, once again, and redemption. Not even Tyron would dare accuse him of fakery after this—

He only got halfway down the hall before he blacked out a second time. When he woke again, it was to find himself lying on a couch in Master

Keileth's office, with an old man in Healer Greens examining him. He looked up into the old man's aged face to see warm blue eyes, half-hidden in wrinkles, regarding him with compassion.

The old man was speaking, he realized vaguely, but not to him.

"—not an illness. My guess would be dazzle-headaches, though they don't usually come with fever like this." The old man was saying. Then he noticed Lan's open eyes, and he passed his hand over his bald head. "Ah, awake are you? How do you feel?"

"Awful," Lan croaked. The pain hadn't abated one bit, and the light hurt his eyes.

The old man nodded, helping him sit up enough that he could drink a potion he recognized by its taste. "Send him home, Master Keileth, until this attack's passed. That's all we can do for such things once they're well started like this one. I'll take him home in my carriage, talk with his parents, and leave another medicine at his house that should help prevent them in the future."

Master Keileth gave a sigh that was half exasperation and half relief. As the pain potion took hold, the Healer helped Lan to his feet and got him out the door, down the stairs in the chill air, and into the carriage. He was amazingly strong for such a wizened old fellow. Once there, safely outside the walls of the school, Lan's relief was so profound that the medicine worked even faster and Lan let himself fall into induced slumber. His last coherent thought was that Master Keileth was undoubtedly annoyed at the inconvenience of having a pupil pass out in his school, but probably relieved that *he* couldn't be held responsible.

Nor would he have to refund all that tuition money.

HE roused when they arrived at the house, and the servants brought him up to his room with a great deal

of unnecessary fuss. Three of them descended on the
carriage—the housekeeper and two of the manservants. The housekeeper directed the operation like
a shrill-voiced general as the two manservants each
draped an arm over their shoulders, and with Lan dangling between them, took him up the stairs and
dropped him onto his bed, where he sat, blinking owl-
ishly, too fogged to think of what to do next. The
manservants stripped him to his skin and threw a
nightshirt over him, then bundled him into bed with
brisk and impersonal efficiency.

His mother was home already, for some reason, and
followed them up, right behind the old Healer. When
Lan was settled into bed, she faced the Healer with a
tight-lipped expression, waiting for an explanation.
The Healer was not at all cowed by her, which Lan
thought was incredibly brave of him.

"Madam, your son is not *seriously* ill," he began,
"although I can tell you that what he suffers from is
not in the least feigned. And although his pain is in
his head, so to speak, it is not in his mind."

I'd better . . . try to stay awake for this, Lan thought.
Neither the Healer nor his mother paid any attention
to him, but that was hardly an unusual occurrence.
They conducted their conversation over his head, as
he fought the medicine to try and listen.

But struggle as he might, his eyelids closed on their
own, and all he managed was to hear a few words of
the Healer's explanation.

". . . often come on in adolescence . . . not common,
no, but not abnormal . . . girls more often than
boys . . . stress, upset . . ."

It was on that last word that the medicine overcame
Lan's determination to stay awake, and he lost his
hold on consciousness.

He slept, woke in darkness to gulp down more medicine to kill the pain, and slept again. He woke again
and repeated the dose, as much to avoid having to talk
with anyone as to numb his head. If he was asleep, no

one would bother him, and right now, he didn't want to have to explain himself.

But by the next evening, the time for the inevitable interview with his mother arrived.

He woke clearheaded, though apprehensive, for at some point during his slumbers, he had managed to form a decision. Tyron's suggestion—practically a demand—that he *steal* the velvet had been the final pebble that starts an avalanche. He had to at least try to reveal what the Sixth Formers were doing to the rest of the school, himself included.

After the scullery maid took his supper tray away, he heard his mother's footsteps on the stairs, and braced himself. Nelda entered the room and took her seat on a chair that had been placed beside his bed and folded her hands in her lap, looking at him gravely. The candles arranged around the room gave a soft and wavering light that was very flattering to her, making her seem not much older than her son.

"Well, she said, after a lengthy pause. "The Healer tells us that this illness of yours is something he calls 'dazzle-headaches.' He has a medicine that will help prevent them, although he tells me it can't be counted on to work all the time."

"Dazzle-headaches?" Lan replied. It seemed an innocuous name for something that hurt so much. "But why did I get them in the first place?"

His mother frowned. "He *says* that it is probably stress, or emotional strain that brought them on, though what you have to be stressed about, merely going to school, I can't imagine. . . ."

"I could stay home and study!" Lan exclaimed hopefully, taking advantage of her momentary pause. "The teachers said I did so well that I was ahead of the—"

"Out of the question," Nelda said sharply, interrupting him with a frown. "That might work for a few days' absence, but under no circumstances will that do as a permanent solution. You're going to have to decide not to allow your emotions to get away from you, that's all."

That's all? Is she insane? How does she think I'm supposed to do that? In mounting anxiety and desperation now, unthinking, he shook his head violently and blurted out the story of his ongoing persecution, ending with Tyron's demand for the velvet. It didn't matter that this situation was humiliating; it didn't matter that he looked a fool. All that mattered was that she see that he couldn't go back to that school—not unless he had the open protection of the adults, so overt that even Tyron would not dare harass him anymore.

His mother listened, openly growing more skeptical with every word, right up until the point where Lan related Tyron's demands. At that point, she threw up her hands in disgust.

"Lavan Chitward, I cannot make up my mind if you are a coward, stupid, or a liar!" she said, her tone dripping with contempt.

"I'm *telling you the truth!*" Lan groaned. "Why won't you believe me? Why would I make any of this up? Send to ask any of the others, they'll tell you!"

But would they? Would they dare risk the anger of the Sixth Formers if they tattled?

Nelda snorted. "If you aren't a liar, you've allowed these boys to bully and tease you, and you made no attempt to stand up to them." Her lip curled. "That makes you a coward; Sam would never put up with this sort of nonsense."

"But—" Yes, and Sam was tall and strong and no one would *dare* shove him around!

Nelda went on as if she hadn't heard his weak protest.

"And as for that last tale of yours, well!" She shook her head. "Tyron Jelnack's father is the Grand Master of the Silversmiths' Guild, Lavan; why would he do anything like you claim he's done? First of all, I cannot believe that a boy from that fine a family would behave the way you have been describing, and secondly I *do not* believe he would ever dream of making that kind of extortionate demand!"

Lan listened to his mother in a state of shock, numb with incredulity. She *still didn't believe him!* He had thought that she would cover him with scorn for "not standing up for himself," but he had never, ever, thought that she wouldn't believe him!

"The only possible explanation is that they've been making a goose out of you," she scolded him. "Since I can't believe that you would try to lie about all of this, that is the only conclusion I can come to. These boys have been pulling an enormous joke on you, and *you* were too dense to see it!"

A joke? She thinks this was all a joke on me? How could she—how could she even imagine—

She shook her head again, oblivious to his shocked gaze. "Lavan, you are more trouble than all of your brothers and sisters put together. Why can't you be like the rest of them?"

With that, she rose and left him, leaving him alone with the flickering candles and a feeling of complete despair.

Never had he felt so completely alone.

His last possible refuge had been closed to him; his own mother thought he was exaggerating and being duped. Nothing would be done, and he would have to go back to school knowing that he had no other choice but to endure whatever Tyron decided to deal out to him.

No point in trying to tell his father about this; Nelda would give him her own interpretation, and that would be that. Archer would hear no further appeals from Lan.

As for the velvet . . . if Tyron *didn't* forget, the velvet might as well be on the moon. Lan could never get it for him. He had no money to buy it, and his father would never let him have it. As for stealing it— out of the question. Velvet was kept in a locked room at the warehouse, every thumb's length of it measured and accounted for.

Tyron didn't want the velvet. He just wanted another excuse to bully Lan. *He'll just flog me,* he tried to tell himself. *What's a few stripes? He won't kill me.*

No, but the pain and the humiliation . . . and worse than that, the certain knowledge that every student in the school would look down on him the way his mother did now . . . how could he bear that? And there would be years more of this, of being beaten and humiliated, of being bullied and treated as less than the lowest ragpicker.

What he wanted to do was to howl his anguish like an animal, but what came out of his throat was a strangled whimper.

If only he could just drink enough of the potion to sleep forever. . . .

He lay flat on his back as the candles burned out, one by one, a bleak cloud of depression weighing him down. Slowly, silently, tears ran down his temples, leaving behind cold trails on the skin and soaking into his hair.

Finally the last of his candles guttered in a pool of its own wax, and he reached despondently for his medicine. There wasn't enough left in the bottle to let him sleep forever. If only there was!

Well, if it helped with the pain in his head, perhaps it would help with the pain in his heart.

DRUGS only brought an end to the physical pain; they did nothing for his despair. He lost his appetite, but now that he was no longer suspected of having a fever, apparently no one noticed that the trays came down almost as full as when they went up. He took his medicines in apathetic silence, and found a strange refuge in the books he used to despise.

This time it was the Healer who had put a time limit to his retreat; the Healer had said that he should be ready to return to school in three days, so in exactly three days, there was another visit from his mother.

She appeared with the supper tray, and actually gazed on him with a hint of approval.

"Your teachers are extremely pleased with you," she said, neutrally. "You're going to be quite ready for school tomorrow."

He wouldn't look into his mother's eyes. He knew there would be no reprieve.

At breakfast, Nelda handed him a small glass containing some thick, unidentifiable liquid.

"What's . . . this?" he asked, staring at it dully.

"The medicine that will keep you from having those headaches from now on," Nelda replied, with a tart edge to her voice. Now that was *not* what Lan remembered; as he recalled, the Healer had not put things with such certainty. *It will* help *prevent them,* was what Lan remembered. But it was obvious that Nelda was determined that the inconvenience of the headaches would no longer be occurring to disrupt the household schedule.

And if they do—obviously it will be because I did something wrong, that I didn't take enough of the medicine, or didn't take it at the right time, he thought bitterly, his throat closing with a painful lump. *Or because I'm faking it.*

The medicine was nowhere near as bitter as his thoughts, and he swallowed it down without a grimace for the taste. Then he gathered up his books, wrapped himself in his depression as well as his cloak, and trudged off through the bleak half light of a gathering storm to what he could not help but feel was his doom.

He didn't try to hide in a crowd this morning; why bother? Tyron would find him no matter where he was.

Bundled in his cloak, with the hood pulled over his head, perhaps they didn't recognize him. He didn't

make his usual sprint, he walked—or, rather, plodded—straight to the door. And no one stopped him,
or even interfered with him.

But this did nothing to give him his lost hopes back
again. In fact, all it did was increase his feeling of
impending doom. With leaden steps he climbed the
staircase to his floor.

*He's waiting. He's sitting like a spider in the middle
of his web. He knows he can have me any time he
wants, and he's just waiting for the perfect time, with
the biggest audience.*

Silence fell over the classroom as he entered, took
off his cloak, and hung it on his peg near the door
with the rest.

He sat down at his desk without a word to any of
the others. He didn't think it was his imagination that
painted expressions of pity in their eyes, mingled with
a kind of gloating relief. ("He's going to be picked
on, not me!")

The morning classes went far too quickly, and the
nearer the time came to lunch, the more Lan's stomach knotted and the less he felt like even seeing food.
But it wasn't until the rest filed out of the room and
he put his aching forehead down on the cool wooden
surface of his desk, that the answer to his unspoken
prayers broke into his mind.

*I don't have to go down to lunch! There is no reason
why I can't just stay here!*

It was so simple, and so perfect, he could hardly
believe no one had ever thought of that solution before. Perhaps it was only because hunger overcame
fear around lunchtime; but more likely, it was because
the students were used to following routine. The students had always gone down to lunch in the Hall at
noon; hence students always would. He had *no* appetite anyway; if he didn't go down to the Hall, there
was no way that Tyron and his cronies could reach
him! It was strictly forbidden for any student to be on
any floor that was not that of his own Form during

the school day, and not even Tyron was immune to that rule. He *did* have a sanctuary after all!

I don't care about today, he thought with a sigh, putting both arms up on his desk, closing his eyes and resting his head on his crossed arms. *My stomach's in knots anyway. Tomorrow I'll bring some bread in my book bag.* There was always water to drink in an urn in the back of the classroom, and although bread and water was supposed to be punishment fare, not even all Lan's favorite dishes lined up in a row in the Hall would be superior to plain bread in peace.

And if anyone asked why he stayed here—well, he could just plead an uneasy stomach and a fascination with something he was reading. Illness combined with scholarship should be equal to any adult objections.

As his head eased, he got himself a drink and then went back to his desk to pillow his head on his arms. It was so peaceful in the quiet classroom that Lan actually dozed a little, and started awake at the sounds of the others returning to class.

He sat up and opened his book as the rest of his class came in. And he noticed that his classmates eyed him with curiosity. There was no doubt that his absence from the Hall had been noted.

As the next class proceeded, more ideas for escape came to him, for after all, there was still dismissal time to worry about this afternoon, and arrival in the morning. *I can wait as long as I have to for them to leave,* he decided. *And I'll really study, I won't just pretend to.* Although he still didn't care much for his classes, studying was preferable to bullying. And there was one thing that he did like: the reserved approval of his teachers for his progress. Reports were sent to parents at weekly intervals, and Lan's parents had been much better pleased with him of late.

If I do well enough, maybe they'll let me go back to Alderscroft for the summer. . . .

Better not to hope for that. It was enough if Tyron and the others would leave him alone. This ploy might make him late for dinner, but that was no problem. As long as he was safely at school and not running wild with friends (as if he had any), his parents wouldn't care where he was.

At the end of the last class, the third idea came to him, another flash of revelation that answered his final problem. *Sixth Form never gets here much earlier than anyone else.* In fact, he had occasionally gotten in past them because he had arrived before any of them did. *No one at home is going to pay any attention to how early I get up.*

It would be a sacrifice, because of all things he loved best, one of them was to lie abed in the morning. Getting up early was torture.

But if he could avoid the far worse torture the Sixth Formers meted out, it would be worth it.

I'll ask Cook to send one of the boys to wake me as soon as she starts work, he decided. That would be a good time; Cook was up and at her duties a good two candlemarks before any of the family. She might not like it, but he could mollify her by not demanding anything for breakfast that she didn't have already done by the time he got downstairs. Yesterday's bread and butter and jam would be good enough for him! She always cooked up more than anyone could eat; he could pocket the leftovers to serve for his lunch. And if his parents wondered why he was going in early and staying late, his weekly reports would be all the answer they needed.

The Sixth Formers would *never* get up early enough to catch him. Abusing the rest was an amusement for them, and things cease to be amusing if you have to make a personal sacrifice in order to attain them.

They're lazy; even if Tyron manages to bully the rest into promising to come early or stay very late, they'll forget to have someone wake them, or they'll get cold and tired of waiting for me. Tyron himself might stay, but Tyron by himself was just a single large, strong bully. He'd have to catch Lan, and he'd have to do it before Lan reached the street, while Lan was inside the school walls. Lan, on the other hand, had the distinct advantage of a good look-out spot. He could wait until he saw one of the Guard coming toward the school on his regular patrol. If the Guardsman heard a commotion, he'd seek out the source, whether or not it was behind a private wall. A Guardsman wouldn't care who Tyron's father was; he'd see a bigger boy abusing a smaller one, and he'd drag Tyron off and at the least give him an ear-blistering lecture. At *worst* (so far as Tyron would be concerned), he might even haul Tyron in front of a Justice!

I'd like to see Tyron explain himself then! he thought vengefully. It would be painfully clear just who was bullying whom, given Lan's stature and Tyron's—and that was something that could not be explained away. If Tyron claimed he was administering punishment on the orders of the Schoolmaster, there would be inquiries. A Justice might not take kindly to the notion of the Master of this school permitting the Sixth Form to adjudicate and administer all punishments.

But that was too much to hope for. Quickly, he stifled any rising elation and visions of revenge (or at least justice) at the hands of the Guard.

It would be enough merely to vanish from the minds and memories of the Sixth Form. Let them think his illness still kept him at home.

So when the rest of the class left the classroom, he remained behind, as usual. He took one of the desks in the back of the room, nearest the inside wall, so that if anyone glanced inside they wouldn't see him, just in case one or another of the teachers looked in. There he applied himself to his book with determination, if not enthusiasm, until the light had faded so much that the words danced in front of his eyes.

Only then did he slowly and cautiously rise and make his way to the window, peeking out carefully, to see if anyone was still waiting for stragglers.

The yard was empty; so was the street outside. Al-

ready the lamplighters had finished one side of the
street and were working their way up the opposite
side. It was *very* late; he'd have to run if he didn't
want to be too late for supper.

He gathered his books and flew down the stairs and
out into the gathering room. For the first time in a
very long time, his heart felt as light as his feet.

FIVE

STRETCHING aching muscles, Herald Pol pulled the blue-leather saddle off of Satiran's muscular back and regarded his Companion Satiran with a lifted brow. "Did you have to take that obstacle course *quite* so fast?" he asked the pearly ears tilted back to catch his words.

:*You're getting soft,:* Satiran replied, with a complacent swish of his silvery tail. :*All you ever do is stand around classrooms. It's my duty to keep you fit.:*

Pol heaved the saddle up onto the rail of Satiran's open stall with a grunt. "If you keep wrenching my shoulders and legs out of their sockets, I'm not likely to agree to run the obstacle course anymore, and then how do you accomplish your so-called duty, eh?"

Satiran turned his head on his long neck and looked straight into Pol's face with his lambent blue eyes, then bared his teeth in a mock snarl. :*I could chase you all around the Collegium. I'd not only keep you fit that way, I'd amuse the children.:*

"You would do that, wouldn't you?" Pol sighed, removing the blue wool blanket and draping it next to the saddle. "Is that fair?"

:You want them to retire you?: Satiran countered, shaking his head vigorously. *:You're fifty this month, and your hair is as silver as Herald Vanyel's. If you don't keep proving how fit you are, they'll force you to stay at the Collegium, and you'll die of boredom.:*

"Don't you mean *you'll* die of boredom?" Pol asked, but knew better than to wait for an answer. Satiran was never happier than when they were out in the field; the Companion seemed to thrive on bad weather and rough forage. He wasn't even *damp* after that rather enthusiastic round of the obstacle course, and Pol was dripping with sweat. "Why did I ever get Chosen by such a *hearty* soul?" he asked, eyes turned upward so that it seemed he addressed the roof of the Companions' stables.

But it wasn't the roof that answered.

:Because someone had to keep you fit,: Satiran replied, then produced a whinny that was entirely like a snicker. Lifting his silver hooves precisely, even daintily, he backed out of the stall, then turned and trotted off to Companion's Field where he dropped to the grass and rolled enthusiastically in the sun, just like any common horse.

Pol laughed in spite of aching shoulders and calves, stretched again, and headed for his quarters in the opposite direction, boots ringing solidly on the wooden floor of the stables. He wasn't going to be fit to encounter until after he'd had a bath and a change of clothing.

This had been an ongoing source of teasing and amusement between himself and his stallion since he was Chosen. Pol was, by nature, rather indolent, and freely admitted it. He liked living at the Collegium, and although he didn't *dislike* going on circuit, if he didn't have to, he would much rather be here. He had been born and raised in Haven, and loved his city and everything in it.

If only being a Herald didn't require leaving Haven so often! There's no city like this in the world, I think.

Even now, although the fine, bright days of autumn were past and Haven had taken on the gray cloak of early winter, he still thought it lovely.

He wouldn't have minded being permanently assigned to the Collegium, although truth be told, he wasn't an indispensable teacher. In fact, his main value to the Collegium lay in a rather peculiar fact. Unlike many other Heralds who taught here, aside from very strong Mindspeech, he didn't have a second strong Gift. Instead, he had a very little of *everything*.

There wasn't another Herald like him; others might have had many, many minor Gifts, but they weren't like Pol. For him, every single minor Gift, however weak, was active and usable.

As a consequence, although his Gifts were not in and of themselves terribly useful, he could literally teach younglings with any possible Gift or combinations thereof, even the most rare and esoteric. He could fill in until specific teachers could be brought back from other duties to tutor them past the beginning levels. At the moment he was coaxing a youngster with Animal Mindspeech through the first, tentative uses of his ability. Pol had to be in physical contact with an animal to speak to it or understand it; this young Trainee was going to be able to look through the eyes of any creature within leagues when he was ready to go out on circuit.

Before then, one of the two Heralds Gifted with strong Animal Mindspeech would have come back to spend a few moons at the Collegium and give him the benefit of an expert's teaching, but until then, Pol would do. Whenever there was a new trainee with a rare Gift, it was often Pol who was summoned to return to the Collegium once the youngster had settled in and his Gift was identified.

Pol was perfectly happy with any opportunity to help the young Trainees, however much Satiran might fret and long for "adventure."

"Adventure" is usually synonymous with discomfort,

not to say pain, Pol thought to himself, as he reached the door of the Herald's Wing and opened it. *"Adventure" is never the exhilarating experience that the would-be adventurer thinks it is.*

:I heard that,: Satiran snapped.

:*You were meant to.*: Pol chuckled at Satiran's mental snort of contempt, and headed for his room to get a fresh set of Whites, the full Herald's constant uniform that identified him as the proxy of the King himself—dispenser, discloser, and adjudicator of the law of Valdemar.

Ah, yes, a *fresh* set of Whites—clean, mended, and ready for him whenever he needed them. That was another benefit of being here, and not on circuit. A packhorse could only carry so much, and he got very tired of wearing the same clothing for days on end.

And that assumed he was on circuit and not pulling messenger duty, which meant riding for days on end, sleeping and eating in the saddle. He'd only had that duty a few times, but it was definitely *not* his favorite. *Thank the gods there are other, much faster riders than I!* he reflected, feeling every one of his years as he walked down the dim, quiet hallway toward the men's bathing room.

He hadn't been the only one out on the obstacle course today; several of the other teachers had taken advantage of the empty course to take some much-needed exercise. The Heralds had to take the times when it wasn't being used by the Trainees, who were, after all, the ones it had been built for. Pol was met at the door of the men's bathing room by a cloud of steam and the greetings of his fellows.

"Good run out there, Pol!" called Herald Isten, invisible in the steam hanging above his bathtub. "You ran that course like a man half your age!"

"And I feel like one who is twice my age," he replied, with a groan that was only half feigned, stripping off his filthy Whites and dropping them into a laundry hamper. "You haven't used up all the hot water, I hope?"

Isten laughed and fanned away the steam, so that his round, red face crowned with curling tendrils of dripping hair, darkened by the damp, appeared like a disembodied spirit in the mist. "I saved you enough, I promise."

"That's good, because if my old bones can't have a good soak, I'm going to have to thrash you." Pol eyed his colleague sternly.

Isten chuckled, knowing the bluff for what it was, and let the fog hide him again as Pol took a free tub and ran water into it from the copper boiler that served this bathing room. He checked the fire beneath the boiler, and added a stick or two of firewood while the tub filled. The boiler's supply of water was topped off from a reservoir on the roof of their wing, the same reservoir that supplied cold water directly.

Pol added some herbs and salts to his bathwater and climbed in with a sigh of utter content as the hot water soothed his aches.

And that is another thing entirely missing on circuit. Give me a hot bath, and I am a happy man.

:Deprive you of one, and you are intolerable.:

:That's because I care if I offend people with my odor,: Pol retorted. *:You might not mind smelling like a horse, but I do!:*

He was rewarded by Satiran's mental snicker.

There was, after all, another and equally compelling reason for Pol to spend at least half his time here at the Collegium, and her name was Elenor.

His youngest daughter Elenor.

He smiled at the thought of her, as he always smiled, as anyone who ever encountered Elenor smiled. She was a child who seemed to have been created to bring happiness to everyone around her. She was neither pretty, nor plain, but her personality sparkled so that no one ever thought her anything but lovely. Her sunny disposition brightened the gloomiest day; no one bent on a quarrel could sustain anger in her presence. As a Mind-Healer she was fulfilling every expectation of her teachers at Healer's Collegium. Her mother Ilea was every bit as proud of her as her father was.

Her mother, however, was needed elsewhere at the moment. Like Heralds, Healers had duties that superseded their own personal preferences, and the need for Healers to tend the wounded on the Border with Karse was of prime importance at the moment. Although the conflict between Karse and Valdemar had not erupted into open warfare lately, there was constant skirmishing and a constant stream of wounded. All the Healers of the Collegium took that duty in turn; Ilea had been excused as long as her youngest child was below the age of thirteen, but once Elenor was well into puberty, the duty could be put off no longer.

Neither Pol nor Ilea wanted to leave Elenor totally without a parent's presence, so Pol had been very glad when he was called back to Haven.

He wondered now and again, though, if she really needed him. Elenor at fourteen was as cool and level-headed a girl as many twice her age. She seemed to have another Gift, that of good sense, and never got into the tangles and trials that the Trainees of all three Collegia of Heralds, Healers, and Bards, often found themselves embroiled in. In fact, Elenor was often found in the midst of their trouble, patiently sorting it before any of the adults realized that there *was* a problem.

My little girl is not so little anymore. Maybe when this last pupil was thoroughly grounded and it was time to hand him off, Pol ought to volunteer for field duty again. There were never enough Heralds for all the work, and eventually Ilea would be back again.

Time never stood still; both of Elenor's sisters had grown up and gone off on their own, after all. Kaika was somewhere north of Haven, a Bard making the same sort of rounds that a Herald did, but with the difference that she was the collector and disseminator of information and entertainment. Or rather, information disguised as entertainment. She'd gotten her Bardic Reds a good three years ago. Her sister Amaly had gotten *her* Greens three years before that, and a husband to boot. She and Ranolf were raising their own brood and tending to the hurts of a fairly sizable village in the southwest. Both of them had their own lives now, and in the not-too-distant future, so would Elenor. He couldn't guide and protect her forever, no matter how much he wanted to.

You'd think that after two of them growing up and flying away, I'd have gotten used to the idea that children never remain that way, he thought with a physical pang. He bit his lip to still the quiet ache in his heart. *But, oh, how I wish they did. . . .*

:It's never easy to see them go, Chosen,: came the soft words in the back of his mind. *:We both have reason to know that.:*

Pol sighed and wordlessly agreed. Satiran had more reason to worry and grieve over his own offspring than Pol did; *his* eldest had come to a premature end, with his Herald, at the hands of the Karsites.

He turned his mind out of that path before he started to worry about Ilea. The Karsites didn't kill Healers, they weren't *that* barbaric, but they made major efforts to capture them. And Pol knew Ilea; she had a heart like a warrior, and never let danger keep her from rushing to the aid of the injured. He only hoped that Elenor's good sense was inherited from Ilea's side of the family as well as his, and that Ilea would know she would cause more harm than good by going into danger.

The water was cooling, and he thought briefly about running more hot water in—

But that *would* be slothful, and he pried himself up out of the tub, feeling unaccountably much heavier than when he'd gone in, and got himself dried, clothed, and presentable. It was nearly time for dinner; he'd have just about enough time to dry his hair before he had to join the courtiers.

And after dinner, provided his pupils left him in peace—he did have responsibility for more than just his little Animal Mindspeaker Kedd—he wanted to see if he could follow up some odd indications he'd felt over the past few weeks. It had *felt* like the first stirrings of a Gift, but if it was, it was a Gift unlike anything he had encountered before.

Pol was the one Herald who was at all sensitive to the odder Gifts, thanks to his own abilities, but since his strength was minimal, he couldn't reach much outside the walls of Haven, and about half the time, nothing much came of these vague sensations. Just because a Gift *began* to stir, it didn't follow that it would actually wake to full flower. Children often lost the use of Mind-Gifts as they entered puberty. The owner might successfully repress it and wall it off. Life changes might send a Gift into limbo again, particularly tragedy.

Still, Pol felt he had to follow up where he could, identify what the Gift he sensed was, if possible, and even find the owner. Usually, though, the Companions beat him to the last.

Pol sat in the open window of his room and combed his hair dry in the waning sunlight; he had a fastidious dislike of going out in public with wet hair. It was a comfortable little room, neat and well-ordered, shared most of the time with Ilea. With so much of white and blue surrounding him, and so much of green surrounding Ilea, Pol's personal tastes broke out in a certain peculiar rebellion in his furnishings. He preferred what Ilea called "earth colors," which were warm browns, wheat golds, and smoldering oranges. Fortunately, so did she. Geometrically patterned weavings softened the white walls and served as curtains; heavier pieces carpeted the floor from wall to wall. His blankets, collected over the years from the most skillful craftspeople he encountered, were splendidly patterned and as soft as swansdown, made from the silky hair of chirras and the wool of lambs. An enormous coverlet, pieced together from the skins of brown, black, and white sheep, could have decked the bed of the King himself.

In fact, one very like it did; Pol had brought it as a gift from his last foray into the field.

Ilea's touch was present in the fragrant wreaths of grapevine and dried herbs, the knitted wraps folded neatly atop one of the chests, waiting to be snuggled into on a chill evening, needlework pieces on the walls, the embroidery basket in the corner. And, hidden behind the doors of the wardrobe, her store of a Healer's Green robes were keeping his Herald's Whites company.

He smiled a little at that. At least if *they* couldn't be together, their uniforms could!

When the sun faded into twilight, he moved to a stool in front of the fire. When his hair was finally dry, he bound it into a thick tail at the nape of his neck with a plain silver clasp, and went on to dinner.

All Heralds present at the Collegium automatically had a place at the uppermost table of the Court, directly below the High Table itself; not all of them availed themselves of that privilege, though. Some preferred to dine with the Collegium, Trainees and teachers together; some preferred a solitary (or not so solitary) tray in their rooms. Pol enjoyed dining with the Court, however; his Gifts were not so sensitive that being with so many unGifted rubbed him raw, and he derived a certain amusement watching the little dramas that went on around him. The Court was full of drama, and although Pol had very little to do with the courtiers themselves, that very freedom gave him an impartiality that allowed him to find the jousting for place altogether hilarious. He had a knack for spotting a piece of trouble abrewing; sometimes all he could do was to alert others to potential difficulties, but at least they had that warning.

He was in good time. People were just now filing into the Great Hall, and Pol joined the traffic with a nod to one or two of the courtiers he *did* know, and a smile for a couple of the other Heralds who were either highborn themselves or for their own reasons preferred to dine here.

He took his place at the Herald's table with the rest, settling into his chair with a glance at the High Table. King Theran and his young son Clevis were laughing at something that King's Own Herald Jedin had just said; Queen Fyllis wasn't in her chair, but that was hardly surprising since she was still suffering from the nausea that always plagued her in the first two months of a pregnancy.

Poor Fyllis! Pol thought with sympathy; he knew the Queen quite well, better than most. The King and Queen both had been Chosen when Theran was still the Heir. At the time she (Herald-Trainee, the third daughter of the Duke of Brendan) met and fell in love with Theran, everyone had agreed that the marriage was the best possible match Theran could make; it created a strong bond of blood between the throne and a dukedom right on the far southeastern Border. She had been a pupil of Pol's; her odd Gift was Empathy. It was a very useful Gift for a monarch, but unfortunately, when she was in the first throes of pregnancy, sometimes she inadvertently projected her nausea to those nearest her, to the discomfort of her friends and family and the utter ruin of one formal dinner reception for the heads of the Craft Guilds back when she'd first been with child. That had been years ago; after that single disaster, she wisely absented herself from meals when pregnant. She drank most of her meals during the touchy months, soothing, smooth concoctions of milk, vegetables, fruits, and nuts, with a Healer nearby to help repress the nausea and make sure she actually got a well-balanced diet. Fyllis

claimed it was a small price to pay, considering that
the rest of her pregnancy was always a joy to her;
being with child made her positively bloom with
health and happiness.

The rest of her offspring weren't fit for the High
Table yet; one was in the "terrible twos" and the other
was still a baby. Clevis was a mere five, but was a
very well-behaved boy as long as his father's eye was
on him.

When it wasn't—well—bread rolls and pickles had
been known to mysteriously acquire the power of
flight, aimed unerringly at other children he'd been
quarreling with earlier in the day.

The young mischief maker was firmly sandwiched
between his father and the King's Own today, however, so it was unlikely there would be any food flights
at this meal.

Court meals were slow and deliberate affairs, with
each course punctuated and announced by musicians
or other entertainments. This was part of what made
coming to Court such an exciting and much-
anticipated event for the nobles and achievers of Valdemar; even the meals were grand affairs for those
who didn't often see professional entertainers. And as
for major festivals—well, when those who spent a season or two at Court went home again, they generally
talked about it for the rest of their lives.

It was costly for those who came here, in expenses
for the elaborate garments considered appropriate, in
lodging, and in any meals not taken in the Great Hall.
Some, but by no means all, of the highborn had their
own houses outside the Palace grounds, and a very
few rated lodging in the Palace itself, but for the rest,
suitable houses had to be found and leased, servants
hired, and furnishings supplied for the few months of
attendance at Court. This was an expensive proposi-
tion, multiplied manyfold when there was more than
one female in the family, for women seemed to require more in the way of elaborate clothing than men.

For instance . . . to Pol's right sat the many-daughtered Lord Vertalays, with all of his offspring lined up on their stools beside him, like one of those sets of dolls that fit one inside the other. It was a good thing that he had a ready source of income from his wool and mutton; he'd need it, dowering six daughters. Lady Vertalays, a wise and clever woman, made a virtue out of necessity; she saved money when they came to Court by doing so in winter when she could cut a fashionable figure in *woolen* garments, rather than of lighter fabrics that would have to be purchased. She had all their Court dress made from cloth woven of the wool of their own sheep, and dressed the entire family in the same colors, saving more money on dyes, carefully choosing colors that suited them all. When she could, she did without dying the cloth altogether; they had a set of garments in white, in a heathered gray, in brown, and in black. Instead of velvet, their heavier gear was made of wool plush— an equally lush fabric, but one that could also be home-woven. Instead of silk, they wore knitted lace, made of threadlike yarn of lambswool. All the embroidery was done by the clever hands of the Lady and her daughters, and together they made quite a fine showing. Pol might be the only person present who knew of her clever shifts, since he had once ridden a circuit that included their holdings. They came to Court for the purpose of getting the daughters acquainted with some of the young men they might be betrothed to one day. The Lady felt it was better to wed someone you at least liked rather than a total stranger.

That was more than many parents felt. To Pol's left was a potential source of trouble, and he wondered when it would break out. Young Lady Leana's rigid posture betrayed what her pleasant face did not; the contempt that her husband of a year held her in. *He* was engaged in a torrid affair with someone out in the city; Pol didn't know who it was, although he would bet his last penny that the King's Own did. *She* seethed with frustration and jealousy, and from some of the heated glances he'd seen her exchange with one of the young rakes of the lesser nobility, her frustration was likely to break out into a full-blown affair of her own very soon. She would probably flaunt her conquest in her husband's face; a bad idea, since he was hot-tempered as well as hot-blooded, and altogether too likely to either punish his wife or challenge her lover.

Probably both.

That would have repercussions of its own, since the marriage was a political one. Pol didn't envy the King; he'd have to sort it all out, somehow.

A more amusing feud was currently on display on the persons of Lady Isend and Duchess Abel; if they piled on much more in the way of jewelry and be-gemmed trimmings to their gowns, they might not be able to get up again if they fell over. Each of the ladies considered herself the sole authority on fashion, and spent most of her time trying to outdo her rival. The previous manifestation of the feud had been hats; tall, pointy ones, dripping veils and gold chains, which imperiled everyone around them and forced them to walk with a peculiar, backward-bent posture with the stomach thrust out. *That* had ended when someone new to Court had kindly inquired when they were expecting their babes to be born.

At least the feud had taken a useful turn this past summer, erupting in gowns made of the thinnest, gauziest possible materials—costly, of course, since that meant gossamer linen and silk, and each gown had to be made of three or more layers if the lady who wore one didn't want to reveal every possible bodily secret to the world. Gauze was cool, comfortable, and looked particularly lovely on slim, young bodies; that inspired the other ladies to copy them. Perhaps not every lady looked as ethereal and graceful in such gowns as the youngest and most lithe of the maidens, but at least they were all comfortable and less quarrelsome with the heat.

Anything that made the ladies of the Court less quarrelsome was worth a few less-than-lovely sights, in Pol's opinion.

He detected no other problems during the course of the meal, and when the sweets came around, he caught the eye of King's Own Herald Jedin and made a brief, but significant nod of his head towards Lady Leana. Jedin nodded, and shrugged a little. The interchange hadn't taken more than a few seconds, but Pol was satisfied that Jedin was aware of the situation. Jedin could always come talk to him later, if need be.

That was all he could do for now, and since he didn't particularly care for sweets, he excused himself to his fellow Heralds, and with a bow to the King, withdrew from the Hall.

As soon as he left the Palace and got into the Collegium, he cocked an ear toward the Collegium dining hall. A subdued hum came from it, indicating that the Trainees were still stuffing their growing bodies; for all of the formality of Court meals, the Trainees took as long or longer to eat than the courtiers, for they devoured a prodigious amount of food.

:Satiran, old friend, can you give me a bit of a boost while I look for those traces I touched last night?: he asked as he opened the door to his room. Servants had already been and gone; the fire had been refreshed, and the lamps lit. Pol hoped that tonight none of the youngsters would decide to have an emotional crisis. It would be nice to spend a peaceful evening for a change.

:Emotional crisis is the constant state of the young, Chosen,: Satiran chuckled. *:That's why they can eat so much; they burn it up with emoting. Of course I can give you a boost. I'm as curious as you.:*

Pol laughed a little, settling into his favorite chair and focusing his gaze on one of the lamp flames to bring himself easily and automatically into a trance, where it would be easier to work.

One by one, he called up his own Gifts, bringing them up like tiny flames within his mind, and searched within his limited range for an answering echo.

Even though the many Gifts that he knew had not resembled this odd one, he tried them anyway. It did no harm, and might awaken echoes from another nascent talent out there in his city.

One by one, he worked his way through them all, down to the most obscure, the kind of Gift that allowed one to see the living energy produced by even the humblest of creatures.

Nothing. Not so much as a hint. Whatever it was that had awakened him out of his sleep last night, it did not answer his call tonight.

When he had exhausted his repertoire, he came up out of his self-induced trance with a little grunt of frustration. As his trance state faded, he became aware that he had sat in one position for far too long. He felt as stiff as a wooden doll; his right shoulder hurt, and his mouth was dry.

:I know how you feel,: Satiran said, as he opened his eyes to see more than a thumb length of candle gone. *:There was something about that—stirring—last night. I don't know what it was. It bothered me then, and it still bothers me.:*

:Emotion is what it was,: Pol replied, getting up to stretch and walking slowly toward his fire. *:Very raw emotion, and a great deal of it, with no control to speak of.:*

:Adolescent,: Satiran confirmed. *:Yes, that's it. A Gift waking under pressure of emotion? That's not a comfortable thought—and, gods, I do hope it isn't Empathy!:*

:I can't think of anything worse than an Empathic Gift bubbling up under such circumstances,: Pol agreed, and yawned. *:On the other hand, if that's what it is, there isn't a better place than Haven for someone*

*like that to appear. We've an entire Collegium full of
experienced Healers prepared to deal with that sort of
thing.:*

Satiran "absented" himself briefly from the close
conference with Pol; he was probably conferring with
the other Companions for a moment. Pol took advantage of the free moment to check his time-candle and
decided that it was late enough that he wouldn't get
any visitors tonight. Using all of his Gifts in sequence
like that was tiring, especially calling up things he
didn't often have an occasion to invoke.

He blew out all but his bedside candle, unclasped
his hair, and stripped for bed, wistfully regarding the
empty half of the bed where Ilea should have been.
He was under the covers and reaching for his bedtime
reading before Satiran got back to him.

*:No one else has any more idea of what it was than
we do,:* the Companion told him. *:And no one else but
you felt it. So that means that, whatever else it is, it
isn't* Empathy.*:*

:So it's something really odd.: Pol cheered up a little
at that. If there wasn't a Herald here at the Collegium
that had felt the surge last night, that meant that there
wasn't anyone here who could *teach* whatever it was.

So if this Gift manifested rather than being re-
pressed, Pol was guaranteed at least another few
months within Collegium walls. That meant more time
with Ilea, when she returned.

Of course it was even odds which it would do—
manifest or submerge. *:Are any of the Companions
feeling restless?:* he asked Satiran. That would be one
indication—if the nascent Gift belonged to a presump-
tive Herald, the Companion due to Choose him would
start sensing that his or her time was near. Or at
least, nearing.

*:Not that I've noticed, and nobody has volunteered
that information, but . . . whoever it is might not. No
one likes to be disappointed in public.:* Satiran himself
had experienced two "false alarms" before he was

drawn to Pol, and the Companions often felt a certain guilt when an expected call didn't come. Pol had a good idea why that should be; there was always the feeling that there was something that one should have done . . . that if, just perhaps, a vague urging had been followed, there might be one more badly-needed Herald.

:Well, you might as well get some sleep. Or whatever,: Pol replied lightly, and was rewarded by a mental chuckle.

:Whatever. Not that it's your *business!:* came the taunting reply.

:Oh, thank you! When you know that Ilea is hundreds of leagues away from me! Twist the dagger, why don't you?: he taunted back.

:Chastity is good for you. Think how much more you'll appreciate her when she comes back!: was the retort, and Satiran dropped out of the front of his mind.

Pol laughed, and opened his book. He had decided to stay awake a little longer than usual, just in case that unknown with the odd Gift was only manifesting in sleep himself.

That might be the case, and might account for why he hadn't touched off an echo when he looked for it.

That would also account for the raw emotions, the sort of uncontrolled feelings that occurred in dream-sleep, when all the inhibitions of the day were gone.

But he was nodding over his book in short order, and finally decided to give up and call it over for the night.

Whatever it was *would* appear again—or not. But if it did, he wouldn't be caught unaware the second time.

SIX

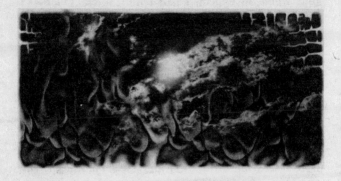

THE next day brought the start of the autumn rains; there had been occasional showers before, but Pol woke up to the kind of steady downpour emerging from solid gray skies that meant there would be day after day of rain for the next several weeks. There would be breaks in the rain, but the sun would have to fight its way through the overcast and, for the most part, would lose the fight. By now the fields outside were getting soggy, which meant that there would be no more grueling circuits of the obstacle course for some time. Satiran didn't care about rain, but he hated mud, and the obstacle course would be a morass until the rains ended. Back when Pol had been a Trainee, they hadn't had any choice but to run the course when they were ordered to; now that they had that choice, by common consent they avoided the place during the autumn rains.

Sadly, the rains also brought the cool, crisp days full of brilliant colors to an end as well. A quick glance out his window told Pol that the damage had already begun, with leaves dropping as steadily as raindrops.

This was the time of year when the leaves quickly faded to brown and dropped from the trees, leaving skeletal fingers silhouetted against a uniformly gray sky. Right now the Trainees in their own gray uniforms trudged about the Collegium grounds, hooded heads hunched against the rain, covered by the waxed cloth of their gray raincapes. At the moment, they looked like bits of scudding rain cloud themselves.

Pol rarely had to leave the Collegium wing himself when he taught here; the classrooms where the Heraldic classes were held were all within the wing. He greatly appreciated the warm fires in every classroom, though every time an outside door opened, a cold, damp wind whipped through the halls. The classrooms were just a bit bigger than his bedroom, and had a friendly warmth to them.

His particular specialty was in geography; Herald-Trainees needed to learn first how to read maps, then needed to memorize those maps, for one day they might have to find their way without the benefit of a map. Many things could happen to a Herald on circuit; the loss of supplies should never mean *becoming* lost.

This lot evidently had clean-up duty at breakfast today; they came into the classroom heat-flushed and scrubbed, with cheerful faces and suppressed giggles. The Collegium Cook was a huge woman without an ounce of fat on her body, who looked as if she ought to be wielding a sword, not brandishing a ladle. She also had a bottomless fund of jokes and a finely-honed sense of humor that made kitchen duty prized above all other chores.

Trainees got the benefit of *some* servants, but for the most part, they had to pitch in to keep the Collegium running. It was good for all of them. Trainees from the farms and cottages discovered leisure and servants, and the highborn learned what it was like for those not fortunate enough to have been born with a title. Trainees took turns at all the chores, from working in the kitchen to waiting at table, from helping in the laundry to stocking the closets, from chopping wood to making certain every room had a filled wood carrier, from mending uniforms to making them. The only thing they didn't do was cleaning; they had to keep their own rooms clean and tidy, but the classrooms, bathing rooms, and hallways were cleaned by the Collegium servants.

The same discipline held in Healer's and Bard's Collegia; it made all students equal, as did the uniforms all Trainees wore. Everyone in the Collegia wore uniforms that identified their status as students. In the case of Healer-Trainees, the uniforms were of a pale green; the Bardic Trainees wore a rusty color. There were a few highborn students, pupils whose noble families wanted them to have an extended education, and a few commoners whose *uncommon* intelligence bought them entry to the same education, who were not affiliated with any of the three Collegia but shared the classes. They, too, wore uniforms, of a light blue. There were no privileges of rank within the Collegia, nor of wealth, though occasionally some students among the highborn tried to break that rule. The King himself usually dealt with such a situation; he was hardly an autocratic man, but there was one thing he wouldn't tolerate, and that was *any* interference in the running of the Collegia.

The three Collegia ran on much the same schedules, and often shared classes. But there was a fundamental difference in the discipline of the Herald's Collegium—if a highborn or wealthy Trainee in either Bardic or Healer's Collegium couldn't abide becoming one among equals, he or she could always leave. Those who abandoned their vocation would always have the shadow of failure hanging over them, and the unused Gift gnawing at them, but they *could* leave. Not so for a Heraldic Trainee. The bond of Herald and Companion was not a thing that could be abandoned.

Not that any Trainee had ever seriously tried. There

was always a Trainee or two who had troubles, but with help, they always worked through those troubles and adjusted. No one was ever Chosen who could not adapt to the regimen of the Collegium and the responsibilities of the Herald. The Companions themselves saw to that. *They* were the final arbiters of who became a Herald and who was unworthy of the honor, and only once, in all of the history of Valdemar, had one ever made a mistake—and even then, it was not in whom she Chose, but that she did not help him when he needed her the most, repudiating him in her anger at what he had done.

Pol had that ever in his mind when he faced his classes of young Trainees. Every Herald did. Never again would there be another Tylendel.

But there was no sign of any trouble in the younglings he was teaching this year. Most of them were the offspring of farmers, craftsmen, and small traders. The two or three highborn had adapted cheerfully, and even eagerly, to their new duties. There were conflicts of personality, of course, and love affairs, broken hearts, and quarrels, mistakes, misunderstandings, and adolescent rebellion, but no tragedies abrewing.

The next class came in dripping, smelling of wet wool; before Pol's class this lot took archery practice, even in the pouring rain. They chattered among themselves much more cheerfully than he would have, given that they'd gone straight from breakfast into the cold rain.

Classes were small, no more than six pupils at a time, so that teachers could give each student individual attention. In Pol's case, he taught a total of five Geography classes over the course of the day, and sometimes filled in for a teacher in who was ill. There were two classes in the lowest level of difficulty, two in the second, and one in the third. After a Trainee finished third-level Geography, he or she went on to Orienteering, the skill of dead reckoning in completely unknown territory.

"Well, Derrian," Pol asked the first one to sit down, "How did you manage this morning?"

Derrian grinned impishly. "We did all right," he said, with a hint of a smirk on his freckled face. "M'pa would have skinned me alive if I'd been too stupid to learn to keep m'bowstring dry by now."

"Derry showed us all what to do," the smallest and youngest of the class piped up, with a worshipful glance at Derrian. "Weaponsmaster actually *smiled!*"

"Good for you, Derrian!" Pol applauded. "Good for all of you, and well done." He turned and drew a map symbol on the slate board behind him with a chunk of chalk. "Now, since you've been so clever, Derrian, perhaps you remember what *this* symbol means?"

By the time the class was over, the Trainees had thoroughly dried out and the room no longer smelled of wool. The third class hadn't undertaken anything out in the wet, and after that class came the break for lunch.

Pol habitually met with three other teachers for a card game over lunch; today it was his turn to host, so he sent a page down to the kitchen for provisions and set up the chairs and the table at the back of the room for a game.

The players were a mixed bag, and he reflected as he arranged the cold meat, sliced breads, and the rest on his desk that they would never have met, much less become friends, if they hadn't been Heralds. Damina was the eldest of the group, a tough old woman with a perfectly unreadable face and a wicked sense of irony. Like Pol, she was a native of Haven. Tevar was highborn—the highest, in fact, since he was the King's youngest brother, but you would never have known it from the company he preferred to keep and the subjects that interested him. In point of fact, he was the specialist in wilderness survival and flora and fauna; he also taught Orienteering and took final-year Trainees out into the wilderness and trained them to survive with only the clothes on their backs and what they had in their pockets. The youngest of the group, Melly, taught History and Literature, and was one of the tutors for students having difficulties. She was assigned permanently to the Collegium, unlike the other three, because she was the best teacher that anyone had ever seen, with the talent—almost, one could say, the Gift—for getting younglings interested and excited about learning. That—and her size. She couldn't have been any taller than the average thirteen-year-old. Riding circuit required physical abilities that she didn't have, but that didn't matter. She could, and did, ride messenger service during any emergency. She could, and did, take her turn out "on circuit" within Haven itself. She had dodged Karsite arrows and bandits, had come into Haven reeling in the saddle with exhaustion. Melly might not take the most arduous of duties, but no one could say that she didn't take the most hazardous.

And she was a deadly card player.

Melly was the first to arrive, with the other two right behind her. "Pfui!" Tevar said, knitting black brows as the wind drove a gust of rain against the window glass. "I hate this time of year!" He pulled his chair back with a scrape, and dropped into it, pulling his tail of sable hair to the side so he wouldn't get it caught between his back and the back of the chair.

Melly cast a glance at the window herself, peering from beneath a thick brown fringe of bangs that made her look like a cheerful little pony. "I don't know; I rather like it, as long as the weather's out there and I'm in here."

"Makes you feel sorry for the ones out there, though, doesn't it?" Damina asked, as she helped herself to food, then settled into her chair. "Then again, it isn't like this everywhere."

"It's still fine down in the south, and in the north the rains are over by now," Pol agreed. "For that matter, it isn't everywhere that gets these autumnal downpours, either, so you could be wasting your pity, Damina."

"Oh, the gods forbid that I should waste anything so precious as *pity!*" she exclaimed wryly. "I have so little of it to spare!"

"And far too much breath," Tevar retorted. "Are you going to talk, or play?"

With a chuckle, Damina cut the cards, and they began their usual fierce combat until the Collegium bells warned that classes were due to begin.

At the end of the day, Pol decided against dinner with the Court and opted for a seat with the rest of the Collegium. A Collegium dinner was the best possible antidote to a gloomy day.

He went in early, while the Trainees were still washing up, taking his favorite seat at a table over near one of the fireplaces. Those tables were generally kept clear so that the adults could claim them, perhaps out of pity for their "old bones!" There were two or three other teachers there, and a group of Heralds entered right after he settled himself, Heralds who had just gotten back from their assignments and had not yet gotten new ones. He waved them over, although he didn't know any of them personally; they would have news of their sectors, and would be willing to share it. They were all fairly young, probably in their first decade of serving as full Heralds; all aggressively fit and lean. The three young men, two very dark, one less so, reached him first, followed by a blonde woman.

"Jonotan, Lake Evendim," said the first to sit down, shaking Pol's extended hand, giving his name and the circuit he'd been on, just as a fifth Herald, an older woman, entered, looked about, and headed for his table.

"Kiela, Staghorn Forest," the young blonde woman told him with a nod.

The broadly smiling dark man introduced himself

next, as "Lerrys, the Fells," followed by a shorter, but equally dark fellow who was "Wernar, Torgate."

The last was another woman, middle-aged with gray streaking her mousy hair, that Pol knew very slightly. "Charis! Good to see you!" he welcomed her. "What sector this time?"

She settled into place with a weary sigh. "Karsite Border," she said, and got the immediate attention of the others.

"And?" Pol asked, assuming the duty of the questioner as host.

One of the Trainees came by about then with a platter of hot bread and a bowl of butter, and Charis made an unmistakable gesture toward him with her eyes. They waited in silence for the boy to get out of hearing distance, and in the meantime, the hall began to fill with chattering youngsters, making it easier for them to converse without being overheard.

"I'll give you the worst news first," Charis told them, as they unconsciously bent toward her, all of them with grave expressions. "There's going to be war. Maybe not this year, though *I* think it will come by Midwinter, but next summer at the latest. It's not bandits raiding the Borders anymore, and not Karsite outcasts desperately clawing out some sort of life, it's Karsite troopers, little squads of them. We finally caught some of them, and there were uniforms in their saddlebags." She shrugged. "The Sun-priests claim they were acting on their own, but we know better, obviously. Not even a Karsite is immune to a Truth Spell."

They all let out their held breath as one. Pol shook his head. "So they've started testing us, have they?"

"That's the general assessment," Charis agreed. "The current Son of the Sun is cautious. He isn't going to move until he's built up his troops there, built them up slowly so we supposedly won't notice, and that is going to take time. At least we're forewarned."

Another set of Trainees came along with platters

and bowls, and the discussion ended for a moment while the Heralds helped themselves. When the servers moved on to other tables, Jonotan asked the next question.

"Is there any *good* news?" he said, mouth twisted in a wry attempt at a smile that was not succeeding very well.

"We've got warning, and we've got time," Charis pointed out. "I just finished reporting to the King and Council; everyone is going to know by tomorrow. We're going to have to build up our own troops, I suppose; maybe evacuate the villages nearest the Border."

"If you can," Kiela pointed out. "A lot of those people are Holderkin; they wouldn't move for any mortal, and I sometimes doubt if they'd even move for their gods."

Charis made a face, but didn't contradict her.

"While you were there," Pol put in hesitantly, "did you happen across a Healer named Ilea?"

To his surprise, Charis laughed out loud, her gloom broken. "Actually, I did, just before I left. There was an outbreak of little-pox in a Holderkin village, and the Elder had actually unbent enough to call in our Healers. When I last saw her, Ilea was politely, gently, and thoroughly telling off the menfolk for not helping the women with the sick. 'If they drop with exhaustion, *they'll* be sick next, and who will cook, clean, and tend to you when *you* fall ill?' she said. And by all that's holy, the Elder was bending his head like a little boy being scolded!"

Greatly relieved, Pol laughed as well; he could certainly picture Ilea doing just as described. That broke the tension, and the conversation moved on to the news the others brought with them; after all, there was nothing to be done about the Karsites at this exact moment, certainly nothing that half a dozen Heralds could do.

Pol took his leave of the others long before they

finished their meal; younger appetites were heartier than his, and they hadn't eaten anything but their own cooking—or army cooking—for the last two years or so. Heralds traveling to and from their assignments stayed in inns along the way, but those on circuit camped, sheltered in waystations, and tended to their own needs. That was so that no one could play host to a Herald and then try to exert influence over him, so that no one could claim a Herald was playing favorites in judgments.

It was certainly a wise policy, even though it was a bit hard on Heralds riding circuit. However snug those waystations might be, they were still very spare of comforts, and the provisions stored in them made for simple and tediously similar meals. And if one wasn't a particularly good cook—Well, after two years, the meals at the Collegium would start to assume the character of gourmet feasts.

Pol returned to his quarters, to find one of his youngest students waiting for him, with a face so full of woe that he thought immediately that the youngster must have received bad news from home. Malken was barely nine years old, and very young to be Chosen, but he was by no means the youngest on record to have shown up at the Collegium with a Companion. Certainly the King's pages were as young or younger, and with his cherubic features and ingenuous brown eyes the Queen had threatened to steal him for her service more than once.

"Malken, what's the matter?" he exclaimed, as he closed the door to his rooms behind him, indicating that he was not to be disturbed.

Malken burst into tears and attached himself to Pol's legs like an animate burr. Pol held and comforted him; as he patted the child's back, he thought with a twinge of how often he had sat in this very fireside chair, comforting one of his own children for some childish woe. . . .

But this was evidently much more than a quarrel

with a friend, or one of the highborn children bullying him. Malken was positively hysterical; it wasn't a case of *would not* stop weeping, it was *could not*.

While Malken sobbed, he racked his brain for some idea of what could have the boy in such a state. If there had been a tragedy in the family, the Dean of the Collegium would have been notified first, so that someone Malken trusted could be with him when he heard the bad news. There hadn't been any sign of anything wrong when Malken had his Geography lesson with the first class this morning, and Malken wasn't the sort to have had a major falling-out with a friend that would leave him so brokenhearted.

Whatever it was, it was serious; the child wasn't even listening to him. Finally, when nothing Pol could do would serve to comfort him and calm the little boy, he rang for a servant and sent him for a Healer.

Not surprisingly, it was his own daughter Elenor who arrived at the door within a few moments, her pale-green cloak thrown hastily around her shoulders, little tendrils of her warm, brown hair escaping from the hood and dripping onto the floor.

"Who is this?" she asked, as she knelt beside her father to take the child in her own arms. Her heart-shaped face was full of concern, her cheeks pink from the cold, raindrops sparkling on her eyelashes.

"Malken. He's about ten," Pol said, as she bent over the sobbing child. He took advantage of her arrival to get a handkerchief to wipe the poor thing's face and nose. Malken continued to howl, oblivious.

"Malken," she murmured in his ear, holding him close, "Malken, sweetling, it's all right—"

Malken clearly didn't think it was all right, but Pol felt his own faint Gift of Empathy wake in answer to his daughter's more powerful abilities, and recognized her soothing touch on the child's mind.

Slowly, carefully, she insinuated herself between Malken and his own hysteria; slowly the child's sobs began to weaken, his howls to fade. It was a mercy that people were used to children in distress seeking Pol out, otherwise someone would surely have charged into the room by now, intent on beating whoever was frightening Malken into a bloody pulp.

At last, at very long last, Malken hiccuped once, and lapsed into silence, collapsing with exhaustion into Elenor's arms.

Pol took the boy from her, picking him up to carry back to his room. Elenor stood up shakily, her face pale, pulling herself up with the aid of her father's chair. Malken was clearly in no shape to be questioned about what had set him off.

But maybe his Companion had picked out something from Malken's mind that would explain all this.

:*Already noted, but you were a bit busy to talk to,*: Satiran told him instantly, with none of his usual smugness at having anticipated something Pol wanted. :*Hayka thinks his Gift decided to come on him all at once just after dinner. He says that Malken was reading, when something in the book triggered a vision of fire, of people burning to death by the thousands. Hayka is fairly shaken himself; all I can get out of him is that it seemed as if the entire world was going up in a storm of flame. And—*:

Satiran hesitated. When Satiran hesitated, Pol worried.

:*And?*: he prodded. :*Forewarned is forearmed; and what, Satiran?*:

:*And somehow you were deeply in the middle of it. That was why he ran to you.*:

"Let's get Malken to bed. Did you bring something to dose him with?" Pol asked his daughter, feeling more than a bit of concern for her as well. She was clearly troubled by the strength of Malken's hysteria; had she gotten an inkling of Malken's vision? He didn't want her to worry. Eventually, he would have to tell Ilea, and that would be bad enough. "I think he ought to sleep through the night, after this."

"No, but I can put him to sleep and make him forget what set this off all by myself," she told him, her pallor fading and her authority as a Healer reasserting itself. She gave him a look that told him she wouldn't allow herself to be persuaded otherwise; the tendrils of curling, red-brown hair falling over one soft brown eye made her look absurdly like a stubborn little foal. "That's much safer in a child this small."

She looked so much like Ilea in this mood that Pol couldn't help but smile; he covered his smile lest she misinterpret it as condescension rather than pride, and led the way to the dormitory and the Trainees' rooms.

Down the long corridor and through a door at the end, then up a wooden staircase lit at intervals by lamps with the flames turned low, he led his daughter to the second floor and the beginning of the dormitory rooms for the Trainees. Each child had his own room; not large rooms, but each had his own to himself, with a door he could close and even lock on the rest of the world if he chose to. Malken's room was on this floor; there were four more floors above this one, with the library at the top, and there were signs that the Collegium wing would have to be expanded again soon.

That thought made Pol uneasy; it hadn't occurred to him until now, but—

But when we're about to go to war, more Heralds are Chosen than usual.

As if to be ready to replace the ones that would inevitably fall to the enemy. Especially when the enemy was Karse, whose Sun-priests hated Heralds and their Companions with a fury that defied rational explanation.

He paused at Malken's room, so denoted by the little plaque with his name on the door, and nodded at Elenor. His daughter opened the door for him, and followed him inside, lighting a candle at the fire, then turning down the bedcovers so her father could place the boy in his bed.

Pol tucked him in, removing only his boots; he

didn't want to risk rousing him enough to start him on his hysterical weeping again. Elenor knelt beside the bed for a moment with one hand on Malken's pale forehead. When she stood up again, the little boy sighed once, deeply, then curled over on his side, the very picture of natural slumber.

They tiptoed out, closing the door behind them.

Elenor waited until they were in the stairway to confront her father.

"Satiran told you something, didn't he?" she demanded from behind and above him on the stairway. "I saw your face—I know he did! What in Kernos' name did he tell you? That child was *terrified!* What frightened him so?" In this temper, her changable eyes had gone to a stormy darker color, with flecks of green.

"I'm not entirely certain," he temporized. "He had a vision—"

"A vision!" she replied, sounding more like her mother than he could have imagined. "I think that's too mild a word for something that sends a child into screaming hysterics!"

By this time they had reached the ground floor, and he turned to face her. She looked up at him with pursed lips; he looked down at her wearing his best card-playing face.

Eventually she made a petulant little stamp of her foot. "I can see you've no intention of telling me anything more," she said sullenly, sounding more now like herself, a fourteen-year-old who has been cheated of an adult confession.

He smiled. "I'm glad you understand," he replied mildly, as she glowered at him.

"I *don't* understand, and I *don't* like it, but I also *don't* have a choice, do I?" she grumbled, tucking her wayward hair back into the snood she wore to keep it out of the way.

"No, you don't," he agreed, and reached out to take

her stiff body in his arms for a good hug. As he'd expected, she thawed, and returned the embrace.

"After all," he murmured into her damply fragrant hair, "I am your father. I should be able to keep some secrets from you."

"Why?" she retorted, her good humor restored as she reluctantly pulled away from him to go back to her own quarters. "You're only a mere *man*. Men can't possibly keep secrets from women; we know what you're going to do long before you do it."

"You are learning far too much from your mother," he accused mockingly, then kissed her on the forehead. "Thank you for coming."

"Thank you for trusting me." She gave him one of her dazzling smiles, and turned to run silently down the corridor, pausing once to wave brightly before darting out the door into the rainy night.

He returned to his room, dropping his cheerful facade, and sat down in his fireside chair, propping his head on one hand to stare into the flames.

Flames. . . .

What could such a vision mean?

:I suppose it could have been a hallucination and not a vision after all,: Satiran offered tentatively.

:But you don't think so. And neither do I. A hallucination like that would have to have some physical cause, and if there'd been a physical cause, Elenor would have spotted it and Malken would be in the charge of a full Healer right now.:

He felt Satiran's reluctant sigh. *:True. Which leaves—ForeSight. Hayka did say that the cause was his Gift coming on him all at once. Of all creatures, Hayka should be the one to really know what happened. Let me have a word with Jolene.:*

:Certainly.: Jolene was Herald Evan's Companion; Evan was currently the teacher in charge of Trainees with ForeSight. Whatever the vision *meant*, there was one thing certain; Malken had better be under Evan's tutelage tomorrow. When a Gift appeared full-blown,

it needed training, and the Trainee needed close attention, even protection from his own abilities. And when it appeared that young, the child wasn't at all prepared to deal with it alone.

:There. Taken care of. They'll see to him as soon as he wakes up,: Satiran was back. *:Right, then. Flames and the world on fire could be representative of a general condition of war.:*

It was his turn to sigh. *:Yes, it could. Malken has never seen warfare; his mind might only be able to grasp the concept as a great conflagration devouring everything it encounters.:*

:And given what Charis had to say tonight, that makes perfect sense. You're a senior Herald. If there's a war, you are *going to be in the middle of it,:* Satiran observed with gloom.

:His vision could have been triggered just because I was thinking about a war with Karse.: Now that his mind had started down this road, it seemed more and more plausible and explanation. *:If he happens to be sensitive to me, just from so much contact with me— I'm the nearest thing he's got to his father right now. The timing is right, he went into this just about when Charis was talking to us.:*

:Karse—the Sun-priests—yes, flame images would certainly be appropriate.: He felt Satiran suddenly shudder. *:They burn their prisoners, you know. Especially Heralds.:*

The same thought had occurred to him. He faced it resolutely. *:Forewarned—visions of the future can be changed. That's why ForeSight is one of our most valuable Gifts. We're warned now, Satiran; we can take steps to prevent getting ourselves into trouble.:*

:We can try,: Satiran replied. There was a long pause. *:Yes. You're right. And it's a good thing I'm having Hayka speak with Jolene tonight and give Jolene all the details. It will be easier to keep* you *out of trouble if all of us know what's been Seen. Unlike certain times in the past when no one knew but you. . . .:*

"Hey!" he exclaimed aloud, but Satiran was right this time. :*All right. Spread the word, then. After all, if that interpretation is right, I won't be the only Herald in danger.*:

:*No,*: Satiran agreed grimly. :*You won't.*:

Pol left it at that.

SEVEN

O N the fourth day of Lan's self-imposed exile from the dining hall, Owyn stayed behind when the others left. The younger boy lingered beside his desk, gazing at Lan with an intensely speculative expression.

"You're avoiding them, aren't you?" he said, suddenly. "You're hiding out from them up here." There didn't seem to be any condemnation in his tone, but Lan couldn't be absolutely sure. After all, Tyron could be using the boy as a tool to find out what Lan was up to.

Lan waited for a moment before answering, using the time it took to unwrap his packet of bread and butter before answering. "I suppose you think I'm a coward," he replied bitterly, with a shrug. "If it's cowardly to avoid getting punished for no reason by people who are big and mean, then I suppose I'm a coward. And, you know, I don't care who says I am." *So much for Tyron. He can call me all the names he wants.*

"Why do they let you stay away from lunch?" Owyn asked curiously, giving no sign that this was what Tyron had sent him to find out.

"Which 'they' do you mean?" Lan answered with a question of his own. "If you mean the teachers, no one has said anything to me, and I don't suppose they will. For all *they* know, I just take a little extra time to go down and hurry through the meal so I can come back up and study. If you mean—*them*—you don't suppose I was going to ask permission of them, do you?" A certain apprehension tightened his belly for a moment. "Have they figured out what I'm doing? Have they said anything about me?"

"Not yet," Owyn told him, and the knot in his gut relaxed. The younger boy fidgeted a little. "I was going to ask if you minded if I stayed, too. I brought apples. . . ."

As Owyn stared at him, hope naked in his eyes, Lan found his lips stretching into a rare smile. "Mind? Why should I mind, and why would it matter if I did? I don't exactly own this room, you know. You have as much right here as I do. But I *wouldn't* mind trading some of my bread for one of your apples."

Owyn sat back down with a thud, and dug in his book bag, coming up with a really fine, red fruit, which he handed to Lan in exchange for a slice of buttered bread. "How did you think of staying up here?" he asked around a mouthful, gazing at Lan as if he was some sort of wizard for coming up with so cunning a solution.

Owyn's admiration made him feel smug and embarrassed, at the same time. Lan did his best to try to look modest. "It was obvious, once you get past the idea that you have to eat something besides bread for lunch," he replied, with a touch of humor.

Owyn gazed at him with something approaching hero worship, and swallowed. "Half the time, when I know they're going to have at me, I can't eat anything anyway," he confessed. "I even get sick, sometimes. They've never flogged me, but I keep thinking they're going to. And—" his expression turned fierce and angry, giving the impression of a puppy in a rage, "—I *hate* it when they do something that makes people laugh at me!''

"I think that was why I was having those fits and headaches," Lan admitted, "but no one at home believes me about *them,* and what *they* are doing to us. My mother pretty much called me a liar and a whiner when I told her what was going on."

Owyn nodded sadly, and Lan felt a crumb of comfort in discovering he was not alone in being ignored by his parents. "I know, I tried, too. And you should *see* Tyron when he's where any of our parents will see him! It's sickening! He pets little ones and talks to them like he was their best friend, he brings them little toys or sweets." His mouth turned down in a bitter grimace, and his eyes grew bright. "My parents think I'm just trying to get him in trouble because he's supposed to be in charge of discipline, and that I'm jealous of him just because all the parents and teachers think he's so great—" He had to stop for a moment, as his emotions overcame him. He sniffed angrily and wiped his eyes with the back of his cuff. "All I want is for *them* to leave us alone!"

Lan looked aside, so as not to embarrass the younger boy by noticing his tears. "My mother said that it must have been my fits that made me say such things about *them,*" he told Owyn, gazing steadfastly at his desk until the boy got himself together. "She went on about what a good family he came from, and how no one from such a good family would ever act that way."

"Huh. What about all the black sheep that get the maids pregnant and gamble away their mother's jewelry?" Owyn retorted, with a worldly and cynical glance at Lan that surprised him. "What about the slick uncles that are so nice to the littles, and—never mind." He shook his head, and bent to his bread and butter, leaving Lan to wonder just what "the slick uncles" did in his family. There wasn't much more conversation after that; Owyn seemed to feel he'd said more than he meant to, and Lan didn't have much to say for himself. But the silence wasn't unfriendly; for once, Lan was actually relaxed around another student.

Lan and Owyn were well into their books by the time the rest of the class returned, and no one remarked on Owyn's absence from the Hall either. The next day, though, it wasn't just Owyn that remained behind with Lan, it was a timid, mouse-plain girl named Liss. She didn't come empty-handed either; she shyly proffered a chunk of sharp cheese to each of them, as if she thought she needed to supply a sort of toll in order for them to permit her presence. Lan had begun bringing extra bread and butter, and by this point they had quite a comfortable lunch.

That was the last of the classmates from this room to remain behind, but Owyn whispered that there were others, not only in their form, but in every form but Sixth, who were rebelling against the Sixth Form tyranny and staying in their classrooms over lunch. Everyone who did so, it seemed, agreed that starvation was preferable to being harried and hounded as the price of a meal.

And the Sixth Formers couldn't do anything about it! The teachers of Sixth Form personally made certain that the Sixth Formers went to the Hall, since *they* were the ones in charge of keeping the place under control during the meal.

"We have to be careful not to leave a crumb behind, though," Liss whispered, after a week of peaceful meals. "We ought to sweep and clean when we're done, otherwise they'll *make* us go downstairs again."

"Why do you suppose they've left us to eat alone up here?" Lan wondered aloud. "By now some of the teachers have to have noticed not everyone is going to the Hall to eat."

Owyn snickered. "Because part of our tuition goes for our meal, and with fewer of us eating, that's more that Master Keileth gets to keep. You don't think he's going to stop something that puts *more* money in his purse, do you?"

Lan nodded, because that made perfect sense. The teachers were paid just enough to ensure that they did their jobs properly; if their pupils failed to learn, *they* lost part of their pay. But they weren't paid to do anything more. That was probably how disciplining the younger students had devolved on the Sixth Form, and probably why the task remained with the oldest pupils—no one had to *pay* them.

Master Keileth, he had learned, was motivated largely by profit. The teachers were motivated by a system of debits from their pay. As long as nothing went drastically wrong, neither cared how the pupils felt, only that they passed their exams and absorbed the information laid before them.

"It can't last forever," he told the other two, carefully folding the muslin bag he brought his bread and butter in and stowing it in his book bag. "At the end of the year, they'll be gone."

Owyn had gotten the broom, and Liss the dustpan; while they swept the floor, he polished the three desktops. "But there are others," Owyn pointed out. "There are bullies in Fifth Form just *waiting* to go up to Sixth."

"And next year we'll be bigger and stronger, too," he replied. "If we can't find a way to talk them out of bullying us, and we're not big and strong enough to *make* them leave us alone, well . . . we'll just keep staying in our classroom for lunch."

Owyn looked doubtful, but didn't argue. Liss didn't look up at all, but that was normal. Liss usually didn't look anyone in the eye, not even when it was just the three of them.

But Lan had been growing more and more confident that his scheme was working with every passing day. The longer he avoided the Sixth Formers, the more he surely faded from their memory. Eventually, they would forget he was a student here altogether.

When the end of the year came and they were dismissed to whatever fate their families had planned for them, they would lose their solidarity as a group.

And then. . . . He had his daydreams. Someday, one of *them* would find himself facing Lan, at a time when the odds favored Lan. In his fondest, sweetest daydreams, it was Tyron who groveled at Lan's feet, begging for some favor.

The daydreams never went much farther than that, because Lan himself couldn't quite make up his mind about what he wanted to do when the situation came up. Would he be magnanimous, or would he smile politely and let Tyron hang? Or even give him a little push over the edge of whatever abyss he teetered on?

In some ways, being magnanimous would carry the most satisfaction with it. After all, Tyron would then have to go on with his life, knowing that *he owed Lan.* And that he would never, ever, be able to pay off that debt and return things to their former footing.

On the other hand, watching Tyron rot would be awfully satisfying, too.

Lan's teachers had been cautiously indicating that they thought his talents lay in the direction of becoming a Caravan Master, the man who was in charge of everything having to do with the transport of goods from one place to another. So far his parents hadn't said that they were opposed to the idea. Lan's current daydream involved Tyron as an impoverished caravan guard, begging Lan to hire him. The idea of Tyron in rags, groveling, was very satisfying; even more satisfying was the extension of the daydream, where Tyron got drunk on duty and Lan casually ordered him flogged.

Lan was, in fact, in the process of elaborating on that daydream, imagining Tyron's current girl, grown up and even prettier, being conveyed in Lan's caravan from Haven to—say—Hardorn.

When the last class was over, the rest of his schoolmates and the teacher cleared out, and the schoolroom fire was left to burn down the coals, he stayed at his desk with a book open, but eyes unfocused. He imagined Anjeyla as she might be in another four years, turned from pretty into stunningly lovely. For good measure, he turned her hair from dark blonde to a golden cascade, subtracted from her waist and added to chest and hips.

She would, of course, be very impressed with Lan, in his suit of silver-washed chain mail, well-used sword at his side, his weather-tanned face and a few attractive scars showing his courage and experience, and a devil-may-care smile telling of his past conquests among the ladies. *"Don't I know you?"* she would ask, a little puzzled. *"I don't think so,"* he would say, with a careless chuckle. And about that time, the chief of his guards would interrupt, with Tyron, dirty and hung over, being dragged along behind him between two more guards.

"Sir, this scum was drunk on duty last night," the guard-chief would say.

"Which one is it?" he would bark in reply, straightening his back, a man of action and decisiveness. Anjeyla would sigh with admiration.

"Tyron, sir," the chief would reply. *"I regret I ever recommended him to you."* And as Anjeyla gasped in recognition, the chief would grab Tyron by the hair, and pull his head up, so that there could be no mistake about *who* it was.

Anjeyla would make a little pout of disdain, and pointedly move away from Tyron and toward Lan, perhaps even placing her hand on his bicep. Tyron would see, and he would look sick and dismayed.

Lan would wait long enough for all the implications to sink in, then bark, *"And what do you have to say for yourself, scum?"*

"So this is where you've been hiding," Tyron replied.

For a moment, Lan stared at the door in confusion; *that* wasn't what Tyron was supposed to say! Then, with a snap, he came back to himself, and his hands clutched the sides of his desk involuntarily.

Tyron leaned against the doorframe, surrounded by the rest of his gang, an indolent smile on his face. "I wondered how you were managing to get past us every day, you little sneak," the Sixth Former sneered. "You never got past us at all. You've been hiding up here all along."

"You—you aren't allowed to be here!" was all Lan could manage, in a faint accusation, his voice breaking on the last word.

"In school hours," Tyron corrected. "After school hours, and before, we can go anywhere in the building we choose."

Full of dismay, his heart pounding and sweat breaking out on his forehead, Lan sought desperately for something that might make Tyron and his band of bullies go away. "I'm studying," he said, ducking his head submissively. "It's too hard to study at home, there's too much noise."

The printed page wavered and blurred before his eyes. "Oooh, poor little Scrub!" Tyron mocked. "You know, somehow I don't believe you. *I* don't think you have any trouble studying at home at all. After all, you managed very, very well while you were playing sick, didn't you?"

Lan glanced up, feeling sick. Tyron unfolded his arms, straightened, and moved away from the doorway, followed by the rest of the bullies. "I don't believe that you were studying just now at all. I must have stood there for a quarter candlemark, and you didn't *once* turn a page."

Lan tried not to cringe, as Tyron stopped right next to him, towering over him. "You, little Scrub, are making things v-e-r-y difficult for me. You're eroding my discipline, and setting a bad example for the others. Why should they obey, when they know all they have to do is stay in their classrooms and they can avoid their just punishments?"

Lan averted his eyes and stared at his book, hands clenched around the sides of the desk, his knuckles turning white.

Tyron was just starting. "And, I believe, *you* have a just punishment coming to you. Doesn't he, Derwit?"

"Setting a bad example, ten strokes," said a cold voice from Lan's other side. "Eroding discipline, ten strokes. That's twenty."

Twenty strokes! Lan's head reeled and a wave of dizziness overcame him. Not even his father had ever flogged Lan with more than five strokes of a cane!

"Oh, but that's not all, not by any means," Tyron purred. "Unless, of course, you happen to have that velvet I told you to bring me squirreled away in your book bag—"

Lan's head shot up, and he stared at Tyron in shock, all conscious thought driven out of his mind. *I thought he'd forgotten about that by now!*

Tyron smiled tenderly, but his eyes were as cold as a fish's. "I thought not. So what would that be, Derwit?"

"Twenty strokes for refusing to obey, ten strokes for lying about being sick, ten for lying about not being able to study at home, and ten for avoiding punishment by lurking up here," Derwit replied with gloating satisfaction. "That's seventy strokes in all."

Something hot and angry began to stir sluggishly down in the farthest depths of Lan's mind, but he still couldn't think, or even move. At the moment, it was panic that had control of his body; the same panic a trapped rabbit feels when it freezes. Two of the bullies pried his hands away from the desk and hauled him to his feet by his elbows.

"I don't think we ought to deal them out to him all at once," Loman said thoughtfully. "We're not allowed to break the skin, you know. No wounds. Master Keileth was very forceful on that point."

"Oh, *really,* Loman, when have you ever known me to be so clumsy as to break the skin?" Tyron chided, leading the way as Lan was hauled bodily out of the classroom and down the stairs. "Still, you have a point. We can't lame him so that his parents would take exception. Perhaps we can spread the punishment out over a few days. Say, four. We can bring the total up to eighty strokes just to keep things even; add another ten for encouraging the others to avoid us by hiding in the classrooms."

Lan dug in his heels and tried to resist, but the others were so much stronger and taller, they just hauled him right off his feet altogether. In a nightmarishly short time, they had him down all four flights of stairs, and into an unused classroom on the back of the building, far from the street. No matter how much he screamed and yelled, no one would hear him here.

"You can fuss all you want, but no one is going to hear you," Tyron pointed out helpfully, confirming his thought. "I do encourage you to do so, however; it lets me know that I'm doing a good job."

Lan gagged, as his stomach surged with nausea. There was a single, straight-backed chair in the middle of the room, and four leather straps on the seat of the chair. It was pretty obvious what they were going to do with that chair.

"Want us to strap him down, Tyron?" asked one of the two monsters holding his arms.

Tyron was playing with a willow cane, experimentally bending it and swishing it through the air. "Not yet. Why don't you just play with him for a little until I'm ready."

Lan didn't get much chance to wonder what *that* meant. The monsters dropped him; he stumbled, not quite falling, and before he could get his balance, the first one shoved him, hard.

He hit the wall with bruising force, knocking some of the breath out of his body, and another of the bullies grabbed his arm, wrenched him away from the wall, and shoved him at a third.

They passed him from one to the other, alternately catching him and knocking him into the walls. And as they did so, that sullen little spark of heat began to grow, driving everything before it, and filling him with a white-hot rage that burned away his thoughts and contended with the panic and fear for supremacy.

RAIN sheeted down, drenching everything in sight—which wasn't much, as the rain curtains obscured most objects farther away than ten horse-lengths. Pol pulled his hood a little closer around his face, and kept his eyes fixed on Satiran's neck.

Malken was no longer Pol's pupil; in fact, Malken was no longer *anyone's* pupil except Herald Evan's. The child's ForeSight was so very powerful that he'd been pulled out of all his classes to concentrate on getting it under control.

Poor Malken didn't just see *the* future, he saw many possible futures, and at the moment, he couldn't tell which was the more likely. That left the child confused and directionless, alternately afraid to act and afraid to hesitate, afraid to warn and afraid to keep silent. Evan had taken him right away from the Collegium altogether, and out of Haven, to one of the many Crown hunting lodges where there were few people, so that he and Malken could begin to sort things out far from the interference of other peoples' lives.

Pol was the only other person allowed to come near them, because Malken had begged Evan not to keep Pol away. So Pol arranged for a holiday, long enough to ride there, stay for a few days to reassure the little boy that he had no intention of taking part in any world-wide conflagrations, and ride back.

At the moment, a world-wide conflagration was the least of all possible fates for him! Drowning was more like it. It was just his luck that he had scheduled himself to ride straight out into the pouring rain. Not that it hadn't been raining, off and on, for the past several weeks, but he'd hoped that things might slack off a bit before he started out.

No such luck.

:*It could be worse,*: Satiran said, after four solid candlemarks of riding in such a steady downpour that he was beginning to have the feeling that the offending clouds were actually moving with them.

"I'd rather not think how," Pol replied, peering forward between Satiran's ears, from under the dripping hood of his rain cape. Satiran's hooves made an unpleasant, squishy splash when he set them down, and an equally unpleasant sucking sound when he picked them up. The ground was completely saturated after all these days of rain. There was nowhere for the water to go, and some people were finding the ground floors of their homes unlivable as water seeped steadily up through the flooring. And there were floods, of course, though most people who lived in areas prone to flooding were encouraged to build houses on stilts, and most did.

:*I can think of any number of ways. For instance, you could have a hole in your cape, right at the nape of your neck.*: Satiran was in a teasing mood, and knew how suggestible his Chosen was; for a brief but unpleasant moment, Pol actually *felt* an icy trickle down his spine, until he convinced himself it was only his overactive imagination.

Both he and Satiran had waxed-canvas rain capes, though Pol also had his woolen winter cape beneath the rain cape, for the rain was one short step above the temperature of ice.

"I wonder what's going to happen with Malken when his Gift stabilizes?" he wondered aloud, hoping both to tease some information out of Satiran and to distract him from any more tricks. Of all the Gifts, ForeSight was the least amenable to control. It tended to come when it felt like, and show you what it wanted to. Pol had the feeling that the Companions were taking a very close interest in Malken's progress.

:Actually, I think little Malken will be able to invoke it at will, but it's always going to show a multiplicity of futures, and there won't be much of a way to tell us how to get to any of them.: Satiran sounded thoughtful, as if he had been working on that very question for some time. *:Still—the worst possibilities can always be guarded against, or planned for.:*

"That's better than having no warning," Pol agreed. "I take it you and the others have been talking about this?"

:Off and on. Malken probably has the strongest single Gift in the entire Heraldic Circle, poor thing. That's a heavy burden to bear at any age, much less such a young one.: There was no doubt that Satiran felt very sorry for the youngster; well, if that was the case, so did Pol. The strong Gifts were sometimes as much of a curse as a blessing to the one saddled with them.

:And right now,: Satiran continued, *:What he's Seeing is a confused jumble of the worst possible events that anyone could imagine. That's what Hayka and Jolene say, anyway. There's no way of telling even where in time those possibilities lie.:*

"Not really useful," Pol remarked.

:Not really, no,: Satiran, replied. *:For instance, if he were able to ForeSee things like a tree falling on you—:*

Afterward, Pol remembered those words with a sense of heavy irony; at the time, though, all he noticed was an odd, creaking sound off to his right—

Which was quickly followed by Satiran's startled neigh and shy to the left, the confused impression of something very large rushing at him—

And then, nothing at all.

LAN had stopped thinking some time ago; now all he was doing was *feeling*. It was pure fear, and barely contained rage that consumed him, the ice of panic, the heat of anger, contending for his mind. There wasn't much room left over for thought.

He struggled to hold in the rage; somehow he felt dimly that if he couldn't keep control over it, something terrible and irrevocable would happen. But the part of him that tried to hang onto a little rational thought was also the part that *hurt*. The blinding pain of the worst headache he had ever felt without passing out entirely was slowly eroding his ability to hang onto his anger.

Abruptly, with a final shove, Tyron's bullies sent him sprawling at the ringleader's feet. He panted, both with exertion and the flush of heat that consumed him, on his hands and knees.

The pain was excruciating, the fear held him paralyzed still, and the anger raged against the bonds containing it.

His ears filled with roaring, very like the thunder of a river in full flood. He barely heard Tyron say, "Strip his shirt off, and strap him down."

A haze of red clouded his eyes. When two of Tyron's henchmen grabbed him and pulled his shirt off over his head, they exclaimed as they grabbed his bare arms. "Tyron—he's as hot as a branding iron!" said the one on his right. "If he's got a fever, maybe you should leave him alone for now—"

"I've left him alone for long enough," Tyron replied with irritation, and to punctuate his intentions, he took his first stroke on Lan's bare back while he was still held between the two bullies, the cane whistling through the air with the savage force that Tyron put behind it.

The pain of the lash was worse than anything Lan had ever felt. It cut right through the headache, broke his paralyzing fear, and left him with only instinct.

He *had* to get away! *He had to get away, and now!*

The fear joined the anger, and together they destroyed the last of his rapidly eroding control over that overpowering rage—and the terrible thing that his rage had summoned.

A moment of utter silence as Tyron pulled back for a second blow.

It fell.

The entire room erupted in flames.

The three who were the closest, Tyron and the two bullies, Loman and Derwit, who were holding his arms, went up like oil-soaked torches, screaming with agony. Tyron blundered backward and into the wall, hitting it, and dropping to the floor. The boy to Lan's right howled and whirled in circles aimlessly. The one to his left ran straight into the fireplace.

Lan himself only noticed this with a tiny part of his mind that was numb and frozen with horror, unable to act or think, only able to observe. The rest of him was consumed with flame, *was* the flame, and existed only to feed itself.

It reached for the nearest source of fuel; the chair, the three bodies already afire and silent now, the other boys, who were trapped. *He* was between them and the door, and the fire was hungry . . . and very, very, angry.

Flames blossomed all around him, sending his hair rising upward, propelled by tiny flames that licked the air savagely, a nimbus of fury that nevertheless did not touch *him*. One of the boys tried to dash past him, making for the door.

The fury inside him recognized the attempt at escape, and intercepted him before Lan realized what was happening. The boy exploded into flame like the other three and dropped like a shot bird to the floor.

The others shrieked in uncomprehending terror.

Their reaction only fed the fire further; it pulsed out to fill the room, as the boys backed up in a pathetic attempt to evade it. One of them shouted the first actual word that any of them had spoken until that moment, staring past the flames to Lan.

"Please!" he screamed, as the fires touched his flesh. *"Please!"*

Something snapped inside him again. With an agonizing wrench that sent him to his knees, Lan wrested back some control from the thing that was consuming them.

The flames receded, pulling back just enough so that the burned and blistered boys could stumble past him and out the door to freedom.

Lan wrestled with a force that didn't want to be controlled, that resisted him with his own strength. The flames flared again, and the walls of the room began to smoke.

Outside, someone had caught sight of the flames and sounded an alarm. There was shouting, screams, a confusion of noise. Lan ignored all of that, battling with the rage inside himself, grappling with a thing that had taken on an evil life all its own.

Now it was even turning its fury on its host; it was Lan's turn to scream in agony as the flames licked his flesh. But that was the power's undoing.

Lan simply could not bear anymore. He slumped over as darkness, a cool, welcoming darkness, beckoned to him to fall into it. His eyes cleared once before that final dark, and saw without comprehension, the flames around him flickering, and dying out, leaving only a few spots of sullenly burning fire in the room itself.

He did not want to think what fueled those fires, for there were four of them.

But the hold that the anger, fear, and fire had over him was gone. Obedient at last, his mind gave itself up to darkness and his body toppled to the floor of the burned-out room.

EIGHT

WHEN Pol first opened his eyes, he found, much to his bemusement, that he was in an unfamiliar room. That was not necessarily an unusual circumstance, but this wasn't a waystation or an inn, which would have made sense; it was a pleasant, but rather bare chamber with pale green walls, and that didn't ring any notes of familiarity.

Then the Healer came in, and he remembered, with unnatural clarity, the rain, the wind, Satiran's neigh of surprise, and something rushing at him. He didn't know this Healer, a lean, hard stick of a man, with his hair going sparse around the temples, but any Healer at the Collegium would be a good one. As always, the Healer wore garments in the standard color of deepest green, but he chose a long tunic and trews rather than floor-length robes.

"A tree fell on me?" he said aloud, incredulously. "A *tree* fell on me?"

"That's what your Companion tells us," the Healer replied, with a dry chuckle. "Evidently the soil was too water-soaked to hold it anymore; from what the rescuers had to tell me it was a giant. They took a while cutting you loose." The Healer raised Pol's head and tucked another pillow behind him to get him propped up. "Your Companion couldn't get out of the way fast enough, but *you* were the one that got a solid blow to the head. He was just battered and bruised; pinned, but conscious, and able to summon help."

Pol groaned. If that just wasn't his luck! It seemed that anytime he was involved in *anything* that produced injuries, he was the one that got the worst of it.

On the other hand, I'm not dead yet, so maybe I am lucky.

"You're really quite lucky," the Healer echoed his thoughts, taking his chin in one hand and turning his head to both sides, examining his eyes, then the bruises around his face and head. "From the look of things they tell me, a little more or less to one side or the other, and you'd both have been hit by a main trunk piece and not just a branch."

"Have I missed anything?" he asked. "Anything important happen? How long have I been unconscious? Is my skull cracked?"

"Yes, but nothing to worry about, four days, nothing in Collegium or Court, but there was some excitement down in town." The Healer left off prodding at Pol's bruises; apparently he'd taken a solid hit, but his scalp hadn't split open, since his head wasn't bandaged. *Or else it did, but they mended it quickly and washed the blood out of my hair. Or the rain did.* He didn't have much of a headache either, so the Healers must have put in some serious work on his skull.

The Healer frowned a bit, though not at Pol. "The Merchants' and Crafts' Guilds had set up a sort of Collegium of their own to educate their brighter children, the ones who weren't falling right into their parents' Guilds. There was a fire there three days ago; four boys were killed, and several burned badly."

That made him sit right up straight, which *did* start

his head pounding. "Good Lord!" he exclaimed. "How did that happen?"

"That's the strange thing; nobody seems to know," the Healer replied, pushing him back down in the bed and putting a soothing hand on his forehead that erased the pain. "The boys have a peculiar story about the fire coming from out of nowhere." His frown deepened. "They *also* have no explanation for being in the building, in an unused classroom, at that time of the late afternoon. Classes were long over, and they should have been home. If they were staying after hours, studying, they should have been in their own classrooms."

Pol pursed his lips, thoughtfully. "You think they started the fire?" It wouldn't be the first time that adolescents started a fire as a prank or to vandalize and had it get away from them.

"I think the Guard thinks they did," the Healer replied. "They're questioning all the boys that are fit to talk to. I'm not so sure. I'm treating one of the injured, the youngest of the lot."

Pol looked inquiring and attentive, and the Healer continued. "The thing that bothers me is that all but one were in the same age group, the same clique. The odd one was a new student, and was in one of the much lower classes. They shouldn't have had anything to do with him, so what was he doing with them at that time of the day?"

Something had roused the Healer's suspicions, that was certain. "Where's that particular boy?" he asked, sensing that this Healer, at least, wanted *someone* with authority to get to the bottom of this.

"Here. He's been unconscious since they were dragged out," the Healer replied, mouth set in a hard line. "Look, Herald Pol, I'm not trying to cause trouble, but I don't like some of the things we've uncovered, or the way those other boys are acting; it seems to me that they want desperately to hide something, and it has to do with that younger boy. It's hard to tell, under the burns, but we think there's a lot of bruising all over him that doesn't look accidental, and it definitely looks as if he's been caned."

Pol hadn't been around the Court as long as he had without gathering a fair understanding of how "ordinary" children sometimes acted. "You think he's being bullied, knocked around—"

"I think he was being tortured," the Healer interrupted, icily. "That's what we'd call it in an adult, and I see no reason to call it by a lesser name in children. I've been trying to get the Guard to call in some of the other, younger children of the school to find out what those older boys could have been up to, but they haven't paid any attention to me. They keep saying that the younger children couldn't possibly know anything about it."

Pol eyed his physician with a lifted eyebrow. "You've had some . . . personal experience with bullies, I take it?"

The Healer's mouth twisted into a thin smile as ironic as Pol's own. "I was an incipient Healer—which means empathic and sensitive—in a Holderkin family. What do you think?"

Pol winced. He had taken one circuit in Holderkin lands; male children were raised to be *manly men*, autocratic rulers of their children and (multiple) wives, rough, taciturn, and without emotion, as warmhearted as granite. Females were expected to be subservient in all things, bowing to the will of any male older than ten. No child growing up with the Healer's Gifts could survive long in such an environment without becoming the target of attempts to "toughen him up," and "make a proper man of him."

"Well, the Guard *has* to listen to a Herald," he replied, deciding—as he was sure the Healer had intended he should—to take a personal interest in this case. After all, Haven `was his circuit, in a sense. If the current Heralds assigned to the city hadn't seen the implications that this Healer pointed to, Pol could deal with it. "You'll have to get me fit for duty, though."

The Healer responded with a tight smile. "No fear of that," he replied. "The Guard has requested to be present when he wakes, to question him."

"Then I will tell the Guard that I need to be present as well." He paused. "Just what *do* you think the other boys were doing to him—exactly?"

The Healer lost his smile. "I think they were roughing him up, then went on to beating him, but were planning on doing something that involved fire— perhaps burning him with coals, or branding him. Something went wrong—perhaps one of them had long sleeves that caught fire—and they reacted in panic. The fire spread, and the ringleaders were killed. That leaves the followers and the victim, and the followers haven't got enough imagination or cohesion as a group to come up with a story to cover themselves. The problem is, if this takes too long, their parents are likely to concoct a story for them."

Pol nodded. "Right. I'll be asking the younger children about that. Meanwhile—" he gestured to his head. "Fix this, please, and I'll get to it when you judge me fit for duty."

THERE'S nothing like a Healer with private motivation, he thought a day and a half later, as he pulled out a seldom-used formal uniform from his wardrobe. *It's amazing what can be done when your Healer really wants you on your feet.*

:Is that why you never have so much as a sniffle?: Satiran teased. The Companion, so Pol had been told, had fretted so much during his period of unconsciousness that he'd lost a fair amount of weight. Now that Pol was awake and recovered, he was making up for

that by stuffing himself, and no one begrudged him, least of all his Herald.

:Of course, but that's also self-interest,: Pol replied with a chuckle. *:Ilea doesn't want to catch anything from me, after all.:* He changed trews and shirt, and began lacing up the white, blue-and-silver-trimmed doeskin tunic. *:Think you can be ready to go into Haven when I get done talking to the Guard in charge of this case?:*

:I would be ready even if I wasn't ready,: Satiran replied instantly. *:I do agree with that Healer of yours; something very rotten has been going on in that school, if bullies thought they could torment a victim inside the building and didn't worry about getting caught.:*

Pol nodded, as he made his way to the Guard barracks. That was another point that no one else had considered. Perhaps some might have dismissed it as irrelevant, but it bothered him. Taken with everything else, this school needed looking into. Just who, exactly, was in charge?

The Guard in Haven that stood sentry on the Palace and Collegia and patrolled the city itself had their barracks on the Palace grounds, connected to the Palace by a private entrance that only a few that were not of the Guard ever used. A clerk-Guardsman in the uniform of midnight-blue and silver on duty at a desk inside the main entrance directed him to the Captain in charge of city patrols and investigations.

The Captain was not anyone that Pol had worked with before, but Pol wasn't worried; people who were inflexible and difficult to reason with didn't last long posted to Haven. The King himself saw to that.

The Captain was in his own tiny office, hardly more than a cubicle crowded with records, and was hard at work on some other paperwork when Pol tapped on his door and entered his workspace. The Captain waved him to the only other seat in the room, absently scribbling down a few more lines.

Pol took a stack of documents off the chair and sat

down. With a sigh of relief, the Captain signed and sealed the paper he was working on, and shoved it into a box with a dozen others like it. He was about the same age as Pol, and just as fit and trim as any active Herald, with a few streaks of gray in his thick, wavy brown hair, and intensely curious hazel eyes.

"What can I do for you, Herald—?" he asked.

"Pol. I'm going to be doing some investigation on that fire at the Merchants' School," he said—or rather, stated.

The Captain tilted his head to the side. "I would have thought that was fairly simple. An unruly lot of adolescent troublemakers started a fire and it got away from them. That's what the Schoolmaster thinks."

But Pol shook his head. "The Healers found marks of a beating and a caning on that boy who's still unconscious, and he was several years younger than all of the others. The rest were the same age, and very much larger and stronger than he is. They don't have a satisfactory explanation for why they were in that room, nor why they were there after hours, nor why they were with a boy they *should* have had no contact with. Taken with this Schoolmaster's story, I think there's a great deal that needs looking into, not only in the incident itself, but in the school."

"What if the Schoolmaster himself caned the boy as punishment?" the Captain countered.

"Wouldn't he have mentioned it?" Pol replied. "Wouldn't he have pointed to that specific boy as a troublemaker? I should think that would be the first thing he would have said; it would have given a logical place for the investigation to start, and a logical perpetrator."

"Hmm. And if the young one has influential parents?" The Captain now looked more interested than he had before. "Wouldn't that preclude any finger-pointing?"

"Please. Four boys, presumably with equally influential parents, are dead, and more are injured. I

should think that under the circumstances the Schoolmaster would be grateful to have *one* boy he could
blame." Pol raised an eyebrow and the Captain nodded, once, slowly.

The Captain drummed his fingers on the desk for a
little while, thinking. Pol waited, quite ready to sit
there all afternoon if need be. But the Guardsman
was not the sort of man to take very long in making
up his mind. "All right. Can you take over the incident entirely?"

Pol nodded in agreement; that was what he had
hoped the Captain would ask. Best that the Guard not
get involved unless he needed them. It was beginning
to sound as if this might involve stepping on some
political toes.

With a faint hint of relief on his features, the Captain took a couple of papers out of a cubbyhole at his
left and quickly scribbled something on them. He
shoved them across the desk to Pol, who picked them
up. The topmost was the initial report, with a note
appended to the effect that Herald Pol was taking
over the investigation.

"Thank you very much," Pol said, gathering up the
papers and standing up. "I hope I can get to the bottom of this for us all."

The Captain smiled back and reached over the desk
to shake Pol's hand. "The last thing I'm going to fight
is to have a Herald come in and take over a case like
this one," he replied. "I wish you Heralds would come
in and help out like this more often!"

Pol laughed. "I'll mention that around," he promised, and left with the papers.

One of them proved to be just what he wanted
most; a list of the pupils of the Guild School, their
parents, and their addresses, what Forms they were
in, and what classes within the Forms.

He searched until he found the class that the youngest boy—who he now knew was named Lavan Chitward—was in. That was where he would start. Stowing

the papers in a pouch he slung over his shoulder, he stopped long enough at his room for his woolen cloak. It was cold out there, through the weather wise predicted the usual false summer around Sovvan.

Classes had been canceled for a week, so Pol knew that the children he wanted to talk to should be at home. :*Ready for that trip into the city?*: he called to Satiran, swinging his cloak over his shoulders.

:*Already saddled,*: was the prompt reply. :*And waiting for you at the gate.*: With that came the mental picture, and Pol nodded his approval. Satiran had asked for and gotten the full formal rig-out, with barding, bridle bells, and all. The more impressive they looked, the less it was likely they would have to argue with possibly nervous parents.

He pulled on white doeskin gloves and held his cloak shut against a blast of chill wind as he left the barracks, walking briskly to the Herald's Gate in the wall that encircled the Palace-Guard-Collegia complex. He saw Satiran as soon as he got out of the sculpted trees of one of the formal gardens, a tiny, toylike white horse against the gray stone wall.

He picked up his pace and shortly caught the chime of Satiran's bells as the Companion shifted his weight from hoof to hoof to keep from stiffening in the chill.

"Business in town, Herald?" asked the Gate Guard. "Or just pleasure?"

"It's never 'just' pleasure, I assure you," Pol replied. "But, yes, I'm in charge of investigating that fire a few days ago. I'm Herald Pol, assigned to the Collegium." It wouldn't hurt to have word spread; if any of the Guard had heard anything, they'd know who to come to with it.

"Yes, sir, I understand." The Guard saluted, and opened the Gate for them; Pol mounted, and he and Satiran went out into the city with every step marked by the chiming of bells.

Streets in Haven were built in a mazelike spiral configuration, a leftover from the days when the city itself might expect enemy attack. The establishments closest to the Palace walls were the homes of the highborn, enormous manses with extensive gardens and galleries. Some were as old as the Palace itself, and had been rebuilt, added onto, or remodeled at least as many times as the Palace, with mixed results. Most of these were the property of some of the oldest families in Valdemar, with a rotating population that depended on what branch of the family wished to come to Court, who was superfluous on the home estate, who was serving as a representative, not only of the family, but of the district, and who wanted to get something accomplished that could only be attained at Court. A few were as rundown and imperiled by lean times as the families themselves. Two had, in Pol's time as a Herald, been acquired by new families and either extensively repaired or torn down altogether to make way for a new Great House in the most modern style.

A full circuit of the city brought him to the next level, where the homes owned or leased by lesser families were located. The houses here were half the size of those of the greater families, the gardens—

Well, there were no "gardens" attached to each house; there was a single pleasure garden for each, a small herb garden for the kitchen, and a courtyard just past the gates. There were, or so Pol had been told, even a few very wealthy private citizens living here with no inherited titles whatsoever to their names.

Round another circuit, and he was in the district of the wealthiest; merchants mostly, with a sprinkling of those who had inherited wealth and built it higher, and one or two adventurers who had discovered wealth or wedded it. This, however, was not where he was going. The offspring of these folk were either educated privately, by tutors, or if the child was exceptional, by the Collegia and the Master Artificers.

One more round brought him to the moderately wealthy; those who had attained Mastery in their Guilds and had their own flourishing trade or kept a workshop full of Journeymen and Apprentices. This was where he would find his first subjects; Owyn Kittlekine and his parents.

Finding their home was a simple matter of asking two or three of the servants being blown along the street by the harsh wind, off on errands. Master Kittlekine was a Leatherworker, as the gate of his house, with its sign of the stretched hide worked into the wood in bronze, proudly proclaimed. Pol rode straight up to the gate and knocked on it with the butt of his purely ornamental riding crop, without dismounting. Someone peeked through a peephole to one side of the gate, and an unnerved servant opened it hastily.

"M-m-master Herald, sir, there was no word, nothing—" the servant stammered.

"I know," Pol said, simply, with gravity, but without too much of a stern demeanor. "I wish to speak with Owyn."

"Owyn?" the servant squeaked. "But—but—but— the Master is not at home, and the Mistress is making calls—"

"It is very cold," Pol interrupted, "and this is a matter of some urgency. It is Owyn with whom I wish to speak, and not the Master or Mistress of the house."

The servant evidently decided that the wishes of a Herald overruled whatever orders he'd been given, and escorted Pol into the best parlor of the house while Satiran was taken into the hothouse that the Kittlekines had in place of a garden. There, he would at least be warm. In the parlor, with a good-sized fire to thaw him, Pol waited for someone to bring Owyn to him.

There were whisperings and the scuffling of feet behind him; word of a Herald in the house must have spread quickly. Pol pretended to be oblivious.

:Are you the new creature in the menagerie, Chosen?: Satiran asked. *:I certainly am. I've got half a dozen servants out here gaping at me.:*

*:They're not being that obvious about it, but yes—
ah, someone's bringing the boy!:* Pol heard two sets of
footsteps, one lighter and quicker than the other, and
stood with a swirl of his cape that he knew would be
particularly effective.

A different servant, probably the housekeeper, had
brought young Owyn to him. She curtsied with great
diffidence and immediately absented herself, leaving
Owyn alone and distinctly uncomfortable.

A bookworm, Pol immediately assessed, looking at
the ink-stained fingers, the slight stoop of the shoulders from bending over reading, and all the other little
signs of the confirmed bibliophile. *And a ready target
for a bully.* Young Owyn was small for his age, with
large, dark eyes and curly dark hair. Pol approached
Owyn, held out his hand with his warmest smile, and
said, "I am Herald Pol, Master Owyn. I would like
you to answer a few questions for me."

"About what?" Owyn replied, suspicion warring
with the fact that he had always been taught that Heralds were to be trusted utterly. The war was visible in
his shifting expression, and Pol turned up the sympathy a trifle in his own expression.

"I would like to ask you a few things about Lavan
Chitward, and about your school." He still held
Owyn's hand in a firm clasp; he used that now to draw
Owyn forward and to one of the two inglenook seats
at the hearth. There they could speak without any
danger of being overheard.

Owyn sat nervously on the edge of the seat as Pol
removed his cloak and hung it over the corner of his,
then sat down. "Lavan was in my class and my Form,"
he said, and didn't elaborate.

"I know." Pol decided to treat the Healer's supposi-
tions as fact and see what information that elicited.
He didn't want to use the Truth Spell this early in the
game, nor on such a young boy who hadn't, himself,
done any wrong. "I know a great deal about what was
going on, in fact. I know that Lavan was being bullied

by the Sixth Form boys, I know that they had taken him down to that classroom to beat him, and I know he wasn't the only one, nor the first one, to be bullied and beaten. Was he?"

Owyn's eyes had grown rounder and larger with every word of this recitation, and when Pol concluded his statement, the youngster blurted out, "You Heralds really *do* read people's thoughts!"

:*Ha!*: Satiran said triumphantly.

"No, we don't—not without permission, Owyn," Pol replied gently. "Those were all deductions, but I need more facts, if I'm to be able to do anything about what has happened to Lavan, and the situation at your school. I hope that you can help me."

That opened the floodgate. From what Owyn told him, Pol was very glad that he had gotten to the boy without the presence of the parents, who would either have dismissed what Owyn said completely or try to hush him up. The situation was even more out of hand than the Healer had guessed. The older boys, the biggest bullies, virtually ran the school in all matters except lessons. Pol took copious notes to turn over to the Council, who would probably keep the school intact, since it served a very useful purpose, but would put someone in charge who would see that the money collected from the parents went to the purposes for which it was intended rather than into the Master's purse.

The boy became quite emotional before his recitation was over; small wonder, considering the number of times he'd been humiliated and frightened into submission by what was, essentially, a gang of thugs. Pol hardly dared think what the younglings who had been physically abused would be like.

:*Probably in tears,*: Satiran observed. :*My advice is to take Elenor with you when you interview them.*:

Owyn was a keen observer and a good judge of character himself; Pol got a list of those who had been caned, who had been assaulted, and who had had mean-spirited pranks played on them to humiliate them, but he also got an assessment of who would be likely to talk freely and who would have to be supported and reassured.

"But I don't know anything about what happened to Lan," Owyn said when he had finally run out of everything else he had to say. By this time, the boy was exhausted; venting so much emotion had worn him out, as well it should have! He slumped in his seat, but never took his eyes off Pol's face. "I was home by the time *they* found Lan in the classroom." Once again, conflicting emotions warred on his face, and by now Pol thought he had a good idea what they were.

"You didn't want anyone hurt, but you can't help but feel glad that the worst of that lot is never going to bother you again, right?" he said into the uncomfortable silence.

The boy let out a huge sigh and nodded, looking horribly ashamed and yet defiant.

"Owyn, that's a perfectly natural way for you to feel. I think in your position, I would feel exactly the same way." He sat up and rubbed his hands, easing a little stiffness in the joints. "How can you *not* feel that way? They certainly deserved punishment. One could almost say that they brought their fate on themselves."

"I didn't—" Owyn stopped, and flushed. Pol nodded.

"You were going to say that you didn't want anyone to die, but you did, didn't you? *Of course* you did! But you, yourself, would have helped them if you had been there, wouldn't you?"

Again the boy sighed deeply. "I guess so," he replied slowly, then repeated, with more assurance, "yes. I would have."

"So there you are. You have no reason to feel guilty. But trust me, the adults who were responsible for letting the situation get to this point are going to be *made* to feel guilty, and acknowledge their guilt, before this is all over." He stood up, and let that sink in. "*All* of the adults, including the ones who wouldn't listen to what their children tried to tell them. And I believe that we—the Heralds—will see that there are some apologies tendered."

As it dawned on Owyn that Pol meant his own parents would be confronted with the facts in the case, a certain glee crept into his eyes. Pol didn't blame him in the least; how else would a boy react to being told that his parents would have to apologize for not listening to and heeding him?

:*It isn't going to do them, or him, any harm,*: Satiran observed. :*I think we're finished here. I will meet you in the courtyard.*:

"I think I'm finished here, Owyn—and thank you, very much." Owyn stood up quickly, and took Pol's extended hand in a much firmer grip than before. "I doubt that your school will reopen for a fortnight or more, until we get things sorted, but don't allow that to be an excuse for falling behind in your work."

Owyn didn't snort, not in front of a Herald, but it was clear that he felt this was an unwarranted comment. "I never fall behind, sir," was all he said. Pol managed to keep his mouth from twitching up into a smile.

But that was the last smile he was to have for the rest of the day. The remaining interviews with the youngsters on Owyn's list who were least likely to break down were very uncomfortable. All boys, all had been caned at least once by the bullies, and half had been caned several times. When Pol heard from their own mouths the alleged *reasons* for the caning— including the boys who had been ordered to bring Tyron Jelnack and his cronies special gifts and treats— he was livid. Of all of them, only one had been a punishment specifically assigned by a teacher, and it *hadn't* warranted a flogging.

He and Satiran returned to the Palace and Collegium in a state of suppressed rage themselves. He went straight to the Captain's office, hoping to catch him before dinner.

He succeeded; and by the time he had given the officer the terse, bare-bones facts of the case, the Captain was left sitting in his chair with his mouth hanging open.

"How did they manage to get away with all that?" he sputtered. "Abuse, extortion—and how long has this been going on?"

"Not long, I don't think—at least, not long at this level of abuse," Pol said, some of his anger cooling, although he was still too keyed up to sit. "I suspect a great deal of this was due to the ringleader. Still."

"Still—I'm issuing an order closing the school until the Council has sorted things out and assigned a new Master," the Captain said, scribbling quickly. "That much is in my power."

"That much will do very nicely," Pol told him. "I'll take care of getting this in front of the Council, and I'll get the interviews with the rest of the children on the list."

The Captain shook his head. "We never would have gotten this much out of the children," he admitted, and touched his forehead in a sketchy salute as Pol turned to go. "I'm glad we have you white-coats around."

The Seneschal's Herald, Trevor, took Pol's report in silence. When Pol was done, Herald Trevor tapped his lips with his pen as he sat in thought.

"This isn't a matter for the full Council, but as it affects the Trades and Crafts, I think the Council ought to hear a full report when we've decided what to do," Trevor said at last. "Hmm. I think the Seneschal, His Majesty, Her Majesty, and Jedin and I can make a quick decision." He gave Pol a knowing glance. "There are always more people worthy of good academic positions than there are positions to fill," he observed dryly. "Putting a real teacher in charge of this school should solve most of the problems. I do agree with you, by the by, that it is *much* too valuable a resource to shut down."

"Do you still want me to get interviews with the rest of the children?" Pol asked, cast in doubt by the Herald's quick resolution of the problem.

"Oh, *absolutely*—and take your daughter, the Empath—what's her name? Elenor. Yes, take Elenor with you." Trevor's tight-lipped smile did not bode well for the adults who would be hearing the judgment laid on them. "When we present our verdict, I don't want there to be the slightest doubt in anyone's mind that we were not only entirely justified, but lamentably tardy in discovering what was going on. I also want you to interview this Lavan Chitward, when he recovers. There is still no evidence of what happened in that room, and there are four dead boys to account for."

"Yes," Pol replied instantly. "There are. And even if they richly deserved punishment—"

"—and even if they caused their punishment themselves, by their own actions, we must see to it that we *know* what happened." Trevor rubbed one temple carefully, with the first two fingers of his right hand. "I would like less mystery and more fact—and I would like to be certain that no one can point a finger at the Chitward boy in any way when this is over."

So would I, Pol thought, taking his leave of Herald Trevor, *I just hope we can manage that.*

NINE

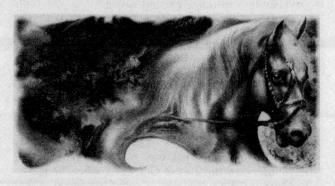

LAN lay floating in a sea of soft fleece, not quite connected to the world. He wasn't in his own room, but in a bright little chamber with soft, green walls and hardly any furniture. From time to time, someone in dark or pale green came in and did things to him, made him eat, or drink, or simply laid hands gently on his head. He knew they were Healers, but he didn't have any inclination to go any further with that thought.

For that matter, he really didn't have any inclination to go very far with *any* thought.

He knew that he hurt, but it was pain at one remove—very distant, and not really affecting *him,* although he heard himself whimpering and groaning from time to time. He knew he wasn't dead, and though he was a little surprised, that didn't matter very much either.

He slept a great deal, and he wasn't entirely sure that the Healers tending him were aware that *he* was aware of them. They certainly treated him as if he wasn't.

He . . . drifted. That was the best word for it. When he was awake, he watched the clouds and the rain through his window, without a single thought interrupting his passive observation for candlemarks at a time. When his eyelids grew too heavy to hold up, he slept, dreamlessly. Something warned him that he didn't want to think about why he was here; whenever any of the Healers said anything that pointed his mind in that direction, he shied violently away from the topic and dove into sleep.

The pain drifted, too—drifted away from him, over the course of two days, perhaps three. As it drifted from him, he became more aware of what was going on around him, whether he liked it or not. And one evening, as the first stars began to shine through his window, he woke up completely for the first time, with his mind clear.

His hands and wrists were bandaged, but they didn't hurt too much. That omnipresent headache was gone. And he remembered why he was here.

But he couldn't explain it, and his memories didn't make any sense. How could *he* have made Tyron and his bullies catch fire? He'd never heard of anything like that, not even in the bedtime stories his nursery maid had told him of gryphons and magic! The idea was simply ludicrous!

Before he could get any farther than that in his thinking, his door opened, and one of the dark-green-clad Healers entered, a tall, thin man who looked like nothing so much as a bundle of sticks made into a man and clothed in a Healer's robes that enveloped him completely, with hair made of a bunch of faded grass just stuck into the top. He smiled when he saw that Lan was staring at him.

"Awake, precisely on time. Very good, Lavan Chitward! There are some people who very much wish to speak with you, but first I have insisted that you have a proper meal." He motioned to someone outside the room, and one of the younger Healers in pale green—

a boy not much older than Lan himself, stocky, blond and a little self-conscious—brought in a tray.

The scent of the food drove all other thoughts from his mind and he fell on it, devouring it ravenously, although it was difficult at first to master the implements with bandaged wrists that didn't bend very well. He had *never* been so hungry before, and when he finished with a sigh, he was astonished at the amount of food he'd eaten. The older man and the young one watched him put away his breakfast without a sign of surprise.

"Recovering from burns requires a great deal of energy, that is why you are so hungry," the young man said—a bit pompously, Lan thought, and from the amused glance of the older Healer, so did his superior.

However, the older Healer didn't rebuke him. The man simply suggested, "Let's see if we can't get you out of bed and clothed. You should be ready for your visitors when they arrive, and it will do you harm to remain too long abed."

They did more than merely get him out of bed; they helped him bathe, get to the water closet, and into a set of clothing he had never seen before. They looked brand new, were brightly decorated with bands of gold-and-black tapestry, and Lan suspected his mother's hand in the selection. However, they were of soft chirra-wool dyed a dark rose, and felt wonderful on his sensitive, pink skin. From the look of things, he'd been burned all over, but his hands and wrists had been the worst.

"Now, it is a fine evening, one of the last we are likely to see until spring, and I would prefer for you to meet with your visitors in the garden," the older Healer said firmly. "Hob will help you get there."

This was obviously more of an order than a request, and although Lan would *much* rather have gone back to his bed to sleep, he wasn't going to be offered a choice in the matter.

With young Hob's assistance, although his legs were very shaky, Lan got as far as the first bench in the Healer's garden, where Hob left him. He took advantage of the momentary isolation to look around, and didn't recognize a single thing.

Where is this place? he wondered, distracted from other thoughts by the novelty of his surroundings.

Although the sky was dark and the leafless condition of the trees around him left no doubt as to the season, the air was balmy, and he thought that it might be somewhere around the time of year that they called "false summer" back in Alderscroft. Right around Sovvan there was a week or two of warm, sunny days and gentle, balmy nights right before the winter set in with a vengeance. There were just enough leaves left to make a semblance of bravery before the cold winds ripped them from the trees.

This was an herb garden, which made sense, given that it was attached to a House of Healing. He sat on a stone bench, still warm from the sun, one of a grouping of four that surrounded a round, raised herb bed. This was one grouping of many; someone had gone to a great deal of trouble to make sure the garden was as ornamental as it was useful. It was perfectly easy to see; there were lights and lanterns everywhere, even in the gardens.

Behind him stood an enormous building; this was where he had been housed until now, and he would have said it was quite the most enormous building he had ever seen—except that now, it wasn't.

It was one of a complex of buildings, three in all, joined by enclosed walkways that formed three sides of a long, narrow rectangle, enclosing this long garden. Beyond this garden, however, were *more* gardens, and more buildings. Or was it just a single, large building? He couldn't make up his mind. The main part of it was huge, and very old, with extensions that must have been added to it over a long period of time so that it rambled in all directions. He just stared at it for a long time, wondering what it could possibly be.

Between him and it was another, fanciful garden, beautifully planted so that even at this late season there were evergreen bushes and trees that kept the aspect verdant. This was a venue meant to be enjoyed in all seasons and times of the day or night, evidently; enormous oil torches stood by, shaped like shallow bowls on pedestals, ready to be lit when night fell, should there be a great occasion that called for the garden to be brilliantly illuminated.

A suspicion had formed in his mind, and he kept dismissing it as nonsense, but the sight of all this kept bringing it back up, for who but a King could afford gardens and buildings like this? Surely this couldn't be— Why would anyone bring *him* to—There was no way this could be—

"Your first view of the Palace, Lavan?" asked someone behind him; he started, and turned around.

A man of medium height with silver hair pulled back into a tail and wearing the uniform of a Herald waited there; with him were three Guardsmen in their distinctive silver-and-midnight-blue uniforms, one of them with the insignia of an officer. The Herald stepped forward first, and stood with one foot up on the stone bench, admiring the view.

He was a handsome man, perhaps forty years old by his face, though his silver hair suggested he was older than that. His firm, square chin and sober mouth suggested he was a stern man, but his kindly, dark eyes and the smile lines around his mouth suggested the opposite.

"Behind you is Healer's Collegium; the building to the right is the dormitory where the Trainees live, the one in the middle holds the classrooms and the library, and the one to your left is the House of Healing itself," the Herald said easily, in a way that made Lan cautiously want to like him. "Out there, that tangle—" He chuckled, waving his hand at the Palace. "Well, that's the Old Palace, and New Palace, and the Herald's Collegium. Bardic is on the other side of Herald's; you can't see it from here. They keep threatening to pull it all down one day and rebuild it because it's such an illogical mess, but I can't imagine them doing so."

"I can't either," Lan replied, dazed at the very notion. "Where would they put everyone?"

"Well, that's the question, isn't it?" the Herald replied, with a wry smile. "One solution would be to build the new structure in a logical fashion first, move everyone in, and tear the old one down. If they ever carry out their threat, that's the only way I can see it happening." He turned to Lan and extended a hand. "I'm Herald Pol, by the way, and I imagine you're wondering why I want to talk to you."

Lan took his hand gingerly, but Pol put no pressure on it at all, just allowed it to rest in his for a moment. His handshake was warm, dry, and neutral. "I don't know why a Herald would want to talk to *me*," he said doubtfully. "I'm nobody."

"Well, you see, four of your schoolmates died in the fire that hurt you, and you are the only one we haven't asked about it yet," the Herald said, and Lan felt his heart stop.

He felt as if the Herald was waiting for him to say something, but he couldn't think of anything. His mouth went dry, and he felt cold all over.

"What exactly were all of you doing in that classroom?" the Herald asked into the silence.

How can I tell him? He'll never believe me! My own parents didn't believe me!

Lan started shaking, and gripped the bench with both hands. "I wasn't doing—anything," he said through clenched teeth.

The Herald raised an eloquent eyebrow. "Perhaps I should rephrase that question. What were the older boys doing to you?" When Lan didn't reply, his gaze

bored into Lan's eyes, prying each reluctant word out
of him.

I can't—

"I—they—were—they were—pushing me about—"
He couldn't get his breath, somehow, and he was
shaking so hard . . . why wouldn't this man leave him
alone? He didn't know anything. "I—it was a kind
of game."

To them, anyway.

"But why did they bring you there?" the Herald
persisted. "What kind of a game is it that involves
large young men tossing a younger boy around? *What
was going on?*"

Maybe if he just told the Herald the truth, the man
would go away! "They were going to flog me!" Lan
blurted in desperation. "Tyron said I was—that—he
said—" He couldn't finish; after all, it was just his
word against that of the other boys, and who knew
what they'd told the authorities? That was why the
Guard Captain was there, wasn't it?

The Herald gave a little nod to the Guard Captain,
as if to say, "I told you so." He continued more gently,
"We've made a point of talking to some of the other
youngsters, and they've been telling us some interesting things. Would you care to talk to us about it as
well?"

He looked so trustworthy. He was a Herald!
Shouldn't I be able to trust a Herald?

But there was a barrier to that. *What if they decide
I'm responsible for the fire?*

And another. What if he really *was?*

No, that was ridiculous. How could he have started
the fire? Impossible. And this *was* a Herald. Surely, if
anyone would know the truth when he heard it, this
man would.

"It depends on who you were talking to," Lan said,
unable to keep sullenness out of his voice, but relaxing
a little. His heart stopped pounding, and he stopped

shivering as much, but he still held to the bench with a death grip.

"Not the young devils in the—what-you-call—Sixth Form," the Guard Captain rumbled unexpectedly. Paper whispered as he took a list out of his pocket. "Young lad called Owyn Kittlekine in your group was the most talkative."

Lan felt tension spool up again. "What did he tell you?" he asked.

"Largely that the leaders of the Sixth Form were using the sloth and negligence of Master Keileth and your teachers to bully and abuse the younger students," the Guard Captain said in disgust. "We've had words with their parents, and that school isn't going to open again until matters are set right."

"But we want to know—*exactly*—what happened in that room, Lan," the Herald interrupted, "I know you don't want to think about it, but when there is even one death, much less four, we have to know why. People are asking a lot of awkward questions, and we must have answers for them."

Oh, gods. They do *think I'm responsible!*

This time, Lan wasn't shivering with cold, he was trembling with fear, and something angry and ominously familiar roused deep inside him. He began to flush as he spoke, feeling anger uncoil in his belly.

"They—Tyron—said I was eroding discipline because I wasn't letting them catch me to beat me up," he began slowly. "And because I wouldn't steal velvet from my father for him. He wanted scarlet for a Midwinter tunic, and he told me to get him some. When I told him I didn't get pocket money, he told me to get the velvet however I had to, and that he'd flog me for disobedience if I didn't." Just the *memory* made him angry, and he felt a headache beginning. Once again, the Herald and the Guard Captain exchanged a look. "He said he was going to punish me for that, and because some of the others were staying up in the classrooms over lunch like I was doing instead of going down to the Hall where Tyron and his bunch could get at them. And he said he was going to punish me for lying about being sick, and for lying about staying behind after classes to study and coming in early to study. He was going to flog me for all of that, and that was why they took me to the storeroom, where nobody could hear me."

"Hmm." The Guard Captain made a note, but said nothing. Once again, it was the Herald that asked the questions.

"And did he tell you just how severe your punishment was going to be?" he asked.

Lan squinted through his headache. "Eighty stripes—I think—" *I can't think . . . why won't they leave me alone? I didn't do anything!*

The Herald interrupted. "All right, you say that the older boys found you in the classroom and took you downstairs to the storage room to flog you."

He *hadn't* said that, he hadn't said where they'd found him, but it was right, so he snapped his mouth shut and tried to think through a pounding headache that misted his vision with red. He just nodded, and the Herald continued.

"Then what happened?"

"Tyron—told me what I told you—and then he told the others to 'play with me' and they started to shove me around." He could hardly speak now, torn between anger at his tormentors, and a terror as great as *they* had given him, but why was he so horribly afraid? What was it that the Herald's questions were pushing him toward? Why did the questions make him want to run away, howling?

Please! Leave me alone!

"So they tossed you about and slammed you into the walls. Then?"

"Then—that was when Tyron said—and they took me to the chair—and they tied—" The red rage and fear rose together, and the Herald *wouldn't* let him alone!

"Then what, Lan?" the Herald persisted. "Then what happened? We have to know!"

He reached out and seized Lan's shoulder in an insistent grip, and the rage and the fear spiraled upward, out of control, and melded into a terrible whole.

"No!" he screamed, flinging himself away, dimly understanding that the unthinking rage and the animal fear would strike at whatever was nearest, whether the target deserved it or not.

He stumbled and fell to his hands and knees at the foot of one of the great torches as the maelstrom of emotion became the monster of flame—but this time, he did not touch anything living.

He sprawled at the base of the ornamental torch, and as his eyes glazed over with crimson, the oil above his head erupted in flame with a sound like the dull impact of a giant fist on flesh, or of something soft and heavy falling to earth. A wave of heat washed over him, and his trailing sleeves caught fire.

By this point, *he* was helpless; the fire held him in thrall. All he could do was let it rage around him, and hope nothing came within its grasp.

Forlorn hope.

Another torch went up, and another, and the nearest bush started to crisp and crackle with flames. The fire spread, and *he could do nothing!* He heard, as from a far country, the cries of alarm, and even someone calling his name, but he was no longer himself, he was the fire, and the flames were more intoxicating than wine, more implacable than a thunderstorm, all-consuming and all-enveloping, and in a moment or two he would be gone and there would be nothing left but the flames.

The little of himself that was left was nothing more than a dry leaf in the firestorm; tempest-tossed, not yet consumed, but doomed, surely doomed—

:Never!:

The word, clear and bright as a trumpet call in a still night, sounded above the chaos enveloping him.

There was a moment of total stillness. Lan, teetering just above the fiery abyss and about to fall into it forever, felt—*something*—reach for him, take him, and pluck him away.

The rage and fear ran out of him like molten metal poured from a cracked crucible. The ragged lightning piercing his brain with unbearable pain vanished. The crimson haze cleared from his sight, and he looked up, saw that the fire around him had died away, all but the flames rising from the torches; saw that he was not alone.

But it was no human that stood beside him, valiantly shielding him with her own body from the Herald and the spears of the two Guards and the Captain.

It was a Companion.

Oh— he thought vaguely, and looked into her eyes.

Once again he fell, but not to his doom.

He fell into a cool, blue world of light; he fell forever and never reached the bottom. But something reached out for him.

Something enfolded him, wrapped and cradled him in an emotion he almost didn't recognize. And when he realized what it was, he wept, and as he wept, he returned it with all his heart, and wrapped the giver in the gift, until it was no longer possible for either of them to have told where one began and the other ended.

They trembled together there, in an embrace so close that there was no room for thought, for a single, deliriously sweet moment. Then they parted, separating into individuals—but never again to be alone, never again without a bond beyond words, joined together by the strongest thing on earth or in the Havens.

He fell back into himself, still gazing into the most wondrous eyes in the world, and heard her speak for the second time into his mind.

:I love you, Lan. I Choose you. I am Kalira, and I will never leave you.:

"Well," said the Herald, in a voice heavy with irony. "This certainly changes things."

POL had anticipated many possible outcomes from his confrontation with Lavan Chitward, but this was not one of them. Never in his wildest imaginings would he have anticipated that Lavan would be Chosen—or be a Firestarter who had nearly immolated himself along with his persecutors.

He managed to persuade Captain Telamaine that the boy was no longer a danger to anyone; he also managed to persuade him that the boy was in no way responsible for what the fires he had called had done to his tormentors. *How* he had done so, he had no idea. It might have been his own feeble powers of Empathic projection, it might have been a miracle. It might even be the work of Kalira, Lavan's new Companion, for there was no doubt that she could, and would, do anything she had to in order to protect him.

Now the four of them—himself, young Lavan, Kalira, and Satiran—were alone in the garden. There was plenty of light to see by, although it was well past midnight. They had gathered, ironically enough, beneath the huge garden torch; there seemed no reason to extinguish it. They needed to have open space for the two Companions, since the Healers wouldn't allow Lavan out of their sight, which meant Pol couldn't carry him off to the Collegium.

Yet.

Lavan stood no taller than Pol's shoulder; short for his reputed age of sixteen, thin, and lanky, with the loose-jointed, unfinished air of a boy who hasn't yet grown into what he will one day be. He had chestnut hair, more red than brown, with a slight wave to it, hazel eyes prone to change colors as his mood changed, and a thin, finely chiseled face, delicate, but in no way effeminate. Not a boy one would have ever suspected as the cause of so much horror.

The Healers had reclothed him and examined every bit of him for new burns, but in the end, only needed to replace the bandages. This time his powers had done him relatively little damage, other than to ruin his clothes. Pol had sent at once for a proper Trainee's Grays; it had reinforced his arguments with Captain Telamaine when the boy reappeared in the garb of a Heraldic Trainee.

Now the only question was—what was Herald's Collegium to do with him?

:What do you think?: asked an unfamiliar mind-voice; female, and there was only one creature it could be. Pol stared at Kalira in astonishment; he could count on the fingers of one hand the number of times that a Companion had ever Mindspoken to someone other than his Chosen Herald.

:Are you—Mindspeaking me?: he asked in shock.

:Of course I am!: she said tartly. *:Don't be ridiculous, Pol. You need to talk to me directly, not through Satiran. And as for what you will do, you Heralds— you will take him, and train him, that is what you will do with him.:*

He gazed at her dubiously. Lavan was oblivious to the conversation, although Pol was certain he heard it; sitting on the bench with one hand and his forehead resting on her flank. He was exhausted, and more than a little befogged by the drugs the Healers had given him.

:How?: Pol asked her. *:How do you train something like—this?:* There hadn't been a Firestarter in the Heraldic Circle in all the time he could remember, not one of any power, at least. He was the only Herald with even a trace of the Gift, and all he could manage to do was light an occasional bit of tinder. A powerful Firestarter came along once every two or three gener-

ations—someone like Lavan, never before. He was
unique—and not a little frightening.

:*How can we deal with this?*: he continued. :*It's not
a Gift, it's a curse! He's got no control over it. It
damned near took him, and the gods only know what
would have been unleashed if it had!*:

Kalira raised her head and stared at him defiantly.
:*I can control it,*: she replied. :*I can, and I will. He will
be of no danger as long as I am with him, and I will
never leave him.*:

:*Kalira—*: Satiran interjected haltingly. :*He has murdered four already. Is this any kind of person to
Choose?*:

Satiran gazed at the other Companion with eyes
dark with fear and worry, and well he might. Kalira
was his daughter.

:*He didn't* murder *anyone; it was part accident, part
horrible bad luck, and part provoked. I Chose him,
Satiran; it is my Choice, not yours. He needs me.
Would you have another Tylendel?*: she asked harshly,
and Pol saw Satiran wince.

He moved to the side of his old friend, and laid his
arm along Satiran's neck, hoping to give him some
comfort, as Satiran had so often given comfort to his
Chosen. "Children grow up and make their own
paths," he murmured. "It's not for us to force them
out of the roads they pick, however much we might
wish to. The Choice is made; now let's deal with it."

Kalira cast him a glance that was half gratitude, half
defiance, then turned her head to nuzzle her Chosen.
What passed between them was not for Pol or Satiran
to hear, but the boy turned his head and looked to
them with a bit more life in his pallid face. And anguish, terrible anguish, more than any boy his age
should have to feel.

"Oh, sir—I didn't mean—" he began, and started
to cry, the sort of helpless, hopeless weeping of one
who is weary far past his strength. His face crumpled,
and Pol heard his spirit crumbling in his tears.

Pol was not proof against that agony. Gingerly, he sat down beside the boy, and when Lavan didn't resist, put an arm around his shoulders. "I know you never meant any of this to happen, Lavan," he told the youngster, and somewhat to his own bemusement, he knew at that moment that he had spoken nothing but the truth. Lavan Chitward had probably fantasized about dealing the bullies the same punishment they'd inflicted on him, but he would never have been Chosen had he been the kind of person who could actually carry out those fantasies. How could anyone blame him for what had happened? Even the mildest of creatures fights back when cornered, and it was just everyone's misfortune that Lavan had teeth and claws that were sharper than swords and more deadly—and hadn't known it.

"I didn't!" Lavan sobbed. "I didn't! Oh, gods, why didn't I die, too?"

:He means it,: Kalira said warningly, and turned her attention back to the boy.

"You didn't die because you don't deserve to die!" Pol said firmly, closing his hand on the boy's shoulder and willing him to believe.

"Neither did they!" Lavan moaned, shrinking into himself.

"That may be. Look at me, Lavan!" He turned the boy's tear-streaked face up so that he had to look into Pol's eyes. His swollen eyes begged for the reassurance that Pol was about to give him. "Now, listen to me! If those boys, out of ignorance, had teased a herd of horses and stampeded them, were the horses to blame?"

"N-no." Perhaps it was the drugs, perhaps the exhaustion, but Lavan had not dropped into unreasoning hysteria. He *was* listening.

"And if those boys had been trampled beneath their hooves, what then?" he persisted. "Do we kill the horses because their panic overwhelmed their reason?"

"So this—thing—inside of me—is like a herd of wild horses?" Lavan said tentatively, his eyes beseeching Pol for the comfort of confirmation.

Pol nodded, firmly. "Very like. Quite as unreasoning. If you had been Chosen and come to us *before* this ability of yours got so inextricably entangled with your fear and anger, perhaps it would have been like a herd of horses harnessed into a team. *But—!*" he continued, holding up a finger to forestall any interruptions. "That is only a 'perhaps'—and a herd turned into a team can still break free and stampede. I don't know enough about your Gift to tell you anything for certain." He sighed and rubbed the back of his own neck. "I don't think anyone ever has."

Lavan scrubbed tears from his face, leaving behind a smear of ash, and sniffed, then gulped. "Now what?" he said, in a very small voice.

"Now we train you as best we can," Pol said, feeling a terrible weight of responsibility descending on his shoulders. "Kalira says that she can control this Gift of yours, and I have never known a Companion to be wrong about something when she is so very certain of her ability."

"What about—" Lavan waved his hand vaguely in the direction of the city. "What about what I did at the school?" His eyes pled for forgiveness, for some sort of redemption.

Pol looked to Satiran for help. What *would* they do? What was the moral and ethical course to steer through this morass? It seemed to him that whatever they chose to do, it would be wrong!

:For now . . .: Satiran pondered. *:For now, nothing. I believe that Captain Telamaine will decide to permit the parents of the dead boys to come to their own conclusions, without revealing that Lavan has any unusual Gifts.:*

Pol wondered if Satiran or Kalira had put that plan into the Captain's head. Then again—probably not. Telamaine would not have been put in charge of the

Guard here in Haven if he was not able to arrive at compromise.

"People are going to find out eventually," Pol protested.

:Perhaps. But memories fade. It is entirely possible that no one will connect Trainee Lavan with Lavan Chitward by then—or put a Firestarting Gift together with the disaster at the school.:

:Even if they do,: Kalira interjected, *:there is nothing they can do about it. I suspect if they dared to bring it up before the Crown, the King would have a few choice words to say about the kind of person who gains his amusement from torturing and abusing the weak and undefended.:*

Pol couldn't help it; however grave the situation, he couldn't stop his lips from quirking into a little smile at the way Kalira leaped to Lan's defense.

Then he sighed. It wasn't entirely a moral or ethical course, but it was the closest he could see to steering one. "Go to bed, Lavan," he said at last, feeling quite as weary as Lavan. "This is more than we can deal with in a single night. Just remember this, every time that you start to feel afraid, or guilty, or angry. *Companions don't Choose wrongly.* That is something we all know, at the core of our souls."

:And if you forget,: Kalira said, half amused, and half fiercely, *:I will certainly remind you.:*

Pol walked Lavan to the door, where the Healers had been waiting impatiently; this time they took him to a different room, one on the ground floor, where a large window could be opened to the garden. These rooms were used for Heralds, so that their Companions could be near them. Kalira settled herself in for the night at the window, and Pol and Satiran walked slowly back to the Collegium, side by side.

"What are we going to do with this one?" Pol asked, unable to see how this situation could ever be made into a success.

:We'll do what we have to,: Satiran replied. *:We'll*

do what we have to. But there's something else I think you should know—:

Pol braced himself. A hundred dire possibilities ran through his mind, but once again, the story of Lavan Chitward was going to surprise him with the unexpected.

:This—is not just Kalira's Choice,: Satiran said hesitantly. *:I think—I think it's a lifebond.:*

TEN

King Theran

POL was not finished for the night, after all.

No sooner had he crossed the threshold into Herald's Collegium, he was surrounded by people; Captain Telamaine, the Lord Marshal and his Herald, Marak—the Seneschal and *his* Herald, Trevor—and the King's Own, Herald Jedin. Pinning him into the poorly-lit entryway, none of them were willing to let him pass until each of them had gotten a say in matters.

The factions were equal and quite clearly demarcated along color lines; the Heralds in their white uniforms on his right, the others in their varicolored court clothing on the other. They all began talking at once, creating a babble that echoed up and down the hallway and rose in sound level as each tried to be heard over the rest. This was an impossible situation, and Pol put his foot down immediately.

"Shut up, all of you!" he roared, silencing them. Heads popped out of doors up and down the hall, and quickly retreated when the rank of those clustered at the entry had been noted. It was too late to hope that

curiosity hadn't been aroused; he could only hope that
the incident was quickly forgotten. "Now, I suggest
we take this to the Lesser Council Chamber before
you frighten all the Trainees and set the Court to making up gossip for lack of concrete information." He
glared at all of them; he rarely invoked his ability to
cow a group, but that made the skill all the more
effective when he displayed it. Without waiting for an
answer, he strode off down the corridor, leaving them
to follow in his wake. The wood-paneled hall remained silent; no more heads popped from doors. Pol
hoped that this altercation was of less interest than
books and interrupted studies.

Once they were out of the Heralds' Wing and into
the Palace proper he breathed a bit easier. Processions
of officials going to and from various rooms at any
and all hours were perfectly normal sights in the Palace. He nodded affably at pages and passing courtiers,
and the others had the wit to do likewise. Through the
maze of hallways and passages they went, occasionally
interrupting a lovers' tryst or sending a group of truant
pages to find some other hiding place, until they arrived at the substantial door of the Lesser Council
Room, which served for meetings of segments of the
Council and three Circles most of the hours of the day.
At this hour the fire was out, but thanks to the warmth
of the evening, the room had taken on no more than
a faint chill. He took a taper from the shelf beside the
door, lit it at a lamp in the hallway, then went around
relighting the room's lamps himself as the others filed
inside. Only when he had seated himself at the head of
the rectangular oak table and the heavy ironwood
door was firmly closed behind the last of the group
did he wait for the others to seat themselves, clear
his throat, and look around with an inquiring glance,
inviting one of them to start. They all hesitated for a
moment except the Captain.

"I don't know what kind of mind-magic you worked
on me out there, Pol," Captain Telamaine began heat-

edly. "But as soon as I got back to my office, I came to my senses about that—that—*menace* in the guise of a boy! I've put guards on him, and I went straight to the Lord Marshal—"

"Which I had every intention of doing myself, although I don't think I would have dared interrupt him if he had already retired for the night," Pol replied, keeping his own voice calm and reasoned. "As for using mind-magic on you—*first* of all, I am appalled that you even considered that I would consider doing so, and second, the only 'magic' taking place during our interview with Lavan was the exercise of your own good sense, which you seem to have lost between Healer's and here."

"Well said," Jedin muttered, low enough that only Pol heard him.

"As for the guards," Pol continued, raising an eyebrow with studied surprise. "What, precisely, did you intend for them to do? The boy is hardly going to evoke his Firestarting Gift on purpose—you saw for yourself that he is terrified of what he can do—and even if he did it by accident, how do you propose to *stop* him with a guard? Have them shoot him dead? Assuming they can, of course. It is possible that the fires would protect their progenitor." The carefully nuanced eyebrow rose again. "And wouldn't killing a Trainee create a fine and confident climate among the rest of our Trainees? A good half of them are afraid of their own Gifts; how are they to take it if members of the Guard start executing people for using Gifts?"

Telamaine flushed, then blanched, then flushed again. "I—" he began, and couldn't get any farther.

The Lord Marshal took pity on him. "You responded as a Captain of the Guard to a situation outside your training, Telamaine," the old man said gruffly, actually reaching out to pat the Captain's shoulder. He rubbed his bushy gray eyebrows with his hand, and then ran the same hand over thick, gray hair. "Putting guards on the boy until you had further orders was in accordance with not knowing what to do about it.''

''And now we will make a reasoned and reasoning response to the situation and correct things before they become a problem,'' Pol pointed out smoothly. ''We need thought, cool heads and tempers, and one thing made perfectly clear. The boy *has been Chosen*. The mare Kalira is no youngster. Furthermore, she made it known in no uncertain terms to my Companion Satiran—who happens to be her sire—*and* to me personally, that she can and will control his Gift.''

''Gift?'' the Seneschal yelped, both eyebrows leaping up like a pair of startled caterpillars. ''You call that a *Gift?*''

''Cool and reasoned,'' murmured Trevor, placing a cautioning hand on the Seneschal's arm. Pol couldn't blame the poor man; he was much younger than any of the others, having come to this position from his previous post as the Seneschal of Theran's country estate. When he wasn't confronted by impossible situations, he was quite a handsome young fellow, and very much the target of the mothers of unwedded maidens.

Seneschal Greeley ran a nervous hand through a thick thatch of brown hair that was growing grayer by the month. Trevor murmured something Pol couldn't hear, and he rolled his eyes, but didn't add any more little comments.

''Nevertheless,'' Captain Telamaine persisted. ''That so-called boy caused the deaths of four of his own schoolmates. Just what are we supposed to say to *their* parents?''

''A *damned* good question!'' Greeley seconded, nodding vigorously.

All four Heralds exchanged a glance. King's Own Jedin took over from Pol. He had more authority than any of the others, and Pol was perfectly glad to let him handle the discussion from this moment on.

''Tell them that there was a terrible accident that

occurred while their offspring were bullying this boy," Jedin said flatly. "That we think there was—lamp oil stored there, one of them threw the boy Lavan into the stack of containers, they broke open and spilled into the fireplace. That was how and why the fire happened so quickly."

For one long moment of absolute silence, the non-Heralds stared at Jedin in disbelief. Finally Captain Telamaine broke the silence with a gasp of protest.

"But that's not true!" he sputtered. "Nothing like that happened!"

Herald Jedin gazed at him from beneath his heavy, black eyebrows. He was a great granite cliff of a man, with a craggy face, precisely barbered black hair, and a naturally forbidding expression that he used to great effect. "I am well aware of that."

"But—" Telamaine protested.

Jedin held up his hand, cutting off the protests before they began. "But would any good be served by telling them the truth? Telling them the entire truth? Including the fact that their sons were essentially torturing other children on a regular basis, ordering them to commit theft and falsehood? Telling them that their sons died because one of their victims was so abused and terrified that he lost control of a powerful Heraldic Gift? And *then* telling them that the boy who killed their children is being made into a Herald himself?"

"Which would, of course," King Theran boomed from the door, "Substantially erode public trust in the Heraldic Circle, upon which we all depend."

They all shoved their chairs back hastily and began to rise, only to have Theran wave them back down into their seats. Pol alone rose and vacated the head of the table; Theran assumed his proper place smoothly, and Pol took another seat farther down along the side, relieved that the pressure was now entirely off him.

Theran *looked* like a King; Pol had often heard children presented at Court exclaim in satisfaction that "he looked just like I thought he would!" Tall, muscular, with even, regular features, a fine head of blond-streaked brown hair that hung down past his shoulders, and a thick, neatly trimmed beard and mustache that matched perfectly, he was one of the most physically commanding men Pol had ever seen.

"I have heard about everything so far," Theran said, without specifying that it was his own Companion that had told him what had gone on. He didn't need to; Theran had a singularly close bond with his Companion, which meant that he knew everything that any Companion in Haven knew. He met the eyes of each of them in turn. "I can appreciate the concerns that the Guard has with this boy," he said, resting his eyes on Captain Telamaine and the Lord Marshal. "Please believe me, I do. I do *not* make my decisions lightly here, but if this Kingdom is to survive and prosper, there are some fundamental principles that we must believe in without question, and one of the most crucial is that our Companions do not make mistakes when they Choose new Heralds, and that when they tell us something is true, we can believe it without question."

The Heralds around the table nodded, relieved that Theran had put this into such plain language. The others looked crestfallen and uncomfortable, but in tentative agreement.

"Now, this child's Companion has told us that she can control his rogue abilities, although he cannot as yet. We must believe this, and Captain Telamaine, this should alleviate any security issues you have."

Telamaine got a stubborn set to his chin, but Theran wasn't done. Whatever the Captain wanted to say would have to remain unsaid. The King held the floor, and was not about to relinquish it. Theran was a powerful man, overmatching even his very powerful King's Own Herald. Jedin could defeat anyone in Court and Collegium at wrestling and practice combat, even the

Weaponsmaster and professional fighters—except the King. Theran rarely used his physical presence to dominate. He didn't have to. And that alone said much about him.

"It seems that his—outbreaks—occur when he undergoes great emotional stress. Therefore I suggest to you that you leave the guards on him, but instruct them to quickly remove anyone who seems to be *causing* this boy such stresses before they trigger another incident." Theran and his Herald exchanged a brief look (barely more than a flicker of amusement) as Captain Telamaine sighed with relief. This *was* something that the Guard could accomplish, and having a task defined evidently made him feel that he had some control over the situation. And without a doubt, Theran had been well aware of this before he even began issuing his edicts and orders.

Theran continued gravely, now giving his attention to his Seneschal. "His Companion also tells us, after minute examination of his memories, that the boy had no intention of killing or even seriously injuring his persecutors. We must also believe this, and thus, in a very real sense, what happened after that was an accident in truth." Theran waited, and this time it was the Seneschal who objected with a raised finger.

"You only said *seriously* injure—" he protested, his hair standing on end from his ceaseless toying with it, giving him the look of a frazzled heron. "So the boy was willing to hurt them!"

Theran snorted; his long friendship with his Seneschal allowed him to handle the man differently than the Guard Captain. "Oh, come now, Greeley! The boy had been beaten to a pulp, slammed into walls, and they'd started flogging him! What do you expect? It would take a saint or a martyr to be forgiving under that sort of circumstance, and although I do require many things of my Heralds, I do *not* require them to be more than human! *Of course* he wanted to hurt them! So would you, so would I, and so would any other man. If these juvenile tyrants weren't already out of my jurisdiction, *I* would be doing significantly more than merely hurting them, and with a certain grim pleasure, might I add! I am sorely tempted to administer a little royal justice to the ones that didn't die!"

Seneschal Greeley ran his hands one more time through his tousled hair, sighed, and shrugged, seeing the justice in the King's statement.

"Now, lastly, the point is that Kalira Chose this boy. Of all things, we must believe that where Companion's Choice is concerned, Companions *are* the final authority." He closed his eyes for a moment, gathering his thoughts—or perhaps, consulting with his own Companion. "Given that, what are we to do with this boy, if not to accept that, and accept him into the Collegium for proper training? Kalira has no intentions of repudiating him. Are we to try and forcibly separate them? I submit that this would be the worst idea yet. Are we to banish them to some remote place? That accomplishes nothing, and leaves the boy untutored, uncounseled, undisciplined. That is an idea as poor as the first. So we accept him. We teach him, we make a Herald of him, we learn what he can do and we make proper use of it." King Theran stood up and swept them all with a challenge in his eyes. "That, as ever, has been and will be *your* duty, and it is a familiar one to all of you. And I will leave you to it."

He nodded to them all, and left the room as he had entered it, calm, strong, and utterly in control, leaving behind silence.

Finally one voice broke the silence; Herald Jedin.

"That, my friends," he said in a voice full of admiration, "is a King."

LAN slept through the night with a gentle murmur of reassurance accompanying his dreams. When he woke, it was to a cheerful whicker outside his window and a *:Come on, lazy one, you can't lie abed forever!:* in his mind. He never had a moment to doubt that this was all real; Kalira saw to that. She was a presence in his mind all night long.

When he woke, with the first morning sun streaming down outside the window, he saw her watching him from the other side of the glass. He didn't exactly leap out of bed—it was more of a crawl—but in spite of what had happened last night, he was still stronger than yesterday. The first thing he did as soon as he got to the other side of the room was to open the window so that Kalira could put her head inside. Throwing his arms around her neck, he put his forehead against hers and closed his eyes, reveling in the mere fact of her presence for a long, blissful moment.

:Do you know how wonderful you are?: he asked her silently, already at ease with this strange form of communication, perhaps because it was with *her*. Already it was easier than talking aloud; instinctive and comfortable.

:Silly boy,: she replied affectionately. *:I'm neither more nor less wonderful than any other Herald or Companion.:*

He didn't argue with her; he didn't exactly have a basis for comparison. *:All I know is that you are the most marvelous person I've ever known.:*

She whickered a chuckle and rubbed her muzzle against his cheek. *:And I feel the same about you.:* She cocked her head to the side, and her eyes twinkled merrily. *:Convenient, isn't it?:*

He had to laugh at that, and she shook her head, tossing her mane. *:Well, what are they going to do to me today?:* he asked her, certain that she would know.

:Pol and Satiran will be coming for you in a little. You should be ready for them,: she suggested. Loath though he was to take his arms from around her neck, he acknowledged the wisdom of her suggestion, and pulled reluctantly away.

This time he dressed himself, though his hands shook and his knees trembled with weakness. When one of the young Healer-Trainees, a pretty little chestnut-haired girl with a lithe graceful figure, entered with his breakfast, she looked blankly at first at the empty bed, then when he moved a little, her heart-shaped face betrayed her surprise to see him sitting at the open window.

"You don't need any help, then?" she said, her surprise turning into a smile. "Good for you!" She brought the tray to him and set the tray down on the window seat beside him, and he saw that she had eyes of mingled green and brown. "You'll be seeing my father in a bit, after he talks with your Healer. You're going to be a bit more complicated to settle in than most Trainees."

"Your father?" Lan asked, and then managed to put two and two together. "You mean that Herald that was here last night is your father?"

She dimpled charmingly. "Oh, I'm afraid so; Herald Pol is my father. It does get rather trying, sometimes, having a father who can keep track of you no matter where you go. I'm Healer-Trainee Elenor, temporarily at your service." She bobbed an impudent curtsy. "My mother is Healer Ilea, but she's in service on the Southeast Border right now. At least I don't have *both* parents hovering over me all the time!"

Lan smiled tentatively at her; he wasn't exactly used to having pretty girls dimple at him, but it was a pleasant experience. She looked to be just about his age, which probably meant she was a great deal farther along in her studies than he. "When did you start here? How long are you going to be a Trainee?" he asked.

"Oh, I've been a Trainee for more than five years, but I won't be one for much longer. Maybe a year," she told him with great confidence, looking around, then seating herself on the edge of the bed. "I don't know how long you'll be one; I suppose it will depend

how much you already know. A lot of the Heraldic
Trainees arrive here barely able to read and write, so
the classes are all planned around that eventuality.
Most of them aren't Chosen until they're twelve or
thirteen, and they generally get their Whites by eighteen no matter how little they knew before they got
here."

"Well, I do know a little more than that," he said,
warming to her cheerful manner. "Am I really going
to be a Heraldic Trainee?" It was hard to believe; he
could picture himself in the Guard, he could easily
picture himself as a Caravan Master, but a Herald?
He'd never seriously entertained the idea of himself
in Whites.

Elenor gestured at Kalira, who was watching both
of them with sparkling blue eyes the color of deep
water. "You've been Chosen, that makes you a Heraldic Trainee. I'm afraid you don't have much of a
choice!" She laughed. "It's not a job you can volunteer for *or* decline, it seems!"

For a brief moment, he felt uncertainty; did he
really want the rest of his life decided for him? Hadn't
he been trying to escape his own parents' plans for
his life? But then he looked into Kalira's eyes and
knew that *she* was worth any sacrifice.

"At least you know what Heralds *do,*" Elenor continued. "Some Trainees don't even know that. Poor
things. They are terribly confused; they've got no idea
why they're here or what they're supposed to do, and
when their Gifts start emerging—"

She stopped abruptly, and blushed, as if aware that
his Gift was the source of a great deal of trouble,
anguish—and tragedy.

"Gifts," he said bitterly. "That's what they're *called,*
isn't it? But it's hardly a *Gift* if you don't want it
and can't control it. It's not a *Gift* if all it does is
bring harm."

She gazed at him solemnly for a little, as if she was
thinking. "I suppose it seems that way, but I can think

of a lot of ways that your Gift could be used for good. If there was a war—" She shook her head. "I'd rather not think about a war, but if there was a forest fire, a bad one, you could use it to start backfires in places it would be too dangerous to send firefighters to."

He had to nod reluctant agreement to that. He had lived in the country, and he knew how devastating a forest or grass fire could be. Sometimes the only way to stop a fire was to set another fire in its path, but that was a very dangerous thing to do, for there was always the chance that the ones setting the fire would find themselves trapped between two fire lines. People had died that way.

"You could herd wild beasts away with a line of fire, too. I'm sure there are other things your Gift would be useful for." She continued hopefully, "We'd just have to work at thinking of them. I mean, the only reason nobody has thought of useful things for Firestarting before is because it's so rare."

Kalira nuzzled him, silently reminding him of her presence and help. *:Pol and Satiran are coming,:* she told him. *:We will have a great deal to discuss.:*

"Kalira says that your father and his Companion are coming," he told the young Healer. She nodded, and gave him a hand to steady himself with as he got to his feet.

"You'll want to talk with them outside," she said immediately. "Like you did last night. That way, Satiran and Kalira can be right there with you."

Yes, and if I lose control again, I won't burn down the building, he added sadly to himself.

:You won't lose control. I am with you, and I will not let that happen.: Kalira answered his unspoken doubt with such passion that he blinked in surprise.

"You know," Elenor continued, as she hovered at his elbow, ready to steady him if he wobbled, "I think Father was hoping that I'd be Chosen by your Kalira instead of becoming a Healer. Then he'd have a double-family team to help train."

"What?" Lan responded, not very cleverly, but that didn't seem to bother Elenor.

"We'd have been entirely family—Kalira is Satiran's daughter, and Pol is my father, you see. The daughters partnered and the fathers partnered. It would have had a nice symmetry."

By this time they were in the garden and saw that the Herald and his Companion were waiting at the bench, so Lan was saved from having to answer, which was just as well. So *his* Companion was daughter to Herald Pol's Companion? He only hoped that there was not as much friction between stallion and filly as there was between himself and his parents.

:There isn't—other than Satiran wanting to protect me too much,: Kalira responded, highly amused.

:If my parents had been half as willing to protect me—: he told her ruefully, not needing to finish the thought. She knew; already she knew him, inside and out, good and bad, and she loved him anyway.

"Good morning, Lan," Pol hailed him with a half wave. "How are you feeling?" This morning all of the sternness seemed to have melted away from Pol's expression; his manner was easy and casual.

"Kind of shaken, sir," Lan replied, then spotted the Guardsman stationed discreetly out of earshot. The man was trying to look as if he was there for some other purpose, but his eyes kept straying back to Lan.

:Is he there because they don't trust me?: he asked Kalira, not at all surprised. *:I can't really blame them for that, I suppose. . . .:*

:It's the Guard's doing, not the Heralds'. When nothing happens for a while, they'll take the watchdog off of you,: she told him, indirectly confirming his guess. *:But there is this—he's there as much to keep people from upsetting you as anything else. If anyone starts to make you unhappy, he's to take them away.:*

Lan wished devoutly that he had gotten the benefit of such a watchdog a long time ago.

"Elenor, is Lan ready to move to Heralds' Collegium?" Pol asked, transferring his attention to his daughter.

"Not yet; a few more days," she told him, with all of the authority of a Healer twice her age. "We want him to have his meeting with his family *here,* before he gets surrounded by strangers."

"Meeting?" he squeaked, taken entirely by surprise. "What meeting?"

"Lan, your parents have to talk with you at some point," Pol chuckled. "You can't escape having a family by being Chosen, you know."

Actually, he hadn't known; somewhere in the back of his mind he must have hoped that he wouldn't have to deal with his parents until he was all trained and a Herald in full Whites, with all the authority of the office behind him. How was he going to explain what had happened to them? They'd blame *him* for all the horrible things that had happened—

But Pol apparently understood his reluctance to face his family. "Don't worry, I think you'll find that they are so overwhelmed by the fact that you've been Chosen that they won't have a great deal to say to you," Pol told him, an amused sparkle in his eyes. Evidently the Herald wasn't at all worried at what Lan's parents might say or think.

Lan blinked and considered that statement. He wondered, now, what they'd been told about the fire and about being Chosen. Did they even know it was his Gift that had caused the fire?

:No,: said Kalira. *:Outside of a very few people, no one has been told. It is being said that the fire was a terrible accident, caused by the boys who were beating you. Which it was, never doubt it, just not in the way that outsiders are assuming.:*

Lan swallowed, and bit his lip. *:Why?:* he asked, as Pol watched him patiently. Was the Herald able to overhear this conversation?

:Because we are protecting you; the real story won't help anyone and will *hurt you.:* She tossed her head.

:Now, your parents will have nothing to reproach you for, will they? I think you just might actually impress them.:

Well, becoming a Herald *was* a great honor, and it wasn't the sort of thing that his parents would have predicted for him. For that matter, it *was* the sort of surprise that could set them off-balance. He felt his spirits start to rise. This might not be so bad after all.

"Do you feel up to seeing them this afternoon?" Pol continued. "After that, I can explain what you're about to go through and get you ready to move into the Collegium with the others, figure out what sort of classes you'll need to take, that sort of thing."

Classes! He didn't sigh, but the idea of facing more classes so soon was a trifle depressing. He was so tired of being stuck in the middle of a bunch of *children*—

"You'll probably find that you're the youngest in some of your classes, the oldest in others, and smack in the middle in the rest," Pol continued, apparently without noticing Lan's reaction. "We get Trainees from every possible nook and cranny of the Kingdom, from fisher folk from Lake Evendim who can barely read to some of the highborn who've had tutors from the time they could talk. And *all* of them wind up being the worst in their classes at something. You'll also be learning things like fancy riding, tracking, path finding, weapons' training—those are all classes as well."

Lan brightened considerably at that thought. "If you can get my family to interrupt their work to come here, I would like to see them as soon as it can be arranged," he said carefully.

Elenor smiled. "You're doing them a disservice, Lavan," she chided gently. "They've been here every single day. They're very concerned about you."

"They have? They are?" That thought left him as bemused as the idea of being a Heraldic Trainee.

Herald Pol nodded. "They have, every single member of the family; in fact, they were *all* here until they knew that you were going to be all right. Since then, each of your parents has been here at some point every day to find out how you were."

"Then I guess I'd better see them," Lan finally responded. He was still trying to wrap his mind around that, when Kalira suddenly looked up, off into the distance.

:Actually, they're here now,: she told him. *:I didn't expect them so early.:*

"I didn't either," Pol responded with surprise, and it was only at that moment that Lan realized that Kalira could talk to both of them, if she chose to. Well, that could turn out to be very useful.

"Are you up to seeing them right now?" Pol asked him.

He shrugged; what other possible response was there? "I suppose," he said dubiously. "Just as ready as I would be this afternoon, I guess."

Elenor jumped to her feet—did the girl ever do anything at a leisurely pace?—and ran off, calling back over her shoulder, "I'll have them sent out here!"

"She has plenty of other things to take care of at this time of the day," Pol explained, as if he needed to supply an explanation for her abrupt departure.

A few moments later, Lan's mother and father appeared in the doorway nearest them, and approached tentatively down the sanded path. Tentatively! They looked at him with expressions he had never seen directed at himself before; they had nearly reached him before he recognized it as respect. Archer looked as he always did; well-groomed and dressed in tunic and trews of fine cloth of a subtle indigo. But Nelda's auburn hair had been carefully bound in a knot on the top of her head with silk ribbons, her gown was one she usually wore only for parties, a handsome, deep-scarlet wool with panels of her own embroidery set into the bodice, the front of the skirt, and the sleeves. She had taken a great deal of care with her appearance; probably because of the setting in which her son had found himself.

He stood up to meet them; his father extended his hand stiffly, as if Lan had become a stranger. Lan took it gingerly.

"How are you?" his father asked, anxiously. "How are you now, I mean? Are you feeling better? Do you remember anything of what happened to you?"

Lan shook his head, not trusting his voice. "Mostly the fire," he said truthfully, "and not much of that."

His parents exchanged an unreadable glance, and some of the tension ran out of them. It was his mother, though, who flushed an unbecoming plum color, and said, "I—Lan, I'm very sorry that I didn't believe you."

That was the closest she was ever going to come to an apology, and Lan knew it. He also knew how much it cost her to say that much, and he sensed a different sort of strain building up among the three of them.

:Hold out your arms, silly,: Kalira whispered in his mind, as he stood there awkwardly and feeling completely at a loss for what to do or say next. Clumsily, he obeyed her, and that did, indeed seem to be what they were waiting for. They both embraced him, just as awkwardly as he.

The embrace didn't last long, but he felt much better after they broke it. He even managed a tentative smile for them.

"So. You're going to be a Herald, then." His father rubbed the back of his neck with one hand, and looked from him to Kalira and back again.

"Not immediately," he told them both, and scrubbed the toe of his gray boot in the dirt a little. "I have an awful lot to learn first."

"Still." His father smiled slowly; his mother didn't exactly beam at him, but she certainly gave him a healthy dose of silent approval. "A Herald! We're proud of you, Lan, that we are! It's hard to think of you being a Herald, but there you are in your uniform, and with your Companion and all—"

"Her name is Kalira," he replied proudly, and Kalira stepped to his side and nodded her head to both of them.

:Suggest that you all walk in the garden,: Kalira prompted.

"Why don't we all take a walk while we talk," he echoed. "There in the garden—" He waved his hand vaguely in the direction of the Palace gardens with their ornamental torches.

His father gaped. "Us? Walk in the Royal gardens?" he stammered.

"I don't see any reason why not," Pol put in casually. "That's what they're there for." He turned his attention pointedly to Lan. "A walk for about a candlemark wouldn't be too taxing for you, and I have some things I must do that will keep me for about that long. I'll meet you back here when I'm finished; you go show your parents where you'll be living for the next couple of years."

Herald Pol took himself off as quickly as his daughter had—little doubt where she'd gotten *that* trait from—and Lan was left alone with his parents and Kalira.

He took a deep breath, and stood up as straight as he could manage.

"Well," he said to them. "Shall we go?"

ELEVEN

Tuck, Elenor and Owyn

WITHIN a week, false summer had collapsed, and autumn returned with a vengeance. There were no more afternoons sitting in the garden for Lan, but Pol found plenty of things to occupy his time. A storm in the night blew most of the leaves away, and Pol began to look forward to the day when he could move Lavan to the Collegium; his own walks to and from Healer's were bleak and uncomfortable.

Meanwhile, he tested Lan on a variety of subjects to figure out what classes he needed to take. One area surprised him; the boy knew the maps of Valdemar as thoroughly as any full Herald, and how to dead reckon by the stars or sun equally well. All in all, Lavan Chitward was no farther behind or ahead than any other Trainee his age.

On a cold, gray, windy day, Pol helped his young Trainee move into his room at Herald's Collegium.

A carter had brought a box of Lan's personal gear the day before, a luxury many of the Trainees never had. Lan was inclined to tire more quickly than he *thought* he should, largely because he attempted more than he was ready for, but the Healers were confident that he was ready for the active regime of classes and training. A stack of new uniforms and other basic necessities waited for him in his new room, and Pol had walked him all over the Collegium the previous day. He met Pol at the door to the gardens, and the two of them bent to the wind and plodded cheerfully enough to his new home.

A ground-floor room had just fallen vacant, and Pol had quickly claimed it for Lan before anyone else did. The window opened onto a sheltered nook of the garden, so if it became necessary at any time, Kalira could even be temporarily housed there, right within reach. The view was somewhat restricted, but he didn't think that Lan would mind.

In fact, Kalira watched them with great interest through the window as Pol introduced Lan to his new quarters, with the still-packed box in the middle of the room. It was very much an average room, depersonalized by the removal of the belongings of the previous occupant who was now on her first circuit in company with an older, experienced mentor. A small but adequate fireplace in the center of the right wall held a cheerful, clean-burning fire of seasoned oak, protected behind a metal fire screen. The furnishings were entirely utilitarian: bed, desk, chair, bookcase, and wardrobe. The bed was tucked in beneath the window with a pile of Trainee Grays and linen piled atop it, the wardrobe and desk arranged on the left wall. The bookcase, which had done double duty for the previous Trainee as a nightstand, was still next to the bed. Lan's class books were already in it, and a candlestick atop it. There was one oil lamp on the mantle, and a second on the desk. The walls themselves were whitewashed plaster—freshly whitewashed for the new tenant. White canvas curtains covered the window, and when pulled back, hid the shutters that could be closed against the worst storms, although in this sheltered corner it wasn't likely that Lan would

ever use them. The youngster looked around, and
smiled slowly.

"I like this place, Herald Pol," Lan said. "I like it
better than my room in my parents' house; this one
has a view. All I saw from my old room was the wall
of the next house. Better than that—it's a view with
trees in it."

"Good, I'm pleased to hear it," Pol replied. After
learning just how well-to-do Lan's parents were, he'd
been a bit apprehensive about the boy's reaction to
what was a very small and unexceptional room. Some
of the highborn Trainees reacted poorly to being assigned to live in something that was the size of a closet
by their normal standards.

On the other hand, the largest houses in the well-
off Merchants' Quarter were not likely to come vacant, which left a newly-wealthy merchant the option
of either taking a relatively smaller house in the fashionable district or building a bigger one in an unfash-
ionable district where no one of any note would ever
see it. His parents must have opted for the former.

"Your schedule is on the desk there, and a map of
the Collegium—" Pol nodded toward the small stack
of notes resting on the surface. "I've already given
you the tour, so you know where everything is, and
you'll start in your classes tomorrow. Don't hesitate
to ask anyone you might meet for directions or help,
and if you need me, you know where to find me."

He wanted to encourage independence in the
youngster, and the best way to do that was to leave
him to his own devices before he developed any
dependencies.

:He'll be fine,: Satiran said. :He's got my daughter,
after all.:

"Thank you, Herald Pol," Lan said, and offered another of his slow, careful smiles. He opened the door
himself, and waited politely for the Herald to take
himself out, a good sign that the Trainee was ready
to stand on his own feet.

Which was a very good thing, since Pol had a class to teach. No matter what disaster transpired, no matter who descended on the Collegium, the classes went on.

WHEN Pol closed the door behind him, Lan turned his attention back to organizing his new room, although with Kalira right outside it already felt more like home than the place he had inhabited since arriving in Haven. The one thing that he didn't have to put up with was his mother's hand at decoration. *She* wanted reds and yellows, relentlessly cheerful colors that irritated him rather than raising his spirits.

He wasn't particularly neat by nature, but he didn't want to start things off with a bad impression, so he quickly stowed away all the clothing in the wardrobe, the towels on the wardrobe's shelf, and made the bed with the linens he found folded there. Virtually everything was spotless but showed some wear, and that was oddly comforting, suggesting that no one was treated with any more deference than anyone else here.

Once the things on the bed were put away, he reflected, looking at the clothing hanging in his wardrobe, that he was going to have a little difficulty getting used to wearing something other than faded black. At least it wasn't as grindingly cheerful as the things his mother tried to make him wear. And as a color, gray wasn't that bad . . . though he still couldn't get his mind wrapped around the notion of himself in pure white. The uniforms were comfortable, and the boots, so he'd discovered, were the one things that were made exactly to the measure of every Trainee. Ill-fitting footwear was worse than none at all in the active life of Herald or Trainee, and boots were never handed down. He had one pair on his feet now, and two more in various stages of construction in the cobbler's workshop.

That left the still-unpacked crate in the center of the room, which by the weight had been stuffed with far more than the few things he had requested. :*At least it won't be clothing*,: Kalira pointed out mischievously. :*No matter what they've sent you, even your mother won't dare send Bardic or Healer colors to a Heraldic Trainee.*:

He untied the latch, reflecting that the sturdy wooden crate itself would be useful for storage, and threw the top back on its hinges.

"Huh!" he said in surprise, examining the wealth of blankets and a down comforter that graced the top few layers. They were all brand new—and, thank the gods, in reasonable, muted earth colors, mostly shades of gray and gray-brown. But he hadn't been brought up in a cloth-merchant's household without recognizing that these bedclothes were made of the very finest of materials. The comforter was stuffed with pure goosedown and protected with a soft cover of wool plush. The blankets were woven of chirra wool, patterned in wide stripes and checks.

He wondered what had prompted such generosity— not that he was going to object! With a bed placed right underneath a window, the more warm coverings he had, the better. Still, he doubted that his parents indulged even themselves in such luxury; such things were for the highborn and the astronomically wealthy. Granted, there was a great deal of profit figured into the prices of such luxuries, but that didn't make them cheap, even for a cloth merchant.

"Maybe they're trying to make up for not listening to me," he muttered to himself.

:*A guilt offering? That's certainly possible*,: Kalira agreed. :*In fact, I think that's probably the answer. They were not very apt at apologizing the other day; this may be their apology. At least it came in a useful form!*:

He removed the bedcoverings in heavy armloads and laid them on his plain, rough-woven linen coverlet, then tackled the next layer. Cushions, this time, three of them that fluffed up fat and soft, and as luxurious as the blankets. Then a lighter bedspread of ramie and linen, also new, probably for summer. Then, at last, the books and personal keepsakes he had asked for.

After distributing these objects on desk, window ledge, and wardrobe top, he turned back to the box again. The one final layer proved to be rugs and small tapestries—geometric designs rather than pictures, something he recognized as weavings from the southwestern Border. At first he laughed at the idea of putting things up on the walls; wasn't that just like his mother to want to priss things up for him?

:*Wait now, look around a bit.*: Kalira cautioned. :*It looks like the inside of the room at Healer's—are you sure you want all that white wall around you when it's nothing but snow outside?*:

He considered that for a moment, and reluctantly agreed that she was right. With the help of a hammer and a few nails, the tapestries did a lot to soften the hard whiteness of the walls, and the two rugs fit nicely by the side of the bed and in front of the hearth.

When he was finally done, he broke into a surprised smile and a quiet laugh. Now *this* was more like it! Somehow, despite almost all of this being a guilt gift and brand new, it was closer to his real room in Alderscroft than he'd ever expected. His old room had been much like this, without any sign of his mother's meddling hand. The real difference was that there the bedcoverings and things had been old and worn, commonplace, or scavenged from the attic, and the walls hadn't needed anything, since they were already hung with the old tapestries that had been there for generations.

:*Makes me wish that I was human so I could curl*

up by your fire!: Kalira chuckled. *:That's quite a cozy little nest you've built for yourself!:*

Just then, the bell for luncheon sounded, and he started a little at the sound. This wasn't a small hand-bell, it came from a bell tower on the roof and could be heard all over the Collegia and Palace and their grounds.

:And on that most opportune note, I'm going to go have a gallop and a bite. Shall I see you at the Field after lunch?: Kalira's casual tone did a great deal to offset the nervous lurch of his gut at the idea of lunch in a room full of strangers. After all, he didn't have very good memories of his last similar experience.

Hesitantly, he left his room, and stepped out into the hall. A steady stream of people, ranging in age from around ten to at least eighteen and about equally divided between males and females, were all heading in the direction of the dining room that Pol had shown him. They chattered away at the tops of their lungs quite cheerfully, a welcome contrast to the nervous demeanor of the students of his school.

"Heyla, are you Lavan?" someone called from behind him. He turned to see a boy his own age emerging from the room next to his. There could not be anyone more unlike his friend Owyn; he was covered in freckles, with bright green eyes, hair of a carrot red, and a huge, gap-toothed grin. His sturdy frame marked him as country-bred, and Lan felt an instant kinship with him.

Lan nodded, and the boy clapped him on the back. "Good to have you! I'm Tuck. I'm from a little village up north, you won't have heard of it."

Lan felt an unaccustomed urge to smile as they joined the rest of the Grays streaming towards their meal. "Try me," he suggested archly.

"Briarley Crossing—" Tuck began.

"Between Lower Devin and Endercott, just off the Nodding Hill Road," he interrupted, and had the pleasure of seeing Tuck's jaw drop.

"I won't ask how you know that, it'd spoil the fun. Want to sit with me and m'mates?" the boy asked, full of admiration. "And would you mind sussing out where they come from if I ask?"

"I can try," he said modestly, secretly pleased not only by Tuck's reaction, but by his invitation.

They entered a room which was physically nearly identical to the Merchants' School dining hall—but, oh, what a difference in the contents of the room! The first thing that struck Lan was the noise—the babble of dozens and dozens of people freely chattering, well mixed with laughter. The second was the monochromatic austerity—a sea of gray, interrupted here and there with small groups of white. Tuck led him over to a table with benches lining both sides, already crowded with other students. "Shove over, then," he laughed good-naturedly, tapping two of his friends on their shoulders. "This's Lavan; he's going to be eating with us. He's just arrived."

With giggling and a little elbowing, the others made room for both of them, and one of them passed down plates, mugs, and eating utensils to the rest from stacks on the end of the table. A basket of bread followed by a dish of butter went up and down the table; a student came by and left pitchers of water and cider, a second followed with a huge bowl of stew. Both got shared out in an egalitarian, if somewhat random fashion, while eating and talking went on simultaneously. A student came 'round at intervals with more bread and stew, offering more helpings to those who were still hungry.

During a gap in the chatter, Tuck called out to a girl on the other side of the table, "Hey Fyllia, tell Lavan your village!"

"He won't have heard of it," the thin, dark-haired girl protested.

Tuck grinned. "Just tell him."

"Forbay," she said, with a shrug.

"On Lake Evendim, a little south of the midpoint,

the end of the Hollyton Road," he said instantly. Fyllia's mouth formed a little "O" of surprise, and everyone at the table clamored to see him perform.

By the time the baked apples in cream came
around, he had attracted the attention of the occupants of the tables on either side. He was greatly enjoying himself when the bell rang, sounding clearly
over the chatter, warning them all that it was time for
classes again.

The rest of the Trainees hurried off to their classes,
except for the ones whose task was to clear up after
the rest. Although it was not strictly his job today, he
decided to help, his spirits buoyed by his first encounter with his fellow Trainees.

"Thanks," said one of the older girls, one of the
ones who was probably about eighteen, as he handed
her a stack of plates. She piled them into the hatch
of the contrivance that took them down into the
kitchen. "You were with that scamp Tuck, weren't
you? What were all of you chattering about over
there?"

"Tuck found out that I've got a pretty good chance
of recognizing where a person's home is," he said honestly and modestly. "It looks like a conjuring trick, I
suppose, but it's only because I've got most of the
trade routes memorized, at least in Valdemar proper."

"You do? That's better than we can do at your
age," the girl said with surprise. "Are you that youngling from a Merchant family that was in the fire in
Haven?"

He nodded, and she tilted her head to one side. "I
wondered what it was they could be studying in that
school of theirs; trade routes, hmm?"

"And accounting, and currency conversions, and—"

"Enough!" she laughed, holding up her hands in
surrender. "Obviously, there's a lot more to being a
merchant than I thought. Forgive me for my unchari-
table assumptions!"

He laughed and went back for another stack of plates.

When the dishes were cleared away, he nipped back to his room for his cloak. It was far too cold to venture out without it today. This was going to be his final day of freedom from classes, and he intended to make the most of it.

Out the door he went, wrapping his cloak closely around himself, heading across the gardens to the fence that separated Companion's Field from the rest of the Palace grounds.

Kalira waited there, the river between her and the largest portion of the Field. *:It's about time,:* she teased. *:You're spending too much time with other women. I'm going to get jealous!:*

:If you think you'd be of any use cleaning up after a meal, you're welcome to join me,: he retorted. *:The only thing I can think of is to use your tail to dry dishes.:*

:Ugh! What a vile idea! I'll meet you in the stables instead.: She trotted into the long building that housed the Companions in bad weather and cold nights; he sped up to enter the door on his own side.

She had already found a stable hand, or he had found her; the two were standing side by side waiting for him next to a stall with her name over it and her tack hung and draped on its sides.

"Training ride, or pleasure?" the stableboy asked, reaching for one of the bitless bridles that Companions used.

"Pleasure ride," Lan replied, wondering why he had asked. "Ah, actually, it's my first ride with her."

The stableboy turned back to look questioningly at him. "You didn't arrive here with her, then? Done any riding at all before this?"

"A lot, actually." Lan wondered why all the questions. "I used to have my own hunter."

"Ah, then! That'll be good." The stableboy grinned, and took down, not a saddle, but a light pad with a bellyband; hardly more than a couple of layers of cloth cut in the shape of a small saddle. He threw this up over Kalira's back and pulled the girth tight. "D'ye need a leg up, or can you hop up yourself?"

:Is that a bareback pad?: he asked Kalira, not wanting to ask the stableboy.

:It is, and you'll like this,: she replied.

He'd heard of bareback pads, but he'd never seen one; used either by the most excellent of riders or with the most exquisitely trained horses or both, the pads were a more secure form of bareback riding than doing so with only a blanket as the wild Shin'a'in were said to do. There was just enough material between the rider and the horse to avoid chafing the skin of either.

"I think—" He wanted to say that he could mount without help, but a sardonic glance from Kalira made him change his mind. "I think I'd better get a leg up," he admitted sheepishly.

The stableboy cupped his hands and braced himself to take Lan's weight without comment. Lan put his left foot in the hand and tried to put as little of his weight on it for the shortest time he could manage, quickly swinging his right leg over Kalira's back and settling onto the pad.

"Them reins is mostly to give you something to grab to and balance with," the boy reminded him with a wave. "Have a good ride."

Kalira walked out of the stable sedately enough, but once out in the open she broke into a brisk canter. Lan found himself moving with her rhythm within a few paces, and was swept up in the most incredible surge of joy he had ever experienced in his life.

She trumpeted a neigh and moved into a full gallop. The wind caught Lan's cloak and blew it out behind him, but he was too exhilarated to be cold. They pounded across one of the bridges, Kalira's hooves making a sound like bells on the hard surface, then out into the wooded expanse of Companion's Field itself.

She took him on a whirlwind ride around the perimeter; up the river to the wall surrounding the entire complex, then along the wall marking the perimeter. Lan had never gone so fast in his entire life, and Kalira's pace was so smooth he would never have believed she was galloping.

The wall curved in and out, not following any sort of straight line; trees interrupted by meadows flew by. They rode up and down gentle hills, and twice leaped a meandering stream. Lan had always understood that Companion's Field was big, but it was *enormous!*

Without warning, they were at the river again, downstream from where they had left it. Now Kalira slowed down to a trot; even her trot was smooth and easy to sit. They trotted along the river for a bit, then Kalira cut away from the stream and walked into the thick trees.

:How long can you run like that?: he asked her, amazed that she was not even sweating.

:Candlemarks,: she told him matter-of-factly. *:A day and a night, more if I have to, but I need a good feed and a long rest after.:*

He blinked. He had never owned or ridden a horse that could keep up a gallop for *one* candlemark, let alone for a day and a night!

:But we aren't horses,: she reminded him gently. *:We only look like horses.:*

:I think I'm beginning to understand that.:

They moved deeper into the trees; a thick blanket of leaves rustled and crackled under her hooves. He thought he caught a glimpse of something ahead. Was it a building?

:It used to be,: she answered his unvoiced thoughts. *:I'm taking you to see the bell tower and the chapel ruins in the Grove.:*

The Grove! He shivered, both in anticipation and with the kind of thrill he got when he was in a place where ghosts were said to walk. Surely if there was any place in the grounds that was haunted, it would be here!

:Heralds and Companions have better things to do than to sit around spooking youngsters when we don't need our bodies anymore,: Kalira laughed at him. *:Why drift about like a bit of mist when you have a much nicer place to go?:*

"Well, what about people who *aren't* Heralds or Companions?" he asked. "Haven't there been enough people who've died here to make the place haunted?"

:Not, I think, while we have anything to say about it. This is our place, you know.: This was a new mind-voice, a very masculine one, and Lan saw another Companion waiting to greet them beside the ruins of an old chapel.

This was a stallion, no larger than any of the others, but somehow he gave an impression of being larger and more imposing. He was beautifully turned out, every strand of mane and tail braided, his coat brushed until it shone with the silver gleam of moonlight, hooves polished to the patina of old silver.

:This is Rolan,: Kalira told him, with a nod of respect to the stallion. *:He's the King's Own's Companion. He wanted to see you for himself.:*

:Yes, and with your permission, I should like to examine you as well, young Trainee,: Rolan told him gravely, with a slow swish of his braided tail. *:I mean no disrespect to you or to Kalira, but I wish to be able to assure my Chosen, and thus every Herald in the Circle, that your power, though dangerous, is under control.:*

He sighed, a little bitterly. "Even if the control isn't mine."

:That is hardly your fault,: the stallion replied instantly. *:Your Gift was forced to ripeness, in order to defend itself and you. In a better world, you would have felt it slowly, slowly, stir; in four or five moons, as you began to feel that something odd was happening*

to you, Kalira would have come for you, and you would have had your Gift come upon you here, and after Pol had identified what it was.: Rolan sighed gustily, and Kalira echoed him, her flanks heaving under Lan's legs. *:It is not a better world, and we must deal with things as they are. May I?:*

Belatedly, Lan realized that Rolan was waiting for his answer. He *could* say no, but why should he? Actually, he felt rather better about the Companion rummaging around in his head than some strange Herald. And at least Rolan had asked permission first. "Go ahead," he replied.

He didn't know what to expect; what happened was the oddest sensation of having someone actually *in* his head with him, taking control of what he was thinking. He was whisked along at blinding speed through his own thoughts and memories; he didn't even have time to identify what they were before being flown through the next.

It happened so quickly that before he had quite grasped what was happening, it was over.

He shook his head dizzily, clutching Kalira's mane, the world trying to spin with him as the center.

:My apologies,: Rolan said, as his head steadied and the Grove stopped rotating. *:Some effects are unavoidable. Thank you; you have allowed me to confirm Kalira's judgment and Choice. That can only be good for all of us.:*

"I hope so," he sighed. "I really hope so."

Unexpectedly, Rolan took a pace forward, and briefly touched Lan's leg with his nose. *:It is hard, having to prove yourself over and over, I know,:* the Companion said sympathetically. *:Please remember, when this happens so often you are sick of it—you will never have to prove yourself to us. Come to the Grove or the stables, and you will be surrounded by no one but friends.:*

Lan looked down into Rolan's eyes, a much deeper sapphire than Kalira's sky-blue, and was moved for a moment almost to tears by the Companion's extraordinary promise. "Thank you," he said softly aloud, "I will."

He hadn't noticed another person had entered the Grove until a severe-looking, raven-haired man actually walked up and placed his hand on Rolan's shoulder. "Let's hope Rolan never has to make good on that promise," the Herald said, his lips slowly curving into a smile. "If I have my way about it, he never will." He held out his hand to Lan, who accepted it; the Herald's grip was firm without being intimidating. "I'm Jedin, and I'm pleased to meet you in person, Lavan."

It broke on Lan at that moment that the man who was shaking his hand was the King's Own Herald—the third most important person in the entire Kingdom! No wonder he looked as if that severe expression was habitual. "I—the—the honor is mine, sir," he stammered out.

Jedin's smile widened. "Not that much of an honor, I assure you. Plenty of people will tell you that they'd much prefer to see rather less of me than more. Did you realize that along with one rare Gift, you have a second?"

Lan shook his head, unable to think of anything that would pass for a Gift.

"You have the ability to inspire Companions to not only trust you, but to leap to your defense without ever actually meeting you themselves." Jedin raised one eyebrow. "I wish I knew why, but there you have it."

Kalira looked innocent; Rolan enigmatic. Lan could only shrug helplessly. "I don't know, sir," he said, as honestly as he could. "It doesn't make any sense to me."

"Hmm." There was a look in Jedin's eyes that made Lan want to squirm, a look that suggested that even though Lan didn't know any reason why the Companions should offer their friendship and defense, Jedin could think of one or two.

"Well, you'll have some learning to do before we find out, anyway," Jedin said after a pause. "And we two have some exercising to do, if we aren't to get fat and ugly." He slapped Rolan on the shoulder, and the Companion neighed laughter.

:Too late,: Rolan taunted, as Jedin put both hands on Rolan's back and vaulted into place without having to use anything to help him. *:You're already ugly.:*

Without waiting to hear Jedin's reply, the Companion cantered off under the trees.

"Were we supposed to hear that?" Lan asked aloud, a little aghast.

:We aren't horses, but we aren't some sort of heavenly creatures either, my love,: Kalira told him, moving out of the Grove in a slightly different direction. *:We're a lot like our Heralds.:*

It seemed that every passing candlemark brought another surprise or revelation; a breaking of one assumption, the bending of another. He wondered if he'd ever get used to it. Or would things settle down as he began to learn what life as a Herald would *really* be like, past the tales and the blaze of silver-and-white uniforms, the dazzle of Companions?

:You aren't the only case of bad timing right now,: Kalira went on as they came out of the trees and within sight of the stables. *:Just the more serious of the two. Lada is in foal, and had to go after her Chosen with less than two moons to go. Poor things! Lada is probably going to drop tonight, and Wrenlet hasn't been here more than a fortnight! They're both going to have a bad night, I think. The stable has fireplaces, but it's drafty, and Lada's a bit on the small side. They'll be up all night at the least.:*

"Is Lada's Chosen going to wait out the night with her?" he asked, all sympathy, for he had once taken foal-watch on one of his ponies.

:Oh, yes; how could she not?:

"That's a good point." He remembered how he'd felt about it, nervous, anxious, excited, and afraid—and that had just been a pony! He couldn't imagine how wrought up he'd be if it was Kalira who was going to drop a foal! He'd be worse than any anxious father in a joke!

:Well, you won't have to worry about that with me; I never saw a stallion worth going through that *for,:* Kalira said lightly, easing the sudden surge of anxiety the thought provoked. *:Now if you were a stallion, I might consider it, but not for anyone else in the herd.:*

He blushed, pleased and embarrassed, but not sure why. "Not even Rolan?" he ventured.

:Not even Rolan,: she replied firmly. He felt absurdly pleased by that, though he had no idea why he should be, and he held that feeling close inside to keep him warm as he walked through the chilling wind back to the Collegium.

TWELVE

The Collegium

LAN passed an old account book back to his teacher, who waved it at the class and addressed them all. "Now, presented with this set of accounts and the story I've told you, what sort of judgment would you make? All of the clues you need are there."

This was Herald Artero's class, one called "Field Investigations." Other than the ability to read and write, this class had no special requirements, but it was one that every Trainee had to take. Here the students were presented with stories and sometimes evidence connected with cases that other Heralds had dealt with while on their circuits, and asked for their own conclusions. As often as not, a Herald on circuit would spend a great deal of his or her time being investigator, jury, and judge; even if a local judge had already made a decision, any case could be appealed to a Herald. The easy cases were those whose intricacies could be solved by application of the famous Truth Spell to one or more of the plaintiffs or defendants. This class did not concern those.

This class was about cases where evidence had to

speak for itself because either some of the witnesses were dead or fled, or it was something where there were no witnesses at all. Mostly the cases were trivial enough, a dispute over a boundary, or ownership of land or property. Sometimes, though, a life could hang in the balance. And sometimes it wasn't life, but honor—which some would hold more precious than their lives.

This time the question concerned a curious case. A merchant had died, and his grown son had accused his stepmother of appropriating money that, according to the accounts, *should* have been there in his cash boxes. The Truth Spell had revealed that the stepmother was not guilty of helping herself to the money stowed in the cash boxes, but where *had* the money gone? Suspicion was rife in the village by the time the Herald arrived. Although people had refrained from making actual accusations, all the tension had poisoned relationships throughout the area.

The Trainees knew all of this, and that a solution to the puzzle had been found. Their teacher had given them a great deal of background, and the last bit of physical evidence: the account books.

The account books were passed from hand to hand, and each of the four students had a chance to examine them carefully. Lan had noted something awry, and he wondered if any of the others had.

"I checked the addition, and he hadn't made any mistakes there," said Tuck, scratching his head. "That was the first thing that I thought of, that'd he'd just been bad at arithmetic."

"Anyone else?" Artero was physically very like an older version of Tyron, which had rather put Lan off at first, but his personality could not possibly have been more different. Artero never sneered, never was anything other than intense and earnest. When he was excited about what he was teaching, his eyes positively glowed. "Lavan, you took a long time over those pages. Did you see anything in them to give you a clue?"

Lan hesitated a moment, then reminded himself that the case was long over, and presumably had been solved correctly. Nothing he said would make any trouble for anyone now. "The addition was right—it was the *numbers* that were wrong," he said at last. "No one dealing in small items like spices ever makes a bargain that ends in round numbers like that. And I think that some of those debits might have been too low, but I don't know enough about foodstuffs to tell for sure." The merchant in question had trafficked in spices and dried or preserved fruits; not exactly Lan's area of expertise. But he *did* recall vividly going with his mother to the market as a small child, and her spirited bargaining over every clipped copper coin.

"Were the numbers altered in any way?" ventured another Trainee, a girl named Mona. "Could someone besides the widow have taken money? Or did someone alter the books to make trouble for the widow?"

"No, to all three questions—and I have a set of altered books to show you some of the common ways in which documents can be changed, and how you can tell, but we'll get to that in a moment." Artero smiled at Lan encouragingly. "Now I'll draw on our newest student's experiences with merchants and traders, and ask Lavan if *he* can think of a possible scenerio that would suit the evidence."

Lan thought very hard, and something else popped up in his memory. The widow, who had been as sharp as she was pretty, was a merchant herself, crafting jewelry in silver and gems, and as such, had been meticulous in making certain that she was not wedding into a failing business. It had taken her elderly suitor a long time to persuade her that her own earnings would not be used to support his trade. In fact, the match was as much a business transaction as a marriage, as was often the case among tradesmen and merchants. Surely she would have checked the books before signing the marriage contract!

On the other hand—much to the son's anger—the spice merchant had been totally besotted with his much younger bride. He had been courting her for three years, and had brought her to the marriage after many gifts, assiduous attention, and many sincere love letters. They hadn't been married more than a couple of months when the old man died. The son had even accused the widow of murdering his father for the inheritance, until it transpired that the old man's will made him the heir to the lion's share of the ready cash, and his wife the heir to the house and goods. Neither house nor goods would have been of any use at all to the son.

"The dead man probably had two sets of books, this one on paper and one either hidden, or in his head," Lan said at last. "The books we looked at were created to make his business look a lot more prosperous than it really was, so the girl he was courting would marry him. So the money wasn't missing, it was never there in the first place."

The other Trainees looked at him with surprise and some skepticism, but Artero slowly nodded, his smile broadening. "And why didn't our widow notice this in the first place?" he asked.

"Because she's a jeweler; they always deal in round numbers, and the finished piece is always worth a *whole* lot more than the components." Now that he knew he was right, Lan was a great deal more certain of his answers. "It's like a piece of tapestry. The colored thread is worth next to nothing compared to the finished piece. What you're paying for is the talent and ability of the artist who made it." A speculation occurred to him, and he went ahead and voiced it. "She worked by herself, so her income was pretty irregular, I bet—nothing until she finished a commission, then a lump sum. She would have been wanting a husband with a steady income, and she wouldn't have known what to look out for in his books, because they were nothing like hers. I bet all she did was check out the addition to make sure he wasn't a shoddy accountant."

Artero slowly stood up and bowed to Lan, who flushed with momentary pride. "Very, very good, Lavan. That is exactly what happened; it took the Herald in question a lot more time to ferret the answers out, but that is what finally came to light when he backtracked the suppliers and compared their accounts with the old man's. So the widow was exonerated, and the son had to go home disappointed in his inheritance, but at least certain that he was not cheated out of it. There was even a relatively happy ending; the village settled down, and everyone made up their differences." He turned to the other members of the class. "Now you see why I say it is as important to know about the lives of those who come to us for a judgment as it is to know the bare facts of the case."

He pulled a ledger out of his bookcase and laid it open in front of them with a smile. "Now, here is an artificial set of account pages that *have* been altered. We've got a sample of every sort of alteration we've ever seen in here. I'll show you where and how they were altered."

Lan leaned over the pages with as much eagerness as the rest; he had always known that figures and handwriting could be changed or forged, but he had never seen any examples. And some were truly ingenious; Artero made it clear that they would be spending a great deal of time on these examples, and Lan was not at all averse to that. There was enough there to occupy him for the next couple of moons, not just the fortnight that Artero promised.

For the first time, classes were teaching him something interesting, not *all* his classes, of course, and he wasn't doing any better than average in most of them, but at least they weren't an ordeal anymore. When he had problems, if the Herald in charge of the class didn't help him, one of the other Trainees would, often volunteering to help him before he asked for it. He hadn't understood that until Tuck explained it to him; they weren't in competition for the best place and the teacher's accolades, they were *supposed* to cooperate. They got better marks for cooperating. In fact, in some classes, no one moved up until they could all move up together.

"We've got to work together; there just aren't enough of us to take care of all the problems," Tuck had said earnestly. "You can't hold back something that another Herald needs to know just to make yourself look good—that only makes *all* the Heralds look *bad*. People have to know that one Herald is going to be able to do just as good a job as another, or they won't trust us."

This was one of those classes in which all the participants moved up as a group, and Lan loved it. He learned such fascinating things in it, not only from Herald Artero, but from the other Trainees.

When the class was over, Tuck intercepted him on the way to the kitchen; he was one of the servers at lunch, and servers got to eat early. "Are you spending Midwinter with your family?" Tuck asked. "Or were you going to be here?"

Lan already knew the answer to that question, and he had mixed feelings about it. On the one hand, he really hadn't been looking forward to spending the holiday with his family; the times that they had come to visit had been very awkward and uncomfortable. None of them had known how to treat him; it almost seemed as if they were afraid of him at times. On the other hand, when the message had come that they were going to be hosting so many relatives that they wanted him only to come for Midwinter Feast, so they could put his granny up in his old room, he'd been rather unhappy about it. He didn't much relish the idea of languishing around the empty Collegium for a fortnight with nothing to do and no company.

"Mother said that they've got a mob of relations coming, and so I said I'd stay here, and just go into town for the Feast," he said, but could not manage to stifle a little sigh.

But Tuck's reaction was a surprise. "Fantastic!" he enthused. "You can come home with me! My folks asked if you would; they have a farm outside the City; you can stay with us and Kalira can take you in for the family feast in style, fancy tack, bridle bells, and all!" He faltered for a moment at the blank look on Lan's face. "If you want—that is—"

"That would be terrific!" Lan replied, shaking off his surprise and gratifying his friend with his own enthusiasm for the plan. Tuck's parents had come in to see their son twice as often as his own, and he'd been invited along for a dinner at one of the taverns a time or two. He liked them, and apparently, they liked him as well.

"It's a done deal, then!" Tuck slapped Lan on the back and sent him on his way. "I'll send a note to tell them you're coming!"

The Midwinter holiday was only a few days away, and now that he had something to look forward to, Lan was a good deal happier about that than he had been. He hurried off to the kitchen with a smile on his face. He was smiling a lot more these days than he had since he had arrived in Haven!

The Trainees took many of the chores of the Collegium in turn, depending on the abilities of the Trainee in question. All of them *had* to learn things like camp cooking, mending, and leatherwork; out on circuit they might be away from a Resupply Station for weeks, and they weren't permitted to take hospitality from anyone on their circuit except the occasional Healer's House or Temple. But there was also no point in forcing their fellow Trainees to live with poorly-sewn uniforms, or indifferent food either. Those who were no good at mending or cooking therefore got the cleaning chores and other things, like waiting on tables.

Lan was actually rather good at waiting on tables; unlike some, he'd gotten his full growth already, so he wasn't suffering from adolescent clumsiness. He erred on the side of caution, preferring to make more trips with less food, rather than load himself down and risk disaster. As a consequence, he generally got the chore two meals out of every three, and the only one that was a burden was breakfast. Having to get up, get ready, get his room tidied and get down to the kitchen a full hour before everyone else was pretty horrid.

On the other hand, since servers *did* eat first, he and the others did get their pick of the piping-hot bread, the occasional pastries, and other breakfast dishes on offer that morning. So that part wasn't at all horrid.

The luncheon fare at the Merchant's School had never varied; rather stringy beef cooked until it fell apart in an attempt to tenderize it, bread and butter, mashed turnips, gravy, peas, and small ale. No two luncheons were the same here at the Collegium, and Lan sniffed experimentally as he neared the kitchen.

Fried fish! Lan loved the way the Collegium cook made it; battered, and fried in a cauldron of hot oil. "Lake Evendim style," they called it, and there were usually other things fried up in the same oil to go with it. Squares of dough fried until they puffed up like pillows that were sugared or eaten with honey, balls of a different sort of batter, spiced and savory, strips of vegetables battered like the fish. He'd never had any of those things before he arrived here, and he was already addicted. It was a good thing that Cook didn't have a "fry-day" often, or he would have wound up as fat as one of those dough pillows in no time.

He arrived at the kitchen just in time to get a plateful of his favorites, leavened with a bowl of stewed greens to keep from overdoing it on the fried-stuff. He sat down with the rest of the helpers and servers at the crowded kitchen table and gave himself over to enjoyment. On a "fry-day," the helpers had to take turns eating, since the fried foods didn't keep well, and tended to turn tough and nasty when cold. Although everything else could be, and was, prepared in advance, the actual frying had to be done fresh, with the platters being filled and carried off immediately.

The aroma wafted through the Collegium, and most people were as enthusiastic about the rare treat as Lan, so the dining hall filled quickly. Lan was one of the first of the servers to be finished, so as soon as he washed off his sugar-sticky fingers at the pump, he got a platter, waited for someone to fill it, and hurried it out to the hungry Trainees.

Platter after hot platter went out and came back empty; once or twice, Lan paused long enough to fill up a forgotten corner with another sugared pillow, then dove back into the fray. Everyone seemed to eat twice as much on these occasions; it might have been Lan's imagination, but he didn't think so. He wasn't the only person who was addicted to Cook's special fry-ups.

At last, when the greediest of the lot was stuffed full and contentedly trailing out of the dining hall, the servers got to collapse, fortify themselves with the leftover bits of dough and batter fried up and eaten with a sharp sauce or honey according to taste, wash their hands, and hustle off to a class or to a free period, leaving the kitchen to those who were assigned to clean up.

Lan had a free period; study was impossible after being so stuffed, so he usually went for a walk out to the Training Field and the Salle instead. Since his *next* class was with the Weaponsmaster, he had to walk off his lethargy. The last thing he wanted to do was give the Weaponsmaster an excuse to make him an example.

Not that the Weaponsmaster was cruel or sadistic; on the contrary, he was an incredibly kind man. And he would tell you, sincerely and sometimes with genu-

ine distress, that in order to save your life at some
later date, he had to make it miserable *now*. No one
ever doubted him; if they had, the number of full Heralds who returned to thank him in person after their
first circuits, bubbling over with gratitude for the
Weaponsmaster's gentle, implacable drive to perfection, would have convinced even the most skeptical.

Nothing was or ever could be good enough for
Weaponsmaster Odo, an oddly proportioned fellow,
muscular in the legs and shoulders, back and arms,
but so narrow in the waist and hips that he looked
like a caricature of a man. Odo had been in the Guard
before being Chosen, and he had been the Weaponsmaster there, too, so he was often found teaching
certain of the Guard some of the specialized skills
he had acquired over the years, including mastery of
particular techniques and odd weapons.

Snow lay about ankle-deep on the ground, but the
paths were pounded hard and sanded for good footing.
Snow wouldn't stop Herald Odo from having his pupils work outside; if anyone objected, he would point
out patiently that when they were on their circuits,
attackers wouldn't wait politely until they were under
the shelter of a roof before assaulting them. His logic
was impeccable, and most new Trainees didn't bother
trying to change his training plan for the day after the
first few fruitless protests.

:*Out early?*: Kalira asked, when he reached the
Training Field. He squinted against the glare of sun
on snow and looked around; she was nowhere to be
seen, but a white Companion in the distance wasn't
exactly visible against the snow. The sky didn't hold
a cloud that was bigger than his hand today, and the
packed snow reflected as much light as the sky held.
Trees were inky sketches against the blue, still and
stark. There wasn't a breath of breeze, and his own
breath puffed out in frosty puffs to vanish in the still
air.

:*I need to walk off my greed*,: he told her with a

chuckle. :*I don't want Odo to get any more advantages than he's already got.*:

:*I'll come keep you company.*: Off in the distance a flock of crows rose from one of the trees in Companion's Field, cawing derision as they flapped away toward the Palace.

After a moment of walking, with the hard-packed snow creaking under each step, he heard the distant sound of hooves on snow, and turned to wave at her. She came on at a trot, tail flagged, ears up; she looked wonderful with the sun shining on her satin coat, just like an image in an illuminated manuscript. Every movement was achingly graceful, smooth as a trained dancer. Not even Rolan was as lovely as she was, with the blaze of the sun full on her and her mane and tail streaming behind, banners of whitest silk.

:*Why, thank you for the compliments! That was quite poetic, dearest!*:

:*You're very welcome, gorgeous!*: he replied, in high good humor. He tucked his hands under his armpits to warm them; he didn't want to touch her with cold hands.

:*Oh, my—keep saying sweet things like that and I'll make sure to stick around you!*: She had reached him by then and nuzzled his cheek, blowing her sweet breath into his hair. Her breath was warm, a soft caress against his cheek, and he reached up to caress her velvety nose. :*Now, am I correct in thinking our plans for Midwinter have been changed, thanks to Tuck?*:

He reached farther up with his gloved hands and scratched the places behind her ears she could never get at; she sighed, and rested her chin on his shoulder, closing her eyes in bliss. "Tuck's parents invited me to stay with them on their farm. We can go in for the Midwinter Night Feast; it's close enough to Haven, Tuck says."

:*Well, I suppose it would have to be, as often as they come visit him. Delightful! Dacerie and I get along splendidly; we'll have a fine time too, just us girls together, being spoiled by Tuck's sibs! I think I can tolerate having my mane and tail braided and fussed with three or four times a day.:* There was no doubt that Kalira was as happy with this plan as Lan was. *:Since Tuck's been back and forth to the farm several times, his parents will know how to house us.:*

"Which, sadly, is more than I can say for my parents," he grumbled. "They haven't even *asked* about you. I don't think they're even expecting you to come with me, assuming they've thought about it at all. Come to think of it, they've never said anything about you—anyone would think that you were just a horse."

:Well, that's not a problem,: Kalira told him, tossing her head with merry disregard for what Lan's parents thought. *:We'll come here first, and have them load me up with my formal gear. While we're at it—make sure you ask for a formal Trainee uniform as well for the occasion; take care of it some time today. There isn't much call for them, but you can have one any time you ask for one if you give the Housekeeper enough time to have one altered to fit you. When we're both looking just slighly less than royal, we can go to your parents' house and make an impressive entrance. Then I'll come back here. When you're just about ready to leave, call me. I'll hear you, no worries. We'll make an impressive exit as well—I think my arrival all by myself should set some tongues wagging.:*

"I should think!" What a wonderful plan! "It should make some eyes pop, too, when they see how beautiful you are!"

:You're flattering me again,: she teased. *:Do keep it up!:*

"How can it be flattery when it's true?" How he loved being with her! Everything seemed so much brighter and sharper when she was at his side; colors were richer, and nothing could ruin his mood. Didn't people often call their spouses their "better half?" Surely she was just that—his better self.

:I must say that I'm very grateful to young Tuck,: she told him as she walked alongside him. *:Make sure and tell him for me, will you? I believe that this will be one of the better Midwinter holidays I've ever had.:*

Just about then, the first members of his weapons class came trailing toward them over the snow. "Looks like we're about to hear the bell for the class change," he observed, and mock-groaned. "I wish you had hands instead of hooves; when Odo gets through with us, I'm going to want a massage *so* badly!"

:Try a hot soak instead,: she said playfully, blew into his hair, and frisked off, cantering back toward Companion's Field as the bell for class change rang in the distance. He watched her go, floating fluidly across the snow as if she had wings just like the Windrider.

Herald Odo emerged from the Salle, and smiled to see Lan already waiting there. "Walking off the fry-up, lad?" he asked genially. "Probably a good idea, given how much we all seem to eat on fry-days. Start your warm-up exercises anyway. Walking won't stretch out everything."

Lan obeyed, toeing the line cut into the hard-packed snow and beginning the arm and upper torso stretches. The Training Field was just a rectangle in the snow, surrounded by a token fence that anyone could step over. When the snow melted, it would go back to its former shape of a rectangle of sand enclosed by timber holding the sand in, with the fence atop the timbers. Before long he was sweating enough that he didn't need his cloak anymore, and tossed it aside over one of the fence rails behind him. One by one, as the rest of the class of ten arrived, they ranged alongside him and started the same exercises, eventually discarding their own cloaks as well. Odo walked up and down their line and eyed them, correcting a stretch that wasn't quite right, chiding for not extending a stretch far enough.

When he judged that they were all sufficiently ready, he passed out the wooden swords and shields, paired them up, distributed the pairs evenly across the extent of the Training Field, and bade them go through their exercises.

Lan's opponent was an older boy who was just a little shorter than he, Trainee Jirkin. This was all very elementary stuff; each sword stroke meant a particular counter, and they took it turn and turn about, attack and parry. Odo wanted the moves to become second nature and completely instinctive; for now, until those moves were drummed into their blood and bone, they made their strokes to the rhythm of his clapped hands, speeding up as he increased the pace of his clapping. All the time, he strode among the five pairs of students, watching and correcting. Faster and faster the pace went; Lan was sweating furiously now. This was the fastest that Odo had ever taken them, and he felt the strain in every muscle.

:*Relax. Don't fight yourself by thinking. Don't think, just listen, and do. Let do, love. Let go it all go and just become part of the sword and the shield*—:

Don't think? How was he going to know what counter to use? What in the world did she mean?

:*Your body already knows. Trust me. Don't try, just be. Experience, and become part of the experience.*:

Don't think and don't try—if he didn't trust Kalira so much—

But he did, he did; she had never put him wrong yet. Between swings, he told his muscles to loosen; he stopped trying to anticipate the next move—after all, they *were* working patterns, not actually fighting. Instead of thinking, he felt; getting into the way his muscles strained, the hollow *thock* of the wooden practice blade on the shield, the vibrations in his hands and arms as each stroke hit. He stopped worrying about when Herald Odo was going to increase the pace.

He began to feel as if he was in a waking dream; his arms and legs stopped hurting, and his body accomplished the moves all by itself. Was this what Herald Odo meant?

"All right!" Odo clapped his hands, breaking Lan's trance; the student pairs broke apart and dropped their weapons to their sides with groans and sighs of relief. Lan's arms and legs went back to hurting, and he panted with the rest of them, sweat dripping off his nose and landing on the snow, where it promptly froze.

"Go back to stretches, and cool down, Trainees," Odo ordered with some satisfaction. "Then take five laps around the Training Field, at an easy jog. Don't race. Then come on inside and get a small drink."

Lan put his mock weapons aside with the rest and jigged and shook out his cramps. His hands were the worst; it was always hard to get his fingers to let go of the hilt of his wooden sword. He wasn't the first to start running around the edge of the field, but he wasn't the last either.

When everyone had finished running, Herald Odo brought them into the Salle and passed out cups of lightly salted cider. It had an odd taste, but they all craved the salt and drank down their brew without complaint. There in the Salle, he had them practice hand-to-hand moves, looking into a mirror so they could see their own faults. Kicks, punches, blocks, and counters, over and over. Lan stared at his own reflection fiercely, alert for mistakes. He liked this better than the sword practice. There was something very satisfying about it, knowing that using this knowledge, he could probably get away from any bullies in the future.

This building, called the Salle, was one large open space, with an office and storage partitioned off at one end. This was where all of the practice weapons were kept and where Odo spent most of his day. It had a wooden floor, sanded smooth but not polished, wooden walls, and a mirror all along one side. Lan didn't want to think about how much that much mirrored glass had cost; several families could have eaten well for years, surely. But it was worth the expense;

Trainees could see their mistakes with their own eyes and correct them immediately, or at least know to ask for help in getting positioned.

There were no windows on the walls; instead, south-facing clerestory windows near the peak of the roof let in generous amounts of light. No danger of getting the sun in your face in here—though Odo would, no doubt, introduce them to the joy of fighting when sun-dazzled in due course.

There was no fireplace in here, so it was pretty chilly, but better than outside. A certain amount of heat radiated from the one wall where the chimney from the fireplace in the office made a break in the expanse of wood paneling.

When they had practiced long enough, Odo had them cool down a second time, then worked with them individually. When it was Lan's turn, Odo showed him a new move, the way to break someone's hold on his wrist, and had him practice it until he got it right. "Now, combine that with what you know," the Herald said, and grabbed for him.

Much to his own shock, Lan evaded the rush, broke Odo's grip, tumbled the Weaponsmaster to the floor, and spun out of reach.

"Now what do you do, boy?" Odo called from the floor.

"I run like fury!" Lan replied, making good his words and fleeing to the opposite end of the Salle, much to the amusement of the rest of his mates.

Odo got up off the floor and dusted himself off. "Don't laugh, Trainees; he's right. As long as you have an escape, take it. Run. Never stand and fight unless there's no other choice. What if you're carrying a vital message? What if it's bandits that ambushed you and you have to get the Guard? You're not in the business of being heroes, you're in the business of being Heralds, and that means staying alive to do your duty."

He walked over to Lan and clapped him on the

shoulder. "Lavan has the right of it. Incapacitate your enemy, and run like fury." He winked broadly. "Of course, if I had been in his place, I'd have broken a few things to make certain my enemy *stayed* where I put him for a while, but you aren't up to that yet. When you are skilled enough to hold back your full force, then we'll practice those moves on each other."

Lan took his place with the others as Odo called another Trainee out for a session. He hadn't expected to like weapons' training; he was a passable shot with a bow, but he'd expected that the bigger, older boys would be all over him. But there were no bigger boys in this class; there were several who were older, but none bigger. It wasn't all Heraldic Trainees, either; three of the boys were in Bardic Trainee rust, and three were in the pale green of Healer Trainees. The Trainees of *all* the Collegia took the basic weapons' courses. Bards were out in the wild parts of the world alone at least as often as Heralds, and not everyone believed in Bardic immunity. Healers weren't molested very often, but they might find themselves forced to defend a sick or injured patient. Some of the Trainees from the other two Collegia stuck with it through the entire weapons' curriculum, too. Not every Bard or Healer found skill with sword and bow incompatible with his or her other training.

When Odo was finished with the last of his students, he had them all get up and run around the Salle for another few laps, then allowed them to cool down and stretch themselves out one final time. They gathered up their cloaks just as the class-change bell rang outside.

"Off with you!" he said, flapping his hands at them, looking as if he were shooting geese. "Same time tomorrow, and try not to overeat!"

Lan trudged out into the snow with the rest of them, then like the rest of them, broke into a trot, drawn by the prospect of a hot bath to ease their aches and bruises before the final two classes of the day. If they hurried, it could just be managed; it was planned into their schedule.

I'm beginning to think that they think of everything, it occurred to him, with a sense of wonder.

:Well, I should certainly hope so. We've had enough practice at it by now!:

He laughed, and picked up his pace. The hot water was going to feel very, very good.

THIRTEEN

SHIVERING with cold, but smiling nonetheless, Tuck and Lan waved good-bye to the last of their friends at the door of the Collegium. As soon as the last flick of Charkan's tail vanished past the gate, they rushed back inside chafing their half-frozen hands. The Collegium wasn't empty yet, but it would be soon, probably within the next day or two. Those whose parents or relatives were close to Haven were generally the last to leave. Those who had far to go were often granted a few days extra leave time for travel.

Tuck and Lan were going to be gone themselves within a candlemark; Lan had already packed up his clothing and personal gear last night. All that remained in the wardrobe were a couple of clean outfits for when he got back, and the resplendent Formal Grays.

Although he had never considered himself to be particularly interested in clothing, he opened the wardrobe to admire the Formal Grays one more time. When he'd asked Housekeeper Tori for a set of Formals, he hadn't expected anything near that nice; the only way they differed from Formal Whites was in the color—which, unlike the everyday Trainee Grays, was a deeper color, very nearly his favorite charcoal gray. This, so the housekeeper told him, was to make it very clear on formal occasions who the Trainees were. This was meant to keep them from getting involved in situations that they were not yet ready for; in an emergency, the paler color used in the everyday Grays might be mistaken for white. The housekeeper, on learning what he wanted the uniform for, had even brought him to the sewing room for several fittings. The Collegium seamstresses tailored it carefully to him and it fitted impeccably, to the point that his mother would probably be impressed by the figure he cut. It was not new, though it looked it; some other Trainee had needed it, and it had passed through the hands of two or three other Trainees before it came to Lan. Each had worn it once or twice, so for all intents and purposes it was as good as the day it had first been made. The housekeeper had a dozen sets of Formal Grays packed away in an aromatic chest to keep off the moths, and when he was finished with this set, she'd let out the alterations, clean it, and put it back in the chest for the next Trainee near his size who needed it.

Lan closed the wardrobe on the splendid, silver-trimmed Grays, then picked up his packs and wrapped himself up in his cloak. He slung the packs over his shoulder and met Tuck at his door, and the two of them headed for the stables.

The Companions themselves arranged for these staged departures; they were quite a bit more organized than their Chosen. About the time that a Trainee had picked up his packs, his Companion would present himself at the entrance to his stall. That was a signal to the stable hands to tack up that particular Companion, and if everyone got the timing right, the Companion would meet his Chosen at the entrance to the stable, all ready to go. Under ordinary circumstances, a Trainee was responsible for doing his own saddling, but during the crush of holiday departures it was deemed wiser to have as few people crowding the stables as possible.

The first rush was always among those who were getting extra leave for their travels, so sometimes those in that lot had to wait or take the option to saddle up their Companions themselves. By this time, though, the Trainees were leaving in a slow trickle, so Lan was gratified to see Kalira and Tuck's mare Dacerie waiting for them, all tacked up in their travel gear.

:Let's go!: Kalira called, doing a little dance in place. *:I can't wait to see something besides Companion's Field for a change!:*

Lan laughed, and threw his packs across her rump, fastening them to the back of the saddle. In no time at all, he and Tuck were in the saddle and out of the gate, with a cheerful wave to the Gate Guard. As Kalira had predicted, the Guards had gotten weary of watching him several weeks ago, and there was no longer anyone shadowing his movements. Now the Guards no longer noted him as anything other than another Trainee; the Guard stationed at the gate in the special uniform of Palace duty gave him nothing more than the same wave he had given to Tuck.

Outside the walls, they found themselves in the oldest section of Haven, where the houses of some of the highborn with the longest lineage stood. These impressive manses were positively ancient, built in an archaic and very ornate style, covered with carvings, stone lacework, and peculiar little statues in niches, dark with age and weather. The gardens here were not as extensive as those on the other side of the Palace grounds, but their age was easily read in the size of the trees and the thickness of the hedges surrounding the gardens. Lan could only imagine what those gardens looked like—nothing at all like the bare patch behind his parents' house, surely.

It was quiet here, with a real sense of age. Oddly enough, although the Palace predated these mansions by centuries, these places seemed older. He surveyed them with a sense of cynicism. Perhaps it was because they were ossified, preserved like flies in amber in a casing of unchanging tradition and petrified pride. The Palace was always alive with change; it looked to Lan as if no one dared so much as move a rock in the garden of one of these places.

"I love coming through here," Tuck said, his eyes shining with enthusiasm as he admired the buildings, the height of which was only rivaled by the ancient trees in the gardens. "These places are so *solid,* you know? You can feel the history and all the lives and events that have passed through their rooms; it's wonderful!"

Lan looked over at him in surprise. "I would have said stifling, myself. I should think that anyone who lived here would be as boring and dusty and moth-eaten as an old stuffed bird, and just about as flexible."

Tuck shook his head. "No, no, no—it's not stifling at all! Well, you know, Daria, don't you? And if you know her, I know that you like her!"

Lan nodded slowly. He did, indeed, know Trainee Daria, a tall brunette with a slow smile; she was in the year-group just before his. Nothing she ever did or said drew attention to herself; she was quiet, vaguely pretty, but not outstanding in any way but one. And that one—was simply amazing. She was the most *competent* person he had ever seen. She never put a foot wrong; when something was needed, she was the first person there, with the required object in her hand. When she didn't know the answer to a question or problem, she invariably knew who did. And although self-effacing, she was so quietly friendly and cheerful that, as Tuck had said, everyone who knew her liked her.

"Well, she grew up right over there." He pointed to a particularly matronly manor. "Her blood's near as blue as the King's. And *she's* not petrified!"

"I have to admit you're right, there," Lan replied. "Huh."

"Daria's going to take me to see the place one of these days, come spring, and let me rummage through the family papers," Tuck went on, fired with enthusiasm. "You know, some of these older Great Houses had their own Chroniclers? They've got records going back centuries, some right back to the Founding! And antiques and artifacts stored up that are nearly as old! Just think about it—stuff like that just brings how the people lived right to life when you look at it and handle it, read their letters, see how they lived!"

"You sound like the Herald Chronicler yourself," Lan teased, only half joking.

"I'd like to do that," Tuck replied, not joking at all. "I'd like that a lot. But I've got a long way to go before I'm ready for that, and a lot of circuit riding! My only Gift is strong Mindspeech, so it's not like I have anything special to teach when it's time to retire from field duty."

Lan blinked, a little surprised by this unexpected depth to his friend. "To tell the truth, I don't know what I want to do. What I *really* wanted was to be in the Guard, but when my parents put their feet down on that idea, I kind of gave it up. Then I thought that I'd like to be a Caravan Master, but I guess that's out of the question now—"

"Riding circuit on the Border, that's what you want," Tuck said firmly. "You work with the Guard a lot, and you help local villages organize militia if there's a local problem. You make sure that if there's a noble estate near enough to help that the lord or whatever is doing *his* duty to help protect his people. Plus there's all the usual circuit-riding stuff."

"And eating my own food—bleah!" Lan teased, as both Companions whickered their own form of laughter.

"Then you'd better learn to cook better!" Tuck retorted. "If you don't want to ride circuit, there's always working with the Guard directly. Then you'd get army rations."

"Hmm." Lan considered that notion as they left the last of the Great Houses behind, crossed through a gate beneath an ancient wall, and entered a section of newer estates with more extensive grounds. "I hadn't thought of that."

"If you've got a Gift that makes you really useful to the Guard, that's probably what you'll be doing after you do your internship circuit," Tuck told him with an emphatic nod. "And if it's really, really useful to the Guard, you may do your internship with one of the Guard Heralds on the Border itself."

"Really?" This was the first Lan had ever heard of such a thing, and he smiled, slowly. If he could do that, it would not only be his childhood dream come true, it would be *better.* "I'd like that. I'd like that a lot."

"I wouldn't, but it takes all kinds, eh?" Tuck grinned broadly. "Me, I'd be happy if they'd let me teach History here, maybe run messenger or courier in an emergency, and apprentice to the Herald Chronicler."

"All right, apprentice—what can you tell me about all of these places?" Lan waved his arm at the walls surrounding the road, over which much newer buildings looked down at them haughtily.

"Not much history here—and these places are more like to change hands than the Great Houses," Tuck said, in a dismissive tone. "Newer nobles, Kingdom Guildmasters, and the very wealthy. I *wish* they'd pay more attention to their own history, actually, but they seem determined to leave it all behind them once they build or buy in this quarter. It's like they want to become someone entirely different and turn their backs on where they came from."

"But they aren't the same people anymore—" Lan objected.

Tuck gazed at him with an unusually solemn expression. "Oh? And would you say that *you* aren't the same person you were before you were Chosen? You can't just forget all that and discard it—it *made* you what you are now! Erase it, try to forget it, and what do you get? Nothing but pretense! And that's just phony, and more pretentious than just enjoying what you've made of yourself, *I* think."

"I guess I can see that, sort of. I mean, I don't always get along with my folks, but they don't pretend that they sprang out of nowhere, or that they've got some sort of fake blue blood in their background."

Lan considered that. What *would* that do to a person's head? Could you remake yourself in another image? And if you did, what would you have? Wouldn't it just be a false image?

"And if these people discard what *they* were, what does that make them?" Tuck persisted. "If they try to convince themselves that their own past has no relevance anymore?"

This was the most philosophic that Tuck had ever been, and it aroused an equally thoughtful mood in Lan.

"Not . . . much," Lan thought aloud. "Kind of hollow. No substance, no debt to the past."

"My point exactly," Tuck said with satisfaction. "And maybe that's why so many of *their* children turn out badly. Too much of trying to give their children what *they* didn't have, and not enough giving their children what the *did* have that made them so successful and prosperous."

And maybe that explains Tyron and his bullies, Lan thought, with a twist of his gut. "You're unaccountably wise today, Tuck," he said lightly, changing the subject a trifle. "I hardly know you!"

Tuck laughed. "That's 'cause most people don't pull my history string and find out what's attached to it. Pure passion, I'm afraid; it's the one subject that I can go on about for days at a time. Blame yourself; you *could* have started me on bad puns or limericks instead, but *nooooo*—"

"That," Lan replied with mock-solemnity, as they passed the last of the mansions and turned down a street lined with shops, "would have been worse. Or should I say, verse?"

Tuck pulled off his cap and hit him on the shoulder with it, as Lan ducked and laughed. A few of the folk walking along the side of the street heard their laughter, turned their heads, and smiled to see two Trainees in such high spirits.

The farther they went from the Palace, the more crowded the streets became. At first, all of the traffic was on foot, but before long they were sharing the pavement with ox-carts, pack-laden donkeys, and a few horsemen. Their pace was leisurely, but was never so slow that either of them felt impatient, and both Companions gazed in every direction with great interest. Lan rather enjoyed looking around; this was yet another part of the city he hadn't yet had a chance to see. In this weather, there were few open stalls, but the shops seemed to be doing a brisk business. The stalls that *were* there tended toward hot food and drink: handfuls of roasted chestnuts; hot tea and cider; mulled ale; hot pies. The only aromas on the cold air were savory—stewing meat, the spices of mulled ale, the hearty scent of hot chestnuts, the sweet intoxication of pastry. Pie vendors also walked the street with trays of pies. One of them approached the boys, and Lan bought a pair of apple pies to share with Tuck. A small child ran up with a gift of a carrot for each Companion. They munched the spicy treats as they continued on out of the city. The streets were very narrow here, and quite noisy. Besides people talking at the tops of their lungs, oxen lowing, donkeys braying, hooves clicking on the pavement, and wheels clattering, there were the sounds of commerce. Butchers wielded cleavers or made sausage with much clanking of gears, tinkers mended pans, blacksmiths shoed animals or beat out utensils, knives were sharpened, wood hewn, furniture built. From the taverns, singing

and laughter drifted out every time a door opened.
From cookshops, a hundred different dinner dishes
added their aroma to the breeze, and a hundred cooks
and all their helpers added to the clamor.

Lan loved it. This was his home village writ large;
he adored the bustle, the fact that there were things
to be seen no matter where you looked. He could
have spent an entire day just watching the people at
all their myriad activities.

Gradually, the bustle ebbed, the buildings were
spaced farther apart, and traffic eased. There were still
plenty of people around, but they didn't have to shout
to be heard. Children shrieked and played; there
wasn't much snow around, since most of it had been
trampled hard or swept away by now, so they bobbed
along, bundled up like so many balls of clothing ready
for the laundry, in clumsy, complicated games of tag.

Then, suddenly, a final wall loomed up in front of
Lan and Tuck, this one attended by a pair of
Guardsmen in the lighter blue and silver of the regular
troops. It was taller than any of the buildings around
it, a real defensive structure, with watchtowers at intervals and more Guards patrolling atop it. The Trainees passed beneath it, and were out into the country.

This was not one of the more heavily-trafficked roads
into Haven, so there weren't any of the big wagons that
brought in farm produce or carried away goods. Instead,
there were a few small carts on the road, and one or
two riders, and the two of them. A wide meadow, snow-
covered and dotted with sheep and milk cows, stretched
on either side of the road all the way up to the wall. It
was kept cleared to prevent anyone from approaching
without warning. This was common land, and anyone
who wished to could tether a cow or a sheep, or run a
flock of geese out here. Many folk clubbed together to
put their animals under a common shepherd, cowherd,
or goose girl. There were no geese out here now—a sign
that the Midwinter Feast was near. They were being

fattened on grain in pens, in preparation for their appearance on many a table.

"Want a gallop?" Tuck asked, now that they were out in the open.

For answer, Kalira launched herself like an arrow from a bow, Tuck's Dacerie following her with great enthusiasm. Lan bent low over Kalira's neck, laughing, as Tuck caught up with them.

This wasn't a race. Instead, they were matching their paces, so perfectly that they could probably have traded mounts in mid-gallop. Full Heralds with more practice *could* do just that, and before he and Tuck finished their riding lessons, so would they.

The Companions slowed to a fast walk as they reached the end of the common land and reached the first farms. Neither of the Companions were even breathing heavily, and Tuck and Lan were laughing with sheer exhilaration.

"Now that is something we'll be able to do as much as we like!" Tuck promised. "Da and Ma don't mind, as long as we don't scare the stock!"

"We'll just stay out of the milch-cow pastures," Lan promised. "I've been a country boy, too, you know, and I don't think it's particularly amusing to stampede the cattle. But—how's the hunting?" He waited hopefully for the answer.

"Good bird hunting, especially pheasant," Tuck replied, smiling at the gleam in Lan's eye. "We don't bother the foxes unless they go after the yard fowl. If you *really* want to go after something big, we can organize a deer- or a boar-hunt, but we're careful about how many we take from the home woods."

"I'd like that, but I'll be satisfied with rabbit and birds," Lan replied truthfully. "We'll only have a fortnight, after all, and I don't want to intrude on your time with your family."

"Oh, don't worry, you won't!" Tuck chuckled. "And I'd better warn you about Merry, my little sister. She's just discovered boys, and she falls in love every time she meets a new one. You're not bad-looking *and* you're going to be a Herald, so she'll probably start making calf eyes at you the minute you cross the threshold."

"I'll try not to hurt her feelings," Lan promised.

:And I'll try not to tease you about it too much,: Kalira chimed in.

"We can always stay out of her way most of the day, and Ma won't let her make too big a loon of herself in the evenings," Tuck chuckled.

The farms they passed looked virtually identical; thatch-roofed, snow-covered buildings with big stone barns, hedges dividing the fields with wooden stiles built for humans and dogs to cross, cattle and sheep pawing through the snow to get at the grass or feeding from bales of hay left out for them. In the farmyards, chickens and ducks jostled each other for grain and vegetable peelings while pigs grunted hopefully in their sties attached to the barns. Some farms boasted a pond full of geese and ducks as well. The figures of the farm folk, made small by the distance, made their way among the buildings at their chores.

"I'll help with the chores," Lan said, suddenly moved to offer by the recollection of how many chores a farm family usually had. "I don't mind, and that will make sure you get some time to have some fun, too."

"That'll make things easier, thanks," Tuck said gratefully, without any awkwardness over the offer. "I usually get wood chopping and water carrying when I'm home—we don't have a pump in the kitchen, so we fill a cistern above it; there's no well under the house, so we're kind of stuck. That's a lot of water."

"Well, it'll be half of a lot of water," Lan laughed. "Which ought to be *some* comfort to you!"

THEY reached Tuck's home just at sunset, with scarlet light streaming across the white snow and the entire sky on fire. Tuck's home looked very like every other farm they'd passed; the house was a trifle larger, perhaps, but otherwise it was the same: stone building, stone barn, thatched roofs, chicken coop with its own thatched roof, dove cot, pig sty, and cows coming in from the field to be milked. This was primarily a dairy farm, close as it was to Haven; the income came from milk, cream, butter, cheese, and eggs, and the vegetables and animals they raised mostly went to their own table. As a consequence, the barn was enormous. The cattle were a pampered lot, cosseted and petted. Each had her own stall with her name over it; each was cared for tenderly. Tuck's family didn't even slaughter their own cattle for beef; weaned bull calves were sent elsewhere, and the cows who could no longer give milk were allowed to play nursemaid to the newly-weaned female calves until they were old enough to join the milch herd.

Not that they *didn't* eat beef; they traded for it. They also raised a few sheep as well as pigs for meat, but no one was allowed to make a pet of them.

All this Lan knew from Tuck's stories of his family, and it all made very good sense to him.

As they turned off the road and took the path leading to the farm, someone came out of the house and spotted them. Waving wildly until they waved back, the figure jumped up and down, then turned back and ran into the house. A moment later, more figures poured out of the house, until there were a good dozen waving at them and shouting greetings.

Tuck and Dacerie launched into a gallop; Lan and Kalira continued at a more sedate pace. When Tuck reached his family, he spilled out of the saddle and into their arms for a hearty exchange of embraces and back slapping. Lan grinned, although he couldn't even imagine his own family indulging in such antics.

By the time he and Kalira reached the group, most of the greeting was over. He dismounted with a bit more dignity and took the hand that Tuck's mother extended to him.

"I can't begin to thank you for this hospitality, Mistress Chester," he began, when the rosy-cheeked woman waved his thanks aside, and clasped his hand in both of hers.

"Call me Ma, youngling," she insisted. "Or Ma Chester, if you'd druther. No formal nonsense amongst friends in holiday, I always say."

Ma Chester's ginger-colored hair and sparkling green eyes were the duplicate of her son's, and although her figure was ample enough, she was by no means the roly-poly dumpling that farm wives were portrayed as in city stories. She worked hard, and she was as sturdy and well-muscled as any of her sons.

"Well, you still have my thanks, Ma Chester," he replied, grinning. "And I promised Tuck I'd share his chores with him, so don't you try and sneak him off to do them alone!"

"A promise is a promise, so I shan't," she agreed, smiling broadly. "Pa Chester's a-milking, so you'll see him soon's you take the ladies to the barn, and about half the rest of the brood, but I'll make you known to the flock—"

She introduced him to her four youngest children, who stared at him merrily from blue or green eyes. One boy and three girls, they were, with the youngest being the boy—Sheela, Trinny, Cassie, and Jan. The rest of the mob were servants or hired workers, whom she introduced just the same as her children. The hired workers took the morning chores, allowing the master and his children to sleep a little past dawn; in return, the master and his children took all the evening chores, permitting the hired hands to have their dinner and go home to their own families early.

With the introductions over for the moment, the crowd returned to dinner, and Lan and Tuck led their Companions into the barn.

A dusky light filled the barn; carefully shielded oil

lamps placed in wrought-iron cages fastened to the great beams that supported the hayloft gave off a diffused illumination. The cattle were all in their stalls, some munching placidly on their hay, the last few being milked. A sweet odor of hay and milk filled the barn, and the swish-swish of milk spurting into pails was the only sound besides the munching of hay and the occasional hoof stamp or snort.

"Aye, Tuck!" called Pa Chester from the back of the barn. "Ye're here, then! And hallo to ye too, young Lavan!"

"Heyla, Master Chester!" Lan called, "Glad I am to be here! I've given your lady my thanks, but you must take them as well."

"Ah, 'tis naught, we're glad for your company, youngling!" Pa Chester replied. "And you'll be calling me Pa, same as Tuck, an' ye please!"

"Yes, sir!" Lan replied, stifling a chuckle.

He followed Tuck, who led Dacerie to the rear of the barn, and there were two stalls—open, box stalls, with ample mangers filled with hay and oats, hock-deep in sweet, fresh straw, and buckets filled with fresh water. The stalls had no doors, so that Dacerie and Kalira could come and go as they pleased, exactly as in the stalls in the Companions' Stable at the Collegium.

Greatly pleased, though not surprised, Lan unsaddled Kalira and gave her a good rubdown, covering her with her special fitted blanket. Saddle and saddle blanket went over the sides of the stall, bitless bridle was hung on a peg at the front, and then he picked up his packs and left Kalira to her meal. He emerged just in time to be introduced to the rest of Tuck's family.

These were three boys and two girls; Merry, who as Tuck had prophesied, immediately began to make eyes at him, her sister Ajela, and Tuck's brothers Hal, Stane, and Guy. Pa Chester he already knew, a hearty blue-eyed, straw-haired farmer, plain as a post and cheerful as a sparrow. The boys were like him; Tuck clearly took after his mother. Merry was blonde as well; Ajela a true strawberry blonde and much the prettier of the two, though Lan doubted that she was aware of the fact.

With dusk fading and the stars beginning to come out, the group trooped into the kitchen for dinner, as cheerful an affair as any meal at the Collegium. Tuck's brothers and sisters bombarded him with questions about the Collegium; Lan kept quiet and listened. Tonight's meal was rabbit pie, mashed turnips with sweet butter, scones, clotted cream, and plenty of jam. There was more than enough for everyone; seconds, and even third helpings were the rule in the Chester household. Everyone worked hard and had the healthiest of appetites.

There was one other member of the family that Lan had not yet met, to whom he was introduced before dinner. This was Granny Chester, Pa Chester's mother. Though very old, she was not at all frail; it was she who still spun most of the wool knitted into stockings and winter garments for the family. She did a great deal of the knitting itself. She taught the girls to sew, weave, and embroider—taught the boys, too, if anyone could catch them often enough to make them sit still for the lessons. Tuck was one of the few boys at the Collegium who had the skills to help out with the sewing and mending, and he made no bones about the fact that he greatly enjoyed being the only rooster in the henhouse.

Lan bowed over Granny's hand like a very courtier; she snatched it away from him and gave him a playful rap on the knuckles, but dimpled with pleasure like the girl she once was. Snow-white hair peeked from under her cap in flossy curls; her blue eyes, surrounded by a maze of fine lines and wrinkles, twinkled at him.

After dinner, the family cleared away the plates and

everyone helped to wash up; Lan took his turn drying the heavy pots. They pushed the table aside and brought in the cushions and easy chairs; the huge kitchen did double duty as a sitting room in winter, for there was no reason to heat two rooms when one would suffice. The sitting room was kept shuttered and closed off from the rest of the house until spring, when it would be opened up and used as a retreat from the heat of the kitchen.

Granny Chester got pride-of-place right next to the fire in the chimney corner; the girls brought out knitting or fine sewing, the boys carving or more knitting. Even Tuck dashed upstairs and brought down a basket with a half-finished pair of stockings, evidently left from the last time he was here.

Seeing what they were up to, Lan rummaged in his packs, which were in a corner of the kitchen, and got out a book. He cleared his throat, and the others looked up at him, some with curiosity, but Tuck with a glint of anticipation.

"I thought maybe some of you might like to hear a tale or two before bed?" he half asked.

He needn't have been so tentative; his suggestion was met with an enthusiasm that would have charmed a practiced Bard.

The book he had brought with him was, in fact, one of the ones that the Bardic Trainees were taught from. As with all songs, many things were left out of the great songs that were famous all throughout Valdemar; this book, and the others that Lan had brought with him, filled in the blank spaces of many of these famous songs.

"I know you've all heard the Bards sing 'Berden's Ride,' but there's more to the story than that," he began, opening the book to the first page. "And here is how Berden's story really began. . . ."

As they all listened raptly, knitting needles clicked and knives whittled tiny slivers, and the fire crackled and popped, making a comfortable, domestic background to the story.

When at last he finished—telling them, for the first time, how Berden settled down at the Collegium, minus a leg but plus his own true love, to live to a respected and ripe old age teaching the Trainees what it meant to be a *real* message rider—they all sighed with pleasure.

"I do believe that's the finest I've ever heard anyone read, young Lavan," Pa Chester said, speaking for them all. "And a fine thing it is to hear the whole of a tale!"

"Aye, to that," Granny Chester agreed with satisfaction. "Me own Ma used to call me Curious Kit, because I was allus asking 'what else happened,' and she could never tell me!"

"Well, I have enough tales in my books with happy endings to read one every night I'm here, if you like," Lan offered, tickled by their response. From the clamor that followed this offer, it was very clear that everyone did, indeed, "like."

Ma Chester produced a round of warm cider and chestnuts to roast; fierce betting ensued as to which chestnut would "pop" first. When the last nut was a memory, and the last sip of cider was gone, Granny ordered them all to bed.

Lan was not at all averse to bed; it had been a long day. He and Tuck fetched their packs from the corner of the kitchen and headed up the stairs with the rest.

The bedrooms were chilly, even the ones arranged around the central chimney, but hot bricks had been placed in the beds right after dinner. Lan shared Tuck's bedroom, taking a trundle that rolled out from beneath Tuck's bed.

"Well?" Tuck asked, after they had both burrowed under their warm blankets, and the candle was blown out. "Think you're going to be able to stand my family for a fortnight?"

"Huh! I think it's more whether they're going to be

able to stand me! This is going to be great, Tuck, and thanks again for asking me here."

"Happy to," Tuck muttered, pleasure in his voice. "You know . . ."

But Lan never did find out what Tuck was going to say, because at that point, he was ambushed by sleep.

FOURTEEN

THE Collegium was uncharacteristically silent, the hallways dim. The one or two Trainees who remained here over the holiday had already been "adopted" by those who had families here, and were spending the day with those families. Without fires burning, the building itself was cold, but it did not have the forlorn sense of abandonment that Lan had expected. Instead, the feeling as he walked down the hallway to his room was of a rest before activity resumed, as if the Collegium were taking a welcome breather until the Trainees returned in force.

His arrival had been anticipated, however, and despite the fact that this was a full holiday, someone had been in his room, built up the fire, and brushed and laid out his Formal Grays for him.

There was even a brand new pair of boots to go with them, something he had not expected, adding the perfect touch of completeness to the uniform. The fire had been going long enough to warm up his room completely; he banked it to await his return before going to the bathing room and cleaning up.

He had gotten up before dawn in order to get to the Collegium before noon. He wanted to arrive on his parents' doorstep just before the servants put out the array of finger foods that would sustain the guests until the great feast just after dark. He would stay through the feast, then leave and spend the night at the Collegium before returning to the Chester farm in the morning.

Fully scrubbed, carefully turned out, he surveyed himself in the full-length mirror at the end of the hall. He straightened unconsciously, and was astonished at his own reflection. A sober-faced stranger stared back at him, clad in a form-fitting, silver-trimmed uniform that lent him a personality somehow more impressive than his own.

:Time to stop admiring yourself and get out here!: Kalira laughed. *:If you want to make a properly-timed arrival, that is.:*

Lan grinned at his reflection and went to fetch his cloak.

This time he took the gate opposite the one that led the way he and Tuck had used to leave the week before. With a cheerful wave to the Guard, he and Kalira stepped out onto the street outside the walls. Although there were many impressive mansions here as well, these were of the newer sort. And from the look of things, they were all full to bursting with guests—probably relatives come in from outlying areas, for Midwinter Festival at Court was a time of great festivity, fetes and balls, for seeing and being seen, and went on for the full fortnight. Every window held a candle, and garlands of greenery festooned the doors and lower windows. These homes had gates of wrought iron rather than the solid wooden gates of the older homes, and as Lan and Kalira rode past, they saw hordes of happily shrieking children at play in the snow-filled gardens. He hoped that on the other side of the Palaces, the ancient walls of the Great Houses were echoing with as much laughter.

Things grew quiet again as they entered another section of shops and workshops, mostly workshops with shops attached. A variety of craftspeople worked here; chandlers, booksellers who rebound their wares in fine covers, craftsmen of strictly ornamental objects. There wasn't a sign of anyone in this part of the city; even the most ambitious shopkeeper knew better than to try to compete with Midwinter Feast. Only where there were taverns and inns was there any sign of where people had gone. Ah, but a turn of the street later found folk gathered around street entertainers in a tiny park filled with lanterns, and the sound of music and dancing echoed through the empty shops. A few enterprising vendors had set up temporary stalls with hot drinks and pastries, and there was no doubt that a good time was being had by all. Another turn, and a different sort of music met Lan's ears as the cheerful dance tunes faded; the sound of hymns from one of the temples, a chorus swelled manyfold by the folk crowded inside its walls.

Turn again, and he was in the quarter he knew well; passing Leeside Park where even now a group of brightly-clad young folk trotted their horses, and another group skated and slid on the frozen ice of the central pond. With houses full to bursting with relatives—most of whom insisted on treating adolescents like infants at this holiday season—this lot would probably stay in the park as long as they could get away with it. Vendors of hot food and drink with semi-permanent stalls lined one side of the pond, and at the other side was a warming shed where skaters surrounded an open fire, perched on encircling benches. None of them gave him more than a curious glance, and he didn't stop to examine them very closely, although he thought he recognized several from the school. He was no longer a part of their world, nor they of his; if he *did* recognize either former acquaintance or foe, he really would be at a loss for what to say to them.

:I'd like to see Owyn, though,: he told Kalira as they turned away from the park and into his parents' street. *:Maybe not right now, but some time soon.:*

:He was a better friend to you than either of you expected,: Kalira replied. *:I think you should.:*

Here, the houses were festooned with more greenery than their little gardens ever saw in the height of summer; even the lamp posts were twined with garlands of evergreen and hung with bunches of mistletoe. From the tiny yards behind the houses rose the sounds of more children playing—not with the same boisterous abandon as the ones out in the park or the streets, but still having a good time from the sound of the laughter.

Kalira's bridle bells chimed cheerfully, echoing up and down the street, and the sound drew children out of the yards to come see what made it. Lan sat up straighter as round eyes peered at him and took in the familiar sight of a Companion, but the unfamiliar uniform. He heard murmurs of speculation, and suppressed a smile.

But then, as he drew nearer to his own house, the offspring of his own relatives piled out of the yard, and one of them finally recognized him. A cousin, a very young one, stared at him with mouth and eyes going equally round, then suddenly burst back into the house through the front door, squealing at the top of her lungs.

"Mama! Mama! It's Cousin Lan, an' he's a Captain Herald!"

That brought a veritable flood of relatives out into the cold, giving Lan exactly the hoped-for opportunity for a dramatic arrival. Kalira went into a parade gait called a pavane, a kind of slow-motion trot with feet raised as high as possible, as Lan sat very straight and still in the saddle.

As his mother and father pushed their way through the rest, Kalira came to a graceful halt. With a flourish of his cape, Lan swung out of the saddle, and tied his

reins over the pommel. With a brief but very low bow
of her head, Kalira whirled on her heels and returned
up the street at a now-brisk canter.

Lan turned and faced his parents—and the rest of
the family—who were all, from the oldest to the youngest, staring as open-mouthed as the first to recognize him.

"Lavan!" his father blurted, "Your horse—"

"*Companion,* Father," he said gently. "It wouldn't
be proper nor polite for her to stand about in the yard
with no shelter and no comforts. We've no place for
her here, so she'll be back for me later."

His father stared at him as if he'd spoken Hardornen; his mother looked at him as if he was a stranger.
He had never seen them look at him that way
before—

Or had he? Hadn't they been odd with him when
they'd come to visit him at the House of Healing?

And was that *fear* he saw, faintly, before they forced
smiles of welcome onto their faces?

They didn't give him a chance to examine them any
closer. "Well, let's not all stand about in the cold any
longer!" his father said, clapping him on the back.
"Come along inside, everyone, and let's get back to
our Festival!"

Lan was carried away on a tide of relations, in
through the front door where he was relieved of his
cloak, revealing the true splendor of his Formal Grays,
and on to the sitting room, where his younger cousins,
terribly impressed, made him sit down and plied him
with plates of food they carried off from the side-
boards just to present to him. He couldn't have moved
if he'd wanted to; he had no idea where the rest of
those his age were at the moment, though he shrewdly
suspected they were at the park. The adults had commanded the parlor, and at this point they were probably bombarding his parents with questions of their
own. He wondered what they were telling everyone,

given that his father hadn't even thought that there was a difference between a horse and a Companion.

It was the children who saved him from further awkwardness. They were dying to hear about what being a Heraldic Trainee was like, and inundated him with questions. Was his Companion really smart enough to come get him? Did she talk like a human? How could she speak in thoughts? Where did he live? Was the Collegium really in the same place as the Palace? Had he met anyone important? He'd met the *King's Own?* Had he ever seen the King?

The answer to each question only gave birth to a dozen more, which prevented him from having to make conversation with the adults. That was just as well, for they kept drifting over from the parlor in little clumps to listen as he spoke to the children; he could feel their eyes on him all the time. If the children treated him as one of their own who had returned from a far country with incredible tales, the adults watched him as if he had changed into some new and strange creature utterly unlike a human.

He had become, unwittingly, the main source of entertainment for the afternoon. Although the adults didn't stoop to asking him any questions themselves, they certainly didn't hesitate to listen while he answered the children.

He tried to concentrate on them rather than anything else. *They* were certainly excited and happy to see him and pelt him with their questions, and after all, it certainly was the first time that any of them had gotten close enough to a Trainee (much less a Herald) to ask all the questions that they wanted to.

It was only after darkness had fallen and a servant had gone around discreetly lighting the candles that his mother appeared in the parlor, clapping her hands to get their attention. Nelda was not dressed in her absolute finest, which she reserved for important meetings, festivals, and parties involving Guild functionaries. Instead, she wore something much more casual, a simple-cut gown of soft brown wool, bound around with a hanging girdle embroidered, not by her own hands, but by Macy—it had been last year's Midwinter present. Her hair was done in a single loose braid down her back, and Lan thought she looked much better and softer than when she wore her best.

"Enough questions for now, little ones!" she called, just a shade too heartily. "It is time for the Feast!"

Since Lan would certainly be around after the Feast to continue to question, the children abandoned him for the pleasures of the table.

The children ate apart from the adults in the kitchen, the parlor, or anywhere else that small tables could be set up for them. The adults had the dining room to themselves. And Lan could tell at a glance that there had been some last-minute reshuffling of the seating arrangements. *He* was escorted to the seat of honor that Sam usually took, at his father's right. Two of the cousins who hadn't spoken to each other for years had somehow gotten placed side by side, and his brother Sam had been positioned between two very pretty but (matrimonially speaking) completely unsuitable country relatives. Neither of these seating accidents would ever have happened if his mother had been paying attention, so evidently his arrival had flustered her.

Or—not his arrival, but his appearance. She had probably expected that he would appear on foot, in his rather forgettable Trainee uniform. Clearly his parents had not bothered to tell anyone of his new status. As usual, the adults would have dismissed him from their minds as entirely unimportant. His theatrical arrival had completely thrown all of her expectations into the dust.

That wasn't entirely unsatisfactory, although he would much rather have been where Sam was. It would have been rather nice to have both his pretty cousins making calf eyes at him over their cups.

As it was, he was between his grandmother, who

had displaced him from his own room, and his father.
Well, at least he wouldn't be required to make conversation. Grandmother was as deaf as a rock, and his
father clearly was reluctant to make conversation
with *him*.

Grandmother evidently considered his new clothing
to be some sort of clever invention of his mother's;
she looked him up and down, then announced loudly,
"I'm glad you managed to get the boy into something
presentable, Nelda! He finally looks like a Chitward,
and not like a ragpicker's son." Then she applied
herself to her food, blissfully unaware of the nervous
giggles from the foot of the table or Nelda's embarrassed blush.

The chief ornament of the Feast was a remarkable
dish composed of a brace of deboned quail stuffed
into a deboned pheasant, stuffed into a deboned
capon, stuffed into a deboned duck, stuffed into a deboned goose. It must have been cooking all day, but
at least it ensured that there was plenty of bird to go
around without burdening the table with five different
platters. The rest of the table groaned beneath the
huge variety of dishes thought necessary to the Midwinter Feast; mashed, roasted, or candied root vegetables, bowls of five different bean concoctions, mashed
peas, stewed greens, four kinds of bread, two kinds of
rolls, plain butter and butter creamed with honey, gra-
vies, jellies, stewed fruit, pickles, pitchers of cream,
small ale, wine, cider. . . .

Lan knew that they wouldn't eat it all, but at least
what wasn't eaten would be carried with great ceremony to the nearest Temple of Kernos to be distributed to the hungry before it even had a chance to
cool. Grandmother would lead the procession, pushed
in her canopied, wheeled chair, just as she had back
in Alderscroft, with Nelda on her right and Macy on
her left. Those female relatives who cared to would
accompany them. The priest would pronounce a solemn blessing on the creators of the dishes who were

so generous as to share them, paying special attention to the matriarch of the clan. Grandmother loved every moment of it; it was her opportunity to be the queen of the family.

At least everyone got a Midwinter Feast that way, for the poor were waiting right there in the temple to be fed.

"So, Lavan," one of the unsuitable cousins piped up from farther down the table, fluttering her eyes at him. "Are there many pretty girls being trained as Heralds?"

Lan was torn between saying the expected, "None as pretty as you," and the indifferent, "I hadn't noticed."

He compromised on, "Most of the time we're all being worked so hard that we're too tired to tell the girls from the boys, and the rest of the time we're trying to catch up on sleep."

"Oh, come now," a particularly obnoxious uncle said, in a patronizing tone of voice. "There can't be *that* much to learn! What does a Herald do, anyway, but ride about and look important, maybe settle an occasional feud between farmers?"

Lan took a very deep breath before answering to remind himself to keep his temper, ignoring the frantic look on his mother's face. "Well, as it happens, I get up about a candlemark before dawn, unless I happen to be one of the people who has morning chores to do and in that case, I get up two candlemarks before dawn. There's breakfast, then I put my room ready for inspection. Then I have classes in History, Geography, and Field Investigation, then hard riding exercises, then maybe afternoon chores, then lunch, then more afternoon chores or study, then Weaponswork, then Mathematics and Accounting, then a class in court etiquette and how to handle situations involving the nobles, then a special class—right now I'm doing a short class on how to take care of injuries or illness in an emergency until a Healer can get there. Then perhaps evening chores. After that is dinner, then archery practice or a free candlemark, then study until bed." He got some satisfaction in seeing his uncle's eyes bulge a little more with every class he added. "Later I'll be getting lessons in how to use my Gift, how to invoke Truth Spell, another short class about Bards. I'll learn how to survive in the wilderness with no supplies and no tools, I'll learn how to rescue people from drowning, handle a rowboat and a sailboat, how to organize fighting a forest fire or a house fire, how to organize local people into a militia and train them to defend themselves, and how to be a judge. That's just what I know about; I'm sure there are a lot more classes I don't know about yet."

"Oh," his uncle said weakly. Well, what else could he say? Lan took great satisfaction in having managed to put the man in the wrong without ever being in the least impolite. It was the first time in his memory that anyone had ever been able to shut the man up.

No one else seemed to be able to think of anything to say to him, which was just as well. There were a few awkward moments of silence, then another cousin asked the discomfited uncle about a matter of trade in a slightly shrill and nervous voice. The uncle loudly proclaimed his opinion, and conversation resumed, flowing around Lan without touching him.

He ate his meal in silence, wishing that he'd stayed with the Chesters instead. Maybe there wouldn't have been any quail-stuffed-inside-pheasant-stuffed-et cetera, but he would have been a lot more comfortable.

Finally, the interminable meal came to an end with the requisite toasts. When it was Lan's turn, he decided to actually make one instead of passing, as he usually did on the rare occasions when the opportunity arose.

After all, I'm in the place of honor. Why shouldn't I?

His father was just beginning to stand, when Lan pushed his chair decisively back and rose to *his* feet, glass held high. His father sat back down hurriedly, and a silence descended on the table with a thud.

Lan stared at the wine the color of old embers glowing in the heart of his glass. "I would like to toast my family," he said, taking an absolutely malicious pleasure in choosing words heavily weighted with irony and loaded with a definite double meaning. "For without your actions, I would not be where I am and what I am at this moment."

Macy looked puzzled. Sam went pale, as did his father. His mother flushed. But what could they do or say? For all they knew, he was being entirely sincere, although surely they knew he *meant* what he had said in every possible interpretation. The rest of his relatives looked askance at each other for a moment, as if wondering just how they should react to this.

It was his grandmother who broke the impasse; he'd spoken loudly enough for her to make out what he'd said. "Properly done, boy!" she declared, "here, here!" and drank her own glass down. That broke the spell holding the rest, and they followed the old woman's example. With a faint smile, Lan took a sip from his glass and sat down, feeling that he'd gotten ample revenge for the uncomfortable meal he'd just endured.

The Feast ended just after that, and the women descended on the kitchen to each take possession of a dish for the procession to the Temple. The children enveloped Lan and rushed him back to the sitting room, and the men retired to the parlor for wine and discussions of their own. Lan had no doubt that he would be the main topic of conversation, though more likely for his borderline insolence to his uncle than for the toast, which his father and brother were likely to avoid discussing.

This time, the youngsters Lan's age and older joined the children, although they would not normally have done so. In past years, the older ones, if they did not escape to some other venue such as moonlight skating, sledding, or sleigh riding, generally would gather in two groups, the boys to discuss girls, and the girls to discuss boys. Once again, he was going to provide the entertainment for the entire lot of them; he didn't much mind, since Kalira would arrive for him in a candlemark or two. There wasn't that much more of this for him to endure.

It turned out not to be an ordeal after all; the relatives of his own age were just as curious and full of admiration as the little ones. It was an entirely new experience for Lan to be admired by anyone in his family; he relaxed and answered questions cheerfully and frankly. The world of the Heraldic Trainee was entirely new to everyone here—well, it had been unknown to him as well, until he was Chosen—and for the most part, the members of the Chitward family had never had anything to do with Heralds. Why should they? Any disputes were settled within the Guild Courts, no one broke any laws, so they never had occasion to more than note a Herald passing at a distance, read about them in a tale, or hear about them in a ballad. If any of them had ever daydreamed about being Chosen, they had probably dismissed the idea with the typical practicality of a merchant family.

I wonder if any of them will start to dream about it now, he thought as he answered another question and watched how the eyes of even the oldest children were shining.

The ladies returned from the Temple, with Grandmother loudly proclaiming her pleasure in the ceremony. That signaled a round of activity, putting the youngest children to bed, collecting all the scattered members of the families of those who lived nearby, farewells and polite thanks from the ones who were going home tonight.

As Lan stood back out of the way, he heard Kalira with relief. *:I'm nearly there. Ready to go?:*

:Your timing is perfection,: he told her. *:Let me go say good-bye to Mother and Father, and I'll meet you outside.:*

He waited while another of the Chitward cousins, burdened with a baby and a toddler, paid their respects to his parents before going out the door. He edged past them as they pushed their toddler toward the door, and approached his parents with his cloak in his arms.

"It's time for me to leave, too," he told them as they turned toward him. "It's been quite an exceptional Feast this year." That, he thought, was diplomatic enough. "I suspect everyone is going to be talking about this one for a long time."

"We thought we'd save you as a sort of surprise," his mother said, in a tone that told him that she hadn't thought any such thing; she hadn't thought about him at all, as he had suspected. Or if she had, she had dismissed his presence as required, but negligible. But her expression softened a little as she looked at him; her hazel eyes took on a glint of pride—in him.

"I certainly was that." He smiled, very slightly. "From the way the youngsters acted, I was better entertainment than the puppet show Uncle Lerris had three years ago."

"Well, the puppet show was only there for a candlemark," his father pointed out, with, at last, a hint of humor, and a faint smile. "They had you captive for the entire afternoon and evening. I hope you weren't too bored with them."

He shrugged. "I didn't mind; it's a good thing for them to find out what we are, what we're like. Maybe it destroys some of the mystery, but it also removes ignorance." He didn't say anything about the obnoxious relative; he didn't have to. "But now, I really do have to go."

His parents embraced him; his father heartily, his mother awkwardly. At that moment, he made up his mind that next year he would decline the invitation, even if he had to make up a reason why he couldn't come, even if the Chesters *didn't* invite him back. Maybe when he was finally a Herald, he'd start coming for the family gatherings occasionally, but not right now.

He drew back from them and nodded formally. "You'd better get back to your guests," he said. "I'll show myself out."

Without waiting for their response, he turned and headed for the door. But just before he reached it, his sister Macy squeezed between two of the adults crowding a doorway and rushed up to him. "Here," she said, pressing a small, thin package into his hand. "I made this for you."

As she waited expectantly, he unwrapped it. Her gift was one of the most beautiful pieces of embroidery he had ever seen her create. It was very much a miniature tapestry; a perfect copy of the crest of Valdemar, with every star in the background picked out in silver, every link in the Windrider's broken chains delineated completely.

"Good gods—I should think you'd go blind doing work like this!" he exclaimed, much to Macy's satisfaction; she dimpled with pleasure as he kissed her cheek. "Macy, it's gorgeous. As soon as I get my hands on a needle and thread, I'll put it right on the shoulder of my cloak where everyone will see it! Thank you so much!"

"If it's all right, I'd like some hair from your Companion's mane and tail eventually," she said, "I want to make some woven jewelry."

:*Have her come out and pull some right now,*: Kalira interrupted. :*As much as she likes, as long as she doesn't snatch me bald.*:

"Kalira's outside, and she says to come and get some," he told her, and was rewarded with her wide eyes and enchanted smile. She didn't even stop to get a cloak; she followed him right outside, and gasped in delight to see Kalira standing at the door, shining in the lamplight.

"Is it really all right?" she asked the Companion, much to Lan's amusement.

Kalira snorted and bobbed her head, and Macy carefully approached her. With great delicacy and care, Macy separated out individual hairs to pull, gathering them carefully into a thin, silvery hank. Long before Lan had thought she would be satisfied, she patted Kalira's neck and said, "Thank you! Thank you so much!" and stepped back.

"I'll save the hair from her currycomb for you," Lan promised, tucking the embroidered patch into a pocket, and mounting.

:And I'll remind you.:

"Will you? Thank you, Lan! Can I come visit you?" She was the only person who had shown any real interest in visiting him, and even if it was more to see Kalira than to see him, Lan was touched.

"Surely. Give me some warning, so I can make time in my classes, but absolutely." He found himself warming unexpectedly to her, and looking forward to her visit.

"I will! Thank you again! I've got to go in, I'm about to freeze—" She flashed him another smile, and darted back inside the door. A trifle bemused by this unanticipated epilogue to the Feast, he and Kalira turned away from the door and started up the street toward the park.

:I hope your Midwinter Feast was more fun than mine,: he said to her, breathing in air that wasn't overheated and too-heavily scented for the first time that evening.

:I wish yours had been as enjoyable as mine,: she replied with sympathy. *:Never mind; we'll be back with Tuck tomorrow, and you'll have—:*

Her head came up, startled, as people suddenly emerged from both sides of the street to block their way. Deliberately.

Kalira paused, but Lan felt her gathering herself for a leap or a run—or both.

A woman with an angry, tear-streaked face stepped forward. Her clothing was mourning of the deepest, most complete black to the least button and bit of embroidery, and very rich. She looked up at him as if at a monster. "Are you Lavan Chitward?" she asked, in a harsh voice.

He nodded. "Yes, Lady. I am."

She stepped forward again and seized Kalira's reins. *"You murdered my son!"* she snarled, as Kalira shied and tried to dance away from her. She held on with the strength of the demented. *"Murderer!"* she continued savagely. "I know not how, but *you* killed my boy, my Tyron! And I will have justice, no matter what the Guard may say!"

Lan sat frozen with shock; Kalira's wide eyes and twitching muscles seemed to indicate that she was, too. Torn between fear and guilt, his heart pounded—and his head began to ache—

Apparently the people with her had not anticipated this sort of confrontation—or perhaps, they had not anticipated that Lan would turn out to be a Heraldic Trainee. A tall man with Tyron's square jaw and blond hair, wearing clothing that was a match with the woman's, stepped out of the crowd and took her elbow. "Leave it, Jisette," he hissed at her. "You're overwrought. Can't you see that this is a Companion?"

"A Companion with a murderer?" she sneered. "This is just a trick! His family thinks they can fool everyone by tricking him out with a uniform and a white horse, but they can't fool me!" Her eyes showed the whites all around, and she shook Kalira's reins furiously. "I know better! Liar! Slanderer! Murderer! *Murderer!*"

The man looked both at her and at Lan doubtfully, not sure whether to believe her. Lan felt as if he was going to have to double over from the pain behind his eyes, and that terrible red mist began to creep over his vision. He knew, he *knew* what was coming, and he wouldn't be able to stop it!

But that seemed to shake Kalira out of her shocked trance. *:I think not!:* she said crisply, and with a toss of her head, somehow slipped out of the bridle entirely. She ducked her head and whirled, leaving the woman with the empty bridle in her hands, and before Lan had any idea of what she was doing, she was pounding back down the way they had come, leaving the Jelnack entourage uselessly blocking the street.

The surprise of her action jolted Lan out of his paralysis, and as he lurched forward, he seized her mane to steady himself. As soon as he had gotten a double handful, she changed direction, quick as a cat, dashing down an unfamiliar street.

His stomach spasmed, and his head pounded, but the mist faded as she changed direction again. This time she raced straight down a broad street meant for huge cargo wagons, which was as empty now as an avenue through a cemetery. Her hooves rang on the cobblestones, but there were no noises of anyone following, and when she came to a dead end, she slowed and finally stopped.

:Hush, and hold still,: she ordered. There was an odd sort of *snap* in his head, a single stab of pain from one temple to the other. Then his headache was gone completely, and with it the cramps and heaving of his gut.

:There.: She sighed gustily. *:And don't you even dare think that crazed woman might be right! You are* not *a murderer, and if you ask me, it's pretty easy to tell where Tyron learned how to be a sadistic manipulator.:*

Lan, who'd had his mouth open to say something of the sort, shut it.

:And no "buts" out of you either!: Kalira continued, shaking her head angrily. *:Miserable woman! I wish I'd had something to leave on her shoes!:*

The unsubtle image that accompanied that was enough to get a feeble chuckle out of him. She snickered.

:Never mind. We'll see what that family has to say when the Guard comes tomorrow to charge her with stealing my bridle. She'll have a hard time convincing

anyone that I'm not a Companion then!: She turned
and proceeded at a walk back to a cross-street. *:I hope
they lock her up as a madwoman. It would serve her
right. Now—let's go home.:*

She picked up her pace to a trot and took a long
and complicated route back to the Palace. It was after
midnight when they entered the Palace gate, and although Lan wanted to take off her tack and groom
her himself, she ordered him to bed.

:We're leaving in the morning so that you *don't have
to have anything to do with those wretched people,:* she
told him. *:You'll need all your sleep.:*

He wrapped his cloak tightly around him, and
trudged up the pathways to the Collegium. He was
quite, quite certain he wasn't going to get that sleep.
By now the fire in his room would have burned out
even though he had banked it, and the room would
be icy—and he couldn't rid himself of the certainty
that Tyron's mother was right. . . .

But when he opened his door, warmth met him, and
there was a mug with a note on it from Elenor, ordering him to drink what was in the mug or suffer unspec-
ified consequences.

Evidently Kalira had been having some choice
words with . . . someone.

He was too tired, mentally, emotionally, and physically, to argue with anyone. He hung up the Formal
Grays, drank the mug, and crawled into his bed. And
the next thing he knew, it was morning.

FIFTEEN

Herald Jedin

ACCOMPANIED by two Guardsmen on horse-back, Pol rode Satiran down into the quarter where the Jelnack household had their imposing home. Lan was well on his way to the Chester farm by now, but before he had left, Pol had gotten an earful from Kalira via her sire. He had a clear and precise picture of what had really happened. As Kalira had said so venomously, Companions did not have the luxury of forgetfulness.

As a consequence of last night's debacle, Pol had called an emergency meeting among interested parties that included himself, the Seneschal, Captain Tela-maine, and King's Own Jedin, thus covering all au-thorities. To his great relief, even the Captain was full of righteous indignation at the Jelnacks' high-handed assumption of authority after the Guard had already made it clear that the case was closed. As a conse-quence, Telamaine had been only too ready to assign him a pair of escorts to reinforce his authority. Herald Jedin had been ready to go himself along with Pol, and would have, had his presence not been required by the King. As for the Seneschal, even Greeley agreed that the Jelnacks had to be dealt with, and swiftly. If one powerful family flaunted the law and the authorities and got away with it, others might well decide to make their own laws as well. When that started, it could end with feuds and blood in the street.

The one good thing that had come out of this disgraceful episode was that Kalira had amply demonstrated her ability to control Lan's Firestarting Gift. In fact, she had more than controlled it, but explaining that, as well as the "how" of it, would have only confused the non-Heralds.

Pol had promised Jedin that he would give him an explanation later, but hadn't specified a time. Knowing Jedin, though, he could expect to be interrupted at almost any time with a demand for information—

:Pol? Are you there yet? Are you busy?: As he had expected, it was Jedin, right on cue.

Pol suppressed a smile in spite of how angry he was with the Jelnacks. *:Not even halfway; everyone and his horse seems to be out on the street this morning. I suppose we can blame all the Midwinter Fairs outside the walls for that; it's not enough anymore to go to the one nearest you, evidently the current fashion is to see all of them, and clog the streets in doing so. I take it you have a moment for that explanation?:*

:Please.:

Jedin had one powerful advantage as a Mindspeaker; he had Rolan for a Companion, who could boost his powers to an unmeasured extent. He could, if he chose, probably reach any Herald within the borders of the entire country of Valdemar at need.

:According to Kalira, Lavan's Gift has only two modes; completely inactive and full force. Whether that was because of the way his Gift was forced, or for some other reason, she doesn't know. And at the moment, he can't consciously call it up; it only manifests when he's threatened and it's linked to his emotions. The angrier

or more frightened he is, the quicker it rouses, and the stronger it is.:

Pol waited courteously for a donkey-cart to cross in front of him as Jedin digested this.

:So his Gift obviously manifested last night—:

:And Kalira knew that if she let anything leak, the Jelnacks would know that Lavan had started the fires that killed those wretched boys. So she had to help him keep it clamped down, and that was why she ended the confrontation by slipping her bridle and running.:

:Ah! Very wise of her!: Jedin had evidently been puzzled about that. It was unlike even a Trainee to abandon a confrontation when calling for help would have brought reinforcements within a reasonable time and running could confirm doubts or accelerate a dubious situation.

:But—: Jedin now thought of the obvious ramification of Kalira's actions. *:If Kalira was helping him keep his power dammed, he must have been in agony.:*

:He was. And when she got him safe, she took care of that, too. She bridged all that pent-up force into herself, all at once, like a bolt of lightning. It was the only way to clear it quickly.:

He felt Jedin's involuntary wince of pain. *:She did what? I don't want to think about that too hard.:*

Neither did he. *:She only told me that Companions are just made to deal with things like that. She didn't seem to have taken any harm from it.:*

:Thank the gods they are. Well, I'm satisfied to learn the whys and wherefores of his Gift, and what Kalira can do with it; if she can handle what happened last night, she can handle him whatever happens. Thank you for the explanation.:

With the King's Own satisfied, the King would shortly be informed of what had transpired. And that would lend Pol the full authority to say and do whatever was required in the next candlemark or so. He wasn't going to do anything to bend or even stretch the law, but he was going to assume a great deal of authority.

All things considered, he hoped he would be able to dump the really unpleasant duties on Jisette Jelnack's own family members. He was certainly going to try, at any rate.

The Midwinter Fairs started the day after the Midwinter Feast and ran for the next seven days. Most folk who could afford to took the day after Midwinter Feast as an additional holiday from work, which was probably wise, given the amount of food and drink that was consumed the day before. It was supposed to be the children's day—this was when they got their presents, usually waiting on a table for them in the morning. Perhaps the entire custom of giving the children their gifts now instead of at the end of the fortnight when the adults exchanged presents was to keep them quiet while their elders recovered from their overindulgence. . . .

At any rate, Pol could count on the entire Jelnack clan being home, which was why he had not wanted to delay *his* confrontation.

The house in question was hard to miss; instead of being decked in green garlands, it was swathed, windows and doors, and the gate in front, in sad swags of black mourning. Pol's mouth twisted, and he felt as if he had bitten something sour. Given what they (and everyone else involved) surely now knew that Tyron had been like, such over-ostentatious mourning was in questionable taste.

He rode to the gate, waited for one of his escort to open it, and rode into the minuscule front court. The Guard who had dismounted led his horse to the front door, and while Pol waited, still mounted on Satiran, the Guard pounded three times on the door with the pommel of his sword.

It was shockingly loud; it was meant to be.

The door flew open, and an angry manservant stood there. Clearly he had been about to deliver a scathing dismissal to whoever it was that had pounded so rudely on the door, but when he saw not one, but *two* Guards *and* a Herald, he was so overcome with shock that he just stood there, hand half raised, mouth hanging open.

"Is this the house of the Master Silversmith Jelnack?" the Guard asked, sternly.

The manservant nodded, dumbly.

"And is he the husband of the lady Jisette Jelnack?" the Guard continued, frowning.

"Y-yes, sir," said the manservant at last. "W-w-would you care to come in?"

"I would *not*," the Guard snapped. "There is a serious charge of theft and endangerment to be laid, and you will summon them here, this instant. If they will not appear of their own accord, instantly, the charges of evading the King's justice and resisting the King's officer will be added to those already accumulated. *And leave the door open.*"

By now, there were eyes at every window in the neighborhood, and likely ears pressed to cracks in the fence.

:*There are,*: Satiran confirmed. :*I do believe we are more entertaining at this moment than the prospect of going to the Fair.*:

Good. Pol was counting on public humiliation to force the rest of the family to deal sharply and decisively with Jisette, who, according to Kalira, was the ringleader last night.

The manservant fled, and in a surprisingly short time, returned with a man and a woman clothed head-to-toe in black. The man pushed to the front, and Pol could tell from his expression that he was going to try bluster and bluff first.

"There must be some mistake," he began.

"There is no mistake," Pol said, using the authoritative Voice, a skill all Bards and most Heralds mastered. "Last night, in the presence of many of your household, you and your wife unlawfully detained and accused a Heraldic Trainee, one Lavan Chitward. You endangered his safety, threatened him, and stole the formal bridle of his Companion, said object made of blue leather and adorned with silver fittings and silver bridle bells, engraved with his Companion's name, said object being worth twenty crowns. I should think that as a Master Silversmith you would recognize this article I have just described. Do you deny this? I should warn you that if you do deny this, I have the authority to have the truth from you by means of the Truth Spell."

The blood drained from Master Jelnack's face; he knew now he wasn't going to be able to bully or bluff his way out of the situation. He also knew that now *every* neighbor knew what his household had been up to last night.

"Cast your spell, Herald!" Jisette said shrilly, pushing past her husband despite his efforts to keep her out of the way and quiet. "That creature you claim is a Trainee murdered my son and slandered him after his death! Nothing you can say will make me believe otherwise! I demand justice! The blood of my son demands justice!"

"You, lady, have already *gotten* justice for your son," Pol told her angrily. "Whether you believe it or not, it's no odds. Your son tortured and abused dozens of smaller, younger children for his own pleasure, forced them to act as his servants and even steal for him. The only person to be blamed for his death is Tyron Jelnack. Had he not been the kind of sadistic bully he was, he would be alive now. And you—" he concluded, again in the Voice, seeing that Jisette was about to launch into a tirade, *"You will be silent!"*

The use of the Voice, directed at her and only at her, and with all of the force of Pol's minor Gift of Empathic Projection behind it, struck her dumb.

Now he turned to Master Jelnack. "I am sorry that your son's death has so clearly deranged your wife's mind," he continued crisply. "And given that it is obvious that she is not thinking clearly or able to act rationally, the Crown may be willing to drop the charges, provided the bridle is returned *and* that you are able to demonstrate your ability to keep your wife under control until her clarity of thought returns. I must say that I am very much surprised and disappointed that she was able to sway all of you to believe in her delusions, but now that you know the truth, I trust you will treat her fantasy as it deserves to be treated, and ignore it."

Master Jelnack had seemingly also lost his power of speech, but he did nod. He swallowed once or twice, then half-turned and whispered something to the manservant, who vanished.

Satiran stamped decisively. "I must warn you that if you fail to keep this afflicted lady from acting on her delusions, she will have to be confined by the Crown," he continued. "And, of course, the charges will be reinstated. I believe you know better than I what such a reinstatment would mean to your reputation and career."

If it had been possible for Master Jelnack to grow any paler, he would have. Pol knew very well what would happen. With even a charge of theft laid against him, Jelnack would lose his position as Guildmaster.

Jelnack clamped his hand on his wife's wrist, and pulled her behind him. "We'll see to it that she is watched over and gets proper treatment," he said fervently. "I'll talk to the Healers myself."

"See to it that you do," Pol replied, remaining stony-faced as the manservant reappeared with the bridle. With a wave of his hand, he directed the Guard at the door to accept it. Then he backed up Satiran a pace, turned him, and led the way out of the courtyard into the street. The mounted Guard followed, then the last Guard mounted his horse, and took up the rear. Master Jelnack watched them leave, silently, afraid to make any show that might be interpreted as disrespect until they were out of the court. Only then did he close the door—very, very gently.

There wasn't a sound in the street; if it hadn't been for all the watchers, Pol could have believed that there wasn't a soul about. The hooves of the two Guards' horses clicked on the stones; Satiran's made that distinctive chiming sound that only Companions produced.

:I would have said that you were too hard on him, except that he should have figured out last night that Lan really was a Trainee,: Satiran remarked. *:I mean, really! A silver-worked bridle, the sound of Kalira's hooves—you can't counterfeit those! If he'd had any sense, he would have been at the Herald's Gate with the bridle in his hands, begging for forgiveness within a candlemark of Lan's return.:*

Pol sniffed. *:The only reason I wasn't harder on them is because I don't want to push things too far. They would be within their rights to demand that Lan undergo Truth Spell, and then the cat would be out of the bag.:*

Satiran put his ears back. *:Huh. I hadn't thought of that. That would be messy.:*

Pol wished he'd dared to take the woman into custody there and then and turn her over to the Healers—in protective custody, of course, with a Guard on her; he couldn't explain why, but he neither trusted her nor felt he could depend on her husband to keep her out of mischief. She was clever and entirely used to getting her own way. That was a bad combination.

But he'd done all he could for the moment. Keeping Lan away from family celebrations was the only other thing he could think of to do.

:That won't be difficult,: Satiran retorted. *:I think it would be harder to force him to go.:*

THE Chesters had made a second, and much more palatable, Feast for Lan. He was greeted as enthusiastically as if he had been gone for a month, and when he walked into the cottage, a dozen delicious odors hit his nose and nearly bowled him over. It was clear from the preparations that they were not going to feed him with leftovers.

He was doubly, triply glad now that on the way here he'd stopped to use the Midwinter gift of money his mother had sent to his room at the Collegium this morning (another guilt offering, perhaps) to buy gifts for everyone in the Chester household, from Granny on down. There was a Midwinter Fair in full swing outside the gate he'd left by, and he'd taken great care in selecting things he thought would please.

He presented them now, straight from the packs, in part to let their pleasure help erase the bitter memory of last night.

"I've got a few things for you all, to thank you for opening your home to me," he said, as he passed them out, casually, hoping that they would not think themselves obliged to respond in kind. "I hope you like them. Granny, these looked useful to me for stitching in the winter," he continued, handing Granny a set of gloves with cut-off fingers that left the last joint uncovered, made of chirra wool. He'd observed her rubbing her knuckles and wrists as if they ached, and he wondered if something like this would help. She tried them on, looking puzzled at first, and then delighted as the warmth penetrated her hands without impeding her dexterity. "And I *know* that these will help you, Ma."

This time what he handed out were another sort of gloves, or rather mittens, with leather palms, the kind that some smiths who worked very small pieces used to handle hot metal. She saw that they were intended for immediately.

"Oh! Just the thing for handling hot pans and things from the oven!" she exclaimed happily.

Yet another set of gloves for Pa Chester came out of the pack, this time work gloves thickly padded on the back, with rough leather palms, triple-stitched to prevent tools from slipping. These had been quite new to Lan, and from the admiration with which Pa regarded them, they were new to him. "Why didn't some'un think of this before?" he asked rhetorically, passing them to Ma and Granny to see. "Brilliant! These are jest brilliant!"

For the girls, Lan had brought various trinkets; a box of brightly colored or pearly shells from Lake Evendim to be made into ornaments and jewelry, a box of glass beads for the same purpose, a bunch of ribbons and a hank of lace; those were for the three oldest. And for the two youngest girls, doll heads of wax-over-porcelain, to replace the battered, featureless heads of two of their own dolls. Both little girls immediately rushed to their room to pick out the dolls to have the transplant. Glass-and-stone marbles in a pouch for the youngest boy, and new pocketknives for Tuck's three older brothers, each of whom solemnly presented him with a groat in exchange, in order that the knife not be a gift, for it was held that the gift of a knife would cut the friendship. And last of all, for Tuck, not a pocketknife, but a real dagger. Lan knew good steel when he saw it, and this dagger had been the outstanding example in a collection of lackluster second-hand blades. Tuck took it with his mouth dropping open, and almost forgot to get a groat to give him in return.

"You'll probably get your Whites long before I do, and I want you to have something to remind you that I'm still getting belabored by the Weaponsmaster," Lan joked. Tuck's radiant smile told him he'd picked the right present.

"Well, now, let's cap this by a good meal," Ma Chester said heartily. " 'Tis only a stewed bird, that nasty old hen that pecked at the girls one too many times, but I reckon revenge'll make her tasty!"

Lan couldn't believe that the hen had ever been old, for the meat fell off the bones, and all the fixin's that Ma had made to go with her were just as good. Lan ate with a much heartier appetite than he had yesterday, and when the dishes were cleared away and cleaned, he and Tuck went out for a ride before milking. Pa had promised to teach him how to milk—it looked like a very soothing sort of occupation—saying that no learning was ever wasted, and he might need to know how to some time.

"So was your Midwinter Feast really horrid?" Tuck asked sympathetically.

"It wasn't as bad as I thought it would be. I surprised my parents with the Formal Grays. Most of the family didn't know what to think of me, but the younglings thought I was the best entertainment they'd ever had." With a sigh, he urged Kalira into a canter, hoping that Tuck wouldn't ask any further questions. He didn't want to talk about the Jelnacks or Jisette Jelnack's accusations.

There was just enough truth in what she'd said to make him sick with guilt. No matter what, there was one thing that was irrefutable. If he had not lost control of his power, no one would be dead. It might have been an accident, but it was still because of him that it had happened.

Tuck didn't ask any more questions. Instead, he turned the conversation to what Lan wanted to do in the next few days.

"Well, the first thing I want is a good gallop!" Lan replied.

"What, so the wind can play a tune, whistling through your ears?" Tuck teased, and without warning, he set off in the lead.

The one thing he didn't have to worry about was that either Companion would step in a hole and break a leg. They seemed to know exactly what lay under the snow, and never put a foot wrong.

Kalira stretched out her neck and went into her top speed; Lan tucked his head down and held on for dear life, his heart pounding with excitement. It was wonderful, and just as wonderful, he had to concentrate on the mechanics of riding and couldn't think of anything else.

He wanted it to last forever; it couldn't, of course, but if he'd had his way, it would have.

When they finally returned to the farmhouse, Tuck filled up the silence with cheerful chatter of his own, mostly about past winters and the prodigies that had occurred. "If we're *really* lucky, we'll get snowed in and get a couple more days of holiday," he said, as they brought their Companions into the barn for a thorough grooming.

"And I think ye'll not, young jackanapes!" said Pa Chester from the back of the barn, where he was readying the stalls for the cows. "Never have heard of a snow so heavy yon Companions couldn't get through, so don't be thinkin' ye can cozen more free days that way!"

"Oh, *Pa*," Tuck moaned.

"An' none of that, neither. *If* there be a blizzard, I'll be callin' on ye both t'give me the truth of what yer Companions have t' say about it." Pa Chester came out of the stall and winked. "Now I'm thinking ye'd best get these fine ladies taken care of for the night, eh?"

"Yes, Pa," they both said obediently, and made sure that both of the "ladies" were groomed to the sheen of silver and well provided for.

"Now, Lan," Pa called, as the cows filed into the barn all on their own—it was a wonder to Lan that they could be trusted to come in out of the pasture all by themselves when milking time came, and each would go into her own stall and not that of another. Pa beckoned from the stall of a fine brown cow with a white blaze on her nose. "Come ye here."

Obediently, Lan gave Kalira a pat and went to the stall where Pa Chester waited.

"This 'un be Brownie." The farmer gave his charge a fond pat. Lan had already noticed that the names of the cattle did not show much imagination, but then, it didn't seem likely that a cow would ever demonstrate enough personality to require an imaginative name. "Now, set ye down on this stool, an' I'll show ye the trick of it. Brownie's a good gel, she won't be kickin' the pail over, nor tryin' to slap yer face wit' her tail. Be gentle wit' her, she'll be patient with' ye."

Pa Chester directed Lan to put his hands atop the farmer's so he could feel how the milk should be coaxed from the udder, with firm, steady, pulling strokes. Then he let Lan take over, and after a couple of fumbles, Lan found that he was milking just as well as Pa had. He leaned his forehead against Brownie's warm flank, breathing in the scent of fresh straw and warm milk, and watched the white streams hiss into the pail. It was somehow a very soothing experience, though by the time he'd filled the pail and Brownie had nothing more to give, he discovered that his hands were tired and a little sore.

He brought the pail to Pa Chester, who took it with a grin after a quick glance inside to measure the level by eye. "Good lad! Ye've a natural hand for it, I see. Fingers sore?"

Lan nodded, flexing them.

"That's expected. Takes practice, just like anything else. Think ye can do another?" Lan took a glance around and saw that Tuck had already joined his brothers at the chore, so he nodded, and Pa Chester gave him a new, clean pail and carried off the full one to the dairy house. Lan got his stool from Brownie's stall and wondered which cow he should try next.

"Take Swan, she's gentle, but watch her tail," Tuck called; Lan looked around at the nameplates until he found one for "Swan," with a white cow munching hay in the stall beneath it. He approached the heifer making the same soothing noises he'd heard the others make, and when she looked around at him with mild, curious brown eyes, he put one hand on her haunches and ran it along her side. He put his stool down beside her and got into position.

Just as he got his hands on her udder, something warned him to turn his head aside, and as he did, he caught a blow on the back of his head that stung. "Hey!" he said indignantly, as the cow turned her head guilessly to look at him again. "What was that about?"

"Warm your hands up; she hates cold hands," one of the other boys said. "Well, how would *you* like cold hands on you there?"

"I don't have a *there,*" Lan retorted, but he saw the point, and stuck his hands in his armpits until they were warmed up. This time when he tried his luck, Swan sighed and let down her milk for him.

He milked one more cow before his hands refused to cooperate anymore, but by then, most of the milking was finished anyway. He went into the dairy and washed up, then helped to pour the pans for rising; Pa and Ma insisted on a scrupulously clean dairy.

Dinner was concocted from the leftovers of the noon meal, but the food was no less tasty for coming around the second time. After dinner, one of the older boys showed Lan how to carve, using the old pocketknife that Lan's gift had replaced, and he spent the remainder of the evening whittling on what he hoped would be a reasonable boat for Tuck's youngest brother. This time Tuck took the turn at reading, and did a tolerable job at it. Granny kept holding up her warm hands to admire her fingerless gloves, which tickled him considerably, and before everyone went off to bed, Ma produced an apple pie and a wedge of cheese for a treat.

When Lan and Tuck went up to bed, though, Lan kept staring into the darkness, thinking about Jisette Jelnack, unable to sleep.

"Stop thinking so loud," Tuck whispered, finally. "You're keeping me awake."

"Am I really?" Lan whispered back, startled.

"Well, not thinking loud; I'm not *that* good a Mind-speaker. But you are keeping me awake. What's wrong? Was it something that happened back in Haven?" Tuck's acuity startled Lan; he hadn't expect that sort of insight from his friend. "You might as well tell me. If I don't get it out of you myself, Kalira will tell Dacerie and Dacerie will tell me."

"Isn't there anything secret to them?" Lan replied, both irritated and touched by his concern.

"No. Get used to it," Tuck replied promptly. "Now, spit it out so we can both get some sleep."

Slowly, reluctantly, Lan told him what had happened when he and Kalira had been waylaid by the Jelnacks, and for the first time, he told someone besides Pol just what had happened that night in the school. "What's bothering me is that she's right. I *am* responsible—"

"Huh." Tuck didn't immediately launch into assurance, which in a curious way, comforted him more than that assurance would have. He wasn't going to give Lan a comforting answer just because he was Lan's friend. . . .

"All right, I can see your point. And you *are* responsible; I mean, if they'd been picking on someone other than you, nothing would have happened. *But* that doesn't mean that the old bag is right either. You're *not* a murderer."

"How am I not—" he began, then stopped. "Because I didn't intend to kill them?"

"Right. And maybe that seems like an irra—erra—" Tuck searched for the word he wanted.

"Irrelevant?" Lan suggested.

"Right. That kind of difference. But it's not. It's a *big* difference." Tuck sounded quite sure of himself, and a moment later Lan found out why. "I've had First Level Judgment, and in the law there's a big difference. There's premeditated murder, and that's where the guy plans it out and goes and does it in cold blood, on purpose. Then there's simple murder, where maybe the guy gets into a fight with someone, and instead of backing off, gets a weapon out and kills the other guy. Now, that didn't happen with you, because you never got a chance to defend yourself, and you were ganged up on. That's the *law*. So you aren't a murderer."

Tuck was so sure of himself that Lan began to believe him. "So what am I?" he asked, uncertainly.

"I'm working that out; give a fellow a moment, I haven't even gotten a test on this yet!" Tuck replied a little crossly. "Now, what's next?" Silence in the darkness, then, "Ah! Got it. There's manslaughter, where a guy kills someone by accident, but that isn't you either, because it has to be someone helpless, and that toad Tyron wasn't helpless, *you* were. So what that leaves is accidental death in self-defense." Solid self-satisfaction filled Tuck's voice. "That's the one that fits, all right. *You* were the helpless one, you got ganged up on, they wouldn't let you go, and they were going to hurt you a lot. *You* couldn't help it if your Gift got away from you—heckfire, you didn't even know what it was and you hadn't got any training in it! How could you *do* anything with it? And how could anybody expect you to?"

"I don't know. . . ." Lan was still troubled, but Tuck wasn't listening to him, he was plowing straight ahead as if this was just another classroom exercise.

"Eyah, that's it. And the law says 'not guilty.' That's the *law*. You can't hold somebody responsible for what happens when they're pushed to the edge and things get out of hand." Now Tuck seemed to recollect that Lan was the subject of this exercise, and his voice took on a coaxing tone. "Honest, Lan, I'm positive on this one. Cross my heart!"

:I told you,: Kalira seconded. *:Now you're heard it from me, from Pol, and from Tuck. Would you like me to ask Rolan's opinion? I already know that Jedin would agree with Tuck, and for that matter, so does the King.:*

Lan gulped. The King? The *King* knew about him?

But when it all came down to it, it was Tuck, honest, clear-minded, transparent Tuck who convinced him. Tuck couldn't lie if he wanted to; it was as if a permanent Truth Spell was working on him. And *Tuck* was convinced of his innocence.

"I think I'm still going to feel horrid—" he ventured.

"Well, you'd be a miserable dog if you didn't!" Tuck retorted, "and I wouldn't be your friend anymore! But you don't have to feel guilty. So let's get some sleep; morning comes early around here."

"All right," he replied. "Thanks, Tuck."

"No problem," Tuck mumbled, already half asleep.

Lan yawned, closed his eyes, and after a few moments more of thought, followed Tuck's example.

SIXTEEN

WHEN everyone got back to the Collegium and back to lessons, no one said a word to Lan about his encounter at Midwinter. Lan breathed a great deal easier when it looked as if no one had heard a word about it. He really didn't want to say more to anyone than he had to; if the entire Collegium and Circle chose to ignore what had happened, he was perfectly happy to go along with that.

As classes resumed, he found himself absorbed more and more into the life of the Collegium. Tuck's circle of friends accepted him without question; he often ran into Elenor on walks or visiting her father. She had taken a great interest in him, probably because of her specialty. He reckoned that to a Mind-Healer he must be fascinating, given all of the horrible things that had happened to him. She was a nice girl, though, and didn't make it obvious. And she was good company.

Of all the places where he had lived, he felt most at home and happiest here. Even if he didn't always enjoy his classes, there were none he disliked, and most he found fascinating.

And above all things, there was Kalira. She was more wonderful every day; he often thought that he could happily live in a desert as long as she was with him.

The third week after Midwinter, he returned to his room to find a message waiting for him from his sister Macy. She wanted to pay him that promised visit. Since the day after the next was one where he usually had a free afternoon, he dashed off a quick reply to that effect, and made sure that he still did have that time free.

Not only did he have it, but Tuck did as well, and his friend volunteered to wait with him at the gate for Macy's arrival.

So the two of them waded through fresh snow up to their knees on the appointed afternoon, with more snow gently falling all around them. It was a particularly pretty, fluffy snow, falling through air that felt deceptively warm, covering bushes and coating the limbs of the trees. Daylight, filtered through clouds and falling snow, seemed to come from everywhere, gentle, soft, and pure. As they passed the Palace proper, courtiers and highborn were spread throughout the gardens, with the more high-spirited engaging in snow fights while the rest admired the scenery. Their handsome cloaks and coats of every possible hue, ornamented with fur and embroidery, made a fine show in the falling snow. The younger women, the Queen's handmaidens, dressed in various shades of blue ornamented with white fur and silver embroidery, watched and whispered among themselves as their suitors and would-be suitors showed off by pitching snowballs at targets and, occasionally, each other.

"Huh," Tuck said, amused. "They wouldn't think it was such fun if they couldn't duck back into the nice, warm Palace and have servants rush up to them with dry clothes."

"Probably not," Lan agreed. "But d'you know, there's no harm in them enjoying it either. Nothing better than a good snowstorm when you've got a nice fire in front of you—and who was it wanted us to get snowbound back home?"

"Dunno," Tuck replied, trying to look innocent and failing utterly.

They passed the formal gardens and the kitchen gardens, where the vegetable and herb beds, protected under mounds of straw, now had a smooth, insulating blanket of undisturbed snow on them that brought them up to the boys' waists. No one would dare plunder the kitchen gardens for snow for snowballs, not even during the hottest battle. The cooks and their helpers would have served a fricassee of the culprits' ears for dinner afterward.

A scraper pulled by a team of horses was clearing the road to the gate just as the boys got there, so the last part of their journey was on cleared paving. The Gate Guard was warming his feet at a brazier when they arrived, and greeted them cordially.

"Sister, eh?" the Guard said, when they explained their errand. "Older or younger?" A young man, well-muscled and good-natured, not terribly handsome but not ugly either, he obviously was not averse to a bit of flirting with a Trainee's sister.

"Younger," Lan replied, and the guard feigned disappointment, shaking his head so that snow that had accumulated on his fur cap fell around him in little clumps.

"And you've none older?" he persisted, grinning hopefully. "No chance there might be two sisters coming instead of one?"

"He doesn't, but I do," Tuck spoke up. "Two older sisters, very pretty, or so I'm told, and very friendly. And I *might* see my way clear to introducing them if you'd look the other way when I come in late some night—"

The Guard laughed and shook his head reprovingly at Tuck. "No use asking *me* to do that," he chuckled. "The ones they pick for night-watch are all older fellows, with daughters of their own, probably daughters the same age as your sisters! They don't take kindly to lads who want to sneak out to town for a bit of fun and overstay their curfew."

Tuck sighed gustily. "*Just* my luck!" he complained aloud. "I think I've finally got a use for the girls and it turns out they *still* don't do me any good!"

Lan interrupted any further complaints. "There she is now!" he exclaimed, waving, as he recognized Macy in her brown wool cloak edged with fox fur, driving up the road in a hired pony cart painted red. She handled the reins quite neatly, but then back at Alderscroft she had done a great deal of the marketing in her own little two-wheeled cart when their mother was too busy or too deep in a project to go.

She waved back, but didn't urge the pony to go any faster. Then again, she might already have discovered that it was difficult to get a hired beast out of a fast walk. Both pony and cart were plain and reliable, and exactly the sort of conveyance that Lan would have expected her to pick for herself.

"You didn't tell me she was pretty!" Tuck exclaimed, his green eyes as round as gooseberries, just before she got within earshot. Lan didn't bother with the obvious answer that it hadn't occurred to him; it also hadn't occurred to him that Tuck might be smitten with his sister. He certainly hadn't had that reaction with any of Tuck's siblings! *What a thought— Tuck taking a fancy to Macy! I wonder if she's likely to fancy him back? Wouldn't that be one in Mother's eye. I reckon she's got her mind set on wedding Macy off to some Guildmaster's son or even a highborn.*

Smitten or not, Tuck had recovered completely by the time Macy brought the cart to a halt in front of the gate and got out to let the Guard inspect her cart and its contents. Tuck introduced himself, jaunty as ever, without waiting for Lan to do the honors.

"Oh, you're the Trainee he was visiting!" Macy said in recognition, tucking her dark auburn curls under her hood. "That was awfully nice of you. I wish *I* had someone to go stay with over the holidays. It got quite horrible at times with all the children getting into fights over toys, Granny complaining and passing judgment on everything and everybody, and Mother wanting me to run errands for everybody, and never mind what I was already doing." She sighed. "I want a holiday like we *used* to have, without cramming more relations into the house than it can hold."

"Sounds right miserable," Tuck sympathized.

Instead of getting back in the cart when the Guard finished his inspection and waved her inside the Palace walls, she led the pony forward. "Mother had another Guild meeting at the house, and Cook baked an indecent number of honey cakes for it," she said to both boys, as Tuck and Lan walked on either side of her. "There were *piles* of leftovers, so I thought you and your friends might as well get the benefit of Mother trying to impress the other Guild members."

Lan caught the not-so-faint hint of exasperation in Macy's voice with surprise; evidently his sister was getting tired of their mother's obvious attempts at social climbing.

"I wish she'd go back to designing and stitching, and spend less time—or should I say, *waste* less time—toadying to anyone with any influence," Macy concluded. "I'm tired of having to dress up and interrupt *my* work to help hand around trays. I'm tired of interrupting my work to go run errands."

"I can understand that," Lan said soothingly. "Maybe what you ought to do is spend more time at the Guild Hall with the other apprentices instead. If you aren't there at hand in the house, if you're actually *in* a lesson with another Guild member, she can't drag you into helping when you should be learning. It would be dreadfully bad manners to take you away from a lesson with someone that might be her peer or superior, and if there's one thing Mother won't do, it's display bad manners."

"That's a good idea," Macy mused, brushing aside her hair with one hand as she led the placid pony with the other. "I mean, when we were back at Alderscroft, there wasn't anyone else to learn from but her, and nowhere else to work but at home, but that's not the case here."

Lan smiled. "You might even learn something she can't teach you. She doesn't know *every* technique, after all. I've never seen her knit a great deal, for instance."

Macy laughed and changed the subject. "She doesn't know fancy braiding. I learned that all by myself—which reminds me; here—"

Macy reached into a pocket of her coat, and pulled out a shining white, seamless band. "Here, this is for you," she said. "I made it from Kalira's hair, that's what I wanted it for."

Lan took it; the intricate braiding amazed him, and he literally could not see where the ends of each horsehair were. It looked to be about the size for a bracelet and he slipped it on over his wrist, smiling to feel Kalira's hair lying smoothly against his skin.

"See? Mother doesn't know how to do that." Macy was quite pleased with herself. "I made a set for myself, and everyone who sees it wants one."

Lan laughed. "Don't think you can make a business out of this!" he warned. "We can't have you denuding our Companions of hair just so silly women can wear jewelry made from it!"

Macy laughed, too. "I don't intend to make it from Companion hair; I'm going to see if I can't braid it from horsehair and silk yarn. I don't think *everyone* should have Companion hair, it's too special for that."

"Maybe fine silver wire," Tuck suggested speculatively. "Wire that fine would cost you, though."

"True, but it's a good suggestion." Macy beamed on him, and Tuck basked in her approval. "I could practice on copper at first; the maids would probably appreciate my practice pieces."

"How much of the Collegium do you want to see?" Lan asked, as they neared the stables for the ordinary horses. "We can leave the pony and cart here and come get them when you're ready to go home."

"All of it!" was Macy's reply.

So show her all of it, they did, from one end to the other, stopping at Lan's room to leave the laundry basket of honey cakes she'd brought him, for she really had not exaggerated the amount of leftovers. There would certainly be a merry little party in their section of the students' quarters tonight!

Macy was suitably impressed, and their friends were in turn quite taken with her. Lan lost no opportunity to display her handiwork, and she left with several skeins of Companion hair, each neatly labeled, and the commission to make more bracelets like Lan's. The Companions were just as taken with the notion as their Chosen, and quite insisted that she get more than she needed, even though it meant pulling perfect hairs afresh.

"Can I see Healer's and Bardic, too?" Macy asked when their tour was over. Lan scratched his head.

"I don't know anyone in Bardic, but there's someone in Healer's who could probably show us around, if she isn't busy," he said. "Let's go find out."

Tuck was not willing to let Macy do without his escort as well, so he came along as a willing third as they hiked across the grounds to Healer's Collegium. When they reached the building and stepped inside, Macy looked around with great interest. In the interest of cleanliness over anything else, the floors and walls were tiled in pale green ceramic, and the lighting was all accomplished with glass-chimneyed oil lamps. Healer's was a bit different from Herald's Collegium in that there were not as many structured classes as such. Instead, the Trainees did a great deal of study on their own, and worked directly with the teachers, one at a time, in each specialty, until they found the one they were best suited to.

As a consequence, there were not many classrooms, but there *were* a number of rooms in which animals suffering from various injuries and illnesses were housed. In the earliest stages of their training, Trainee Healers were rarely allowed to work on human patients, instead tending to animals brought to the Collegium by their owners. This aspect of the Collegium made it very popular with farmers and pet owners, and there was never a lack of subjects for them to learn their craft on. Even wild animals were sometimes brought here for tending.

Somehow, instead of resembling a crazed blend of barnyard and zoo, there was very little evidence of what these rooms were for out in the hallway. Peace and quiet reigned, with only the occasional call, bark, or whistle to show that the place was full of birds and animals. And as far as scent went, the stalls and cages were kept so scrupulously clean, as were the patients, that the only aroma was that of the clean straw used for their bedding, overlaid with the scent of herbs used to repel vermin.

Lan motioned for Tuck and Macy to stay near the entrance, while he asked several teachers or Trainees if any of them knew where Elenor was. As luck would have it, she was not far off at that very moment, and since the teacher in question was going in her direction anyway, he promised to tell her of Lan's arrival. Lan thanked him profusely as he bustled off.

They didn't wait long. Lan spotted Elenor at the end of the hallway hurrying toward them with a bright and expectant expression, and he waved at her. As she neared and saw he wasn't alone, for some reason she faltered, and her face lost some of its brightness.

"Elenor!" Lan called. "You know my friend Tuck, and this is my sister Macy. Macy wanted to get a tour of Healer's. Do you have time to give us one, or could you find us someone who can?"

"*Your* sister?" was Elenor's reply. "Not Tuck's? I thought Tuck was the one with all the sisters."

It was a curious question, or so it seemed to Lan, but since it didn't seem to signify anything, he assumed it was just curiosity. "No," he answered, grinning. "Macy's mine. She just looks more like Mother than I do."

"Which is a blessing," Macy retorted, poking him in the arm teasingly, "since you'd make an *ugly* girl!"

Elenor brightened back up again, and Lan decided that it was only shyness that had made her expression change. "As it happens, I have just enough time to show you about, and I would be happy to!" she said, and proceeded to give them a whirlwind tour.

Macy was fascinated, although she blanched a bit at the room where people were actually cutting into a dog to remove a growth, and backed out of the one where a wound that had gone bad was being cleaned out. Lan didn't blame her; it was a wonder to him how gentle Elenor managed to observe all of this with equanimity.

"I can't show you where the older Trainees treat people, of course," she said apologetically. "That would be rude to the people; they aren't on display, after all!"

"Well, I wouldn't want strangers who weren't even Healers parading into my room if I were ill either," Macy smiled. "Thank you very much for showing us around!"

"You are *quite* welcome!" Elenor said, gracing them with a dazzling smile of her own. "It's nice to meet some of Lan's family."

Lan traded a glance with Macy; she grimaced.

"Some of Lan's family who don't want to treat him like a freak, that is," Macy replied. "I can't believe how well he kept his temper at the Feast."

Elenor raised her eyebrows in a way that suggested she agreed with Macy, but didn't say anything.

Elenor had to be about her own duties, so she left them at the door and hurried back to whatever she had to do. Macy walked between Lan and Tuck into a garden so quiet that every tiny creak of a snow-laden branch was clearly audible. Snow was still falling, and the fading light warned that Macy would have to start back soon if she wanted to be home by dark.

She kept giving Lan the oddest looks out of the corner of her eyes as they walked toward the stables to get her pony and cart.

"How long have you known Elenor?" she asked finally.

"She was one of the first people I met, while I was still hurt," he said, wondering why she asked. "Her father is Herald Pol, the one who's my—I guess you'd call him a mentor."

"Ah," she said, as if that explained far more than just the content of his words. Then she turned to Tuck, and began plying him with questions, until Lan completely forgot her curious behavior by the time they had reached the stables.

THE tack room of the Companions' stable was perhaps not the best place for Lan's first lesson in using his Gift, but it was the only one that would work at all. It was absolutely too cold to try to teach Lan outside, for Pol didn't have the strength to teach him and keep them both warm at the same time. The first consideration in this set of lessons was that Kalira had to be with him, which ruled out most of the rooms in the Collegium. He'd asked for a tiled room in Healers, but there wasn't one available. That left the tack room, the only heated place in the stables that wasn't also too near stored straw and other flammable substances. Pol wished that it was spring, when these lessons could have been held safely outdoors, but this was too urgent to wait until spring. Just to be on the safe side, though, he had a pail of water nearby.

Not that a pail of water is going to make much differ-

ence if he really *loses control . . .* Pol told himself sternly to dismiss the idea. Kalira had already demonstrated she could control Lan's power. If he let himself doubt that she could, he could undermine her ability to continue to do so.

So he sat down at a small table, across from his pupil, and put himself in the calmest and most confident state of mind he could conjure. Lan looked up at him and smiled, faintly, and reached out to touch Kalira who stood at his elbow.

"This is the usual first step for a Firestarter," Pol said, placing a small piece of oil-soaked lint in the middle of a saucer in front of Lan. "Needless to say, in your case, the reason we're starting small is not because you need to increase your power—" here he raised an ironic eyebrow at Lan, who flushed, "—but because you need to increase your control. Or rather, you and Kalira need to work together so that you two can accomplish something besides blasting. So. Light this gently. You'll probably get a reaction-headache, Lan, unless Kalira has managed to work out how to keep that from happening too."

Kalira gave Pol a distinctly superior look, which made Pol wonder just what she had been concocting. Companions had this addiction to secrecy sometimes . . . and took a distinct delight in coming out of nowhere with a surprise for their Chosen.

:What is she up to?: he asked Satiran, who stood just behind him, watching the proceedings.

:I have no idea,: his Companion replied. *:You know children. When they're planning something, the last person they tell is a parent.:*

Lan bit his lip and stared at the bit of lint apprehensively.

"I expect you're going to have to get worked up about something," Pol told him. "It's going to be a while before you can access the power of your Gift without getting emotionally—"

"Overwrought," Lan supplied, unhappily.

"Well, yes. But just remember that when you two *do* get it under control, it's going to be easier to access, reliable, and very useful." Maybe it wasn't such a bad thing that Lan was unhappy about his Gift, seeing that it was so linked with emotions. . . .

"Try it," he urged. "The only way things are going to get better for you is to get everything under control."

"And the only way to get control is to practice." The boy sighed, but nodded. "Right." He closed his eyes.

Pol was enough of an Empath to feel the unhappiness that Lan was conjuring out of his memories. The tension increased moment by moment, and Pol's stomach tightened in response.

Time crawled by, and Pol's shoulders and neck began to knot up as well. He felt sweat trickling down his back, nervous sweat, since it certainly wasn't that warm in the tack room. Soon it was at the point where he began to worry that Kalira's confidence was *over*-confidence, that the plate would explode in his face in a moment. Lan's face reflected anger, fear, and unhappiness, and Pol had to force himself to remain where he was, looking calm and confident in case Lan looked up.

He felt as if *his* head was about to burst.

Then it happened. With a tiny sigh, the bit of fluff in front of him blossomed into a lovely flame that unfolded like a flower to feed on the lint and the oil.

Lan's shoulders slumped and his eyes opened; the anger drained from his face, then the fear, and he looked at the little flame with wonder.

"I—we did it!" he said, with great surprise. "And my head doesn't hurt!"

:*I should hope not,*: Kalira said smugly, for the benefit of both the Heralds. :*I've been working on that. If I hadn't been, you'd have been waking up with a reaction-headache every time you had a bad dream.*:

She tossed her head proudly and arched her neck, waiting for Pol to congratulate her.

"Aha! You clever girl, you! You've found the key, it's to take care of the problem before it's a problem!" Although Lan still looked baffled, Pol understood immediately. "You're draining off energy as he produces it!"

:And leaving just enough for him to use. Right now I'm directing it, too, but if you let him link in and show him what to do, all I'll have to do is manage the draining.: Kalira had lost a bit of the smugness, but she was still very proud of herself, as well she should be. It was the best possible solution for now, although poor Lan would have to weather a great many emotional ups and downs in order to access his power.

"How are you doing?" Pol asked. Lan chewed on his lip, and looked anxiously at his mentor, but slowly the anxiety was fading.

"My stomach's upset, but I guess I'm all right," he admitted.

:A cup of tea from Elenor will take care of that,: Kalira soothed, though to Pol's experienced ear, she also sounded just a trifle impatient with her Chosen. She knew they could do this, now, and she wanted him to keep trying.

Lan didn't, but he knew that if he wasn't able to learn to control this ability, it would control him. It already had twice, after all, and he knew the consequences of that. While he thought, the bit of lint flared and went out, leaving a tiny pile of ashes.

"Let's . . . do it again," he said at last.

"Good lad!" Pol replied, and replaced the bit of lint on the saucer. "Now, try again."

This time, it seemed to be a little easier. It certainly didn't take as long. Pol ran him through the exercise a few more times before changing the focus.

"Right; let's take a break here—or at least, a break for you." Pol smiled at Lan's look of relief. "Kalira will link you in to me, and you'll see *how* this is done."

"Why can't Kalira show me?" Lan wanted to know. "If she can control the power, why can't she show me how to do it myself?"

:Because I'm not handling the power the way that you and Pol will,: Kalira replied. *:I'm doing something only a Companion can do. We're born in energy and live in it all the time, that's why we're white. This kind of energy bleaches every live thing that it contacts after a time.:*

"It is?" Lan asked, intrigued. Even Pol was intrigued; this was new information to him. Usually Companions revealed very little about themselves; he hadn't realized that they were so intimately involved with the force behind the Gifts.

:Indeed. You can't dye us either,: she chuckled. *:We bleach right out in a few days.:*

"Annoying of you," Pol put in. "It would be so much more helpful to Heralds who are trying to gather information unobtrusively if you could just become an ordinary chestnut color once in a while."

:Learn from adversity, Herald; we won't do everything for you.: Kalira was still highly amused, and Pol sensed that Satiran was, too.

But her sire was willing to put up with only so much insolence from his offspring. *:Respect your seniors, Companion,:* the stallion chided. *:At this point in his life, Pol has accomplished more than you have ever dreamed of doing. Let's get on with this.:*

:Sir!: she replied promptly; obedient, but with a hint of amusement, still.

Pol felt Kalira form the link between himself and his pupil. This way Lan was not directly in his mind, nor was he in Lan's. This was a much better way of dealing with the task; he didn't want Lan privy to his uncensored thoughts, and he certainly didn't want to experience the poor lad's uncensored emotions.

He shifted his concentration to the lint, not that he had to concentrate a great deal. What he did have to do was slow things down so that Lan could see exactly what happened.

It wasn't spectacular; basically, it was very similar to using the Fetching Gift at a very tiny scale. Although he no longer had to think about how he did this, he *vibrated* the materials until the heat they generated ignited them. He moved infinitesimal bits of the oil and lint so that they rubbed against each other, creating heat by friction, until the lint burst into flame.

When the lint flamed, he looked up at Lan, and saw the Trainee's eyes narrowed, his brow furrowed with concentration, but his mouth forming a slight "o" of surprise.

"So *that's* what's happening!" he said, looking up into Pol's eyes.

"Basically, yes; just very, very quickly. And in your case, it's—" he tried to think of an analogy, "—hmm. Like an avalanche instead of a single, aimed stone. You just pour out power, and everything in its path goes up in flames. Things that are very flammable burn immediately, things that are around or near fire have flames jump to them, channeled by the power."

Lan winced, but nodded. Pol was deliberately reminding him of what had happened, because he also wanted these sessions to desensitize Lan to what had happened by accident—

—because one day, he might have to do it on purpose. He couldn't keep wincing away from creating a major fire. He had to be able to create it when and where it was needed, even offensively.

Pol was privy to information known only to the King, the King's Own, and a few other, carefully selected members of the Council. What no other Herald teacher in the Collegium knew was that the situation on the Border with Karse was getting more serious with every passing day. They were taking advantage of the milder southern climate to increase their probes along the Border. If there was a war—ready or not, Lan might be needed.

Trained or not, he may be needed. It was a sobering thought, and one that kept Pol lying wakeful at nights. If—no, *when* war came, more Trainees than Lavan would be thrown into Whites, all unready, and sent out to the South. More young Healers would follow; and young volunteers to the Guard.

Best to end it quickly, and for that, it might be necessary to unleash Lavan Chitward's power, unchecked, unhindered, in all its ferocity.

"So, do you think that if Kalira controls the amount of energy you get, you can replicate what I just did?" Pol asked.

Lan drummed his fingers restlessly, his eyes looking off at some far distant point while he sorted things through in his own mind. "Not yet," he decided. "Can you show me again, three or four more times, I mean?"

"Certainly." Pol was actually relieved to hear Lan's caution. "Kalira, if you would be so kind? Link and hold the link for four repetitions of the exercise?"

:*Certainly, Pol,*: Kalira said cheerfully. She insinuated the link with great skill and delicacy; Pol spared a moment to admire her touch.

Four times, he ignited tiny balls of lint, going so slowly that it was possible to see a minute coal form at the heart of the ball before the flame rose. Four times, Lan "watched" with his eyes closed in concentration. The third and fourth time, the furrows in his brow eased, and he nodded slightly when the lint caught fire.

After the fourth iteration, he looked up and smiled.

"I can do it, Herald," he said with confidence. "Let me try again, doing it right."

Pol placed another lint ball on the altar of sacrifice, and Lan stared at it.

In three heartbeats, as Lan's smile increased to a grin, it was nothing but ash.

Pol was flatly astonished. He had *never* had any

pupil with one of the odder Gifts catch on so quickly before.

On the other hand, their problem was usually in accessing their power, not in controlling it.

Only young Malken has had the same problem as Lan, it occurred to him. *And Malken is* not *ready to control it.* Poor Malken had been so overwhelmed by his ForeSight that Herald Evan had finally decided to shut it down altogether. It was a temporary measure, but until the child was older and stronger, there was no way he could understand what he was seeing and why he was seeing it so he could control it. *"I am not risking a child's sanity,"* Evan had said flatly. *"Nothing is worth that."*

He'd gotten no argument from anyone on that score.

Pol lined up lint balls, directing Lan to ignite them in a specific sequence; after a bit of fumbling, Lan did just that. He made the piles of lint bigger, then smaller. Finally, he took the bucket of water, extinguished the tack-room fire, and had Lan relight it with the remainder of the lint as kindling. In order to get the now-wet wood going properly, Lan had to concentrate his force on the fire until the water had evaporated and the wood could burn.

"Enough!" Pol ordered when that exercise was over. Lan was pale, but triumphant; he looked eager to keep going, but Pol knew weariness when he saw it. "That's enough for the first day, Lavan. Quite enough. We'll start on real targets and more distant targets tomorrow. How are you feeling?"

"Tired. And my stomach's in knots," Lan said truthfully. "I don't like having to get angry like this, but— but I don't think I have to get quite as angry now as I did when we started."

"That's good." Pol hoped he was right. "Go on back to the Collegium and your classes; I'll clean up, and I'll see you here tomorrow."

Lan turned to go, and Pol called after him, "No practicing on your own, promise me!"

"I promise," Lan called back over his shoulder. "No fear."

:I wish that was the only thing we had to worry about, Chosen,: Satiran said soberly.

Pol sighed. "The sooner we can say he's fully trained, the more likely he is to be sent out—" He shook his head. "Gods. Now I know how the Weaponsmaster feels."

:I always did,: said Satiran, and left it at that.

SEVENTEEN

Weaponsmaster Odo

POL paused for a moment with one hand on the latch of his room, and the other massaging his own shoulder. The hallway was cold, and his room would be warm, but he was very nearly too tired even to open his own door. It had been a long day; a very, very long day. Why *he* should have been selected to be on the elite committee of Those Who Knew What Was Going On With Karse—

Bother. He knew why. Lavan Chitward—or Firestarter, as the King had begun to call him—was the reason why good old dependable Herald Pol should suddenly be counted among the important minds of this land. The boy was shaping up to be a very important player in the coming war, and Pol was his teacher, his mentor, and his friend. Pol's Companion was the sire to Lavan's Companion, giving him yet another source of insight into Lavan's young mind. If Pol and Satiran knew what was coming, they could prepare the boy to face it.

Pol was dancing on the edge of his energy, though; he was forced to juggle teaching, tutoring Lavan, and meetings with the Select Council, along with whatever incidental tasks came up. He wasn't young anymore, and his body reminded him of that sad fact rather frequently these days.

So, for that matter, did Satiran, who nagged him about slowing down at least once a day. Not that there was anything Pol could do about it. His body, mind, and spirit were not his to command.

At last he opened the door of his room, and stared in bewilderment to see his daughter Elenor in her mother's chair by the fire, waiting patiently for him, with a tray full of covered dishes beside her.

"Elenor! What are you—" He stopped himself in mid-sentence and shook his head in mingled disbelief and dismay. He *couldn't* have forgotten the weekly dinner they always shared, could he? "It's not—I thought it was—"

"Yes, Father, you've lost track of time again," Elenor sighed. "When you didn't come to Healers', I knew you'd forgotten what day it was. I also thought that you'd probably forget you were supposed to have dinner at all, so I had one of the servants bring dinner here."

The fire crackled cheerfully as Pol shook his head at his own forgetfulness, and took his chair across from hers. "I'm glad you did. I'm so tired I probably would have just opted for some fruit and cheese."

"Assuming you remembered to eat anything before you went to sleep." Elenor began uncovering the platters and fixing a plate of food for him. "I won't ask why they're running you out like this, but I hope it ends soon."

He didn't say anything; he couldn't. He knew very well that the secret meetings wouldn't end until the entire Kingdom knew that Valdemar was at war with Karse—and then, it wouldn't just be meetings that she would be worrying about. The only thing he could do was something he already had done. He'd extracted a promise from Theran that Elenor would never have both parents on the front lines of the fighting at the same time. This was not to say that they wouldn't both be down near the Border, but they would never be near the fighting simultaneously.

Elenor had ordered a wonderful meal, and he gave it its due attention, although he didn't neglect conversation to do so. He told her what he could of the doings of Circle and Collegium, and she shared stories of the interesting or the funny from her end of the grounds. But when they reached the dessert, Elenor brought up a subject he had not been anticipating.

"So, has Lavan found a sweetheart among the Trainees?" she asked, so casually that Pol didn't believe for a moment that she felt casual about the subject.

Oh, gods, no—he thought, with a sinking heart. There was only one thing that could prompt a question like that; Elenor was smitten with the boy. *Oh gods. Grant that it isn't serious yet.* His tired mind, which had been sinking into a state of comfortable relaxation, suddenly lurched into frantic activity again. He knew from his experiences with her older sisters that the last person a girl confides her romantic hopes to is her father. Somehow, some way, he had to dissuade her from setting those hopes on Lavan Firestarter. Assuming it wasn't already too late.

But what to say?

"He's not going to. You're more like to see that fire iron take a sweetheart," Pol settled on, with a yawn to cover his anxiety. Above all, the one thing he must not do was appear opposed to her infatuation. Nothing watered and fed the young plant of love like parental opposition.

"Oh, come now, Father, you are never going to convince me he's *shaych*," she replied with a laugh, that faded as he didn't reply. "Is he?" she faltered.

It was so tempting to let her believe that, but she was a Healer, and she would be able to figure the truth of that out for herself without too much difficulty. "No, he's not *shaych,*" Pol replied, and interrupted her sigh of relief with, "But he might just as well be. Any girl who pins her hopes on him as a sweetheart is going to have her heart broken. He's already lifebonded."

He hoped that Elenor would leave things at that, but no. She looked at him sharply, as the fire flared beside her. "I thought you said he didn't have a sweetheart—oh, she's not in the Trainees?" Her brow wrinkled with puzzlement and annoyance. "But he hasn't seen anyone but his sister—" And now her expression turned to one of horror. "He *can't* be lifebonded to his *sister?*"

She jumped to her feet; Pol rose and grabbed both her elbows, holding her fast, so that she had to look into his eyes. "Elenor, listen to me. Lavan is lifebonded to Kalira. There is absolutely no doubt of it."

"Kalira?" She stood very, very still, and he let go of her arms. "Kalira? His *Companion?*"

Pol sat down heavily, and she copied him unconsciously. He nodded, watching her closely. "Kalira. His Companion. There is no room in his life or his heart for any other female except as a friend."

Firelight created changing shadows over her face, a face whose expressions changed as quickly as the shadows. "But that's not possible," she said aloud, hardly seeming to be aware that she was speaking. "That can't be possible."

"It is possible, and it is the truth." Pol said bluntly, now hoping to hammer his point home with repetition.

"But *Kalira*—" She turned her eyes toward her father entreatingly. "A Companion isn't human—a Companion can't be—" She flushed a bright crimson. "A Companion can't—she isn't *human*—"

He decided to be as obtuse and diplomatic as possible. "It doesn't matter. Not when they're lifebonded. They are bound to each other in a way that nothing can change."

But Elenor wasn't going to take the hint. "A Companion isn't a *woman*. Kalira can't be what I—ah, a woman can be!"

"Elenor, it doesn't matter. Listen to me; I *know*. I'm not speculating, I *know*. It. Does. Not. Matter." He leaned forward and took her hands before she could withdraw them, using every voice trick and Gift he had mastered in all his years as a Herald to make her listen and believe. "He will never love a human as anything other than a friend. Don't lose your heart to him, because you'll only end up breaking it over this, and it won't be his fault that you do. I'll comfort you, but I won't sympathize with you."

Her expression gradually settled to one of dazed confusion. He let her hands go, then, and she put her right to her temple. "I just—it doesn't—" she faltered. Then she rose slowly. "I think I'd better go get some rest."

"I think you should, too," he replied soothingly, putting his arm around her as he escorted her to the door. He kept his own feelings behind hard shields; the last thing she needed was to sense *his* aching heart, she already had her own to deal with. "It's been a long day for both of us. Thank you for dinner; I enjoyed it very much, and your company."

She came to herself long enough to give him a wan smile and a kiss on the cheek. "Thanks, Father. I love you, too."

He closed the door behind her, and leaned against it, waiting until she was long gone from the building, well on her way to Healers' Collegium, and as preoccupied as she was, unlikely to sense *his* emotions.

He let his shields down, and metaphorically leaned on Satiran's shoulder, his heart surely as sore as Elenor's was. *My poor baby!* Even if it was only infatuation, it *hurt,* and she'd never had her heart wounded before. Just now, all she knew was grief; she didn't know that grief can heal, or that some can be greater than others. First love was no less real than mature love, and first heartbreak hurt worse. He buried his

head in his hands and hot tears of the sorrow only a
parent can know for the hurts of his child slipped
through his fingers.

:*There is nothing harder than being a father or
mother,:* Satiran said, with an understanding deeper
than the words could ever reach.

:*Yes,:* he replied, and with that one word said all
that could be said.

LAN always thought that this was the saddest part of
the year, the time when it seemed that winter would
never end. The excitement of Midwinter was over;
hard-packed snow blanketed the ground, and an un-
ending sea of gray cloud blanketed the sky. The cold
was relentless, leaking in around door- and window-
frames, sending unexpected chills down the back. You
couldn't escape it, except in bed, and you knew that
when you woke up again, you'd be battling it from
the time you turned back the covers.

Lan hated this time of year. There was nothing to
look forward to; the days dragged on with soul-
deadening sameness until, at last, spring arrived, and
it was impossible to believe in spring when the ground
was frozen rock-hard.

That was not so much the case this year—although
he often felt he teetered on the edge of failure. He
had progressed beyond merely igniting a few lowly
bits of lint, and in the Collegium at least, his Gift was
no longer a secret.

They were starting to call him "Lavan Firestarter,"
a name that pleased him and made him feel queasy
at the same time. He didn't in the least mind shedding
his surname, but he wished that this new one was
less—sinister.

Many things made him uneasy and uncertain about
this new role that Fate had cast him in. Heralds did

so much more than he had ever dreamed they did! Not that Heralds had crossed his mind so much before all of this, but it had never occurred to him that they were more than the mouthpieces of the King.

That was what was occupying his mind as he trudged back from his last class—which was a combined lesson for him and some of the final-year students. *They* were doing archery practice; *he,* however, had taken his Gift into the realm of the practical.

The scenario was simple enough. The archers were firing at moving targets. *He* was trying to incinerate the arrows before they hit those targets. The archers were not launching their arrows singly anymore, but in volleys, as they would in combat. So it wasn't just one arrow he had to get, but many.

He was exhausted. Today he'd had to take a long walk with Kalira after the lesson, to cool down the terrible anger he'd had to raise. It made him feel sick—but something about the cloaked anxiety of his mentor Herald Pol told him that there was a reason, a good one, for the relentless pace being set for him. That in itself worried him. Something was going on, something that no one was talking about openly.

And yet, he seemed to be the only one of the Trainees that was aware of the subcurrent. Everyone else went to classes, to meals, gossiped, complained, and went on with their lives just as they always had.

The regular class load was bad enough without this added, unacknowledged pressure. Heralds did so much! With the Bards, they passed on news, but theirs concentrated on the edicts of law and government. They made certain that everyone actually understood new laws and decrees. They acted as judges and juries, but also investigated crime, or suspected crime. They went for help when needed, for nothing in the Kingdom could travel as fast as a Herald and Companion. They organized and trained local militia; they led militia when something more than simple home defense was needed. They carried secret messages, they acted as spies, and very rarely, as assassins. Some with very specific Gifts—such as his—worked with the Guard and army. They were posted as diplomats, or as adjuncts to diplomats. They had to know geography and history, not only of Valdemar but of the lands around it. Mathematics, orienteering and navigation, rudimentary artifice, sleight-of-hand, literature, manners, the whys and wherefores of many religions—these and many more disparate classes filled his days and nights with study.

No one person could do and be all these things, but that was why everyone had at least rudimentary lessons in them. How could you know what you were good at if you didn't at least try it?

But, oh, the burden of all those classes!

He thanked the gods for a mentor like Herald Pol, who understood as no one else could exactly how much stress he could bear without cracking. A few days ago, Pol had gotten together with all of his teachers and laid down certain guidelines—which included the order that no one, absolutely *no one* was to assign him after-class work for the evening after a Gift-practice. That had given him some breathing space, sorely needed. He'd also arranged that Lan got a tray in his room on those evenings, rather than eating with the rest of the Collegium. His nerves were just too raw to bear the company of even his closest friends so soon after the lessons.

:Oh, my dear, you'll feel better after a hot meal,: Kalira said cheerfully. *:And you have all of the evening for yourself.:*

:I wish it was warm again,: he fretted. He still was not much of a reader unless he read aloud to an audience. That was as much because he had discovered a pleasure in acting things out for others—which would probably thoroughly horrify his mother if she knew, for she would be certain that he was going to have a second career as a mountebank. There was far less pleasure in reading alone.

:*You need something active to do,*: Kalira acknowledged. :*But something other than riding. You're getting
quite enough of that, I think.*:

:*I never get enough of you, Kalira,*: he said obliquely.

:*But you've had quite enough of riding in Companions' Field, I know,*: she laughed. :*Get something to
eat, warm up, and see if you can find something to
read. And if you can't—maybe there are enough of
your friends free to play some taroc.*:

Being warm surely sounded attractive right now. He
was always warm enough when he was using his Gift,
but as soon as he stopped, all the energy ran out of
him and his feet and hands grew cold and numb in
no time, no matter how many gloves and socks he
wore. At least Kalira kept him from having reaction-
headaches now.

He stamped his boots clear of snow at the door, but
little trails of melted water showed that not all of his
fellow Trainees had remembered to do so. There was
a Trainee down at the other end of the hall with a
mop and bucket, remedying the situation until a servant could do a proper job.

The warmth of his room didn't penetrate to the chill
core of him until he had taken off his cloak and boots
and settled down to his tray at the fire. And it wasn't
until he'd finished eating that he saw the small white
square of a note on the floor just inside his door; there
was a bit of boot print on one corner, so he must have
trod right over it when he came in.

He got out of his chair and picked it up, unfolding
it. The paper was soft, erased and reused many times,
since paper was too expensive to be wasted in the
Chitward household.

Lan, I want to go skating in the moonlight, it read,
*and Mother won't let me unless I've got an escort. Sam
said he's too busy; have you got the evening free? Besides, I want to talk with you in private. If you can,
come straight to the house. Macy.*

Well, if that wasn't exactly what he'd been hoping

for! He liked to skate, and hadn't out skating in ages, not since back in Alderscroft. His skates should still be in the storage box in his room, along with a few other belongings.

:Very good!: Kalira enthused, "looking" over his shoulder. *:It's only just dusk, we should get there in plenty of time for a couple of candlemarks of skating. And you can bring your skates back here with you, after. That will give you something active to do. I'll go nudge up one of the grooms, and I'll meet you at the door.:*

Yes, and he probably could organize some of the others for games on the ice, once he started skating at the Collegium. Broom-ball was always fun; skates weren't that hard to come by, you could always make a pair of wooden runners if you didn't have the ready money to buy steel ones. He thought with pleasure of being able to show Tuck how to skate, if he didn't already know how.

Feeling much more cheerful and ready to go, he pulled a heavy knitted garment, shapeless, but warm, over his shirt and canvas tunic, shoved his feet into his boots, and threw his cloak on over all. He left his tray outside the door to be picked up later, and headed back out again, pulling on his gloves as he walked.

The Trainee with the mop was nowhere in sight, but the floor was dry and clean again. He met the cold at the door with determination that brightened when he saw Kalira waiting for him.

:What do you suppose Macy wants to talk about?: Kalira asked, as they passed the Guard, who waved at them as they went by.

:I'm not sure,: he replied. It was so *quiet* out here—he was getting used to the constant buzz of the Collegium, and even in Alderscroft in the middle of winter there were noises from the forest and barns. Here in the heart of Haven, where he had least expected it, he found silence. The homes of the wealthy, enclosed

behind their walls, only showed that they were inhabited by the shadows moving in the curtained, lighted windows. Even the sound of Kalira's hooves was muffled by the packed snow, and he was reluctant to break the silence by speaking.

:She's not the only one who wants to talk in private, though,: Lan continued. *:I want to talk to her about Elenor.:*

The young Healer had been acting very peculiar, to his way of thinking. One moment she was friendly and her normal self, the next, withdrawn and watching him with the most peculiar expression. Tuck was no help; he was completely infatuated with Macy, and kept turning the conversation back to Lan's sister. And he hadn't been able to talk to Macy alone, because whenever she visited the Collegium, Tuck was with them every step of the way.

:Hmm. Not a bad idea. I haven't been with you enough to see how she's acting,: Kalira admitted. *:Macy is probably the best one to ask. I hope Elenor isn't worried because there's something wrong with her father; Satiran doesn't tell me much.:*

That could well be the case. *:Pol's been looking strained and rather seedy lately,:* he replied, now concerned himself. *:I hadn't thought of that. You don't think he's sick, do you?:*

:Not sick, but overworked, and certainly there is something that has him very concerned, enough to prey on him night and day.:

That got Lan's attention. *:I wonder what's on his mind? I hope it isn't me—I mean, I hope I'm not getting horribly behind or something—:*

:Something to do with the Kingdom, not you, Chosen,: Kalira assured him immediately. *:They've put him on the Privy Council, I'm not sure why, but he's spending a great deal of time in meetings.:* She looked back at him over her shoulder, and cocked her ears at him.

:Ah,: Lan said, relieved, and dismissed Pol from his

concern. If it was Kingdom business, there was nothing *he* could do about it.

The uncomfortable silence in the residential district gave way to sound as he and Kalira entered the first street of shops. But here they ran into a slight problem. A furniture shop was taking a delivery—a very bulky delivery—and the street was blocked. A wagon loaded with massive, carved furniture, pulled by four oxen, had backed up to the store front, probably because the wagon was too large to fit into the alley behind it. The wagon and its team completely crossed the street. Nothing bigger than a cat was going to get by for a while. They stopped, and Lan eyed the blockage.

:Bother,: Kalira said cheerfully. *:Well, no matter. I know a way around, but we'll have to go through a rather rotten district.:*

:Rotten or not, they're not stupid enough to bother a Trainee,: Lan replied. *:Are they? I mean, most people know we could call for help.:*

:I was just pointing that out because you'll probably see a lot of unpleasant things.: Kalira sighed. *:You won't like it. It was one thing to be poor in a little village like yours; it's entirely another to be poor in a city. Even Haven has its share of thieves, beggars, and ne'er-do-wells.:*

:But as a Herald, there's going to be a lot of things I won't like. I might as well get used to it. And if there's something going on that somebody should know about, then we can call for help.: That seemed perfectly reasonable to him, and Kalira evidently agreed, for she shook her head and cut down a side street.

The problem with Haven was that once you got off the main thoroughfares, you couldn't necessarily get from one place in the city to another very easily. It was designed that way, to confuse invaders and force them to divide their numbers, thus rendering them more vulnerable to the defenders. Valdemar was long past the time when anyone needed to think about invaders taking Haven, but the main part of the city could not be changed at this late date. Shops and houses were backed not by alleys, but by continuous walls. The only way to get into an alley was through the building. This would be another unpleasant surprise for an invader, and another opportunity to trap small parties of invaders and finish them off.

Lan had no idea of how to get through this maze, but Kalira did, so he relaxed and let her pick out the way. Within a very short period of time, he was in an entirely new sector; a farmer's market. It was empty now, the stalls holding nothing more than a few wilted cabbage leaves or chicken feathers, but the faint scents and the arrangement told him what it was. Kalira picked her way through it daintily, and exited the area through an alley on the other side.

This was another residential district, but a poorer one than Lan had seen before. No silence here; babies squalled, adults quarreled, drunks sang, children played or fought, all at the tops of their lungs. There was light, but it was from oil torches, fueled with something that smoked and had an unpleasant smell. There was no glass in the windows to keep out the cold; just shutters, most of them with rags stuffed into cracks.

Another sound broke through the general babble; the sound of a serious fight. Ahead, two gangs of boys clashed, fists and feet flying—and landing, with muffled *thuds*. They screamed at each other at the tops of their collective lungs, adding to the din. Shutters all up and down the street flew open; people leaned out of the windows, gawking, then shouting to the boys and each other, some laying bets on the outcome.

:*Another detour, I think,*: Kalira said promptly; she increased her pace to a trot, and made a quick turn into yet another side street. He could see, as the noise died away, that this was a dead end, culminating in a cul-de-sac with one of the oil torches at the end.

:*No worries,*: Kalira said cheerfully. :*We just nip*

down this alley and come back out on another street.:
She suited her actions to her words, and made a quick
turn into a dark alley. The only light came from the
street behind them, and Lan looked nervously back
over his shoulder. It was as dark as the inside of a
black bag in this alley, and suddenly Lan was no
longer so confident that as a Heraldic Trainee his
safety was a certainty.

The alley was awfully long—

And why couldn't he see light at the other end?

Then it was obvious why, as Kalira suddenly
stopped, ears up in surprise and radiating annoyance;
this alley was a dead end as well, with a wooden barri-
cade built across it, a few arm's lengths from Kalira's nose.

:This isn't supposed to be here!: she said in indignant
surprise, when a faint sound behind and the flare of
light above alerted both of them.

Kalira spun on her heels; two light baskets now
hung from chains coming from second-story windows
on either side of the alley, and between them and the
exit was a group of villainous-looking men with bows,
arrows already nocked to the strings. Six? Eight?
Too many—

Gods!

Lan sat frozen with shock, unable to do more than
stare as they aimed, and let fly.

Kalira was not so paralyzed; she darted to one side,
writhing to avoid the falling arrows, quick as falcon
and lithe as a mink. She reared up on her hind legs
and twisted her forequarters to the side to present the
smallest possible target. Somehow Lan managed to
hang on, bending over her neck and clinging to her
with both hands tangled tightly into her mane, and
somehow he managed to remain untouched by the
half-dozen arrows.

Kalira was not so lucky.

With a shock they both felt, a bolt struck her hindquarters, driving in deeply in a lance of pain they

shared. She shied sideways and screamed, and Lan screamed with her—it felt as if a red-hot sword drove into his hip and out the other side.

But her pain and danger woke the serpent asleep inside him and roused it in a single instant to action.

Red rage rose within, uncoiling with terrible swiftness, and giving birth to the fire; the next volley of arrows burst into flame in midair.

Arrowheads clattered to the frozen ground beside him, and a drift of ash flew away through the flames.

The volley after that never left the bows.

The arrows nocked to bowstrings flared once; for a moment, arrow-shapes of ash holding for a heartbeat, before crumbling in their fingers. The arrowheads dropped to the ground, as the bows ignited. With startled shouts, the men flung their weapons away.

His sight was filmed with red, and he prepared to strike a third time—

:Lan—hold them. Just hold them. Don't kill them, please!:

Kalira's mind-voice penetrated the rage as nothing else had; with a wrenching effort, he held and redirected his strike.

As they turned to flee, they were barred by a wall of flame that rose between them and the end of the alley. A second wall penned them away from Lan and Kalira.

Lan held the anger in with all his strength as it tried to escape him and take its rightful prey. It didn't feel like a serpent anymore; it felt like a dragon, mindless and raging, and very, very hungry.

Trapped, they lost their heads and their cohesion as a group; they abandoned anything like sense and climbed over each other in a panic, trying desperately to find an escape. When the mounted Guardsmen pounded up to the rescue, led by a Herald, they were jabbering and begging for mercy from within their cage of flame.

The flames licked at them hungrily; Kalira helped

Lan to hold onto control and keep back the fires. Lan wasn't really thinking now; he was consumed by the fires within and without, and only Kalira's aid allowed him to hold onto sanity and control.

Lan sat in his saddle as rigid as a statue until the moment that help arrived. He didn't even realize they were there until a strange mind-voice called to him; he was too intent on what lay within the fire to pay attention to what was outside it. It was so tempting— the fires beckoned so seductively—and it was such a struggle to keep himself from burning those evil creatures to a crisp. Nor was that all; he had to fight to keep the fires where they were, confined within the walls of the alley. If he lost concentration for a moment, they would escape, leap to the wooden building on either side of the alley, incinerating the innocent people inside. Thanks to Kalira, the dragon had been confined, but it was not tame and never would be. If he lost his hold on it for even a moment, all would be lost. His body was so tense he couldn't move a single muscle, and although his head was clear, it was full of the rage and the fire.

:Lavan!: a woman's voice called. *:Trainee Lavan! You can let them go now!:*

With a start, Lan came back to himself.

:It's all right, Lavan. Let them go; that's right. We'll take them now. We're here to help you.:

With an effort, he let the fires die, and with them his anger.

:Good, Lavan, excellent. Thank you——: The Guards had come down off their mounts, and were rounding up the men who had ambushed them; the Herald rode forward as Lan slumped over the pommel of his saddle, then slid down off Kalira to take his weight from her wounded hindquarters.

"I'm Herald Sharissa," said the newcomer, dismounting quickly and going at once to Kalira, who shivered and shook with pain and reaction. Lan could only hold her head and shake, himself; tears poured down his face as he cradled her against his chest.

"Hold on, little one, this is going to hurt." The Herald took hold of the shaft of the crossbow bolt and gave a quick pull; Kalira's body convulsed with the pain when the bolt came free, and she gave a low moan, a moan that Lan echoed as he endured her agony with her.

The Herald took them both in charge, binding a crude dressing on Kalira's wound, taking Lan up behind her, and getting them both away before the Guard had even finished trussing up the ambushers. The streets passed in a kind of blur; all that Lan could think of was Kalira. He was frantic now, wanting to urge Herald Sharissa to greater speed, then wanting to beg her to hold back to a mere crawl. If he could have carried Kalira, he would have.

"Easy on, lad," Sharissa murmured from time to time. "Easy on. She hurts, but she's not in any danger."

But watching Kalira limping painfully behind them, feeling her agony with every step she took, did nothing to convince Lan of that.

Halfway to the Collegium, Pol and Satiran came pounding up, shaking him out of his daze of fear and hurt. He stared dumbly at Pol and was vaguely astonished at the unfettered anger he saw in his mentor's face.

But Pol only looked him over quickly, then he and Satiran moved to Kalira's side. Sharissa's Companion took his place on Kalira's opposite side, and Pol buckled Kalira into a peculiar harness he had brought with him, fastening the other two into it as well. In a moment, Lan saw what they were about; the two stallions were much larger than Kalira, and they were able to take most of the weight off her hindquarters. The relief to Kalira was so great that Lan burst into tears of gratitude.

Now they were able to move more quickly, and

soon Kalira was in the hands of real Healers in her own stall in the stables.

Lan hovered anxiously outside the stall, still full of fear, although he felt everything that Kalira felt, and knew for himself that they were easing her pain and knitting her wound closed with their Healing Magic. He couldn't *see* what they were doing, though, and he couldn't be right with her, and that was horrid.

Finally they all cleared away, and he dashed into the stall to fling himself down on the straw next to her and cry as he had not since he was an infant. His thoughts were a tangle of guilt and anger, guilt because if he hadn't gone into the city, this never would have happened, and anger at those who had dared to harm her. His throat and stomach were one long knot; his cheeks raw, his eyes burning, and still the tears fell.

"This is all my fault!" he sobbed into her neck. "You should never have Chosen me! If you hadn't, you'd be all right!"

"Shh, lad," said Pol, dropping to his knees beside them. Lan had been so hysterical he hadn't even heard Pol approach. He put his arm around Lan's shoulders, dropping the load of blankets he'd brought with him. "If she'd Chosen someone else, she might well be on the Southern Border fighting Karse at this moment. She knows that Heralds and Companions can't escape danger, don't you, little girl."

Kalira raised her head with an effort and looked up at them both. :*I just—wish that danger didn't hurt so much,*: she said ruefully, and nuzzled Lan. :*I couldn't— wouldn't—have anyone but you, Chosen. Ever.*:

Before that could bring a new spate of self-accusation, Pol shook his shoulder a little. "I thought you'd probably want to stay with her tonight, so I brought up some bedding for you, and a hot brick. If you get cold, there'll be a couple more bricks on the hearth over in the tack room. Now, let's get a bed made up for you before you fall on your nose."

Making up a bed in the straw took what was left of

Lan's energy and all his concentration. When Pol left them, blowing out the lantern at the end of the stall as he went, it was all Lan could do to get into his crude bed and curl up with one hand resting on Kalira's foreleg. *She* was already asleep, and he lay there, listening to her breathing, to the mice rustling in the straw, to the occasional stamp of a hoof in one of the other stalls. He thought he would never be able to sleep, no matter how tired he was, but it was very dark in the stable and as warmth crept into him from the hot brick he lay curled around, he felt his knotted muscles relaxing from sheer exhaustion. And finally, his eyes closed all by themselves and he, too, slipped into sleep.

EIGHTEEN

POL'S breath hung in clouds before his face; the icy air was as still as death, and the silence that hung over the gathered crowd made it seem that everyone in the Great Square had been turned into ice statues. Not in fifty years, perhaps even a hundred, had a King of Valdemar held an open Judgment like this, with everyone in Haven that could fit crowded into the Great Square in front of the City Hall. More folk still hung out of the windows or stood on the balconies of the buildings surrounding the Great Square.

Theran sat in stony silence on a temporary platform draped in white, the King's Own on his right, armed to the teeth, his bodyguard of Heralds around him, also armed, and all their Companions ranged in front of the platform. They could have been a grim snow sculpture; there wasn't a hint of a smile on any face in that grouping. The only touch of color other than white was in the form of one set of Formal Grays, Grays worn by Lavan Firestarter, who stood at Theran's left hand. The poor boy's face was as snowy as Theran's Royal Whites, but he was holding up gallantly; Pol was very, very proud of him. *He* was not the one waiting to be sentenced, but you wouldn't have known that from his face.

In a clear space below the platform, surrounded by a half-circle of Palace Guards in their special midnight-blue uniforms, stood the accused. Or perhaps, better to say the condemned, for their guilt was clear and they waited only for a chance to speak before Theran passed judgment on them.

It was not likely that the seven hired thugs who'd accepted the job of murdering Lavan would say much; caught in the act, their guilt was beyond question. But the wife of the Head of the Silversmith's Guild, Jisette Jelnack, was definitely going to speak her piece. She practically shook with rage and outrage, and her face was as pale as Lan's, looking bloodless against the black of her gown. She twisted a handkerchief in her hands, the action suggesting that even now she longed to twine it around Lan's throat and strangle him with it.

Of all her family, only her husband was here, and he stood apart as if in a vain attempt to dissociate himself from her. He stood within the half-circle of Guards, but not himself under arrest. There was not one single member of the Silversmiths' Guild here in attendance, in fact, they were notable in their absence; Pol did not doubt for a moment that by the end of the day there would be a new Guildmaster in that House.

He was warned. If he couldn't keep Jisette from doing something foolish, he should have turned her in to the Guard, and this would never have become a public matter. And he had to know. Hired assassins don't come cheaply, especially ones who are thorough enough to track the target's movements and friends, forge notes, and arrange to block streets with wagons and fighting gangs. Where did that money come from, if not the household coffers? Surely he didn't think she was spending that much money on household expenses!

Hoarfrost rimed every surface of the buildings

around the Square, muting the colors; the sky above, a flat gray, promised nothing and added nothing. It seemed that all the elements had agreed to contribute to the atmosphere of rejection that Theran had concocted.

Theran stood, and slowly scanned the entire gathering, the force of his personality ensuring that every single individual in the Square would be willing to swear later that the King had locked eyes with him, personally. Theran took a deep breath, and his voice rolled over the silent crowd.

"We are here to pass judgment," he said, each word weighted carefully. "*You* are here to bear witness that justice has been done. These seven men—" he gestured slightly at the hired thugs, "—were captured in the act of attempted murder of one of Valdemar's Heraldic Trainees; this boy, Lavan Chitward, called Firestarter."

Pol's swift intake of breath was echoed by many others; this was the first time that Lan's Gift had been acknowledged publicly, and those who knew that he had been one of the boys involved in the Guild School fire would now be putting two and two together. This was no accident on Theran's part, but what was he going to accomplish with this information?

"These seven men stand convicted of that crime, and of the crime of attempted murder and injury of one of Valdemar's Companions, the Companion Kalira, bound to Lavan Firestarter."

Another and more general gasp; for most people, the very notion that someone would deliberately harm a Companion was shocking. To actually see the men who had done such a thing was an outrage to their sensibilities.

"Have you men anything to say for yourself before we pass judgment upon you?" Theran stared down at them; his look one of utter disgust. Pol didn't really expect them to say anything at all, but to his surprise, one of them stepped forward.

"We wasn't to hurt the horse—I mean, Companion," the grizzled, mustached man said defiantly. "And we was just doin' the job we'd been hired to. By *her*—" and he pointed at Jisette Jelnack.

The crowd murmured; there had been rumors flying all through Haven since the attack two days ago, but until now none of that had been confirmed. Pol noticed with satisfaction that if anything, the general sense of outrage had increased.

Theran's expression did not change by a hair. "We are aware of that," he said, distantly. "Nevertheless, regardless of who hired you, or why, you intended to murder, you attempted to murder. The fact that this attempt was on one of our Trainees and resulted in the injury of one of our Companions only compounds the felony. You stand condemned out of your own mouths, under Truth Spell, and duly witnessed. Is that all you have to say?"

The man wilted a little, and shook his head, stepping back a pace.

Theran hardened his expression. "Very well. Your crime is punishable by death." Here he paused, while the condemned looked sick and the crowd radiated approval. "But we have—another fate in mind for you, one that will serve Valdemar. You will proceed under guard to the Karsite Border. You will remain under guard, in heavy chains when you are not performing your duty, in light chains when you are. You will be outfitted in a special red uniform, patterned with a broad black cross on front and back, to make you visible and prevent you from being mistaken for Bards. You will serve the Healers in whatever capacity they deem fit—including and especially the extraction of the wounded from the battlefield during battles." He raised an eyebrow at them, for the first time changing his expression, from one of condemnation to irony. "This will be your duty for the rest of your lives— however long or short that may be. And I do not recommend an attempt at escape. You would not evade my Guards and Heralds for long, and should you think to find mercy at the hands of the Karsites, think again. They burn our people in Karse, and you would never be able to pass yourselves off as Believers in their One God."

He gestured to the Guards surrounding the miscreants, who took the seven away to their fates, to the subdued approval of the crowd. Now his attention turned to Jisette.

The Guards brought her forward at his gesture. Pol knew what was going through the minds of many who could not see her face. *How could this wealthy, pampered, delicate woman have done what she was accused of?* She stared up at the King in defiance, then her gaze went to Lan, and her expression turned to one of pure hate. Lan trembled, and would have shrunk back, if the King had not put a hand on his elbow. Of all of those present, only Pol and King's Own Jedin could know how much it cost the boy just to stand there impassively. It was damnably unfair to put him through this, but worse was to come.

"You, Jisette Jelnack, stand accused and convicted of hiring men to murder Heraldic Trainee Lavan Firestarter. Out of your own mouth you were condemned, under Truth Spell. Have you anything to say for yourself?"

Jisette shook off the restraining hand of one of her Guards and stepped forward, entirely unrepentant. "That—*creature*—next to you is a murderer!" she shrilled, and Pol was not the only person to wince at her tone. "He killed my son! Put *him* under Truth Spell if you dare! I only sought justice for my poor boy when your justice was denied me!"

More murmurs from the crowd, uncertainty this time. There had been rumors of this also—and Theran had decided to deal with them in public, once and for all. He couldn't deny that Lan had, in the sight of witnesses, brought up fire to protect himself and Kalira. People were already thinking back to the Merchants' School Fire. He couldn't have confidence in the Heralds undermined.

So Lan would have to take the blows, and bear them, for his sake, and the sake of every Herald in the Kingdom.

"I intend to," Theran said flatly. "Now, in the sight of all these witnesses, so that there can be no question of the depth of your obsession and insane hatred." He stepped back; Jedin stepped forward as Lan swallowed hard, and waited.

A moment later, Lan was surrounded by a faint, blue glow, clearly visible against the universal white of the platform, the draping, and the white uniforms. Very few people, even those living in the capital, had actually seen a Truth Spell in action, and from the front to the rear they craned their necks, peering up at the platform in avid curiosity.

Jedin wasted no time; after a few preliminaries to establish that Lan was, indeed, Lavan Chitward, and that he had attended the Merchants' School as stated, he went straight to the heart of the matter.

"Describe the situation between the younger pupils and the older," Jedin ordered.

In a strained voice, Lan related everything that Pol already knew about the behavior of the Sixth Form, as the crowd listened closely, and began to radiate disapproval—not of Lan, but of the gang of bullies who had so dominated every other pupil in the school. Jisette Jelnack, however, stirred angrily.

"Lies!" she shrieked, when Lan was finished. "All lies!"

Now the Seneschal's Herald stepped forward and offered Theran a sheaf of papers. "This is testimony from forty other pupils of the Merchants' School, all taken under Truth Spell and witnessed, that corroborate and add to the statements of Lavan Chitward," he said, for the benefit of the crowd. "These include statements from the boys who survived the fire and styled themselves 'Sixth Formers,' and were the followers of the Jelnack boy."

"Lies!" Jisette shrieked again. Theran glared at her, rapidly losing patience—a feat in itself, for Theran's patience was nothing short of monumental.

"Woman, you will be silent unless permission is granted you to speak," he thundered. "If you cannot be silent, you will be gagged. Do you understand this?"

Angrily, she stared up at the King, as if she were the rightful ruler and not he. Then she nodded once, sharply, with extreme reluctance.

Lan was not out from under the burden yet, and Jedin returned to him. "Describe, from the moment that you were accosted in the classroom after dismissal, precisely what occurred on the day of the fire."

Shaking so that his distress must be visible even to the farthest corner of the Great Square, Lan complied, leaving out nothing. He faltered when trying to describe how his Gift suddenly erupted and broke free of his control; rather than coach him, Jedin asked very specific questions that enabled him to give details that would satisfy even the most skeptical that, untrained as he was, and not even knowing what it was that had happened, there was nothing he could have done to stop what had happened once it got started. The blue glow of the Truth Spell never wavered through all of this. Finally Jedin asked the most important question of all.

"Did you intend for anyone to be hurt?" he asked, almost gently.

Lan shook his head.

"What did you want?" Jedin persisted.

"I just wanted them to *leave me alone!*" Lan cried, his voice breaking. "All I ever wanted was to be left alone!"

It was obvious that not only his voice was cracking, but his nerves, and Jedin dismissed the Truth Spell, nodded once to the King, and stepped back into his proper place.

But Jisette could no longer control herself. "You see! You see! He murdered my boy in cold blood! I demand—"

"*Silence!*" Theran shouted, making everyone jump. "Guards, gag the prisoner!"

The Guards, looking pleased for the first time this afternoon, obeyed him with alacrity. Jisette struggled, but uselessly. In a moment, she was silenced, and glared all around her with eyes so wide that the whites showed all around.

Another murmur rose from the crowd, this one of approval. "I'd'a given the bitch the back of m'hand a candlemark agone," one man behind Pol muttered to his neighbor.

"Trainee Lavan, called Firestarter, has demonstrated to the satisfaction of the entire Guard and Collegium that his Gift is now under control," said the Lord Marshal, over the comments of the crowd. "Under attack, he eliminated the weapons of his attackers, and confined them, without harming them."

"Very good," Theran responded with utmost gravity; this, of course, was to settle any remaining unease concerning Lan's Gift. "And there is no doubt that the Companion Kalira's Choice is a true one?"

"No doubt whatsoever, Sire," Jedin supplied. "And everyone knows that a Companion does not Choose the unworthy."

Despite what poor Lan was going through, Pol had to admire the way that Theran had orchestrated these proceedings. Every possible doubt that could arise had been set up, like a target, and neatly knocked down. Only one possible thing remained, an analogy to what had occurred at the school that even the dullest could understand.

Theran stood up, and glared down at the Jelnack woman. Unrepentant to the last, she glared back up at him.

"Woman, your child willfully and intentionally went about that school throwing stones aimed to hurt," he rumbled, as the crowd stilled, the better to hear his words. "He triggered an avalanche with his stones when he aimed at Trainee Lavan. The fact that the avalanche killed him is his *own* fault and no one else's; not the fault of Lavan or even of the avalanche itself. Those who take delight in causing harm would do well to heed his example and his fate."

Pol nodded with satisfaction; Theran must have been working on those exact words for the better part of a day. He could not have chosen a better simile, or one more memorable and graphic.

"As for you," Theran continued, "we have thought long and hard about your punishment. You are very clearly obsessed, for the warning you had and the evidence you have heard was not sufficient; just as clearly, you are no longer able to consider your actions rationally. We do not execute the insane in this land. It is obvious that your family can exert no control over you, and thus cannot be trusted with your custody. Our Healers have enough to do; we will not burden them with the duty of taking care of you. We do not want you in our prison, providing an added burden for our Guards; prison is not the place for one such as you. Fortunately, and due entirely to the consideration of the combined Priesthoods of this land, a solution has been found."

He gestured, and a robed figure in cream-colored wool came forward from behind the platform. Pol craned his neck along with everyone else; this was as much a surprise to him as to the rest of those here. It was a woman, but he didn't recognize the robes of her Order.

"This is Priestess Fayshan, of the Cloistered Order of Kernos-Sequestered," Theran announced, and Pol saw his lips curve ever so slightly as Jisette's eyes widened in recognition. "I see that you know the Order. For the benefit of others, Fayshan's sect normally accepts only the most ardent in their faith, for their way is one of the most *complete* seclusion. In fact, each votary is sealed into her cell for the entirety of her life, receiving her needs and nourishment through a slit in the wall, and daylight through a slit-window. They know when they are sealed into those cells that they will exit their cells only at death. However, given the circumstances, Priestess Fayshan has graciously offered the hospitality of one of her cells, so that you may have the opportunity, through diligent prayer and contemplation, to be cured of your madness, and then, through more prayer and contemplation for as long as you may live, expiate your sin. Like her willing votaries, you will leave your cell only when you are dead."

Jisette began to flail wildly; the Guards took hold of her and restrained her as Priestess Fayshan gazed at her with sorrow thinly veiling profound disgust.

"My Guards will escort her to the Cloister, good Lady," Theran said. "They will see to it that she—behaves herself—until the last brick is in place."

"That—is most appreciated, Majesty," Fayshan replied, and bowed deeply. She beckoned to the Guards, who followed her away from the platform. The crowd divided to let them pass, with the occasional brave soul hissing or otherwise expressing his or her feelings at the unfortunate Jisette. Master Jelnack himself took the opportunity to escape, slinking off to one side and rapidly getting lost among the milling people nearest the platform.

But Theran held up his hand, taking back the attention of the crowd.

"This matter is *closed*," he said forcefully. "And let all of you know, I, Theran, King of Valdemar, will hear *no more* accusations against this boy. Understand that he is the single most valuable Herald in this land, not even second to Jedin, King's Own."

Well, *that* raised some eyebrows, not the least of which were Pol's. And this wasn't part of the original script, either. What had happened since he'd last talked to the King?

"We need this boy's Gift as we have never needed another," Theran continued, actually putting his arm around Lan's shoulders. Poor Lan looked as if he was about to faint. "Fate or the gods themselves have brought him to us at a time of desperate need. People of Valdemar, we are at war."

The word passed through the crowd like wildfire. *War!* Expected for months, yes, but not truly anticipated; now that it was at hand, it sent a shock through everyone assembled. "The land of Karse is, even as I speak, attacking our Border positions. Their bonfires are built and ready for the bodies of our Priests, our Heralds, our Bards, and our citizens. Their demons range along the Border, attacking our soldiers. Only Lavan Firestarter has the power to reach across that Border to strike the Sun-priests who control those demons, and we thank all the gods that we have him now!"

He pulled Lan tight in a sudden embrace, and the crowd, shocked by his announcement, gave vent to a spontaneous cheer.

But all that Pol could feel from the Lan was pure terror.

LAN escaped as soon as he could; it had only been Kalira's presence down behind the platform that had kept him from loosing that terrible Gift of his right in the middle of all the cheering.

He left Theran and the rest of the Heralds as Theran continued his rousing speech about the war, and dropped down to Kalira's side. She still wasn't ready to be ridden, although the Healers had gone a long way toward getting her there. Together, with Lan walking along beside her, they slipped away from the Great Square and headed back toward the Collegium.

Despite Kalira's soothing presence, he was anything but calm.

:What am I going to do?: he wailed silently at Kalira. *:The King said I'm—:*

:The King said what would best work to show the people that you aren't a useless danger, Chosen,: Kalira interrupted. *:He knows you aren't anywhere near ready to be in the war yet. You've got a lot more time to train before you need to think about the war. Months, probably.:*

Her certainty had the effect of lessening his terror a little. A lot could happen in a couple of months— well, look what had happened already! In a couple of months, the war could be over.

But if it wasn't—*:Kalira, I can't even think about killing someone,:* he confessed miserably. *:Not in cold blood. Not at a distance. Not like the King was saying, getting those Sun-priests. If someone was after you or me, directly, and I got mad, but not like that!:*

:Then don't.: Kalira replied. *:There are plenty of ways to handle those Sun-priests. I imagine setting their robes afire would distract them fairly easily without killing them! And if they're too stupid or proud to drop down and roll in the snow, that's their problem.:*

The image she sent along with her words, of a fat fellow dancing wildly as frantic acolytes dealt with the flaming hem of his robe startled a weak laugh out of him.

:In fact, you could probably do as much, if not more, by setting fire to things, and not people,: she continued. *:Hit the tents, the supplies, the weapon stocks. Drive their troops with the kind of fire wall you used to hold the men in the alley. All you have to do is learn how to move them.:*

All! Well, perhaps it was better than setting fire to people. . . .

He couldn't imagine himself in a war; he couldn't imagine what a war was like. When he and his friends had played at Guards and Bandits as children, the combats in their imagination had been very straight-forward. It was all man-to-man, good against evil, no more than a few boys on either side.

This war— Well, the good against evil part was clear enough, but the rest! A combat that went on and on, masses of men clashing—the moment he tried to imagine it, he found he couldn't. He couldn't see his place in that chaos either.

What if he was a coward? Maybe that was why he couldn't imagine it.

He was very glad that the Great Square was so near the Palace, for he was able to get inside the walls long before anyone from that huge gathering could spot him. Right now, all he wanted was to hide.

Kalira hesitated a moment as they neared the Collegium, but he waved her away. "Go on," he urged, "The others will want to hear what happened. I'll—be all right."

That wasn't true; the truth was that he wanted very much to be alone. He didn't want her to know just how close to the breaking point he was. She already had more than enough to worry about. He could tell that she was tired and that she ached all over, that she was even more worried about this war than he was, worried for *her* friends, and her sire. She didn't need any more stress.

She was *so* exhausted that she didn't even argue with him or question him more closely. Instead, she headed straight for the stables, her head drooping.

He sought sanctuary in his room, locking the door behind him. He scrunched himself into a corner of his bed and hugged his knees to his chest, resting his forehead on them.

Give your enemy a face, Master Odo always said. *If he is human, do not dehumanize him. Know him and know why he is your enemy. If your enemy is within you, understand what it is and why you are afraid. Put a face on your fear. When you understand it, and it is*

*no longer vague and shapeless, you will find that your
fear is no longer so formidable.*

That was what he *said,* anyway. But how could you
make a war less formidable and how could you face
an all-too-concrete fear? He began to shake again,
teeth chattering. How could he ever be what they
wanted him to be? He was so afraid, so very afraid—

Someone tapped lightly on his door.

:Lan, you know I know you're in there,: Pol said
patiently, his words for him alone. *:I can understand
not wanting to be pestered by your friends right now,
but I think maybe we can help each other.:* And when
Lan didn't answer, Pol continued, *:I have to tell you,
this war scares the whey out of me.:*

Herald Pol? Afraid? How could that be? But you
couldn't lie mind-to-mind. Slowly, Lan uncurled himself, got off the bed, and went to the door. When he'd
unlocked it, Pol didn't immediately come in. In fact,
Lan was back in the same position on the bed when
Pol pushed the door open, looked around, closed it
behind him, and sat wearily on the side of the bed.

"I've got to make a confession to you, Lan. I've
known this was coming, for some time. That's why I
was put on the Privy Council." He looked up at Lan,
then down at his hands. "Because of you—because
I'm your mentor. If you want someone else now—"

"No!" Lan blurted, then blushed. "No," he said,
more quietly. "You were sworn to secrecy, I bet."

Pol nodded. "I was. I tried to give you some hints,
but I couldn't really prepare you properly. Hellfires, I
couldn't really prepare *me* properly; I was as stunned
as you were when the King made that announcement.
And I have to tell you, I am frightened witless, knowing I'm going to have to go to war."

"Why should you be scared?" Lan asked bitterly.
"You've got *loads* more training than I do!"

"Why?" Pol's expression was as sour as Lan's. "I'm
more than old enough to be *your* father; I'm old, Lan.
I don't move as fast, I don't have your endurance or

your reflexes, and I don't have *any* Gift that's powerful enough to protect me. My wife is probably going
to be in the front lines as well, and do you know what
the Karsites do with captured Healers? If a Healer
cooperates, they put her in chains and force her to
Heal until she burns herself out. If she doesn't, they
tie her to a stake and incinerate her on the spot."

Lan hid his head against his knees. How could he
have not thought of that? No matter what, at least he
could protect himself and Kalira, and he didn't have
anyone he loved facing the possibility of being burned
alive.

"I'm sorry," he said in a whisper. "I didn't think—"

"Why should you? A candlemark ago you didn't
even know there was going to be a war. I've had more
than a moon to brood on this." Pol didn't sound the
least annoyed with Lan, and Lan finally looked up
again. Pol was leaning back against the footboard of
the bed, looking twenty years older than he had this
morning. "Anybody with any sense or imagination is
going to be scared white at this prospect. Lan, you're
not ready—but no one is going to be ready enough,
or trained enough. The King isn't expecting you to do
a fraction of what he claimed, and believe me, when
we get out there, *anything* you can do is going to be
far more than we had before."

Lan sucked at his lower lip. "But if the King doesn't
expect me to do all that, why did he *say* it in front of
all those people?"

Pol chuckled sadly. "You haven't gotten to the the-
ory of *propaganda* in your studies, I suspect. In your
case, he's given people something special to think
about—a gods-sent savior. With you on our side, how
can we lose? He's boosting their spirits, which will in
turn boost the spirits of our fighters. And he didn't
make all that up. With enough practice, you *will* be
able to do all those things."

Lan's eyes widened, but Pol wasn't done.

"What's more, he turned you from a dangerous un-

known, the boy who lost control of his Gift and con-
tributed to a tragedy at the Merchants' School, to the
boy who is ready to sacrifice himself for the good of
all Valdemar. Now people won't flinch when they see
you in the street, they're more like to cheer for you."

Lan flushed. "That doesn't seem—right," he faltered. "It seems like lying."

Pol sighed, and shifted his weight so that the bed
creaked a little. "There, I agree with you to a certain
extent, but Theran and Jedin see it as protecting you.
With this much notoriety, if any more of the Jelnacks
were contemplating revenge, they won't dare try it, because with the entire city intent on your protection,
nothing they tried would have a chance of succeeding.
If they try and hire more thugs in Haven, the thugs
themselves will turn them in. If they bring in outsiders, the
outsiders will be of a certain *type,* and the local thugs will
spot them, know why they are here, and turn them in."

Lan put his head back, and stared up at the ceiling.
Put a face on your enemy. "What—what's the Karsite
army going to be like?"

Pol sighed and stretched out his legs, crossing them
at the ankles. "Despite what you might think, they
aren't *all* fanatics; in fact, most of them aren't much
different than our people. Most of the line troops will
be farmers, or herders, or crafters. Their regular army
will be in the minority, the Sun-priests, a smaller minority than that. What they are, is terrified of *us.* They
think that Heralds are demons, that the Companions
are demons, and that if they are captured, they'll be
sacrificed to our demon gods, slowly and painfully.
That gives them a rather powerful incentive to fight."

Lan brought his head down and saw that Pol was
watching him wearing an expression full of irony.

"Of course, you realize that if you can do even a
little of what we think you can, they are only going
to be *more* convinced that Heralds are demons," Pol
continued, raising an eyebrow.

"I suppose. . . ." Lan rubbed his nose with the back

of his hand. Master Odo was right; somehow an army of farmers like Tuck's family wasn't nearly as terrifying as the faceless, mindless, implacable army he'd pictured in his mind. "Pol, I don't know that I can kill anyone! I already have so many nightmares about the school—"

"So don't!" Pol replied. "I haven't heard anyone suggesting that you should."

So Kalira was right. "Kalira said—maybe I should make fire walls, or burn up their supplies and tents, or something—"

"Very good ideas. What's more, *you* are the only one who can dictate what you will and won't do. No one really knows what you can do here at the Collegium, and they'll know still less on the front lines. You tell the Generals what you can do, or what you're willing to do, and they'll fit that into their plans." Pol actually smiled at Lan's surprise. "You didn't know that things worked like that?"

"No! I thought that—that people would just order me to do things—" he stammered.

Pol shook his head. "You can't *order* someone with a Gift; how can you enforce orders on something that no one can weigh or measure? Our people have decades of knowing how to adapt battle tactics to include some new ability, but they also know how to adapt if the person with that ability is too tired to work, or doesn't have the strength that they thought, as well."

If Pol had intended to bring his fears down to a more reasonable level, he was succeeding. Lan was still afraid, but he didn't feel like crawling into a ball somewhere dark and shaking anymore. In fact, now there was room for another bubble of guilt and anxiety to rise to the surface of his thoughts.

"Madame Jelnack—" he paused, as Pol cast a penetrating glance at him. "If I asked the King—do you think he'd find a different place for her to go?" He shuddered, thinking of the situation that Theran had described. "I mean, walled up in a cave for the rest of her life—that's horrid! She's not sane, but—"

To his surprise, Pol chuckled again. "Don't feel too sorry for her," he replied. "I know something about that particular Cloistered Order. Not everyone who goes there is an ascetic; sometimes it's well-born women who are recluses by nature and want to be away from the distraction of the world to concentrate on religious scholasticism, meditation, and prayer. It's no cave that Jisette Jelnack is going to be walled into, it's a very comfortable little apartment, with its own little bathing room and all. She can have anything her family wants her to have in there. She'll just never get out, and it all becomes the property of the Order after she's gone." He chuckled again. "In fact, I have no doubt that the Order is going to charge her family a princely amount for her keep and comfort, given that she's a prisoner, and it serves them all right."

"Are you sure?" Lan asked, his conscience considerably eased, now that his mental picture of a dank, barren, shadow-filled cell had been replaced by a very different vision.

"So sure that I'll take you there to see for yourself if you need to be convinced," Pol told him. He stood up. "Thank you, Lan."

"Me?" Lan said, surprised. "For what?"

"Talking to you helped *me* to put on a face on the enemy. Remember what Master Odo always tells us." He touched his eyebrow with two fingers in a little salute. "I think that we'll put off practice for today. I don't think that either of us want to be the center of a circle of gawkers just now."

Lan nodded, and belatedly remembered his manners. He scooted off the bed, and went to open the door for his mentor. "If I were you," Pol finished, as he paused halfway out the door, "I'd go out to Kalira. I think she needs you quite a bit right now."

"I will," Lan promised, and before Pol was more than halfway down the hall, he had gotten his cloak and was out the door, heading for the stables at a trot.

NINETEEN

T HE departure of a mere ten Trainees should not
have made *that* much difference in the way that
the Collegium halls felt, but it did. Ten rooms empty,
and the place had a hollower sound to it, the sense
that something was missing, or amiss.

Pol told himself that he was being overly dramatic,
but from the nervous way his pupils were acting, they
felt the same. Laughter sounded forced or strained,
voices were hushed, and jokes were far, far fewer.

Ten Trainees had been hustled into Whites months
before they were due to graduate, and sent off to the
south. They would finish their training the old-
fashioned way, paired with a mentor with the same
Gift, expected to act as his or her backup. It was the
way that Heralds had been trained in Vanyel's time,
revived in the current crisis—and no one liked it.

Weaponmaster Odo, who'd had some choice words
for those who'd thought of it, liked it least of all. If it
hadn't been that the Trainees themselves had been
willing, even eager to go, the whole plan might well
have collapsed at that moment. But the Trainees

themselves talked the Weaponsmaster around, and so they went.

What disturbed Pol more than their leave-taking was that by the end of that same week, twelve Companions had presented themselves to be tacked-up, and had gone out to make their Choices. Twelve! Were they Choosing replacements for those who would soon die in this war? He didn't have the courage to ask Satiran.

All too soon, another set of too-young Trainees would follow the first set. And by spring—if not sooner—he and Lan would follow the same path.

He shook off his worries and headed for the Field, where Lan was waiting for him. Satiran stood at the fence, watching him approach with ears perked forward; he climbed the fence and used it as a help to get onto Satiran's bare back. His Companion carried him deep into the Field, to a spot where straw sheaves set up as targets by Master Odo were just barely visible. Pol slid down from Satiran's back; Lan smiled at his mentor, but his smile could not disguise the fact that he had dark shadows around his eyes, and that he was too thin. He had been working like one possessed, as if by working himself to exhaustion he could drive away the demons that haunted *his* dreams.

I can understand that, Pol thought, reflecting on his own dreams.

"Odo's ready," he said, gesturing at the distant specks, well to the side of the straw targets. "Get the straw bales first, then see if you can surround the practice ground at this distance."

Lan nodded. He was long past merely flaming volleys of arrows; if that was all that was wanted, he could deal with archers from dawn to dusk. Now he was learning to reach distant targets, to create and hold walls of flame much longer and higher than the ones he'd used to pen in his attackers in the alley. Every day his control grew finer, his reach farther. Pol had always known that Lan's Gift was powerful, but until now, he'd had no way to judge how powerful it would be when he had learned to use it to its fullest.

Now he knew, and sometimes he shuddered to think about it. One day, perhaps one day soon, they would not call him Lavan Firestarter anymore. No—no, it would be another name entirely.

Lavan Firestorm.

It wouldn't happen here, though. The kind of raw emotion it would take to fuel a Firestorm couldn't be generated by the memories of old angers, though these days it only took a glance at the scar on Kalira's hip to produce as impressive a fire wall as was needed. The first Firestorm would probably come in a moment of desperate need on the front lines, and when it did—

Pol resolutely turned his thoughts away from that path; troubles enough dogged their footsteps without thinking too hard about that.

Lan shaded his eyes with one hand, the other on Kalira's neck, and frowned fiercely. Pol watched the targets; what Lan was working on now was the control that would permit him to ignite the targets instantaneously, with no smoke or heat to warn of what was happening.

Lan nodded, as if he was counting, and his frown grew fiercer.

Then—*one, two, three, four!*—deceptively tiny fire-blossoms engulfed the far-off targets, and the specks that were Master Odo and his hand-picked Trainee volunteers leaped back. A moment later, the breeze brought the faint sounds of their voices, high-pitched exclamations that told Pol the trial had succeeded.

Frenzied activity around the burning targets ensued, until the fires were out. Then the distant figures gathered together in the center of the practice ground, very much like a beleaguered group of fighters trying to protect themselves and each other.

Lan's face twisted into a mask of anger; his free hand clenched at his side, he glared at the distant grouping. He'd brought up sheltering walls of flame before, but not at anywhere near this distance.

For a moment, as Lan's face grew red with strain, Pol thought he would not be able to manage it this time either. But then, a speck, a gleam of yellow against the white snow, warned him that Lan had managed *something,* at any rate.

Slowly enough that Pol could follow the track, a wavering line of flame encircled the group at a healthy distance. It remained no more than knee-high for a few heartbeats, then finally roared upward, a scarlet-and-golden waterfall in reverse. The flames reached to the height of a house, then stopped. Lan held them long enough to be certain that he could hold them for a candlemark at least, then with a gasp, let it all go.

The fire went out as if snuffed by a giant hand, and the distant helpers broke up their group and milled curiously about, examining the melted lines where the flames had been. That was a good trick, making flames burn on top of snow until the snow was melted enough to get to the fuel beneath. Pol still didn't know how Lan managed it.

"Good job!" he enthused, clapping Lan on the back. "Go report to Master Odo for details, then go take yourself a short rest."

"I will," the boy replied, looking more drained than before, pulling himself up onto Kalira's back. "I need it—"

"And get something to eat, too!" Pol shouted after him, as he and his Companion trotted off. "You're too thin!"

He walked back with Satiran, watching from a distance as Lan discussed his actions with Odo and Odo's assistants, then rode to the door of the Collegium where he dismounted and went inside. Pol purposely hadn't accompanied him; he wanted the boy to learn to do things without being shepherded. When they got to the front, he'd have to think for himself.

He left Satiran at the gate with a pat on his neck,

and went back into the Collegium to report on Lan's progress.

Once inside, young Tuck hurried past him, with his arms full of books and dark circles under *his* eyes. Pol intercepted him.

"Isn't this supposed to be your free time?" he asked.

Tuck grimaced. "If I'm going to go with you and Lan, I've *got* to get a better handle on my Karsite," he replied, and hurried off. Pol sighed.

He's working himself as hard as Lan is. Gods above, what are we doing to these children? Tuck was determined to be with Lan when he was sent out, and had lost all of his lazy habits in an effort to cram as much as he could into every candlemark so that when Lan was sent south, he, too, would be deemed ready. That would give Pol not one but two Trainees to keep track of. On the other hand, Tuck would supply a second hand at keeping Lan settled and in control of himself. Pol knew that very well, so how could he discourage the boy? The best he could do for Tuck was the same he was doing for Lan—try to make sure he ate and slept enough. It could have been worse for both of them. There were plenty of children in impoverished families who would have thought their current situation the equivalent of a holiday.

So many of the Trainees were driving themselves just as hard that Pol hardly knew whether to admire them or despair. Of all of them, however, only Lan had ever been the target of an enemy determined to slay him; they had no idea what they were going to face.

It's a wonder Odo isn't a drunkard. I don't know how he manages to train these children to go out and get hurt or killed, year after year. Of course, that was the case with all of the teachers, but only Odo had that fact shoved in his face day after day.

And yet, the Trainees were better equipped and better warned for what they would face than all those fresh-faced, eager volunteers for the Guard and the army. From cities and towns, from farms and fields, from every imaginable background, they formed up little Companies and marched themselves to the capital. New cadres arrived in Haven daily, to camp in the meadows outside the walls, train for a few weeks under the stern eyes of Guard sergeants, and march on with newly-assigned officers from the seasoned troops. They trained as they traveled and, presumably, would be fit for combat when they arrived at the Border. But even at that, they wouldn't get much more than a moon's worth of battle training before they took up their arms in earnest. Pol was thankful he didn't have charge over them; he'd never be able to sleep at night.

:You don't sleep that well as it is,: Satiran observed correctly. *:You carry enough burdens of your own. Speaking of which, are you going to another Privy Council meeting? If so, they're in the King's quarters, not the Lesser Council Chamber.:*

Trust Satiran to stay on top of things for him. *:Yes I am, and thank you,:* he replied gratefully, and instead of turning left when he passed the door marking the entrance to the Palace, he turned right, and penetrated deep into the heart of the Palace. The closer he drew to the seat of power, the more Guards he passed, until he reached the door of the Royal Suite itself. Instead of the usual two Guards, there were six. Theran was taking no chances with the safety of himself or his family.

Pol nodded to the two Guards actually on either side of the door itself, recognizing both of them. One of them opened the door for him, and Pol stepped right into the midst of the ongoing meeting.

They all stopped long enough to greet him, then returned to the discussion at hand—the contributions of those first ten Trainees who'd been rushed into service. Pol took a seat next to the fire and listened.

Jedin was the one making the report; Rolan was

fully capable of Mindspeaking to any Companion in the country, no matter how far apart they were, so it was Rolan who relayed these reports to his Chosen.

It was fairly clear why Theran had chosen to hold the meeting in his private quarters. Warmth and comfort. Even the Lesser Council Chamber was drafty and chill, and the seats around the Council Table were hard and unyielding. Granted, this did tend to lead to shorter Council sessions—which in itself wasn't a bad thing—but why endure discomfort when you didn't have a reason to? Not that anyone was lolling about by any means, but there were not going to be any long, drawn-out arguments from this lot. Like Pol, everyone here had so much to do that they resented a single wasted moment.

The gist of Jedin's report was that the newly-promoted youngsters were doing as well or better than they had been expected to. All of them had Gifts that were particularly useful in a battlefield situation. Of the ten, six were strong Mindspeakers and acted as communications liaisons all along the front. Two were FarSeers and essentially functioned as scouts, spying on the movements of enemy troops. One, an Animal Mindspeaker, was able to use the birds of the region for the same purpose. The last had one of those quirky Gifts that did not, at first, seem particularly useful until one saw it in action. This youngster had very short-term ForeSight, the sort of thing that led his friends to ban him from games of chance. His range was no more than a candlemark, and he did not actually see anything so much as get a sense of what would happen given the present conditions. But that made him incredibly useful during battles; he could tell those in command where they could expect to see a push by enemy forces far enough in advance of the actual occurrence to bring forces of their own to meet the opposition.

This of course did not guarantee victory by any means, but at least it helped to prevent defeats.

All ten youngsters had fit themselves in quickly, enabling their mentors to spend most of their time in service, rather than in supervision.

When Jedin was finished, Theran's pointed look prodded Pol to speak.

"Lavan is able to hit specific targets at a distance of twenty furlongs, and I have no reason to think that farther distance is going to make any difference in his ability to burn them. As long as he can see something, he can hit it. He can bring up fire walls to surround troops and hold them for a full candlemark, or move them and hold them for a quarter candlemark. His only limitation is how long he can sustain anger." Pol took a deep breath, and answered the unspoken question in every face. "He's as ready as you want, I think. Only practice is going to make him—more than he is now."

"He isn't going to get the kind of practice he needs on bales of straw," Theran said bluntly. "If his only limitation is sustaining his anger, then to provoke his abilities to the fullest he needs to be on the front lines. The first time he sees what the Karsites are doing to our people—"

Pol dared to raise a hand, cutting the King off. "I respect that you have to think of the larger view, Your Majesty," he replied, feeling slightly sick. "But please remember that this is a boy not yet old enough to be accepted as a volunteer in the Guard."

"I never forget it," Theran said, softening his eagle look a trifle, "but there are plenty of young volunteers his age that are lying about their years and going to the front anyway. I know that we aren't catching more than half of them and sending them home. Under other circumstances, Lavan might have been one of *them.*"

Knowing Lan's former aspirations, Pol could only nod agreement; poor Lan might well have considered volunteering and going to fight the lesser evil, given a choice between the Guard and further torment at the Merchants' School.

"So the only question is, how soon can you go?" Theran asked. "You'll be his mentor, of course."

"Not until his friend Tuck is also ready." Pol seized on that as a delaying tactic. "I want Tuck's help; he needs his friends to keep him steady."

"Hmm. I can see that. We don't want an emotional youngster with *that* particular Gift feeling friendless." Theran nodded. "Jedin, have a word with the other boy's teachers. Has he any other friends?"

"Pol's daughter," Jedin volunteered. "Young Healer, well in advance of the rest of the Trainees her age. Ready to go into full Greens, from what I hear. Mind-Healer."

"Which we will have need of there, *and* she can see to it that he stays sane. Good. See if she wants to volunteer as well," Theran decreed.

Pol blanched, but held his peace. There was always the chance that Elenor would not volunteer. . . .

With a chance to follow Lan? You're fooling yourself, old man. He felt even sicker, now. *But they'll be protected; they're all too valuable to let anything happen to them—*

"They'll be as safe, or safer, than if they were here, Pol," Theran added, with a hint of sympathy. "Lavan Firestarter may be the one person who can turn this war for us. When his Sun-Priests start incinerating, the Son of the Sun may think better of prosecuting this idiocy and pull back behind the Border again."

"Lan is all right burning inanimate objects, but he has serious mental difficulties—" Pol began.

Jedin interrupted him. "I have good reason to think he'll lose those reservations when he actually sees fighting," the King's Own said grimly.

What kind of good reason? Is it that *bad out there?* Pol wondered. He'd heard vague rumors of things the Karsite Sun-Priests were doing. Were those rumors based in fact?

He didn't get any time to contemplate that; Theran was already going on. "Given that your daughter will be with you, do you still want to have your wife return to Healer's collegium when you leave?" he asked. "Or would you rather have the three of you together?"

"Let me think about it," he temporized, "and let me see if I can get a message to her. I don't think that I want to make a decision about this without asking her opinion first."

:That may be the wisest thing you've ever said,: Satiran observed.

:Hush.:

"That's a reasonable request," the King agreed. "Jedin, put it on your agenda. We can schedule your departure as soon as we know what your lady thinks."

:Rolan is going to think he's nothing but a messenger service.: This time Satiran was actually snickering. Pol let him; there was little enough these days to be amused about.

The discussion turned to other Trainees, older than Lan, who might be candidates for assignment to the Border, but none of them were as ready as the ones who had already left, or as necessary as Lavan. Pol listened, but didn't often need to give his opinion, and he was relieved when no one, not even the King, thought that there were any more Trainees who should be hurried into Whites. Ten—twelve, if you counted Lan and Tuck—were enough.

Good gods—twelve—and twelve Companions went out. All we're doing is replacing Trainees.: Somehow that made him feel much better.

In Healers' Collegium, and to a lesser extent, Bardic, this same discussion was taking place. If Pol closed his eyes, he could sense the flood of resources, the redirection of attention, to the south. This war did not yet command the entirety of Valdemar, but it soon would, and it would continue to devour lives and resources until it ended.

However it ended.

Valdemar would be perfectly willing to end the war with the withdrawal of Karsite troops back across their own border. Karse, however, would not stop short of destroying Valdemar, unless the war became so expensive that their religious and secular leader, the self-styled Son of the Sun, called a retreat. This particular Son of the Sun was so firmly on the Sun Throne that it would take a great deal before his rule was shaken. And not until then would he give way. This was a holy crusade in their eyes, and they had been planning it for most of Pol's life.

"I believe that will be all for now," the King decreed, and Pol pulled himself out of his own thoughts to rise and bow himself out with the rest.

Had spring already begun down there? He longed for spring with all of his being, and yet dreaded it. Spring would allow the freer movement of troops; with spring, the slaughter would begin in earnest.

:This has been hanging over our heads all our lives,: Satiran observed sadly, as Pol reached his own quarters and went inside. *:And now that it's here—even for me, it doesn't seem quite real.:*

:Ah, old friend, it will be real enough, all too soon,: he replied. *:Be grateful for the respite.:*

He knew that *he* was. He would have to tell the youngsters that they were going soon, and then he would savor every single moment of every day until word came from Ilea. And that, he feared, would be very, very soon.

"SO we're both going!" Tuck said happily, sprawled over Lan's bed, while Lan occupied a pile of cushions in front of the fire, soaking up heat like a cat. "I was afraid they'd leave me behind!"

"I almost wish they would," Lan replied. At Tuck's stricken look, he added hastily, "Not because I don't want you along! But, Tuck, this isn't a lark, or a training exercise—"

"I know that!" Tuck said scornfully, interrupting him. "But you're my best friend, and I don't want you to go off anywhere without me along! Besides, Ma would skin me if I wasn't there; she'd want to know we were together so we could watch each other's backs." He lolled his head over the side of the bed and gave Lan what he probably thought was a reproving glare.

Privately Lan still thought that Tuck had no idea of what they were getting into, but he didn't say anything more. He was touched and comforted, knowing that Tuck would be there for no other reason but that they were friends. *Bless him!*

Tuck would be facing their enemy, not with a formidable Gift at his disposal, but with nothing more than a bow and arrows and Mindspeech. Surely Tuck had more to fear from this conflict than Lan did.

"I don't know why Elenor is coming along, though," Tuck continued, frowning at his fingernails. "She can't even fight, and she's not a regular Healer." He shrugged. "Maybe it's to take care of people who've seen too much fighting."

"I don't know why she's coming either," Lan admitted. A draft touched his neck and he put another log on the fire. "And I hate to sound like I don't like her, but I don't think this is the right thing for her to be doing, and I wish they'd let her stay here."

Tuck made a face. "War is no place for *girls*," he intoned, self-importantly. "She's going to take one look and beg to go home."

Of that, Lan was far from as sure as Tuck. "I think you're wrong there," he countered. "I think she's more likely to try and do too much, and hurt herself trying. She hasn't got all the practice that the older Healers have, so she'd know how to pace herself." He sighed. "It doesn't matter anyway. They said she should go, and she's going to."

The real reason that he wished Elenor wasn't coming along was very personal; he didn't understand her, or the way she was acting around him. Kalira only said *she'll outgrow it,* when he asked his Companion's opinion, but wouldn't tell him *what* Elenor was supposed to outgrow.

For a while, Elenor would be fine, just like always, a regular friend. A little bossy, maybe, but sometimes girls were like that. Then for no reason at all, she'd go melancholy and calf-eyed, and if he pressed her to say something or explain what was wrong, she'd just go sullen. Or worst of all, a couple of times she'd gone bursting into tears and running away. And when he saw her again, she'd pretend it hadn't happened.

He was afraid that she was under as much stress as he was; after all, her mother was already in the fighting, her father was going there, and so were her friends. Though her odd behavior had predated the announcement of war—

But she probably heard things from Herald Pol that no one else did. She probably knew there was going to be war way before the rest of us.

He certainly hoped so; selfishly, he didn't want to have to deal with anyone else's troubles, and he *certainly* didn't want to find himself burdened with a weepy girl on a long trip.

:Not that long,: Kalira corrected. *:Six to ten days, at the most. We'll all share carrying Elenor as the double rider, and you have no idea how fast and far we can go in a day.:*

Six to ten days! Lan would never have believed anyone but Kalira—why, it took the average caravan a full *month* to go from Haven to the Southern Border, and that was on the main road, pushing hard, with fit horses in the traces, not oxen, which would be a lot slower!

He supposed he could put up with Elenor for ten days, anyway, and once they were at their assignment, she'd have too much to do to have time for bouts of self-pity, or whatever it was.

"I know what you're going to be doing, but I wonder what they'll want with me," Tuck said, looking worried and self-conscious as the thought occurred to him. "I mean, all I've got is Mindspeaking—"

"You'll be with me, because it takes everything Kalira has to keep me from—losing control," Lan told him. "*She* won't have anything to spare to Mindspeak anyone but me. You'll be my contact with whoever is giving orders, through the Herald that's with him. We'll be behind the main front lines, somewhere high, I expect, where I can see what I need to hit or herd."

"But anybody would do for that," Tuck began anxiously.

"Oh no. I don't want some stranger!" Lan replied sharply. "I don't want somebody who might grab my elbow, or shout in my ear when I don't respond, or anything else! *You* know what not to do around me!"

"I guess," Tuck responded, with relief and the respect only someone who had seen Lan's latest practice sessions would possess. Lan was just grateful that his year-mates gave him respect and not the poorly-disguised fear that his own parents showed. Of his family, once the secret that *he* was responsible for the Merchants' School fire was out—and the fact that the King himself was Lan's personal protector—only Macy wanted anything to do with him. He'd even gotten a note of groveling apology from that loud-mouthed uncle who had so disparaged Heralds at the Midwinter Feast. If it hadn't given him such a sour taste in his mouth, it would have been funny. It was very clear from the note that the stupid lout didn't mean a word of his apology, he just didn't want his nephew to casually incinerate him in a fit of pique.

Macy, thank the gods, was still just as comfortable with him as ever, and he wished, in a way, that he could take her along as well. But if war was no place for Elenor, it was doubly no place for Macy.

"I wish Macy could come," Tuck said, in a wistful echo of his own thoughts. Tuck rolled over on his back and stared up at the ceiling. "But she'd be lost out there, and probably scared, too."

"I think she'd be more annoyed than scared, and frustrated that there wasn't anything she could do," Lan responded, out of his new respect for his little sister. Macy had not only done what he'd suggested and found new teachers at the Guildhouse, she'd informed their mother in no uncertain terms that embroidery for fancy garments was a waste of time and resources under the present circumstances, and that for the duration *she* was going to be making banners and badges for Guard units. And what was more, *she* was spending her free time making lint bandages for the Healers and knitting socks and fingerless gloves for the archers, and her mother could just hold parties without her help.

The end result was that their mother had been shamed into organizing the entire Guild to do the same. The numbers of fingerless gloves streaming southward would probably ensure that every archer in the Army had warm hands before too long.

"Macy would just drive us all crazy because she couldn't really do anything," Lan repeated confidently. "But if this goes on for very long, I wouldn't bet on not seeing her. She's just as likely to get trained as a Healer's assistant so she *can* follow us."

Tuck brightened so much at that idea that Lan had to smother a smile. :*I hope your mother hasn't got some fat merchant picked out for Macy, because there's going to be a war of an entirely different kind in Haven if she tries to bully your sister into a wedding,*: Kalira observed, for once, without a trace of merriment at Tuck's expense. :*I was in doubt at first, but I think those two are remarkably well suited, and that's not the usual thing for a Herald. If they ever wed, it's usually another Herald, a Bard, or a Healer.*:

:Oh? Why?: Lan asked, curiously.

:*Usually someone from one of the Circles is the only person likely to understand how duty comes first—and understand how important our bond is.:* Now Kalira sounded oddly sad, and he wondered why.

Perhaps she had just seen too many blighted romances. It wasn't at all unusual for brief courtships or even full-blown affairs to spring up between Heralds or Trainees and members of the highborn families. Heralds, after all, could be trusted to keep their mouths shut, which was more than could be said for the members of the highborn class. But in the overwhelming majority of the cases, those romantic interludes were doomed to end. Perhaps Kalira had just told him why.

"Macy likes you, too," he blurted, and was rewarded by Tuck's crimson blush that spread over his ears and down the back of his neck.

"I think she's the best girl I've ever met," Tuck declared stoutly. "She's not anywhere near as silly as my sisters. She's got a head on her shoulders, and she knows what she wants to do. And—"

"Whoa, she's my sister, I'm perfectly aware of her virtues," Lan laughed, glad to have something to laugh about at last. "I think she's pretty fine, myself. And I'll tell you something else, if you were worrying about it. Before she'd let Mother nag her into marrying some old Guild goat, she'd run off barefoot in the snow. And within a day she'd probably have wangled herself not only boots, but a cloak and a traveling pack, and she'd be on the way to somewhere she thought she'd be properly appreciated. Like here, for instance."

Tuck had no reply for that, other than an even deeper blush, but he looked relieved and grateful. "Have you got kitchen duty?" he asked instead.

Lan shook his head. "Pol told me that they were relieving anyone in line to be graduated early from all chores, so we can actually get some rest once in a while, in between practice and study."

"Hooo—well, that's one *good* thing this war's done

for us!" Tuck exclaimed with pleasurable surprise. "I guess it's true that inside every rotten thing there's a touch of sweet!"

Lan decided not to spoil things by replying that he would much rather have a countyful of dirty dishes to wash and not have a war. "I guess that's true," he agreed instead. "So why not take advantage of our exalted status, hog a couple of hot baths, then drift in to early dinner like members of the gentry?"

"Sounds good to me," Tuck responded, and stretched luxuriously. "Take advantage of the bathing room while we still get to use it, eh?"

"Good plan," Lan said. *And hope that the bathing room is all that we miss. . . .*

TWENTY

THEY left at dawn, while the sun barely peeked above the horizon, trying without success to burn through the same slate-gray clouds that had hidden the sky for the past week. Elenor rode pillion behind her father, her belongings shared out among the three of them. Lan, Tuck, and Pol carried very little. They needed no supplies for the road, for they would spend their nights at inns, each journey carefully calculated to bring them to their day's destination three to four candlemarks after sunset. They each carried only enough in the way of clothing to get them to the army. After that, they would be supplied as regularly as if they were at the Collegium. Elenor and her things were no burden to the three Companions.

Halfway between Haven and the Border, they would meet up with Pol's wife, Healer Ilea, at one of their nightly stops. She and Pol would decide then if she would return with them to the army, or go back to Haven. Lan privately hoped that her mother would persuade Elenor to turn back and go with her to Healers' Collegium.

It was cold, mortally cold, this morning. The snow
had thawed and frozen so many times that now it was
granular and crunchy; no one could have made snow
figures or snowballs out of it even if they'd had the
heart to. It wasn't only the Collegium that had lost
young people to this war—it was the Palace as well.
The Court had been decimated by the rush to volunteer, until it was said in the halls of the Collegium
that the only courtiers left were those who could not
be spared, the lame, and the old.

Lan put all that behind him as they rode out of the
South Gate—one he had not yet used—and trotted
through the silent city. A few early risers looked out
of their windows when they heard the chiming hoofbeats of the Companions. Those who spotted them—
or encountered them—waved solemnly or gave little
nods. Lan noted that Pol always returned these little
gestures of respect, and did likewise.

He felt very strange in his new Whites, and he
couldn't forget for a moment that he was wearing his
new uniform. The Whites were made of entirely different materials than the Grays, and were tailored to
him. Trainee uniforms were comfortable enough, but
full Whites were little more than a second skin. Where
the Gray tunics were heavy canvas or wool, the Field
Whites were butter-soft doeskin. The winter shirts that
went beneath the tunics were chirra wool or ramie
and linen; the Trainees made do with wool or plain
linen. Trews were doeskin again—Trainees got canvas.
Hose beneath the trews were finely knitted linen or
chirra wool, where Trainees got stockings of heavier
wool or baggy woven linen. Only in the matter of
boots did Trainees and Heralds fare alike.

After due consideration and consultation with Master Odo, neither Lan nor Tuck wore swords, though
both had daggers and bows. The Weaponsmaster
deemed neither of them able enough with the longer
blade to be effective with it, and Lan was just as glad.
He felt awkward enough with the heavy dagger at his

belt and the quiver on his back, and he was used to using both.

It hadn't snowed for two weeks, and the old snow piled along the sides of the street had gotten to a fairly grimy stage. Everything conspired to produce an aura of depression, from the thin, gray light to the dirty, weatherbeaten snow to the cracked paint and chipped trim on houses and shops that wouldn't be repaired until spring. He was glad when they left the city at last and into the countryside, where at least things didn't look quite as tired and tatty.

Once out of the city, the Companions took up a very peculiar pace—not a trot, not a fast walk, certainly not a canter. It was very like the lope of a wolf, the ground-eating stride that members of the canine family could keep up for candlemarks at a time—or perhaps the long-legged stride that elk used to migrate. It was a comfortable pace for a rider; a smooth, rocking motion. There was an arrangement of straps on Kalira's saddle, now rolled up and tucked out of the way, that would allow Lan to strap himself in so that he could even sleep while she moved onward. He reckoned that he would have to be very tired before he tried *that* little trick, but Heralds had certainly used it before.

Pol rode slightly ahead of Lan and Tuck; from time to time Elenor would look back at them and smile, but for the most part, she seemed engrossed in the scenery, what there was of it. The early part of the morning took them through a patchwork of fields inhabited by sheep or cattle, pawing through the snow to get to the grass beneath, or cultivated fields that waited for the plow beneath a thick blanket of white. Not an unblemished blanket, though; tracks of animals, the occasional human, and birds marked the surface. Once Lan spotted the place where a fox had taken a rabbit or something about that size by the tracks and the churned-up spot; another time the predator had clearly been a hawk, since the only footprints were those of the hare, and they ended in a splash of dark, old blood.

By midmorning they had passed their first village; every person that was about gathered along the side of the road to wave them onward, faces solemn. All three of them returned the salutes this time; only Elenor didn't wave, and that was largely because she was too busy holding to her father's waist with both mittened hands.

No one looked askance at a Green-clad Healer riding pillion behind a Herald; evidently that was just as familiar a sight as that of the Heralds themselves riding south. They were through the village quickly, and out into the countryside just as the first flurries began to fall.

Through air chill and quiet, without so much as a stirring of breeze, the tiny flakes dusted over the old snow and softened the edges of the bare branches. For a while it was a pleasure to ride beneath; he and Tuck actually started a game of trying to catch snowflakes on their tongues before they began to get truly hungry. By the time their stomachs were making embarrassing noises so that even Pol glanced back with a thin smile, they reached a village large enough to support an inn at last.

The Companions slowed to a walk just as Lan spotted the welcome sign hanging over a door, and Pol pulled them all up beneath it. They didn't dismount, though, much to Elenor's open dismay, and Lan's secret disappointment. One of the inn servitors brought hot meat and berry pies wrapped in napkins, and mugs of cider that steamed in the cold air. They ate in the saddle while the servant went back inside—though perhaps ate was too tame a word for the way they wolfed down the food—and exchanged empty mugs and napkins for packets of paper-wrapped sausage, bread, and cheese when the servant returned. Pol saluted the man, tossed him a coin as a tip, and they

were off again before a quarter of a candlemark had
passed.

The snow thickened as they ate, and soon after their
departure it was no longer flurries, it was fat flakes.
The air seemed a trifle warmer and held a distinct
dampness; snow curtained the road in front of them,
and the Companions slowed, although their pace was
still faster than any horse would set.

:This is going to get thicker,: Kalira said at last, the
first that she had actually spoken since they left the
Collegium. *:Not a blizzard, but a thick snowfall.* We
*won't be terribly slowed, but they'll have to get the road
crews out before nightfall.:*

"It's going to take us longer to reach our inn than
I thought," Pol called back over his shoulder. "Are
you all right with that, or would you rather we stopped
at the first inn we find at about the time we expected
to stop?"

The look of agony that Elenor cast back over her
shoulder decided Lan. "Stop when we find an inn,
please," he replied. "It might not be as comfortable,
but we're not used to riding for this long."

"Ah. Right." The startled, then thoughtful look that
Pol gave back to him suggested to Lan that the senior
Herald had understood who "we" really was. His next
move confirmed it, as he directed them all to stop for
a moment and get down to stretch their legs and take
care of other pressing business. The snow was thick
enough now to provide a modesty curtain for them
all, which relieved Lan considerably. The cold made
things awkward enough without the added factor of
embarrassment in front of Elenor.

"She's not doing too badly yet," Tuck observed, as
they washed their hands with snow. "Not a peep out
of her."

Lan kept his doubts to himself, and just nodded.
He really hoped that the rigors of this journey would
convince Elenor to turn back around.

Pol mounted Satiran and extended his hand to his

daughter. He pulled Elenor back up onto the pillion, and she tried not to wince. "No, sweetling, don't sit astride," he told her, as she tried to get her leg over Satiran's rump. "Sit side-saddle fashion. We aren't going to be going that fast, you'll be safe enough, and it's a different position for your legs. You'll be all right." The young Healer obeyed him. Although this was a less stable position, it clearly gave her aching legs a lot of relief, given her expression.

Pol looked back to see that the other two were mounted, and waved them on.

The snow was so thick now that Lan couldn't see more than a wagon's length to either side of the road, or ahead. They might just as well have been moving along on a treadmill, going nowhere. It was an odd feeling.

The snow itself, light and fluffy, took no effort for the Companions to push through. Things might be different, though, if the wind began to blow. Wind would create drifts and pack the snow hard where it collected. He hoped they wouldn't get any before they stopped for the night; it could turn the last hours of the day into a waking nightmare.

Not to mention what it would be like for the poor Companions.

:Thank you for thinking of me at last,: Kalira teased.

:Perhaps I ought to stop thinking of things that can go wrong,: he observed ironically, as a light wind picked up and blew the falling flakes toward them.

:Isn't that like trying not to think of a blue cow?: she replied, and bowed her head into the wind. *:Better fasten your cloak tight while you still can.:*

Lan took her advice, making certain that every clasp on his cloak was fastened tightly and that his scarf was wrapped around his neck and tucked in, tying the strings of his hood tight around his face. Glancing to the side, he saw that Tuck was doing the same, so he must have been warned. Pol, the old hand at this, needed no warning; he must have buttoned himself up while waiting for them to come back from stretching their legs.

The wind picked up noticeably, and as darkness fell, it was impossible to tell where the road was, much less where Pol and Tuck were. Lan just put his head down and closed his eyes, keeping one hand just holding the reins loosely, the other tucked inside his cloak. Wind-blown snow caked his cloak and hood, and after a few futile attempts to shake it off, he gave up and allowed it to collect. As the light faded into a thick, blue-tinged dusk, and from dusk into full dark, there was no sign of anyone living along the road, although Lan knew that they must be passing by farms and even small villages. Candles and lanterns couldn't penetrate this weather.

:*The only way we're going to find an inn is by running into it!*: he said anxiously.

:*No worries; we know where we are, even if you can't see*,: Kalira replied. :*Tuck's keeping track of exactly where the farms are in case we have to go to ground as someone's guest. He just opened up his shields a bit, without actually hearing anyone's thoughts; he can lead us straight to a farmhouse if need be. And Pol and Satiran have been this way a dozen times. It might seem like forever, but we'll be at an inn before they clear away the supper dishes and close the kitchen for the night.*:

He certainly hoped so; with all of his precautions, he was still getting awfully cold. The wind found its way under his cloak in so many places it was useless to try to identify them and close them off. And luncheon was wearing mightily thin . . . he worried off one snow-caked glove with the help of his teeth, biting into the ice-crusted fingertips to hold it while he slipped his hand out. He certainly couldn't *see* well enough to keep track of a loose glove, and as for holding onto it with his other benumbed hand, already clutching reins and pommel, that was out of the question.

He fished his paper-wrapped package of bread and cheese out of his belt-pouch, unwrapped it, managed to stow the paper in his pouch and wriggle his fingers back into his glove without dropping anything. The cheese and bread weren't cut; a small, hand-sized loaf had one end cut out, a hollow made, and the cheese stuffed into it. That made less to drop, and it was easier for gloved hands to hold. He bit into it, getting drink as well as food in the form of the snow that coated every bite. The bread, cold-toughened and chewy, made his jaws ache, but it eased the hunger pains in his gut, and he was glad to have it. There was one thing to be said for tough, chewy bread; it didn't crumble the way pastry would. He had no way of cleaning up a mess at the moment.

Poor Kalira had nothing at all to sustain her, and he saved half of his bread for her, although it wasn't much more than a generous mouthful. He held it down near his knee and felt her turn her head and take it from him. With the bitless bridle that Companions wore, she could chew in complete comfort.

:Thank you, love,: she said gratefully. *:That helps.:*

He wondered how the others were faring. Elenor at least had her father's broad back to shelter behind; she couldn't possibly be as cold as he, Tuck, and Pol were. And she had Pol right with her; for all that he could sense, he and Kalira might have been completely on their own in this storm.

The wind howled and sobbed among the trees on either side of the road. At least, he assumed there were trees on either side of the road, since wind usually didn't make those sort of noises sweeping by itself, unintercepted across an empty plain. He *thought* he heard branches rattling above him, and hoped that none of them were weak enough to come down just as they were riding beneath.

:That would be bad,: Kalira agreed.

Her response didn't exactly comfort him.

Soon, he told himself. *She said it would be soon. If*

nothing else, we'll have something hot to eat and drink, a fire, and a flat place to sleep soon. But it was impossible to tell how fast or slow they were going, and there was nothing to give him any clue to the passing of time. If his life depended on it, he couldn't have told how long it had been since he'd eaten that bread.

:We're nearly there,: Kalira told him as he wriggled his numbing toes in his boots to try and get them a little warmer. *:If we could see through this muck, we'd see the inn windows from here.:*

Wherever *here* was. But his heart warmed, even if his feet didn't, and he sat up a little straighter in the saddle—which turned out to be a mistake, as he immediately let in another cold draft under his cloak. Still, nearly there was accurate; sooner than he'd thought, they were dismounting stiffly in front of a tiny inn, distinguished chiefly by the wooden wheat sheaf over the door. Their hostess herself, a round bundle of cloak, conducted them to the stables after helping Elenor inside.

The stables were nothing but a single, stoutly-built shed, but the shed had thick walls made of mud-brick and a thatched roof, and that freedom from the driving wind alone made it seem as warm as a cozy kitchen. With the help of the hostess, Pol and Tuck dragged in straw for bedding and hay for fodder, while Lan filled buckets of water from the pump and set up more buckets of grain, then stripped all three Companions of their tack and rubbed them down. With straw knee-deep on the floor and blankets of wool patchwork thrown over them, the Companions munched their way gratefully through their belated dinners, and the Heralds followed the innkeeper back into the tiny inn.

Tiny it might be, but it was a snug little place, nicely warmed by a good fire. Elenor huddled beside it, but she wasn't just warming herself, she was tending a pot that bubbled over it.

"Ye be my on'y guests, sir Herald," the innkeeper

said to Pol as they both took off their cloaks and hung them on pegs cemented into the wall of the fireplace. "This's nout a big place, belike—" Her round face was anxious. "Have'na got guest room; on'y me own bed above. Girl can sleep wi' me, but—"

"So long as you have enough straw for us," Pol replied. "We'll make do on the floor, and be grateful."

Her anxious face lightened. "Ne need of straw—got featherbed beg enow for three. Pease pottage suit ye, or ye druther I kill a chicken?"

"*Anything* hot right now is far preferable even to a feast in a candlemark," Pol laughed. "Come along, boys, let's give our hostess a hand."

The inn was nothing more than a single room, really. There was no kitchen; all cooking was done on the hearth. The brick floor was spotlessly clean, though, with any vestige of dirt dug out with ruthless strokes of a straw broom and sent out the front door. With a bake oven built into the sides of the large fireplace, itself big enough to comfortably roast a small pig, and warming shelves built into the upper level, she had everything she needed for a kitchen. Shelves beside the fireplace held her dishes and pots, water came from the pump outside. There was one table, rough-hewn and black with age, two benches, and four little stools. The room was dominated by the barrels ranged along one wall; beer, soft cider, hard cider, and one small barrel of wine. This was not so much an inn as a village tavern, a place to eat a little and perhaps drink a great deal, but not a place intended to house travelers.

Nevertheless, this round, brown little woman was equal to her unplanned task. They all settled on stools on the hearth, wanting to soak up as much heat as possible. She scurried up into the loft after serving them all hot bowls of pease pottage and warm, buttered bread. While they ate, she lugged down a featherbed that preceded her and followed her on the ladder; she shoved the table to one side and piled the benches atop it, spread the featherbed on the floor, and added a couple of patchwork blankets identical to the ones she had supplied to the Companions.

Lan cradled his bowl in his lap, absorbing heat from it as he ate. He wasn't so much hungry now as just weary, and he basked in the heat like an old cat while he took slow bites of his bread, alternating with spoonfuls of pottage and sips of cider. When he finished the bowl, their hostess was at his elbow immediately.

"More?" she asked, taking his bowl. He shook his head. "Just sleep," he told her, handing her his cup as well. As the heat soaked into him, so did weariness. He stood up as she bustled over to the wall, filled a basin with water from a bucket and began the washing-up.

He plodded the few steps over to the featherbed, took the spot nearest the wall, wrapped one of the blankets around himself, and sank down onto the mattress. For once, he didn't even dream of fire.

THE storm ended some time in the night, and finally the sun was not hidden behind a shroud of clouds when it rose. Pol roused them early and got them on the road with only a pause to wash up in the basin and eat a bit of bread and butter. Elenor moved stiffly down the ladder from the loft, washed her hands and face, and remained standing while she ate.

"Are you saddle-sore?" Lan asked, feeling sorry for her, in spite of the fact that he wished she hadn't come along.

She made a face. "Very," she said, looking and acting more like her old self. "My legs hurt so much I don't even want to think about riding. But—if you can do it, so can I." She looked so stubborn that he decided not to remind her that she could turn around and go back whenever she chose. She would be welcome in any village if she chose to give up, and the next Herald or Bard coming through could bring her back home when she was ready.

Apparently she was not going to give up yet.

"Finish your breakfasts," Pol said shortly. "We have a lot of distance to make up today." The door closed on his last word; he was impatient, the first time that Lan had ever seen him like that.

"I ast him if he 'ouldn't wait on gettin' some hot parriche for ye, but he 'ouldn't hev it," the plump innkeeper said worriedly, looking like a fretful sparrow. She was making up packets of bread and cheese, using the paper saved from yesterday to wrap them. "Reckon he's saddlin' now."

With that to warn him, Lan hastily finished his breakfast and put on his cloak, while Tuck helped the innkeeper get the featherbed back up into the loft. He went out into the brilliantly white world, squinting against the glare, and pushed his way through the snow, following Pol's track to the shed.

"You're done, good," Pol said without looking around. "We've got to get going. It'll be slow, pushing through until we get to where the storm ended or where the road crews have gotten."

"Right," was all Lan said; he picked up Kalira's saddle blanket, beat the snow out of it, and threw it over her back. Kalira was nose-deep in her grain bucket, as were the other two, stuffing themselves with food that was much more concentrated nourishment than hay. It was a race to see whether the Heralds would finish saddling before the Companions finished eating, and in the end, the Companions whuffled up the last grains just as Pol pulled Satiran's girth tight.

Tuck brought out the food packets and gave one each to Pol and Lan as they came around to the front with the Companions. The innkeeper came with him, again a shapeless bundle in her frayed-edged, brown wool cloak. They all mounted, and with a wince,

Elenor took her father's hand and mounted up behind him.

"Lady, thank you," Pol said, bending down and handing four road-chits, the tokens used by traveling Heralds, into her hand. A road-chit entitled the innkeeper who got it to a remission of tax, a benefit more valuable than actual payment. "I know that you were not at all prepared for overnight guests, and your hospitality and readiness to deal with us was truly, deeply appreciated."

The innkeeper, who probably had not seen one road-chit in her life, much less four, blushed modestly. "Eh, now, was I s'posed to turn ye inter the road again? 'Twas good of ye t' put up wit' sleepin' on me floor an' all."

Pol just smiled, reached down again, and squeezed her hand. Then he and Satiran turned and began pushing through the snow, back on the road, with Tuck and Lan following.

By midafternoon, they came to the point where the new snow tapered off, and there was nothing much to contend with but a dusting that covered the older, granulated stuff. Then they were able to pick up their pace again, pushing harder than they had the first day. But Pol stopped more often, too; once in midmorning to let them eat their packets of food, once at noon, for luncheon, and once again for another snack when they broke out of the snowfield. Each time, Elenor shifted positions on the pillion, and that seemed to help her.

The next three days were identical, and as Elenor grew more accustomed to day-long riding and the uncertain conditions of inns on the road, Lan gave up the idea that she was going to quit. At least for now, anyway. Maybe when she got to the fighting, and saw what it was like, she might change her mind.

The fourth day was special, and the reason why Pol was in such a hurry to make up the time lost. Healer Ilea, Elenor's mother and Pol's' wife, was waiting for them at the inn where they would make their nightly stop.

Pol's back was a study in tension; Satiran stretched his legs just a trifle more in each step, and his urgency communicated itself to the other two Companions. Even Elenor forgot her aches in anticipation of seeing her mother. For once, the reason for going south in the first place got pushed to the back of everyone's thoughts.

The inn that they arrived at—well after darkness fell—could not have been more unlike their first stop. This was a huge place, three two-storied wings joined in the shape of a horseshoe, with its own courtyard in the center. The stables formed the back side, and travelers entered the center court through a passage made in the center of the front wing. There were torches on either side of the passage, and lanterns in the courtyard; even at this late hour, people were coming and going. From the faint sound of music, and the babble of voices, the inn was popular with the locals as well as travelers.

Stable hands came to take the Companions, asking their names and treating them just as they would be at the Collegium—which was to say, like people, and not like horses. Pol just gave Satiran a congratulatory pat and sent him on his way, following his stable hand without the latter even attempting to lead him with the reins.

:Satiran's told me about this place. We're going to be spoiled outrageously,: Kalira told Lan, with just a touch of greed. He laughed, relieved, and dismounted. She followed her sire, her attendant following *her,* with her ears up and a very light step on the cobblestones of the courtyard.

With a thatched roof, stone walls, and shuttered windows, this inn looked as comfortable as a farmhouse, but built on a massive scale. A myriad of chimney pots poking up through the thatch promised warm and comfortable rooms. They were definitely expected. A servant met them before they even reached the door.

"Herald Pol," the young man said, a statement rather than a question. "If you will all come with me, please?"

The servant led them past the common room, filled with people eating and drinking, a Bard entertaining at the far end beside a fireplace large enough to roast an entire ox. There wasn't an ox on the spit at the moment, only a boar, or rather, what was left of the boar. Most of him was either on plates or already inside patrons, and the mouth-watering aroma nearly drove Lan crazy.

They had a bit of a distance to go; down a long corridor, then up a flight of stairs, and around a corner. But the long walk was worth it; the servant ushered them into a warm and welcoming private parlor with more doors opening off of it. There was already a fire burning in the fireplace, a pitcher of drink and some food laid ready, and a woman in Healer's Greens rising from her seat by the fire so quickly she might have been stung.

She flung herself into Pol's arms, and Elenor joined the embrace. Lan and Tuck exchanged an embarrassed glance, and with one accord, turned their attention to the fruit and bread on the table, turning their backs on the reunited family to give them at least the illusion of privacy.

Só far as Lan was concerned, a welcome interruption came before they finished picking over the light refreshments, in the form of the arrival of dinner. Three servants arrived with trays; the remains of the snacks were whisked away. The family embrace broke up, and the table beside the fire quickly set up for a meal. Juicy slices of pork steamed on a heated platter, garnished with roasted onions and apples. A bowl of mashed turnips topped with butter and brown sugar, a loaf of hot bread, steaming peas, and a whole apple pie completed the repast, and Lan and Tuck had no hesitation in sitting right down and helping themselves.

"So," Ilea said, taking a seat between Pol and Elenor, and meeting the eyes of each boy with a frank gaze. "This is Lavan, and this is Tuck. I'm pleased to finally meet you boys."

Lan put his hand to his breast and gave her a little formal bow, which seemed to amuse her. Ilea was a stunning woman, although her effect was due as much to force of personality as to her looks. Her eyes were huge, dominating her face; masses of dark brown hair surrounded it. She had thin lips, but Lan had the sense that when she wasn't worried, she smiled often and enthusiastically, as she was smiling now. A nose too long, perhaps, for beauty still suited her face and lent it strength.

"Never mind us, m'lady," Tuck said, after swallowing a huge mouthful of food. "You just catch up with your family and pretend we aren't here. Right now I'd druther have food than talking."

That amused her as well, but she took him up on his advice, and turned to her husband and daughter, exchanging tales of what had been going on with them while Lan and Tuck ate.

Lan couldn't help noticing that, while Pol and Elenor (though mostly Pol; Elenor did more listening that talking) were full of gossip and stories about mutual acquaintances and friends, Ilea's tales concentrated on what life was like for a Healer on the battlefield. Though she often couched her stories in such a way as to get a rueful chuckle at the end, the point of each was clear. Day-to-day life was full of hardship, Healers witnessed terrible things with virtually every passing candlemark, and the consequences of being captured were far worse than merely being hurt or killed by a stray arrow.

So her mother doesn't want Elenor to go to the front either, Lan thought, his interest piqued. *Well, good!*

He didn't much like what *he* heard, though, even

given that Ilea might be exaggerating a trifle. Pol was
right; the Karsites must have been planning this for
the past couple of years. Valdemaran forces were only
just keeping the enemy advance to a crawl, but they
were already into Valdemaran territory, and showed
no signs of stopping. Their fighters were well trained,
not unskilled or half-trained conscripts. And their officers were fanatics.

That put a distinct chill up Lan's back. He had
thought that he would be able to frighten the Karsites
with a display of fire; would he really have to actually
hurt people? Or even kill them?

No. I can't, he told himself firmly, as a sick feeling
rose in him. *I can't do that. I'll find a way around it,
or Pol will, or whoever is commanding the army. I
can't hurt anyone.*

I've done too much of that already.

TWENTY-ONE

Ilea and Pol

ILEA closed the door to the bedchamber behind her and put her back to it, giving Pol one of those looks he had come to recognize over the years as significant and serious. Her hair had fallen charmingly over one eye, with a suggestion of flirtation, but the expression in her eyes was not in the least amatory.

"Are you aware that Elenor is in love with that boy?" she asked peremptorily.

Pol sighed. He would have so much preferred not to deal with this until after he'd had Ilea to himself for a while. He took the candles out of their sconces around the room, lit them at the fire, and replaced them to give himself time to think. "I would have said *infatuated* rather than 'in love,' but yes," he replied with resignation. He knew as well as Ilea that Lan was "that boy" and not Tuck, nor any other boy of their acquaintance; there was no point in prevaricating with questions of which boy she meant.

He sat on the edge of the canopied bed, the only furniture in the room, and waited for her reply. "At her age, they're the same," Ilea responded, giving vent

to her agitation in pacing back and forth in the con-
fines of the little room, but never taking her eyes off
her husband. "Well?"

"Well what?" he asked, reasonably, he thought, but
she rolled her eyes upward, as if asking the heavens
for help with his denseness.

"Well, what are you doing about it?"

"Nothing. She's not likely to confide in any mere
male, and especially not her father," he pointed out.
"And it wasn't *my* idea to bring her along, it was the
King's, and Jedin's; they only know that she's Lan's
friend and they want friends around him to keep him
sane. The fact that she's a Mind-Healer was just that
much more reason to send her. I'm hoping now that
in constant contact with Lavan, she's going to wear
out her passion against his indifference. Or failing
that, she'll take one look at the battlefield and beg
you to take her back home."

Ilea relaxed a little, as if he'd put at least one of
her fears to rest, and stopped pacing. "You're sure
he's indifferent?" she asked—begged, rather.

Pol sighed again, shook his head, and patted the top
of the bed beside him. She accepted the silent invitation and sat beside him, pulling her legs up onto the
quilted coverlet and curling up against his shoulder.
"Lan couldn't be anything but indifferent to Elenor—
or any girl, for that matter. He's already lifebonded.
To his Companion," he added, to cut through any
more questions.

Ilea squirmed around and looked into his face, her
own features a mask of incredulity. "You *aren't* joking!" she exclaimed, stunned, and even a little
shocked. "Oh, no! Poor Elenor!"

"And poor Lan, and poor Kalira—that's his Companion—" he replied. "Herald-bond *and* lifebond?
They're never out of each other's heads, and if anything happens to Kalira, Lan just goes—crazy—" He
shook his head. "When she was hurt, he couldn't think
of anything else, and it was no use attempting to get

him to try. No one his age should have to cope with a full lifebond. It's not healthy. He doesn't even know who he is, yet, but now he's inextricably bound up with someone who isn't his age, his sex, or even human."

"But apparently in his case, it's necessary," she brooded, putting her head back on his shoulder with a sigh of her own. "If what I've heard is true. *She's* the controlling force on his Gift?"

"Exactly, and I'm not sure she could do that if they weren't lifebonded. But he's never going to be *himself,* whole and entire, and he's never going to be independent. Is he?" he asked her doubtfully, leaning back against the pillows and making them both more comfortable.

"Ask Elenor. I'm not the Mind-Healer. Or, rather," she corrected hastily, "*don't* ask Elenor. I'd rather she didn't take him on as a Cause; there's nothing more certain of cementing misplaced infatuation into permanency than being Needed."

Pol heard the inflection that turned the word into an icon, and he agreed with her. "I talked with her back when I first saw this happening," he said, hastening to let her know that he hadn't shirked his parental duties. "I tried—I really *tried* to make her understand that she—she couldn't hope to compete— I *tried*—"

Ilea wrapped her arms around him, and he relaxed into her embrace. *Gods, it's so good to be with her again—*

"I know you did, and I know you didn't try anything as stupid as flatly opposing her," she said into his ear. "Nothing feeds romance like opposition, and you know it."

Thank you for that, my love, and for your confidence in my good sense.

"She'll talk to me about it, sooner rather than later, I think," Ilea continued, as her hair tickled his nose and he tucked it under his chin. "I don't know what else I can do, but at least I can keep track of how she's feeling."

"Satiran reminds me fairly often that parents can't cushion the blows our children set themselves up for," he murmured into her ear, breathing in the warm scent of herbs that always clung to her.

"I'm not going to think any more about it until tomorrow," she said firmly.

He was perfectly willing to go along with her on that score.

MIDMORNING, and they were less than half a day from the Southern Border and the war, and yet there was no sign of the conflict here other than the wear on the roads. They were no longer on the main roads; this was the way that Ilea had passed coming up here, and they were all returning to report to the main quarters of the Lord Marshal. This was a pine forest, a very old one; the scent was fantastic in here, but the boughs all overhung the road, completely blocking the sun and leaving them in half-light no brighter than twilight.

Pol led the way, unburdened for once. Ilea was up behind Lan, and Elenor behind Tuck. Ilea was a perfect passenger, actually; she was friendly and made intelligent conversation; Lan much preferred her to Elenor.

"We moved the Headquarters to White Foal Pass just before I left," Ilea told him. "That's why this little road hasn't been trampled to bare dirt yet. It looked to the Lord Marshal as if the Karsites were going to make a big push there. It would be the logical place to go with as large a force as they have. White Foal is the only pass where they get big numbers of men through quickly."

"Not to mention the value of pushing us back at

White Foal Pass," Lan replied grimly. "There's an awful lot of symbolic significance there if even I can see that. . . ."

Ilea nodded. He felt her hair move against his shoulder. Then, before he could continue his thought—

—something dropped down out of the tree head of them.

Frozen between shock and total terror, Lan jerked on the reins, and Kalira shied sideways.

It—no, *he*—landed on the pillion behind Pol, knocking Satiran sideways with the unexpected weight. Hooves skidding on the icy road, Satiran shrieked as his hind feet slid out from underneath him, but the black-hooded man grabbed Pol around the chest and shoulders and pulled him sideways. They tumbled to the ground together, Pol fighting to get his arms free and shouting, Satiran scrambling to get his feet under him again.

Elenor screamed, and kept screaming, a high, thin, terror-filled wail; Ilea didn't make a sound, but her hands clutched Lan's upper arms so tightly it hurt. Lan's stomach flipped, but it was the only part of him that could move. He couldn't even breathe—

The man had a knife, a black-bladed knife that didn't reflect light at all; it drew Lan's eyes and filled his gaze as the man brandished it.

He'd wrapped his legs around Pol's body, trapping Pol's arms so the Herald couldn't get to his weapons. He shouted something as he and Pol struggled on the ground—it was Karsite, something about demons—

:*Lan!*: Kalira shouted at him, but he couldn't shake off his paralysis—

The attacker grabbed Pol's hair, pulling his head back. Satiran, still shrieking a battle cry, whirled. His hooves pounded the ground a hair away from Pol, but he couldn't trample the man and not get Pol, too.

Tuck fought with Elenor to keep her from leaping into the fray. Ilea frozen and rigid, only whimpered.

The dragon within Lan flamed into life with a roar, ready to kill.

Taste of metal, of blood—the taste of anger—

The dragon uncoiled in a rush, craving death, fire, destruction. It lunged at the restraints that held it, raged against the bindings, filling Lan's mind and soul with a dreadful lust.

No! He couldn't. That was a man, not a bundle of straw!

:Lan!: Kalira shouted at him. *:Now!:*

This was all happening too fast, he couldn't think!

Flames washing through him, straining his control—

Only fire would save his friend. He had to let the dragon kill!

No! Pol was—Pol was a fighter! He could—surely he would free himself—Lan couldn't kill a *man*—

As the man struck at Pol's throat, Pol wrenched his head down and to the side and his hands grabbed the man's feet, twisting in a move Lan had seen Odo demonstrate a dozen times. Lan's heart pounded, his head felt full to bursting—

Blood fountained, as the man slashed his knife across Pol's eyes instead of his throat, blood gushing everywhere, staining the snow, dyeing the Whites a terrible crimson.

And something inside Lan parted with a *snap.*

Yesyesyesyesyes!

Pol screamed. Ilea and Tuck screamed. Elenor was still screaming.

Lan's throat closed, his hands clenched on the reins, and his vision tunneled—but the Karsite exploded into flame.

Firedeathragehate—

Ilea scrambled down from the pillion running for Pol. Lan barely noticed. He was bathed in fire, tiny flamelets dancing from the tips of his fingers, floating in the air around him. This was what he had been born for—

The dragon within him exulted in its freedom, and ravaged the Karsite within and without. Bound to the dragon, one with the dragon, he *was* the dragon now, and the dragon was rage and flame and hunger. The Karsite died instantly, but death was not enough, not nearly enough! He spun in a circle of fire and danced a *volta* of revenge as the Karsite burned and burned and burned.

THE knife fell, as Pol tried to squirm out of the way, and the blackened steel sliced across his face.

Gods!

A streak of agony, darkness, the hot gush of his own blood over his cheeks.

He screamed, the sound tearing from his throat, but kept fighting. The next stroke could be the final one—

He held to consciousness and twisted the Karsite's ankles until the man himself shouted in pain, then wrenched himself free of the Karsite somehow, still screaming in agony.

He scrambled away over the snow on hands and knees, horrible pain making him *want* to curl himself into a ball and just lie there screaming. He heard a strange sound behind him, as if something very large and soft had plummeted out of the sky to land in the snow as he scrambled, blind and still howling with agony, toward the place where he thought the rest of them were—

Teeth grabbed his collar and hauled him unceremoniously out of harm's way, dropping him literally in Ilea's lap.

Only then did he fall into blessed unconsciousness.

:LAN! Lan!:

Lan ignored the mind-voice—until it resorted to a sort of mind-*kick* that finally got his attention.

Shaken out of his entrancement, this time the mind-voice penetrated the wash of fire and the terrible joy.

:Lan, enough! Pol needs you!:

Oh, gods—He shook his head and wrenched himself out of the meld with the dragon, fighting to get his eyes open.

Without his full attention feeding it, the dragon found itself quickly enchanted again by Kalira. Sullenly, it coiled itself deep inside his mind, and dropped into uneasy slumber. Jolted back into the real world, Lan opened his eyes on a black patch in the snow that held *nothing*, nothing but a bit of melted metal—not a body, not even bones. Nothing but ashes.

Ilea sat on the bare road, Pol's bloody head in her lap, a frown of fierce concentration in her face. The gash across Pol's eyes closed even as Lan watched, but there was no doubt that the knife had cut right across Pol's eyes, blinding him, perhaps forever.

Gut-wrenching guilt hit him and nearly knocked him out of the saddle. *Oh, gods, what have I done*—

"Don't sit there feeling sorry for yourself," Ilea snarled with a touch of hysteria in her voice, without looking up. "I need hot water and bandages, and I need them *now*. And a fire, before he goes into shock. And don't wallow in guilt until after you've got it going."

Elenor was useless; that much was obvious; she knelt in the snow and sobbed into her hands next to her father. That left Lan and Tuck; Lan went for wood while Tuck slid off his Companion and emptied the contents of all the saddlebags onto the ground.

When Lan returned with the wood, afoot now, with the wood piled onto Kalira's back, Tuck had spread blankets over the snow and Pol lay on them, his face neatly bandaged. There was a strange scent in the air, not of burned meat, but a metallic scent, hot stone and scorched earth. Lan piled the wood near Pol and Ilea and ignited it, turning it into a roaring fire in an instant. As he went back for more wood, Ilea pushed a small pot holding clean snow near the flames to melt for water.

When he returned the second time, Elenor was finally doing something, cleaning some of the blood off her father's face and clothing and helping her mother, although she was sobbing as she worked. Tuck was off getting more wood himself.

Ilea was on the verge of hysteria. "I *can't* stop now!" she shouted at Elenor, in response to a tear-choked entreaty. "I am *not* going to let your father go blind! I *will* Heal him, I swear it, if I have to die trying!"

At that, Elenor took her hands off her mother's and grabbed Ilea's shoulders, shaking her. "And what good will *that* do?" she shrieked, as Ilea went limp with surprise and her head jerked back and forth from the shaking. "You'll *kill* him if you die!"

That seemed to snap Ilea out of her crazed state. She stared at Elenor in shock, then the two of them fell into each other's arms, weeping. Lan stared at them all, and it was only Kalira who snapped *him* out of his trance.

:Drape blankets over all of them and get some more wood!: his Companion said harshly, then actually walked over to her sire and *bit* him on the neck. Satiran's sagging head flew up. Lan didn't hear what went on between them, but he didn't wait to see anything more. Draping blankets over the sobbing women and over Pol, he escaped to the forest again, and a job he could understand.

He went back, and back again, until he was stumbling through dusk that obscured everything in his path and was forced to give up. By then, Ilea was sleeping, and Elenor organizing a crude camp. The three Companions arranged themselves in three sides of a square around the blankets spread on the snow, lying down. Pol lay still unconscious, with his eyes bandaged and his head pillowed on Satiran's flank, between Ilea and Kalira. The fire formed the fourth side of the square. Tuck wearily ate a handful of bread, and Elenor looked up at Lan's entrance.

"Get some sleep," she said shortly, her voice nasal and thick with weeping. "If we can, we'll have to leave in the morning. We've no food and no shelter; we *can't* stay here."

Lan didn't say anything; guilt devoured him and killed any appetite he might have had. He lay down obediently and turned his face away from Elenor, sure that he wasn't going to get a wink of sleep all night.

And he was right. He stared at Dacerie's flank and the firelight flickering on it for candlemarks, stomach knotted with misery while the stars wheeled overhead. He heard Tuck lie down and eventually begin breathing deeply. He heard Elenor gently fall over sideways—

When he looked, *she* was asleep, half-propped by Tuck's body, up against Satiran's shoulder.

He sat up. *:I'll take care of the fire,:* he told Satiran, Mindspeaking so as not to make a sound.

Satiran nodded, ever so slightly, but did not reply. Lan found some relief from his guilt by making certain the fire burned evenly and without smoke, feeding it diligently as the stars paraded overhead.

As dawn neared, he felt a tap on his shoulder.

"I'll take over now," Tuck said, giving him an understanding smile. He nodded, finally so dull with exhaustion he couldn't feel anything. He curled up against Dacerie's shoulder, and knew nothing more.

HE woke to hear Pol's voice.

"—all right," he said, as Lan started up, turning in his mentor's direction. Pol's head pointed toward Lan, and he managed a weak smile. "Lan, thank you."

"For what?" Lan responded harshly, scooting over to sit on his heels beside his mentor. The warmth of the fire bathed them both—and at least *this* fire smelled of wood smoke and pine, and not of burned flesh.

"That will be enough of that," Ilea snapped, swiveling her head to glare at him. "What's better, blinded or half-burned? If you'd gotten the bastard *before* Pol started to get loose, would Pol have ended up cooking with him? What happened is done, and we're all alive, and it could have been much worse."

Lan trembled anyway. The guilt was there; he couldn't exactly wish it out of existence. *He* knew that if he had just *not hesitated*—

It won't happen that way again.

Pol patted Ilea's hand. "He's done you a favor, my love," the senior Herald said, with an attempt at a laugh. "They're hardly going to allow me on a battlefield now." Elenor choked on a sob, and he hugged her with his free arm.

"'The tempest ruined the orchard, but applewood makes a sweet fire,'" Tuck quoted under his breath.

"Exactly," Pol replied.

Ilea's stare went right through Lan, as if she was daring him to display any more guilty feelings.

"Rest," she told Pol. "This is just temporary. I *will* Heal you."

But Pol said nothing, and Lan got a peculiar and gut-twisting feeling that Pol was far from confident that she would be able to do that, and was humoring her with his silence.

Oh, gods—what have I done?

Lan was happy to escape into the woods for yet more wood, although he couldn't outrun his guilt.

BY late afternoon, Pol was strong enough to drink something hot, and was insisting that he could and *must* ride.

"No," Ilea replied, although weakly; he was wearing
her arguments down.

"Yes," he insisted. "I've ridden with worse wounds
than this." He did *sound* stronger, although there was
still an edge of pain in his voice.

"And you were twenty years younger at the time,"
she responded waspishly, trying to cover up the fact
that she was weeping again.

He shrugged and sat up slowly. "I don't think I've
lost too much blood, thanks to *your* quick work. We
can't stay here. Where there was one assassin, there
may be more. We haven't any more food and no shelter. And I can see well enough through Satiran's
eyes—"

"How is that going to help?" Ilea asked.

"I can see to ride," was all he said. "Help me up."

To Lan's astonishment, with Ilea and Elenor on either side of him, he got slowly to his knees. Satiran
went to him immediately and knelt down beside him.
With great effort, and Ilea's help, he mounted. Ilea
unpacked the straps meant to hold a wounded and
unconscious Herald in the saddle, and strapped him in.

Satiran lurched to his feet; hindquarters coming up
first, then forequarters, as Pol controlled his swift intake of breath, producing the slightest hiss of pain.

He stayed quietly in his saddle for a long time, as
Satiran swung his head about. "Yes. This will be fine,
I think. Ilea, come up behind me; I might need a little
help with managing the pain."

How can he do this? Lan wondered. *He's blind!
Shouldn't he be crying or screaming or—something?*
As another stab of self-recrimination lanced through
Lan, the bandaged head swung accurately to point in
Lan's direction.

"Before you start in on berating yourself and deciding that you are the only one to blame for this, Satiran
says to inform you that you have to take second place
to him," Pol told him then offered a hand to his wife.

She refused it. Instead, she motioned to Tuck, who

made a stirrup of his hands for her. She grabbed the high cantle of the saddle, stood in Tuck's hand, and swung her free leg over Satiran's rump up onto the pillion to ride astride, one arm carefully around her husband, the other gripping the cantle for her real support. Lan and Tuck cleaned up the hasty camp, extinguished the fire, and gathered up their belongings, stuffing them any way they would fit into the saddlebags and strapping them all on the pillion-pad of Tuck's saddle.

Elenor chose to ride behind Lan, who was very much of a mixed mind about that. But he wasn't about to voice an objection; he didn't exactly have a right to. Her arms closed around his waist, and she kept sniffling in his ear.

"We're leagues from the battlefield—how did a Karsite *get* here?" Tuck said aloud. "How did he pass the lines?"

Ilea was the first to respond, and though her voice sounded controlled, Lan could see she was still white and tight-lipped. "Why drop down on us as if he was waiting for us? What was he shouting?"

"Death to demons, or something like that," Tuck supplied. "He *couldn't* have been waiting for us, could he?"

Pol put one hand on the saddle-pommel. "Let's hold a moment. We need to let others know what happened to us, so it doesn't happen to anyone else. Satiran?"

The other two Companions moved forward to touch their noses to Satiran's while Lan averted his eyes so he wouldn't have to look at Pol's face or into Ilea's swollen, bloodshot eyes.

I will never *hesitate again.*

Beneath him Kalira tensed with the effort of Mindspeaking; this was no ordinary Mindspeech; the three Companions had joined efforts so that Satiran could warn every other Companion within range of what had just happened—and they would, in turn, warn others.

It didn't take long; a few heartbeats, and Kalira relaxed again, then backed up, shaking her head and snorting.

Only Pol and Satiran remained still a moment longer, and when Satiran moved, there were no signs in him of relaxation.

:*Lan,*: Kalira said, tensing beneath him, :*There's trouble.*:

"We have—troubles ahead," Pol said tensely, as Ilea responded to the words by wrapping her arm tightly around his chest and taking the reins from him with her right hand. "We have to get to the pass. *Now.*"

"You can't—" Ilea protested weakly.

"Satiran can gallop and still keep me in the saddle," Pol replied, though it was clear that he spoke through pain. "We don't have a choice."

Ilea closed her mouth on further protests, just holding Pol tighter than before, as if she did not have as much confidence in Satiran's ability as he did.

Satiran moved into a gallop in a couple of strides with Tuck and Dacerie beside him; Kalira waited until Elenor was secure before doing the same. The headlong pace down the gloomy road left no time for thought, much less guilt, for Lan had all he could do to keep himself down over Kalira's neck and balanced, since he had to compensate for Elenor.

And it was at a gallop that they pounded into the army encampment, a candlemark before sunset.

POL wanted nothing so much as to lie down. His head throbbed, the gash across his eyes felt like a burning brand, and he wanted so badly just to have the leisure to mourn his loss—

But not now. There was duty, and there was Duty,

and Lan was desperately needed. If Lan was needed, so was Pol.

"I don't *care!*" Ilea protested behind him, as someone helped her down out of his saddle. "I don't care how much you need him! You get him a stretcher, and you take him there lying down, and *I* tell you when he's spoken enough!"

Pol wanted to protest but he couldn't. How could he? He could barely sit astride his Companion, even with the help of all the straps. He let himself be taken down out of the saddle and assisted onto the stretcher—and as his head touched the pillow there, he felt tears of relief seeping into the bandage around his eyes.

They carried him into the Lord Marshal's tent. Now Lan was Pol's eyes; all that time that they had spent linked so that Pol could show him the intricacies of his own Gift was serving a dual purpose.

Ilea allowed him to sit up, but only with the aid of several pillows and folded blankets. They sat in the tent of the Lord Marshal himself; the Lord Marshal's Herald watched them solemnly with an unidentifiable expression on his young face. This Herald Turag was a replacement. The Lord Marshal's original Herald Marak had been one of the first casualties of the stand at White Foal Pass. Not dead, but so seriously wounded that he would be months in recovering, and probably lose a leg.

"These new Sun-priests—we call them the Dark Servants—turned up a few days ago; they start in on their business at sunset, and these *things* howl around the tents all night long. Come morning, people are dead in their bedrolls—and the morale of our troops is being hammered," the Lord Marshal said. The man looked very much as if his own morale was in jeopardy; there were huge circles beneath his eyes, and new lines of strain in his face. His thick, gray hair, tied back from his face in a utilitarian tail, was lank and brittle, and his beard hadn't been trimmed or properly cared for in a fortnight.

"We're outnumbered, but more to the point, we're at a profound disadvantage," Lord Marshal Weldon continued. "How can we fight something we can't see? It strikes in the dark, and no one is safe. They've pushed us back every day, and every night we lose more men to their horrors. One more day, and they're going to break through, and they won't stop until they reach Haven."

Lan clenched his jaw, and Pol felt it, but the boy was hiding his innermost thoughts.

"Are they out there now—the Dark Servants?" Lan asked. "Can we see them from our lines?"

"They make damned certain we can," the Lord Marshal said bitterly. "You can see them—and their cursed bonfires—from here with no difficulty at all. We've tried shooting at them, but they're just out of range and no one wants to get any closer."

Pol was suddenly left without eyes—Lan cut off his link. "Please, my lord, I need to see them for myself," the boy said, then just got up, brushed through the tent flaps and was gone.

Pol didn't need to see to know that the Lord Marshal was nonplussed at this very junior Herald's abrupt departure.

"My lord—I think we had better follow him," he said, as the new Marshal's Herald stepped attentively to his side and touched his elbow.

"No—" Ilea said.

"Yes," Pol ordered through clenched teeth.

The stretcher bearers took Pol outside, following the Marshal, and they all went out into the open air.

Once outside, Pol found Satiran gently shoving the young Herald aside with his nose and taking the latter's place. Now he saw what Satiran saw—which was taking some getting used to, since there was a peculiar blind spot straight ahead, but an enormous amount of peripheral vision; one eye saw Pol, while the other surveyed everything on the opposite side. The Lord Marshal's tent stood on the top of a hill overlooking White Foal Pass, where the army of the Karsites spread out beneath them, an ugly blot upon the white snow. Although it was nearly dark, there was enough light to show more than Pol wanted to see.

Bonfires blazed along the front of that blotch, seven of them in all, and Pol saw why the Lord Marshal had called the bonfires cursed. At the heart of each was a stake, and tied to the stake was what was left of a man. Beside each fire was a person in long, hooded robes; encircling the fires at a healthy distance were other folk in the robes that Pol recognized as being the Sun-priests he was familiar with. Despite the distance, the clear air of these mountains made it easy to make out what was there—and Satiran's eyes were exceptionally keen. Lan peered down at the bonfires, one hand on Kalira's shoulder, standing as still as one of the trees beyond him.

"It's when the fires burn down to coals that the *things* start howling. The victims in the fires are no one of ours—none from the army, that is," the Lord Marshal growled. "We try and retrieve the bodies of our own before *they* can get to them, and we've seen them dragging ruffians in Karsite rags to the fires and trussing them to the stakes. I'm assuming that the victims are brigands or thieves."

"Or just some poor fellows who were in the wrong place," Pol replied. "Whatever they are—I doubt they deserved—"

The fires below them suddenly—

—*erupted.*

Once again, Pol heard that strange sound, as of something soft and heavy hitting the ground; it wasn't like thunder, nor like a tree falling, though it had something of the character of both those sounds. Now, though, he realized what it was—what the cause was, anyway. Lan had called the fires, and they had answered.

Between one heartbeat and the next, the bonfires grew—no, *grew* was too mild a word for they way they increased exponentially in size and fury. The burst outward in all directions, and they *ate* the priests around them before the latter could even twitch, licking out, enveloping them and devouring them before the eyes of their followers! The newly-roused fires roared, their voice like a chorus of wild beasts, so loud that if there was any screaming going on down there—and there must be—it was completely drowned.

In the next instant, the fires merged into one, a line cutting across the pass, effectively separating the Karsites from Valdemar. Not a chorus of beasts now—the single fire roared in a solitary voice of triumph, and as it roared, it began to move, spreading toward the Karsite tents.

Pol and Satiran stared, mesmerized. Probably everyone in the Valdemaran lines was doing the same at that moment. For the moment, he forgot his pain, forgot he was tired unto death, forgot everything but the fire in front of him. The flames clawed at the sky, reaching higher than the treetops, high as the mountain peaks on either side of the pass. Little vortices twisted in the midst of the flames, dancing along the burning ground delicately, gracefully. The fire drove forward, chasing the Karsites out of their encampment, driving them back to their own border. Pol felt the heat of it scorching his face even from his stretcher; he couldn't imagine what it was like down in the pass!

Showers of sparks, storms of sparks spun through the sky above the flames, yet none of them landed on the Valdemar side of the fire-line. Choking, black smoke billowed above the fire, yet none of it blew across to fill the lungs of Valdemarans.

:What are our people doing?: Pol asked Satiran, for nothing could be seen of the Karsite side but flame.

Satiran turned his head, and just below them ranged a sea of faces, all staring at the firestorm incredulously, mesmerized by the power and the awful beauty. No one moved; and if anyone spoke or even shouted, it couldn't be heard above the roar of the fire.

Trees actually exploded from the heat, burning pieces flying in every direction *except* toward the Valdemaran forces.

The fire crawled slowly away, and where it had been there was only bare earth and the smoldering remains of stumps. It retreated up the pass, presumably sending the Karsites fleeing before it.

:What's Lan doing?: Pol prompted.

Satiran swung his head about, obedient to Pol's wishes.

Satiran couldn't see Lan's face from this angle, but the boy was no longer standing rock-steady. He swayed a little, and so did Kalira.

That wasn't what made the hair on the back of Pol's neck stand up, though. What he saw was chilling and was probably sending a finger of fear down the spine of everyone else who could see the boy.

Tiny blossoms of flame danced around Lan, flickering in his hair, floating in the air above him, twirling on his fingertips, and the tiny fires swayed to the same directions as the greater fires.

Blessed gods!

If there was anyone who hadn't known of Lan's powers before, they certainly were in no doubt of them now.

Lan's hand spasmed in Kalira's mane; the flamelets vanished.

The boy collapsed, his knees giving out beneath him. He slid down Kalira's side to land in a crumpled heap on the snow.

And the firestorm below faltered.

As quickly as it had begun, it died, until there was nothing in the pass but burning tree stumps, glowing coals, and blackened ground.

No one moved for a long time. Although normally this would have been an occasion for cheers, the sheer and terrifying power of the fire had left mouths dry with unspoken fear—and no one dared to approach the creator of that terror.

No one, except Elenor, who shook off her mother's hand and ran to Lan's side.

Kalira first knelt, then carefully laid herself down beside her Chosen, and Elenor propped Lan's head up against her flank as Pol finally broke his own paralysis and sent his litter bearers stumbling toward them, with Satiran right beside him.

"He's just exhausted," Elenor said, looking up at her father with relief. "He needs to be put to bed, though, and he'll need to eat like a starving man when he wakes."

Pol didn't doubt that in the least and fortunately the young Herald Turag was near enough to hear her. Without being asked to, he moved to Elenor's side, carefully scooped the boy up in his arms, and carried him off, Elenor running alongside. Kalira remained where she was, she was probably just as exhausted as Lan was.

:Turag's Adan will stay with her,: Satiran said, moving in Herald Turag's wake. Pol went with him, lying flat and exhausted on the stretcher himself, one hand still on Satiran's shoulder. They caught up with the Lord Marshal's Herald just as he shoved his way through the entrance of a tent.

"He can have my bed for now," Turag told Elenor as Pol reached for the tent flap and held it open so Satiran could see inside by the light of the lamp that burned beneath the centerpole. There were several cots set up, heaped with blankets; from the clothing scattered about, this tent was shared by several Heralds. Turag put Lan down on one of the cots, and Elenor carefully covered him over, taking a cushion from nearby and settling herself on the floor beside him.

Turag backed away, then turned and motioned to Pol's litter bearers to bring him inside as well. With

Satiran outside—there was no room for him in the crowded tent—Pol was left in darkness again. They transferred him to another cot, as Turag hovered nearby.

"What happened?" the young man asked Pol anxiously. "Did that *boy*—I mean—"

"The boy is Herald Lavan Firestarter, and yes, he caused—all that." Pol waved his arm in the general direction of the pass. "Mind you, his strength comes from anger, and if we hadn't been attacked today, I don't know that he could have. . . ." His voice trailed off, and he shrugged as Turag took in the bloodstains on his Whites.

"I forgot. You were the ones that were ambushed. I suppose that would give him enough anger for anything," Turag replied, his mind clearly more on Lan and the firestorm than anything else. "I'm not really suited for this position, I—" He seemed to suddenly wake up, and looked sharply at Pol. "Sir, would you please be willing to put off your rest for a little longer? I think the Lord Marshal will want an explanation."

Ah, gods, not more—He wanted so badly to sink down into the blackness of sleep, rather than the blackness of sightlessness. "All right—" he began.

"A handful of words!" Ilea said angrily. "And no more!"

The Lord Marshal did, indeed want an explanation. The Lord Marshal also wanted a great deal of assurance that Lan was no danger to their *own* people.

Finally even Pol's patience and strength were exhausted, and Ilea's was already strained to the breaking point. "My Lord," he snapped, his head pounding and his eyes one long streak of agony, "enough."

Ilea took this as her cue to speak the words that had probably been trembling behind her lips for the past candlemark. There was *no* mistaking the anger in her voice. She couldn't revenge herself on the man that had attacked him, but she could, and would, vent some spleen on the Lord Marshal. "With all due respect, my Lord—*you* know the King's position on this boy already, and my husband is tired, wounded, and should have been in a bed the moment we entered this camp! If you must have reassurance, seek it somewhere else!"

Pol knew that tone of voice, and pictured her in his mind without any difficulty, her eyes flashing her head up, quite ready to do battle with the King himself at this moment. The Lord Marshal was no match for her in this mood.

Thank the gods. Pol didn't think he could have stayed there for another moment, and he didn't have to. With stammered apologies, the Lord Marshal sent for servants, who bustled about the tent, fetching food, drink, and a fresh brazier, emptying the tent of all the cots but the ones Lan and Pol were on, and a third one left for Tuck, who was already asleep on it.

Pol got cool cider to drink in short order, and a blanket warmed over the brazier, pain medicine, and piece of bread with cheese melted over it, along with a snow-pack laid gently across his eyes to ease the burning.

When the drug in his drink eased the pain as well, then summoned him down into slumber, he went. Willingly. With his hand clasped in his beloved Ilea's to give him comfort.

TWENTY-TWO

SOME time during the ride to the headquarters, Pol had made up his mind on several points; it had given him relief from the pain to work things logically through in that way. Losing his eyesight was *not* going to be a tragedy, and if Ilea could not Heal him, then he would simply accept that.

The events of the evening only confirmed that belief. He worked through everything as logically as he could during the ride, and during that night and the day and night that followed, in his dreams he was able to employ a technique called directed dreaming to work through things emotionally. It wasn't easy; he exhausted himself all over again, weeping for what he had lost and raging against everyone involved, including himself. But it had to be done, and quickly, and dreams were the best and least harmful place to do so. As a consequence, when he woke, he actually felt remarkably normal.

Ilea was not with him, but Satiran was, lying beside his cot on a thick layer of straw laid over the canvas floor of the tent. That was how Pol was able to see that Lan was still unconscious on the cot on the oppo-

site side of the tent with Kalira beside *him,* a charcoal
brazier warming the air between the two Companions,
and everything else that had been in the tent with
them except for a third cot was gone.

:The other Heralds removed their things last night,:
Satiran informed him. *:They've moved into a different
tent. Just as well; it would have been very crowded in
here. Ilea has been with you most of the time, until the
Chief Healer here came and chased her off to a bed
around dawn.:*

A pile of uniforms lay stacked at the foot of the
cot; Pol sat up stiffly, stripped off his bloodstained
clothing and gratefully donned a clean, new set of
Whites. The only things he retained were his boots.
"Let's go find the Lord Marshal," he said aloud,
standing up with care and one hand on the wall of the
tent, moving to the side so that Satiran had a bit more
room. "I have the feeling he needs more of that
reassurance."

Satiran got to his feet with an eye on the brazier,
once Pol had a secure hold on his mane, the two of
them went out into the cold morning. The scent of
stale smoke still hovered over the camp, and the
blackened pass below was an ever-present reminder
of what had so recently happened. Smoke still rose
from the stumps of trees, giving the oddly discon-
certing effect of dozens of black chimneys sticking up
out of the earth, as if there was an entire village un-
derground down there.

There was no sign of the Karsites. Anything that
had been in their camp was ashes, indistinguishable
from the ashes of trees and bushes; the Karsites themselves were nowhere to be seen.

:Well, given what happened to them, would you *come
back here?:* Satiran asked reasonably. He raised his
head and looked around alertly. *:I believe that the
Lord Marshal is in the command tent, and as you suggested, still in need of a level head to point out that
Lan is no danger to our side. The vista that lies below*

*us did not give him much of a sense of comfort this
morning. I can't imagine why not.:*

Well, Satiran was back to normal, at any rate.

The two of them made their way to the command
tent, and this time Satiran just poked his head inside
without an invitation, decided there was enough room
in there for him, and squeezed his considerable bulk
along one side of the map table, much to the Lord
Marshal's gape-mouthed surprise.

"Sorry, my Lord, but Satiran is necessary," Pol said
apologetically, wedging himself in on the same side as
his Companion. Satiran seized a camp chair in his
strong teeth and pulled it over to Pol, who felt it over,
then sat down in it gratefully. Turag looked at both
of them and then turned to the Lord Marshal.

"My Lord Weldon," he said, "I would like to be
put back on duty with the rest of the army."

Pol was probably as surprised as the Lord Marshal
himself; that venerable gentleman was taken entirely
aback.

"Hear me out," Turag continued earnestly. "My
only Gift is Mindspeech, which, I'll grant you, is very
strong—but I have no battlefield experience, no lead-
ership experience, and this is not the time or place to
get them at the possible expense of making blunders.
Herald Pol has both, you are known to each other,
and even more important, he is the mentor of that—
ah—*remarkable* youngster, Herald Lavan. Please, I
beg you; let me go back to a job I know how to do,
and put Herald Pol in my place."

"Hrmph," coughed the Lord Marshal, fingering his
beard and looking at Pol with speculation. "I don't
want you to think that *you* haven't been doing a good
job—"

"I know my own abilities and limitations, my Lord,"
Turag relied. "I have been doing an adequate job.
You need someone outstanding."

Meanwhile, Pol's spirits rose; the plain fact was that
Turag was right—even without the use of his own

eyes, he would be just as good a Marshal's Herald as
Marak had been. Not that he wouldn't be happy to
hand Marak's job back to him as soon as he was fit
again, but in the meantime. . . .

"Pol, how do you feel about this?" the Lord Marshal asked. "I don't want you to think this is offered
out of pity, because it isn't. You're good—you may
not be the strongest Mindspeaker about, but you're
strong enough, and your Companion can make up for
that. Being the youngster's mentor makes you doubly
valuable to me."

Pol smiled wholeheartedly for the first time since
he had lost his eyesight. "My Lord, I would be pleased
and honored to accept. Herald Turag, I am and will
be forever grateful for your generous offer and great
soul."

Turag heaved a sigh of relief. "You're the generous
one, Herald Pol," the young man replied. "And I'm
the one who is grateful! Now, if you don't mind, I'll
excuse myself and Adan and we will take ourselves
back to the unit we came from!"

Turag lost no time in making himself scarce, which
left Pol and the Lord Marshal alone for a moment or
two—until the next crisis came on.

"How's the boy?" the old man asked, betraying just
a hint of his unease.

"Still recovering. Last night's exhibition was well
out of his normal abilities." Pol felt the edge of the
table and pulled himself closer to it. "I hope you
aren't planning on more of the same, because I'll be
honest with you; I don't think he can do that sort of
thing very often."

"Ah." That seemed to be exactly what the Lord
Marshal needed to hear. "On the other hand, the Karsites don't know that, do they?"

"So any time fires start—" Pol allowed himself a
cruel chuckle. "I can't say that seeing them run like
frightened mice is going to make *me* unhappy. Well,
let me tell you what Lan *can* do on a regular basis."

Briefly he outlined what Lan had been practicing, and the Lord Marshal nodded as he listened. "We can extract a great deal of tactical advantage from having him. Not to mention that *he* can rid us of that nocturnal enemy that gave the Karsites an advantage over *us*. How long do you think he'll need to recover? We can hold camp here for another day or so, if that's all it will take."

:Kalira thinks he'll be up and able by tomorrow morning,: Satiran reported.

"That should be long enough," Pol replied.

"Excellent." The Lord Marshal rubbed his hands together and flexed his fingers. "Now, come over here and have a look at this troop disposition—"

It was Satiran who craned his neck over the map table as the Lord Marshal pushed tokens about, but it was obvious that this made no difference to the leader of Valdemar's armies. Pol bent over the table, holding his head up in both hands, suggesting possible strategies, and felt whole once again.

LAN woke slowly; Elenor wasn't sitting there next to him, but Tuck was, and he was just as pleased with that substitution. It was easy enough to tell the difference even with his eyes closed; Tuck didn't hover over him. *I guess Healers think they have to loom over their patients all the time.* When he finally stretched and opened his eyes, he discovered that there were only three cots set up in the tent, which he recalled as holding more than that.

"Hey," Tuck said cheerfully. "You're finally awake! Wait until you see what you did the other night, out there in the pass! It's pretty impressive!"

"Um." Lan wasn't all that sure that impressive was the proper word for it. "I, ah, just did what I could to get rid of those *things* the Lord Marshal was afraid of. I thought, you know, if I got rid of those Dark Servant priests and chased the rest away, that would— be a good thing—" He really didn't know what else to say at that point.

"And believe me, the entire camp is grateful! Two entire nights without bogles howling around the camp and people dying in their sleep, *and* two days without fighting!" Tuck replied, and threw him a clean uniform from a stack at the foot of the cot. "Lord Marshal wants to see you as soon as you've got something to eat. Can't just rest on your laurels, you know! More things to do, if we're going to scare those beasts back across the border for good and all!"

Tuck's solid, ordinary matter-of-factness was the best tonic Lan could have had. He scrambled out from under his warm blankets and into the chill air, stripping off his old uniform and putting on a new one. "I thought there were more people in this tent," he said, as he pulled on his boots.

"There were, but Pol and I chased 'em out," Tuck said. "Just you, me, and him—and Kalira and Satiran; no more room in the tent for anyone else. He's the Lord Marshal's Herald now, Pol is, so how is *that* for a promotion? Lord Marshal says he sees more using Satiran's eyes than any four people using their own."

Lan's throat closed in a spasm; he swallowed hard to clear it. No matter what he did, he'd never be able to *un*do what had happened to Pol. . . .

And he recalled, only too vividly, a scene that had played out in the tent before Tuck had come to replace Elenor.

"*I can't do it!*" Ilea had wept, quietly, hopelessly. "*I've tried everything I know, and I can't—I can't Heal him, and I never will! He's going to be blind for the rest of his life, and it's my fault!*"

No it isn't, *he'd wanted to shout.* It's my fault, all mine, and I'm so sorry—

"*Mother, you can't do it all at once,*" Elenor had soothed, *taking her mother away.*

He hadn't heard anything after that, for they had been outside the tent, but he had turned his face to the wall and wept into his pillow, crying himself to sleep with the pain of his own guilt.

"Anyway," Tuck continued, blithely oblivious, "Ilea isn't arguing; if the promotion sticks, Pol will never have to leave the Collegium again, and she says she'll stick to teaching."

"That would be nice for them," Lan managed to say, without sounding like he was about to cry. "Where's the food?" Guilt-ridden or not, his stomach was oblivious to his emotions, and wanted tending.

Tuck laughed and gave him a hand up, then led the way to the mess tent. The army was spread out over the expanse of several hillsides, but there were several mess tents, it seemed, and the nearest was not that far from their own camp. It wasn't a very large tent, and served mostly, it seemed, to keep the snow and wind out of the cook-fires. Army rations weren't the most elaborate in the world; Lan got a bowl of grain porridge from a big kettle, and considered himself fortunate to have that. It was sticky and full of lumps, but it was food, and there was enough honey to make it taste all right. Outside the tent, logs had been set up along the hillside to make rough seats, so that was where he and Tuck took themselves; Tuck had decided in favor of skipping a second breakfast. Lan polished off the bowl, ignoring the whispers as some of the fighters recognized him. It made him feel even more awkward and unhappy as some of them left their meals and scuttled off, though.

Joyous. I get rid of the Karsite monsters, but now I'm a monster.

Tuck kept up a bright stream of chatter, and Lan shoveled in his food, forcing it past the lump in his throat. More people crammed into the area outside the tent, staring at him and whispering, and he ate faster.

"Let's get out of here," he whispered to Tuck as he shoved the last bite into his mouth.

"Sure," Tuck agreed, and they left they stood up to leave—

—only to find that the crowd near the tent was the merest hint of the one on the opposite side of it.

Lan backed up a pace; feeling cold and queasy, he stared back into all those strange faces, wondering what they wanted. Were they only curious? Or were they as afraid of him as his own parents were? They pressed in around him, separating him from Tuck, surrounding him on all sides. He couldn't see any officers, much less other Heralds.

What do they want? Where was Kalira? Had they bound her up somewhere so that they could deal with him without her interference?

He straightened up, and faced them squarely; there was a whisper of voices from farther out in the group, but those nearest him didn't seem hostile—

The chant started in the rear of the crowd—a few voices at first. And for a few doubtful moments, he couldn't tell *what* they were saying.

Then it became clear.

"—Firestorm, firestorm, firestorm—"

More voices took up the chant.

"Firestorm! Firestorm! Firestorm!"

Now they were *all* shouting it, and the crowd surged forward, seizing Lan and hoisting him up onto their shoulders.

When they grabbed him, he very nearly passed out—

But the huge grins and enthusiasm quickly persuaded him that they meant no harm, and when he realized that they meant to thank him by parading him around the entire camp, the excitement made it very hard to breathe. More and more people joined in as Lan's bearers trotted him through the lines of tents, swelling the chanting chorus until he couldn't hear anything else. Up and down hills, even out to the sentries and back, running now, so that he hung on to the shoulders of two of his supporters for dear life!

They finally marched up the hill with him, heading

toward the command tent, where the Lord Marshal and his generals were standing, with Pol and Satiran beside them.

For the first time, he wondered what the Lord Marshal would have to say about this demonstration. To Lan's relief, the Lord Marshal had a smile on his face; he didn't look at all angry about it.

:Well, you are the hero of the Battle of White Foal Pass,: Kalira said, poking her head over her sire's shoulder. *:Be properly gracious, now.:*

Lan's supporters deposited him in front of the Lord Marshal, and finally the chanting died away. The old man took Lan's shoulders in both his hands, and turned him around to face the crowd. This was very like being on that high platform in the city square—and very unlike, for these were all people who had no doubts about him. All the smiling faces peering up at him, spreading out in a human carpet down the hillside, made him feel so wonderful he could hardly stand still.

"Fighters of Valdemar!" the Lord Marshal declaimed, his voice carrying easily to the farthest man. "Here is the partner that you have so desperately needed to drive the Karsites back to their own land! While you conquer their armies, here is the gallant Herald who will see to it that their foul demons and insidious trickery can do you no harm; that their vile monsters are sent flying back into the faces of those who would use them against you! I give you Herald Lavan Firestorm!"

Dizzy with exhilaration, Lan thought the cheering would never end.

LAN bent over the map table with the others, intent on the reports of scouts and Heralds with FarSight, although he hardly felt as if he belonged there. After all, what was *he* doing, the youngest Herald in the

Circle, in company with the Lord Marshal and all the Commanders of the army? No one else even gave him a second glance, though, so he held his tongue and tried to concentrate on the reports like everyone else.

There were charcoal braziers going in all four corners of the tent and the flap was shut tight, but it was still cold in here. The white canvas moved in the wind, belling inward and outward again. The Lord Marshal's cot and chests were pushed back against the rear of the tent, giving everyone room to stand around the map table.

Everyone except Pol, that is, whose continued weakness left him sitting while the rest stood.

"The main force of the Karsite army appears to be here," Herald Fedor said, marking a rough oblong on the map on the far side of White Foal pass with his finger. "Right at the moment, they don't seem too keen on trying the pass a second time. *I* haven't seen any more of those new priests of theirs—"

"That doesn't mean that they aren't there, however," the Lord Marshal rumbled, though he did look fairly well satisfied with the current situation. "Best guess from the ForeSeers?"

"Is that they'll move eastward, along here," Fedor replied, tracing a path along the back of the mountain ridge divided by the pass. "You can see that there's a small river running along here, enough to cut a long valley without too many obstacles, and there's something of a roadway beside it. It's not the easiest place to take a major force, but it's the best they're going to get. That's what the two with ForeSight think."

"I wish it was what they *knew,* but beggars can't be choosy about what they get," Commander Releigh sighed. "Well—look at this, if they come along *this* route here, can they come through at us *here?*"

His finger stabbed down at a minor pass, one that came out in a heavily wooded area on the Valdemar side, marked only as Pine Forest. Lan noted thankfully that there didn't seem to be any major habitations there, not so much as a village.

All eyes went to the chief scout, who pulled at his lip, then nodded. "It does go though to their route, if that's the one they take, and it's wide enough at that point to bring them through in numbers. Odds are they aren't going to give up, not at this point. For all *they* know, it was their own priests that did something wrong, and not something we did."

The Lord Marshal grimaced. "And they can make better time than we can to get to that pass; their route is shorter, with fewer obstacles in the way. Damn. Well, pass the word, we'll march in two candlemarks. Are we dealing with anything between here and there?"

"Some pockets here, here, and here," the scout pointed. "Maybe more; we'll find them before they know where *we* are." He sounded confident, and Lan knew that he should be; the Valdemaran scouts had yet to be detected by the Karsites, and brought far more information than the couple of FarSeers, who had to concentrate on areas where they already knew were worth spying on.

"Young Lavan—" the Lord Marshal said, turning to him, somewhat to his surprise. "I want you to work with Fedor and Scout Calum, here, while we're on the march. You're going to be our—catapult. Our way of getting at someone entrenched. If any of those pockets of Karsite force are well-entrenched, I'd rather deal with 'em at a distance than winkle them out like snakes in a crevice."

Lan saluted the Lord Marshal, as he had seen other Heralds do, with a quick snap to attention and a nod. "Yes, my Lord," he replied simply. "I'll need Herald Tuck as well. I can't Mindspeak while I'm—ah—working."

"Take him," the Lord Marshal replied simply, and waved Lan, the other Herald, and the chief scout off, as he and his Commanders got back to detailed battle plans.

Lan didn't at all mind being dismissed; he followed Fedor and Calum out of the tent and into the sunlight. Fedor took his elbow and pointed at a Companion near to a tent on the upward slope of the next hill. "We're over there; make sure there's someone assigned to handle your tent and supplies, then meet us there. And bring the other boy as well."

"Yes, sir," Lan replied, and the scout and Herald hurried away. Already the camp was a sea of activity as tents were broken down and supplies packed up. He ran to the tent he shared with Pol and Tuck.

Word had already been passed, and the Lord Marshal's own chief servant was at the tent with a couple of other servants, packing things up for them. Pol and Satiran were with the Commanders, of course, but Tuck and the other two Companions watched the packing with interest.

"Hey, Tuck!" Lan called, waving, as he ran towards them. "We've got an assignment!"

Tuck's face brightened, and he jumped up into his Companion's saddle; Kalira cantered down the hill towards Lan, who mounted on the run. He was secretly pleased to be able to accomplish the maneuver, especially in front of an audience.

:With a little help from me, of course.:

:Of course!: he acknowledged, as Kalira paused just long enough for Tuck to catch up. Then they loped through the encampment, which now seethed with activity, heading for the Scout camp.

Fedor and Calum and the rest of the scouts who were not currently out on patrol waited for them there, at the edge of the main encampment, supervising the final pack up of their own belongings, such as they were. Scouts tended to pack lightly.

The scout contingent was a very mixed bag. There was Calum, who looked like most of the career fighters in the Guard or army, and a couple more men and women like him, but the majority were nothing at all like professional soldiers. The youngest was no older than Lan, a dim-looking, shaggy-haired youth mounted bareback on a pony that was just as shaggy, whose main article of clothing was a rough-sewn coat of sheepskin and hat and boots to match. The oldest was a stick-scrawny graybeard, whose horse could have been plucked from the King's stable just before a parade, and whose costume seemed to consist of odds and ends he'd picked up over the course of his lifetime.

The rest of the group was just as eclectic, and included a young woman who kept close to the old man and was obviously highborn, a male and female pair of hunters (or at least, that was what Lan guessed their profession had been), a couple of farmers, and five people who were clearly civilians, or former civilians, but whose former professions weren't immediately obvious.

Calum didn't bother to introduce anyone; he just fired off some orders, and roughly half of the scouts mounted up and vanished over the next hill. The rest formed up into a rough group behind him, and with Herald Fedor, followed him over the hill at a slower pace. Tuck and Lan, with Lan leading, worked their way through to Calum's right, since Fedor was already on his left.

"Did you have anything in mind for me, Sir?" Lan asked diffidently.

"We're going to wait at the outermost picket for the army to get marching," Calum replied, with an amused quirk of his lips, perhaps at Lan's diffidence. "Then this lot will spread out and work the leading edge of the march. You Heralds will stick with me, until someone comes back with word—either of a pocket of trouble we already know about, or something we *don't*. I'll decide if it requires the—hmm— *catapult* solution. If it does—" He pointed a finger at

Lan. "You and your friend there will go with the scout to deal with it."

That seemed simple enough, and Lan nodded.

"I hope you've got an arrow in your quiver that's a bit more subtle than what you did at the pass," Calum continued. "We won't need to burn down the forest; in fact, the people that live here wouldn't appreciate that."

"I do, sir, I do!" Lan hastened to say. "I—we—we've never done anything like that before, Kalira and I. I—didn't know we could." If the last words came out in a faltering tone, Calum didn't comment on it.

"Good. That's a relief. Yo, Ben, Diera—come over here and tell the boys what they're likely to be up against, will you?" Calum waved at the old man and the young woman with the magnificent horses, who cut across a line of brush to take their places on either side of Lan and Tuck.

"I'm Diera Ashkevron, and this is Ben Dotes, our Horsemaster," the young woman said.

"Retired, missy," the old man corrected. "Barnebin be every bit the Horsemaster I ever was."

Diera smiled, and continued. "We volunteered, first thing; brought a string of horses from the Home Farm and volunteered ourselves. We don't know this country, but we do know scouting and horses, so here we are."

Diera was *not* an attractive young woman; she had a face like an abused ax-blade, but her friendly and open personality made her face irrelevant. But it was Tuck who identified her, not Lan.

"Ashkevron?" he gulped. "*The* Ashkevrons? Of Forst Reach?"

:Oh, my ears—that's the family that Herald Vanyel came from!: Kalira exclaimed as the girl nodded.

"We're all girls but my one brother, and he *can't* fight, he's laid up with a leg broke in three places," Diera continued. "There's more of us coming, but I was the only one ready to go *now*. Fancied I'd go into the Guard, and been training for it."

"And I wasna about to let her go off alone," the old man added, with a stubborn set to his mouth. "But thas' neither here nor there. We're to tell you 'bout what we know, eh? So les' get to it."

Over the next league or so, the ill-matched pair detailed the three or four pockets of Karsite strength they thought would fall to Lan to eliminate. Rather as he had expected once they began, these places were all small fortresses, manned by no more than twenty or thirty, that overlooked key passes. With that handful of fighters, the Karsites could easily delay the Valdemaran army by a day and perhaps more, if they had Sun-priests with them who could command similar powers to the Heraldic Gifts.

The excitement of being called a hero had long since worn off, and when he realized that he would be expected to burn these people out, he began to feel queasy. Kalira sensed his unease, without knowing the cause, and enveloped him in a wordless blanket of assurance.

There were hundreds, thousands of fighters in the army depending on him, who could—*would*—lose their lives if he didn't do what he was expected to do.

"You'll be able to take care of them, won't you?" Diera asked anxiously. "If you can't—it would be bad, very bad, I think."

I hesitated once. I swore I never would again, and I won't. I won't.

When that didn't extinguish the queasiness, he called up the mental image of Pol with his bandaged eyes . . . Ilea beside him, with a reproachful look aimed straight toward *him*.

That awoke guilt, but guilt was better than indecision. "Just get me there," he told Diera. "I'll do the rest."

SINCE they would travel with the Lord Marshal and the bulk of the army, Pol and his family were left at loose ends until everyone was underway. There were servants to pack up the Healers' gear, and the Lord Marshal's people dealt with Pol's. So Pol found himself with a rare moment of leisure to share with his wife, as they perched on a log with the last scrapings from the mess kettle to eat (nothing went to waste when a Guard-cook was in charge) and tried to stay out of the way.

"What's wrong with Elenor?" Pol whispered to Ilea to get her mind off of her own failure to restore his sight, although he was afraid he already knew the answer. His daughter's listless behavior since Lan had awakened was something he would have called moping in anyone else. Most of her conversation was in monosyllables, and although he couldn't actually see her face, he suspected that her eyes were reddened from secret crying.

"What do you think?" Ilea replied, with a distinct edge to her voice. "Lavan woke up and didn't ask for her, didn't look for her, didn't even thank her. In fact, Lavan hasn't even *looked* at her since your accident."

"Ah." Well, that was what he had expected. Though it would have been better for poor Elenor if her infatuation had turned to anger that Lan hadn't prevented the accident. "And you? How do you feel about the boy?"

"I am . . . mixed in feeling," Ilea admitted. "It's not the boy's fault, but I *am* annoyed with him; I wish he'd at least notice she's in love with him! But he's so thick-headed!"

"Boys that age usually are, if they're unaffected by the girl in question," Pol said dryly. "If they *do* notice, they're generally so embarrassed they try to avoid her altogether, and I can't see where that would be an improvement so far as Elenor is concerned."

"At least it would be rejection, and maybe she could stop trying to convince herself that if she just proves her devotion he'll repay it," Ilea responded, and took the empty bowl from him. There was more irritation in her voice now, and Pol guessed that she was more put out with her own daughter than with Lavan.

"It's Elenor I'm really irritated with," she continued, confirming his guess. "How much will it take before she gives up? The boy couldn't be more indifferent to her, and she's a *Healer*. She has to be able to sense his lifebond with his Companion by now!"

Interestingly, Ilea's annoyance with her daughter lessened Pol's. "She won't see it until she stops believing it isn't there," he told Ilea, and put an arm around her shoulders, pulling her a little closer. She resisted for a moment, then gave in and relaxed against him. "She doesn't want to see it, and at her age, what you *want* seems more important sometimes than what *is*."

"Gods," Ilea groaned. "We may be dealing with this for years, then. Can't you do something?"

"Lan doesn't need me now," Pol replied, after a moment of hesitation. "Not after White Foal Pass. If—*when* this war is over and the Karsites are driven back, perhaps it would be wisest to have him stationed here permanently. . . ."

Even though he was thinking aloud, the idea caught hold of his imagination, and he could see how well it would work out. Elenor would not be allowed to go far from the Collegium; Mind-Healers were too rare, and most people that needed them were brought *to* them rather than the other way around.

And for Lan, this would be the ideal place. He could be left here on circuit for the next two years with a senior Herald, then take over the circuit on his own. If the Karsites dared set foot across the Border again, Lan would send them back with their tails smoking.

"That would be perfect!" Ilea replied, seizing on his idea. "Separate them! She can't obsess about someone who forgets to even answer her letters!"

"We can't do anything until the war is over," Pol cautioned her, as he sensed her relief and enthusiasm. "A great many things could change between now and then—"

"I know—I know—"

"And during that time we're going to have to bear with her tears and tantrums," Pol continued. "Not to mention every other wretched thing that a war can throw at us."

"But I can put out my hand and feel the candle, even if I can't light it yet," Ilea replied, sounding much less anxious already. "Just knowing it's there is enough."

Pol just nodded, and tightened his arm. Sometimes knowing that there would eventually be an end to something *was* enough. Strange, that Ilea could cope cheerfully with the endless flood of injured and dying, and be thrown so off-balance by the mere heartache of their daughter.

And of her own inability to create a miracle.

"I have to go; the Healers should be packed up by now," Ilea said abruptly. "I suppose—"

"You know where to find me," Pol replied, with a final squeeze before he let her go. "You go to your duty, love."

"And you to yours," he responded, and waited until the creak of her footsteps on the snow faded out of hearing range before summoning Satiran.

:*Are we ready to join the Lord Marshal, old friend?*: he asked, as he felt his Companion's warm breath on his neck.

:*Better ask if they are ready for us!*: Satiran replied, with a mental chuckle, as he linked in with Pol and gave him sight again. :*Let's ride!*:

TWENTY-THREE

LAN lay flat on a rocky overhang, peering down at his latest target, with the shepherd Wulaf beside him. Young Wulaf was a native of these parts; he and his shaggy pony could go very nearly anywhere that a goat could go. The boy was far more intelligent than he looked, and so was the pony; Lan and Tuck marveled at how much he knew about the area, and his pony's clever ability to find trails where there was no sign of where to go. Both pony and boy were, in the main, shaggy, untidy, brown. Both surveyed the world from beneath heavy forelocks of brown hair with blond streaks bleached by the sun.

So far Lan had managed to eliminate two potential trouble spots without actually killing anyone; both of the Karsite strongholds positioned strategically above the route the army would have to travel had been simple wooden fortresses, thrown up out of local logs, and just starting a fire that the enemy couldn't put out had driven the Karsites into the open. He burned their fortresses to the ground once there was no longer anyone in them to prevent the enemy from retaking and repairing the places. Once they were no longer protected behind walls and out of local logs, just starting a fire that the enemy couldn't put out had driven the Karsites into the open. Once they were no longer protected behind walls, the garrisons retreated back south and east without even putting up token resistance.

This place, however, would prove a harder nut to crack.

Below Lan, tucked into a flat space about halfway down the mountain, was what had begun its life as a robber-baron's stronghold. Built stoutly of stone, kept even safer within high stone walls, it must have taken a very clever plan to capture it in the past. Subsequently, it had become a farm; mainly raising sheep, goats, and mountain ponies. Then the Karsites took it for themselves, and it became the platform from which they could prevent any passage through the pass below.

"Look, yon," Wulaf said, pointing at the largest building in the complex, with a round, squat construction beside it. "That war yon barn an' silo, an' reckon they bain't took out fodder an' th' like, nah?"

"Huh. Hay burns," Lan replied, shading his eyes to get a better view. "And their main gate is wood. I can take that out, and leave them without a way to keep attackers out."

"Aye that," Wulaf agreed. "Reckon ye burn all what bain't stone, they canna stay. Burn gate, food, beddin', clothes. . . . Start wi' barn, belike, an' silo."

Lan narrowed his eyes, held tightly to the dragon's bonds with both mental hands, and allowed it to wake—a very little.

He projected the power past the slate roof of the round towerlike silo, sending a little spark into it to find tinder.

He sensed it catch.

Then the mountainside beneath him shook with a deafening roar!

The mountain trembled; he and Wulaf clung to their

rocky perch and stared at each other; Wulaf's pony locked his legs in place but screamed with fear, tossing his blunt head upward, his eyes wild beneath his shaggy brindled forelock. Beneath them, a fountain of rock, dust, and snow blew out in an extravagant plume from the spot where the farm had been.

"Get cover!" Wulaf shouted, far quicker of wit than Lan; he and his pony scrambled back beneath the safety of an overhang, while Lan and Kalira followed—and just in time, as a rain of rocks, some half the size of the pony, plummeted down on the mountaintop. For a few moments, all they could do was cower as boulders crashed all around them, chipping ice and rock from their protection, landing nearly at their feet. Every time one crashed near them, the rock under their feet vibrated.

When the last pebble ticked down, a heavy silence descended. The haze of dust hanging over everything made Lan cough.

"Wha' the de'il hoppened?" Wulaf asked rhetorically, and sneezed, his eyes as round and big as prize whortleberries.

"I—don't know," Lan said, who had heard him only through a ringing noise in his ears. He made his way to the edge of the precipice on his hands and knees, testing each step before he took it, and looked down.

The fortress was gone. Where it had been was a tumble of rock shaken down from the mountain above it, a tumble that continued down the side of the mountain and into the valley, seen imperfectly through a thick cloud of dust. Lan's jaw dropped; Wulaf appeared beside him, and whistled.

"Way-ell. That be a nest'a snakes we bain't to handle," Wulaf said, with a studied air of disinterest.

But Lan could only think that once again, the dragon had feasted on blood, for no one in that fortress could have escaped.

They found their way down the mountain with some difficulty; in many places the path was blocked by boulders or small landslides and they had to backtrack to find another route. When they finally reached the scouts, however, they found that the mood was one of elation—and there was no question *there* about what had happened. They had already worked out what had caused the explosive eruption.

"It was a farm, you see?" Diera said as Lan and Wulaf waited for someone to enlighten them. "You must have ignited the grain dust in the silo."

Lan's complete bafflement prompted more of an explanation. "The dust from grain—powdered chaff, pulverized grain, bits of straw—can build up in a silo. And the silage at the bottom can ferment and give off fumes, too—sometimes farm workers drink the stuff to get drunk. Set a spark to *that,* if it's thick enough, and you get what—you got."

"Oh," was all that Lan could think of to say. "Were there any captives in there? Women? Children?"

"Probably not," Diera replied, dismissively. "And even if there were, all you did was set a spark to what would have gone off eventually anyway. Anyone poking around with a lamp, a candle, or a torch would have done the same, and they were obviously too ignorant to prevent it from happening."

Lan didn't answer; instead, he turned to Kalira for comfort. He was doing that more and more as the days passed, going into a wordless communion with her whenever he was troubled. Somehow she managed to make him feel that his guilt was no greater than anyone else's, and that he *must* go on, for the greater good of everyone in Valdemar. He found reassurance in her that he could not extract from anyone or anything else, and a bond of love that was beyond anything he had ever dreamed of. It was not that she loved him unconditionally, it was that she knew the very worst of him and loved him despite that knowledge.

One of the scouts rode back to tell the rest of the army that the way was clear; the rest of the scouts pitched camp where they were, for there could be no safer place to spend the night than one where they had cleared they enemy out beyond question.

Lan went about his chores mechanically, most of his attention bound up in Kalira. Not surprisingly, he was in charge of the fire, and he and Tuck had the task of gathering wood and water. The scouts did not use tents, so a fire was all the more important to their camp; they camped rough, often supplementing their dried rations with game hunted as they moved.

A wind sprang up above them and carried the dust away in a long, trailing plume, but nothing could hide the ugly scar down the mountainside. Lan was grateful for the evergreen trees, for their thickly needled branches hid that scar from him.

When he brought back the first load of wood, he added it to what Tuck had brought and the others had gathered from around the campsite. He built a long fire, rather than a typical pyramid; after all, he could keep anything he chose burning, and this way everyone would have a place right at the fireside to keep warm. With a careless flick of his mind, he set it burning.

Green wood or windfall, dry or wet, it all burned at his touch, and burned totally, leaving behind only ashes and producing very little smoke. He went out into the scrubby forest time and time again, returning to the campsite with loads of wood or great enormous logs. Kalira helped there, dragging the logs in tied to her girth. He laid or rolled the logs down on his fire with Tuck's help; an advantage of having a long fire, since it meant that no one had to chop the logs up to fit. Calum had charge of the primitive cooking by common consent, since he never, ever burned anything. Tonight's catch was hare and squirrel, and very tasty it smelled, too, at the point when Lan was ready to stop hauling in wood.

He accepted his rabbit hindquarter, with a mug of strong tea, and sat down beside Tuck to eat it. Stars bloomed overhead, and it seemed an impossible thing that this place could have been scarred by war only a few candlemarks ago.

Tuck poked him in the side as he sucked meditatively on a rabbit bone. "What're you thinking?" he asked. "I can almost hear your thoughts jabbering to each other."

"Nothing much," Lan demurred. "Just that I don't know what they'll do with me when the war is over."

Tuck snorted, and punched Lan lightly on the upper arm. "No fear of that any time soon. Did you hear the scout reports? This Karsite lot doesn't know when to give over!"

"And we do?" he countered with a dim smile. "But it's our land we're fighting on, so I suppose we can't give up."

"Suppose! You know we can't!" Tuck exclaimed, giving him a peculiar look, as if he suspected his friend had gone mad.

Lan didn't respond; he just dropped back into his link with Kalira, who came to stand behind him.

:When is this going to end? And when it does, what will they do with me?: he asked her plaintively.

:I don't know for certain, but you mustn't fret about it, love,: she replied. *:You will always be needed—:*

Something interrupted her. Her head went up and her eyes unfocused for just a moment. Across the fire, the same was happening with Fedor's Companion, and Tuck's Dacerie as well—and that could only mean one thing. The situation had just changed again, and they were getting new orders.

Kalira snapped out of her trance first. *:No rest for the weary, love,:* she said apologetically. *:Get the tack; we have to ride.:*

Lan had not been aware that the rest of the scouts were watching him, Tuck, and Fedor, but the moment he got up and reached for Kalira's saddle-blanket, the scouts started moving.

"Load and ride," Fedor said shortly, as he and his

Companion came back to themselves. "The Karsites are moving faster than we thought they would. Our job is to get Lan here to a point where he can hold them back until the rest of the army comes up."

Me? They're depending on me?

Although he had been told that something of the sort might happen, the words still put a chill down his back and a lump of cold fear in his stomach. *They are all expecting me to do what no one else can.* He froze for a moment, but no one else even paused in what they were doing.

In fact, if anything, they put a bit more speed on.

His fingers fumbled with the buckle on Kalira's girth until she enclosed him in a cocoon of calm. He couldn't help but feel comforted and steadied; his hands stopped shaking, and he finished his jobs just as quickly as the rest of the scouts.

They all mounted within moments of each other. "Kill the fire," Calum ordered, and Lan, who had discovered that he could extinguish fires as easily as he started them, obeyed. The flames shrank down to nothing in a heartbeat, the coals lingered a moment, then with a metallic clinking, went black. You could put your hand right into the middle of the ashen remains now, and feel nothing more than a bit of residual warmth.

"Right," was all Calum said; he turned his horse's head up the trail, and motioned to Fedor to take the lead. Companions had infinitely better night vision than horses; Fedor and his Companion would find the trail and set the pace.

The pace—in a moment, as Lan and Kalira swung into place behind Diera and in front of Ben—was going to be grueling, at least as far as the horses were concerned. It was a good thing that there was a full moon, and that the snow reflected back so much moonlight. They alternated between a fast walk and a canter, holding the latter as long as the horses could bear up. Only when the first began to flag did they slow; interestingly, the horse that failed first was generally Calum's mount, not the shaggy little pony that Waluf rode.

:Where are we going?: Lan asked, keeping himself low over Kalira's neck.

:A bit farther in than we'd planned to—you're going to be blocking a pass at the southern tip of that pine forest,: she replied. *:On the way there is one more possible Karsite stronghold, but it's another wooden fortress; you can probably burn it out as we go by.:*

True, but he wouldn't be able to do so in a way that would ensure the Karsites got out before he sent it up. *That's just too bad,* he told himself—or tried to. *They're the enemy, after all. They've killed plenty of our people without caring what happened.*

But had they? He couldn't say for certain if this particular batch of Karsites had been cold-blooded killers like those priests, or the assassin that had attacked Pol. They might just be ordinary folks, as troubled in their minds about dealing death as he was. . . .

But if he left them in place, they *would* kill Valdemarans, whether or not they were troubled afterward, so he had no choice.

Far sooner than he would have liked, the time to act came upon him.

Fedor brought them all to a halt with an upraised arm, and motioned to Lan to come up beside him. "See that little dot of light?" he asked, pointing to the mountainside. Lan sighted along his arm and nodded.

"That's the last Karsite post, and it's a wooden fort." Fedor didn't bother to say anything more; Lan already knew what was needed.

Lan gritted his teeth and steeled himself against what he was about to do to those unsuspecting Karsites in what they thought was a safe shelter. *Best to get this over with—*

"*I can't do this!*" In memory, Ilea sobbed in Elenor's arms, the recollection painfully clear in Lan's mind. *"Nothing I've tried is enough! I can't bring back his sight!"*

Never again will I hesitate.

The dragon came up in a rush of fury, and flung itself at the proffered target. On the mountainside, a fire-lily flung open hectic petals to the moon.

His mind closed to anything other than the fires, Lan let the dragon have free play. At least they were far enough away that he couldn't hear the screams. Only when there was nothing left to burn did he haul the dragon back to its lair deep within his soul, only partly sated at best.

He opened his eyes, grateful that he could not see the place where the fires had lately raged. Calum and Fedor put their heads together for a moment, then Calum signaled to the rest of them to move forward behind Fedor. He and Wulaf headed up a trail toward the Karsite fortress to make certain that it had been cleared out.

:Steady-on love,: Kalira said soothingly. *:You did just fine.:* But she didn't say anything about the men in the fortress—and Lan added another load of guilt to the one he was already carrying. *Striking without warning, without giving them a chance to surrender or flee . . . what am I becoming?*

Calum and Wulaf rejoined them some while later— it wouldn't have been at all difficult to see their trail, even with only moonlight to guide them. They weren't trying to hide it, after all; this would be the trail that the rest of the army would follow. And it was no odds if Karsites followed it as well; they'd either be met by fire from the scouts, or fire from the army.

At the pace they were setting, it was unlikely that anyone would overtake them anyway.

Lan hadn't intended to sleep in the saddle, but evidently Kalira had already made up her mind about that.

He wasn't riding anymore. In fact, he couldn't remember where he'd been or why he'd been riding. He

*and Kalira walked slowly and dreamily, side by side
but not touching, through a landscape that was too wild
to be a garden, but too well-ordered to be wilderness.*

*Beside him moved a brightness—Kalira—and it
seemed to him that she had always looked that way.
He wasn't thinking much; his mind was entirely taken
up with simply being.*

*Golden light, thick and sweet, poured down over
them. There were no other people here, but this wasn't
a place that needed people. The birds, animals, and
plants here acted as if they had never seen a human
before. And Lan himself felt so entirely swathed in
peace and loving warmth that he felt no urgency about
anything; for that matter, he couldn't remember if there
had ever been any urgency about anything. Perhaps he
had always been here, and always would be.*

Then he woke, with the sunrise casting long blue
shadows across the white faces of the mountains, the
peace fleeing from him in a rush. He could have wept
like a baby at being thrust back into this world, this
horrible war—

Then, although the peace did not return, the love
and warmth did, flooding from Kalira into him; and if
it did not return him to peace, it did comfort him.

This looked pretty much like every other piece of
country that they had passed through, but Calum
reined in his horse and looked about with satisfaction.

"Good, we've beaten them here," the scout leader
said. "Most of you, rest. Lan, start a fire. Tuck, come
with Wulaf, Fedor, and me. Let's find a place to put
our young friend."

Lan climbed down from the saddle, feeling nowhere
near as tired as the rest looked. While they wearily
dismounted, he cobbled together as much deadfall as
he could find and set it ablaze; as they gathered
around, he and Kalira brought back large branches
and logs and piled them on the roaring fire. By his
third trip, someone had put water on for tea and broken out the field rations.

He was happy enough to help himself to both, and it wasn't long until Calum returned.

The scout squatted down beside the fire and accepted a mug from one of the others. Lan supplied Fedor and Tuck with food and drink as the scout drained his mug in a single swallow.

"We've got a good spot for you, lad, and just in the nick of time," Calum told him, passing his mug over for a refill. "As soon as you get something into you, we'll take you up there and get you settled in. The Karsites will be here in about a candlemark, or so Fedor thinks."

Calum's casual statement chilled Lan to the bone, though he did his best not to show it. He gulped down his own tea, ignoring his scalded tongue, and bolted his ration bar. "I'm ready now," he said, putting on his bravest face.

:*That's my Herald,*: Kalira crooned as he mounted, and he felt a little glow of pleasure warming the chill of fear.

Dutifully, they followed in Fedor's wake; Calum remained behind to direct the scouts to a place where they, too, could guard the pass. Tuck started to follow, but Fedor waved him back. "We'll need you here, youngster," Fedor called over his shoulder as Lan turned to look back. "Lan's job will be simple enough and he won't need anyone to relay him orders."

Tuck nodded and dismounted, gratefully accepting a second cup of tea. Lan sighed and faced forward again. He would have liked the company.

:*Oh, now, you always have me,*: Kalira replied. :*Besides, Tuck always feels bad when there's nothing for him to do.*:

:*That's true enough, love,*: he replied, and Fedor motioned to him to come up beside him.

"This is a very narrow passage," Fedor said, as they rode side by side through a thick grove of pines. "You'll be able to stop them from coming through the pass directly, and we think you'll also be able to block most of the attempts to use the high passes, because you'll be able to see them from where we're putting you. And they shouldn't be able to get anywhere near you; you're going to be on a slope that had a rockslide in the last year or so, there is *no* kind of cover on it."

"Do you know much about what's coming?" he asked, rather shyly.

Fedor shook his head. "Only what they told me. All of the Karsite forces have consolidated for this, so I suppose this is their big push to break us. If that's true, winning here could win the war for us."

"Oh, I hope so," Lan said fervently. Fedor smiled, with understanding in his brown eyes.

"I hate this, too," Fedor said softly. "That's one reason why I asked to be a scout. Blood makes me sick."

"It does?" Lan felt immensely better to hear a senior Herald confess the same weakness he felt. "I *hate* killing people," he said in a rush. "I hate it! I don't care if they're our enemies!"

"And thank the gods you feel that way, Lan," Fedor said solemnly. "Anyone who doesn't is perilously near to becoming a monster. Most of these people wouldn't be fighting us if their leaders weren't forcing them, or at least telling them such lies that they're afraid *we'll* slaughter them if they don't get rid of us."

Lan wanted to talk more to him, but the trail narrowed at that point and he had to fall back to the rear. They came out of the pine trees onto the lower slope of the mountain, and began to climb it on a switchback path rising alternately through more trees and stretches of barren rock.

Only a goat, a mountain pony, or a Companion could have taken this route safely, and Lan's attention was entirely occupied by helping Kalira as she climbed by shifting his balance in the saddle like a tightrope walker on a rope. At times he hung over her neck, at others over to one side, or practically hanging off her tail. He kept his eyes down on the ground—and on the sheer drop-offs just beyond Kalira's hooves. The trail didn't always switch back under itself, and even when it did, the likelihood of catching themselves if they started down was minimal.

It wasn't until Fedor said, "We're here," that he looked up from the trail, and gasped at the vista that unfolded before him.

This place that Fedor and Calum had chosen for him was a little scooped-out section in the middle of the goat trail. A boulder might well have once been here, and been knocked out of place by that rockfall. He had a perfect view of the passage between two snow-covered mountains, and the zigzag valley below. A mist hung over the valley, glowing with the golden light of morning, filling the vale to a point halfway up the peaks. It wasn't a thick mist; he could see the sparkle of a river and the forms of trees perfectly well through it. The mist was nothing more than a tenuous, gilded veil that softened the edges of what lay beyond.

A few puffy white clouds soared just above him, barely touching the mountain peaks, and somewhere in the distance, a blackbird sang. For a fleeting moment, the peace of his dream descended on him. This was so beautiful, so peaceful—his soul opened up to it.

"Dear gods," Fedor murmured. "How I hate mankind, sometimes."

Lan knew exactly what he meant by that. This peace, this loveliness, would be shattered irrevocably in a few candlemarks, and for no more reason but that one group of men desired dominance over another.

"Make yourself as comfortable as you can, Lavan," Fedor said a bit louder, shaking himself out of his melancholy. "If you look up that way, you'll see the signs that they're coming. Then—well, do what seems best to you, and what you can to hold them back." Fedor smiled weakly. "No one knows better than I how unreliable Gifts can be."

Lan was touched and terrified at the same time by the trust implied by that order. He *could*, if he chose, do nothing, and claim that his Gift had deserted him. Not that he would—but he *could*. Of course, if he didn't, more people would die, his own people—they wouldn't die at his hands, but they would die because of his neglect.

"You can depend on me, sir," he said solemnly. Fedor saluted him, and turned his Companion's head to go back down the trail.

Well, if he was going to be here a while, there was no point in sitting on a lump of ice until he became one. Once again he gathered wood, this time from among the tumbled rocks where the remains of smashed trees poked up out of the boulders, the remains of a grove of pines that had once stood here. In no time he had a fine pile of dry, seasoned wood; he made a fire, and warmed himself at it, while Kalira sidled up to the flames on the opposite side. From time to time he looked up to see if there was any sign of the enemy, but the fire had burned through the first feeding and halfway through the second before they appeared.

A moving blackness, with bright glints of metal in the midst of it, crept forward imperceptibly at the farthest range of his vision. Again, a shiver of fear crept over him. Could he do this thing? He was only one person—

:*You can.*: Kalira came up close to him, supporting him with her shoulder. Together they watched the enemy approach, filling the entire valley from slope to slope, announcing their presence with trumpets that frightened the blackbird into silence.

Black anger roiled sluggishly in his gut; they were a pollution, a desecration of this peaceful place. How *dare* they come here with their bows and swords, their warhorns and their noise? How *dare* they trample this pristine place, churning up the untouched snow and leaving the landscape ruined?

They poured through the valley in a sluggish stream, with no end in sight; not only were there glints from their weapons flashing among them, but bands of color from banners waving among them. And a safe distance from the front, something shining moved in the midst of them; something bright gold, reflecting the sun, that almost seemed to float on the surface of the throng, bobbing in the current of humanity.

:That's a shrine to their god,: Kalira informed him.

"Oh, really?" he responded aloud, and a spirit of angered devilment suddenly took hold of them. "Well—I think maybe they can do without it, don't you?"

A whicker and a toss of her head answered his question, and he reached out with his Gift, feeling Kalira behind him, acting as a check on his power.

The shrine couldn't be solid gold, or no one would be able to move it. There was wood, even paper, beneath that gilding—and where there was something, anything, to burn, Lan would find it.

These people burn living sacrifices to that shrine. These people sent a man that took Pol's eyes. There was less grief within him now, and more anger. Much more. He turned took a breath, and loosed the dragon within him, targeting its fury on the shrine.

For some time, the army flowed forward, and nothing outwardly happened. But Lan felt the fire catch and take hold; he held it back to let it build, and then—released it.

An entire bouquet of fire-blossoms burst forth from every opening in the shrine.

Below—pandemonium.

It looked exactly as if he had dropped a burning twig into a seething mass of ants. The little black specks that were enemy fighters surged away from the burning shrine in all directions, as Lan fed the flames in glee. A few, brave believers or full of bravado, tried to extinguish the flames by tossing snow on them, but soon gave up as the heat from the shrine drove them out of throwing distance.

Would that give them pause? Would they decide to turn back, given the defeat of their god?

No such luck.

When the shrine was nothing but ash and puddled gold, the army of dots milled uncertainly for a little while—but the echo of shrill voices reached Lan's perch, and eventually the army crept forward again.

Damn. Lan frowned, anger still controlled, but quickening. He'd hoped to finish this bloodlessly. Well, perhaps he still could. He called up all his memories of the Dark Servants at the pass, of the attack on Pol, of Ilea's despair and Elenor's grief, and let the anger build higher still.

The dragon waited, not at all restless now, for it knew he was going to let it loose again, and this time it would have everything it wanted.

Just before the first of the enemy reached the pass, a wall of flame erupted before them, three times the height of a man, stretching not only across the valley but a good way up the side of the mountains on either side. And as they recoiled from the fires, he saw something that raised the hair on the back of his neck, and made his blood boil.

In the front of the army was another line of those detestable Priests, and just behind them, a line of captives tied together by the neck, frightened fodder for *their* fires.

Oh, no, you won't!

With the surge in his temper, the line of fire below leapt up, rising in height and increasing in ferocity. Even the priests were forced back by the heat, and Lan had the bit in his teeth now—he'd burn the very stone of the mountains before he let them pass!

:Hold hard, beloved.: That was Kalira, a bulwark supporting him. As he exhausted the fuel available in the line of fire, he crept it forward a pace, forcing the Karsite army back again.

:There—look there!: Without needing to be shown *where* to look, he glanced up on the side of the moun-

tain below him, and saw a party of Karsites trying to establish a way around. In a flash, he sent the dragon out to chase them down again. And it looked almost as if an invisible creature was after them; fire sprang up to bar their path, then followed them down to the floor of the valley. Lan let it spread; there was plenty of dry thatch for it to feed on, and as long as it didn't threaten the Valdemar forces, he no longer cared what it did. The tranquility of the mountains was already gone, and they had trampled the beauty under their feet. There was very little he could do that would spoil the valley more than it had been.

Movement below caught his eye, and he set his chin when he realized that the priests were building their horrible bonfires, set in a line in front of the wall of fire.

Now his temper truly rose, and in a fury, he set the bonfires alight with an angry wave of his fist, then surged the fire wall forward to engulf them.

"Bastards!" he muttered through clenched teeth. "Not here—not now! Hellfires, not *ever*."

:Gently, Lan,: Kalira warned, but he was past being gentle with people who burned innocents to call up devils. When another party tried to find a new way along the mountain opposite, he flamed the entire mountainside and grinned to see them tumbling and falling from the trail in their haste to get away.

You won't get past me, you bastards! he crowed, giddy with intoxication. *Try, and you'll fry!*

And he laughed, and spread his arms, daring them to make the attempt, while little flamelets filled the air around him.

TWENTY-FOUR

POL ached from head to toe, every muscle sore from riding, walking, and riding again, but he was well aware that every other member of the army felt the same aching exhaustion. Pushed ruthlessly until they were just about to drop, allowed a brief respite (which was never long enough) to plummet into sleep, then roused and pushed again, the army was, during most of the trek, composed of folk who only differed from walking corpses by having pulses. The Karsites had to cover roughly half the distance that the Valdemarans did in order to reach the next pass northward, and although their path was rougher, both armies were contending with the same winter conditions of ice, snow, and bitter cold. Cold could be as exhausting as marching. Huddled together in piles to conserve heat, wrapped in cloaks and blankets, the fighters hadn't had a great deal of rest during their rest stops. Cavalry and Heralds had it a little better, with Companions and horses to snuggle up to, but it was still so bitterly cold it was hard to sleep.

They'd gotten a full eight candlemarks of sleep in

a complete camp with tents and fires at their last
pause, though it had not made them into fresh men,
just less exhausted ones. Now, with four candlemarks
of marching to bring them to the pass before them,
their energy dared not flag. They daren't come up
exhausted, when no one knew what they'd face at the
end of the march. Pol knew that the Commanders had
some hope that they'd be able to get more rest at the
unnamed pass itself, but the Karsites had put on an
unexpected burst of speed, and now the army was
marching at a desperate pace to meet them. The only
creature with any hope of standing between the Karsites and Valdemar was Lavan Firestorm.

The Karsites were expected to reach the pass about
now—early morning. The Valdemaran army hoped to
arrive before noon. That was a lot of time for something to go wrong; a lot of time for Lan to exhaust
himself or be captured—

:*Lan will not be captured,*: Satiran said firmly. :*Kalira would never allow it. He is holding the pass with
surprising skill. The limiting factor is the amount of
fuel for his fires.*:

If Lan exhausted the fuel, could he still hold the
pass?

:*Kalira learned strategy from me—Lan learned it
from you. We have to assume they won't do anything
stupid.*:

Pol wished he had Satiran's self-assurance that what
he had taught wasn't flawed.

:*How long?*: he fretted. :*How long until we're there?*:

Satiran raised his head from the trail, and pointed
his long nose at one mountain among many piercing
the clear morning sky. :*That's the peak that Lan is on;
I think we will be there in two candlemarks or there-
abouts. Look! See the smoke?*:

Lan's fires produced very little smoke, burning as
hot as they did, but through Satiran's eyes, Pol saw
there was a haze of smoke around the north side of
the peak.

:He's holding a barrier across the narrowest part of the pass.:

Pol nodded; that was what *he* would have done. Depending on how long Lan could hold that barrier, and how much he had to move it when the fuel was gone, he could keep the Karsites back for more than the couple of candlemarks it would take for the army to reach him.

Candlemarks! That was too long—too long! He had to force himself to ride easily and not strain toward that far-off goal. *What wouldn't I give for a way to get us all there now!*

:I can't reach Kalira.: It was Satiran's turn to fret, and Pol felt his muscles straining for a couple of strides, until he realized it would be foolhardy to try and outrun the rest of the army.

:You already knew you wouldn't be able to,: Pol reminded him. *:If he's holding something that large, she'll have all she can do to keep him under control. I wish they'd put Tuck up there with him, though.:*

Satiran's sides heaved beneath his legs as his Companion groaned. *:But when the Karsites start breaking through—and they will—Tuck is more use down with the scouts.:*

Every horseman in the cavalry had a bowman up behind him, and these troops, with the Heralds (also carrying double, with the exception of Pol), were the vanguard of the army. They were already making the best pace they could. Horses would break down under the pace a Companion could set.

"Pol. I want you to relay an order to the Heralds," the Lord Marshal said, cutting across his thoughts and fretting.

Pol turned his bandaged eyes obediently towards the Lord Marshal riding on his right. "Sir?"

"Send the Heralds and their archers on ahead. I know that the Companions can make better time than this—and it may be that a few men in place early can do more than many men arriving too late." The Lord

Marshal paused, and then continued, "You may go yourself, if you wish."

Oh, he wished, oh—*how* he wished! But blind as he was, he would be useless as a fighter, for not even Satiran could help him aim a bow—while here at the Lord Marshal's side, he would be able to relay messages directly to the leader of their forces. "No, my Lord. My place is with you. But allow me a moment—"

:*Heralds!:* he called, his mind-voice given strength by Satiran. :*The Lord Marshal commands that you and your Companions ride ahead, carrying your archers, to hold the line until the rest of us arrive.:*

A ragged cheer greeted his order, and all across the front of the great mass of riders, silver-white Companions, and blue-clad archers leaped ahead like arrows speeding from bows. There were a hundred or so Heralds racing on ahead, with as many additional archers riding pillion behind. It was a thrilling and beautiful sight, the Companions flying smoothly over the white snow with shimmering manes and tails streaming behind them. They hardly seemed to touch the snow as they ran, with their Heralds and archers bent closely down over their backs. Those archers were the finest master marksmen in Valdemar, and instead of baggage, they all carried extra quivers. As they vanished into the trees, Pol and Satiran yearned after them, sending all the strength they could spare to speed them on their way.

LAN gnawed his lip in anger and frustration, tasting blood but feeling nothing but rage. "Leave!" he shouted at the tiny milling specks below. "Why won't you *leave?*" He sneezed as a wisp of smoke tickled his nose. He'd already shed his cloak and gloves; he wasn't cold anymore. Far from it; he didn't need the fire at his side to stay warm anymore.

He'd held them in this narrow passage for as long as the fuel for his fires was there. He couldn't burn air— well, he could, but not for long—and they *still* weren't giving up! He knew now to the thumb's length the size of the barrier he could hold, and if he moved it either farther back or farther forward where there was more fuel, some of them would be able to get around it.

Damn! He sensed the fires below beginning to flicker, and prepared to move them—

Then—a plan flashed across his mind, whole and entire, and he grinned savagely and hugged Kalira's neck, letting her see and rejoice in it a heartbeat before he put it into motion.

He dropped the barrier altogether; gave them a flicker of time to gape in astonishment, another for their officers to order them forward. *Then*—with a *whoosh* like a windstorm—he flung up a new barrier just at the Valdemar side of the blackened, burned strip where there still fuel left to catch fire. It nearly caught the foremost ones, and he laughed savagely to see them spill backward to escape being toasted.

Kalira trembled beneath his arm in reaction to his anger, but the anger was what fed the fires, and he couldn't do this without it.

Now he made a virtue of necessity, as the fire crept back toward Valdemar, allowing a stretch of climbable slope to remain unprotected on the farther side of the mountain. Would they see it? Would they take the bait?

Only fanatics would have scrambled up those tumbled, ice-covered rocks with a fire raging in their faces, but twenty or thirty of the Karsites did just that. And Lan allowed them to slip across. There were, after all, twenty or so Valdemaran scouts on this side, just waiting for a target that they could shoot full of arrows!

But before anyone else took courage from that move, he slid the barrier over, so that the gap was now on the opposite side. But this time, it was a gap bordered by cliff on one side, and fire on the other;

anyone who dared it would not be able to escape by climbing higher if the fires moved again.

No one tried it. Not all the exhortations of the officers could force Karsite fighters into the jaws of *that* trap. Lan chuckled with angry pleasure, as shouts came to him faintly from below. *Good! Fight among each other! The more you fight, the better for us!*

Perhaps it was the presence of the Dark Servants that kept the rank and file from revolting entirely against their leaders. Despite the loss of their shrine and their execution fires, the sinister priests remained at the forefront of the army, given wide berth by the common soldiers, but an ever-present threat against desertion. Perhaps there were more of them at the rear of the army; that would explain why Lan hadn't been able to get the Karsites to retreat.

:There are,: Kalira said shortly. *:The Karsites fear their priests more than our fires. So far they have been too busy preventing desertion to call up any of their demons, but if we give them a moment of rest, they will. They don't need a ritual fire—a knife to a victim's neck will do just as well.:*

More activity down below hinted that the leaders had gotten enough volunteers to agree to attempt the gap—so before they could try, Lan shifted the fireline backward and to the side again, closing the gap, but leaving the slope open once more.

"Try it again, you bastards!" he shouted down at them, keeping his anger as hot as the fires, though his knees quaked with exertion and his hands shook. He balled his trembling hands into fists and brandished them at the men below. "Go ahead and see what you get!"

:POL, we're here in good time! Lavan holds the pass— he's letting small groups through, but we can take them!:

Pol clenched both hands in Satiran's mane with relief. "The Heralds have gotten to the battlefield. Lavan is holding the pass, my Lord," he said to the Lord Marshal. "Evidently he can't keep it completely blocked, but he's managing it so that only small groups are getting through at the moment, small enough that our Heralds and archers can deal with them."

He sensed the Lord Marshal's relief, but it was only momentary. "The boy can't hold forever," came the gruff reply. Pol heard nothing more, but knew that the Lord Marshal had retreated within himself weighing alternate plans.

"Pass the word," Weldon said at last. "I want the light cavalry to drop their archers and proceed ahead at their best speed. Have the heavy cavalry take the archers left behind at their stirrups." A man hanging onto a stirrup could make better time than one without that aid; it would slow this group a bit, but the light cavalry, skirmishers all, were of more use sent ahead. They couldn't be more than a candlemark from the battlefield now.

Satiran tossed his head with excitement, as he and Pol watched the nimble, lightly-built horses, black and sorrel, chestnut and gray, leaping forward into the snow, blue-clad riders bent over their necks, blue-and-silver lance pennons lashing in the wind. Hooves thundered away into the trees ahead, leaving behind only the echoes of their departure rumbling between the mountains above, and the churned-up snow below.

The departure of the light cavalry seemed to somehow give more energy to the rest of the army. Or perhaps it was that the battle was so near at hand—but drooping heads came up, weary eyes sparked with excitement, and plodding feet found the strength to pick up the pace.

More mind-voices gave Pol information. *:He's moving the barrier again—about a hundred got through this time. No casualties so far, but we haven't had to close hand-to-hand yet, we're picking them off from a dis-*

tance. Damn! Archers through this time! One scout, three archers down—:

He relayed all this faithfully to the Lord Marshal, his voice tense with anxiety, although they both knew that these were the merest of skirmishes.

:The cavalry's here! And they're making mince of the Karsites!:

That announcement sent a shiver of excitement through the entire army as it spread from man to man. Another surge of new energy—this time born of the rivalry between light and heavy cavalry, cavalry and foot soldiers.

"C'mon, men!" Pol heard someone shout, back behind him. "Ye want them prancin' pony riders t'steal all the glory?"

A roar answered the taunt, and the pace picked up yet again, to something near what fresh men could manage. Pol and Satiran needed no urging to take a harder pace.

:They're coming through in larger groups now—:

When Pol reported that, the Lord Marshal said nothing, except, "listen; your ears are younger than mine. We've *got* to be getting near them! Can you hear the sounds of fighting yet?"

"No," Pol replied, as Satiran strained his neck forward, as if by doing so he could urge the army on faster than it was going already. "Not yet—" But every step brought them nearer, and as he strained his ears, trying to shut out the closer sounds of hoofbeats, jangle of harness, and grunting of men, he *thought* he heard something—

They breasted their way through tall, thick-grown pines that towered over their heads and muffled sound, following on the track of the mounted fighters that had gone on ahead. Pol looked up at the sky and the mountain ahead. The smoke was certainly closer.

:The barrier's too short. They're coming through!:

"I hear them!" Pol exclaimed, the faint echoes of shouts and shrieks, the clang of metal-on-metal finally penetrating the screen of trees. "They must be on the other side of this forest!"

That was enough; the Lord Marshal gave the signal to charge, and his trumpeter blared out the call, which was picked up by trumpeters all down the line and to the rear. With a roar as of one man, the army of Valdemar charged, beating their way past hanging boughs and lunging through the snow. Pol and the Lord Marshal were carried forward on the rush.

Their momentum carried them through the trees and into a huge mountain meadow, a vast space of snow clotted with fighters. There was no mistaking the curtain of flame rising to their right, nor the horde of tiny figures pouring through on either side of it. In the midst of the meadow, the light cavalry charged, reformed, and charged again, keeping the Karsites already there from forming a defensive square and from launching a volley of arrows at the Valdemarans. Their own archers nearer the pass kept up a steady rain of deadly arrows on those who were pouring through on either side of the flames.

The Lord Marshal's escort and guard shoved at the Lord Marshal and Pol, and by main force kept the little group from being carried along in the charge; they managed to get off to one side of the torrent of fighters, and a squire galloped off on his pony, searching for an elevation with a good view of the battlefield. He came back sooner than Pol expected and led them to a knee of the mountain where they arranged themselves, Pol and the Lord Marshal, surrounded by the bodyguard.

Out in the meadow, the foot soldiers mopped up the nearest Karsites, then formed up in ranks, while the heavy cavalry flattened the Karsites in mid-meadow, allowing the light cavalry time to regroup and face off the next wave coming in.

:Lan—where's Lan?:

Satiran looked up.

There, above the pass and just visible where they

stood, was a glint of fire, and a miniscule, doll-like Companion and Herald. Pol's first thought was that they were horribly conspicuous.

:So are we,: Satiran reminded him grimly. *:So are all Heralds. Especially to Karsites.:*

LAN kept the barrier shifting, back and forth, trying to keep the Karsites from getting more than twenty or thirty men across at a time. He kept glancing at the Valdemar side of the barrier as well, hoping against hope that the scouts were not on the verge of being overwhelmed.

The scouts were perched in a defensive group on high ground above the pass, where they were very difficult to come at, but commanded the field of fire. They'd taken that overlook right after Lan had let the first lot of Karsites through, and they'd seen what he was up to.

The snow was littered with quiet, black-clad figures.

The Karsites were still afraid to dare the gap at the cliff, though it was now twice as wide as it had been when Lan first opened it. They couldn't know, thank the gods, that going over the rocks was far more deadly.

The Dark Servants—I can't leave them free to act—

Now, if ever, was the time to find out if he could manage two fires at once.

He slid the barrier over so that at least he didn't have to keep an eye on the Karsite fighters, and turned his attention to the nearest priest.

:You could always set fire to their robes,: he heard Kalira say in memory.

But it was the priests who were responsible for all of this in the first place. Why should he let *them* escape harm while his own people as well as the fighters the priests led died?

That thought lent him just the extra bit of anger he needed.

A finger of flame lashed out from the barrier, and caught the nearest priest. And for the first time, he met resistance.

The flames splayed out in all directions, as if they had struck a barrier just short of the priest—who raised his arms in a gesture of unmistakable triumph.

With a roar that was audible above, the Karsites greeted this demonstration of their priests' power with hysterical relief.

No, you don't! Lan's response was a lash of rage that drove the dragon to even greater efforts. The wall of flame bulged, then erupted toward the priest, as the air itself ignited in a tentacle as thick as a house, completely engulfing the priest in his moment of triumph, even the air inside the priest's lungs afire. It was over in a flash, for Lan could not burn air for long, leaving behind a black and twisted shape on the ground, still burning with blue-and-gold flames dancing above it.

Yes! Lan laughed aloud, watching the Karsites pull away from the remains of the priest.

He glanced away to check on the scouts, and his heart leaped with joy to see the flood of reinforcements pouring out of the trees. A hundred or more strong, they paused long enough to drop more archers on Lan's side of the pass, then formed up as a barrier along the edge of the trees.

Hah! Lan moved his fire wall again; this time it took the stunned Karsites a little longer to make the run for the opening, but the opening was much larger now, and more of them got through. As they ran, Lan caught sight of another priest near enough to the wall to make a try for.

This one was quicker than the first—younger, perhaps—and as the tongue of flame licked toward him, he managed to sprint to safety. Lan growled deep in his throat, frustrated.

:Lan, he ran from you. That alone will undermine him.:

Perhaps; but he felt the same as a hawk whose rightful prey has somehow left him with nothing but a talonful of fur.

Time to shift the barrier again; fuel was running out.

This time, the gap between the cliff and the fire was *too* big and too tempting; for the first time, fifty or more Karsites flooded through, this time with the priest that had escaped Lan's fire chasing them from behind.

Straight into the arrows of the new archers, and the priest was the first to fall.

Lan jigged in place with savage joy.

But there was no denying the fact that he was losing his effectiveness. Every time he shifted the barrier, more Karsites got through; fighting below was no longer one-sided as more of the Karsites managed to survive the gauntlet of fire and arrows. It was no longer groups of fifty getting through, it was a hundred or more, and the press of those on the other side of the barrier grew as it became clear that Lan wasn't creating the impassible defense it first seemed. Nor could he catch another priest unaware, though he tried—even tried to get them two and three at a time. They were aware of his reach now, and dashed out of the way at the first sign of activity in the barrier. By now they were over the burned area on *their* side of the barrier, and there was nothing to ignite beneath them.

New motion on his side caught his attention—the light cavalry! He felt a surge of new energy as they charged through the trees and into the massed Karsite forces. He didn't dare watch for too long—but surely, surely, the rest of the army couldn't be too far behind!

Please, please come quickly—

It wouldn't be long now before his barrier reached a point where the mountainsides on both ends fell away, and it would be totally ineffective. Already the

scouts and the Valdemaran archers had been forced
to move to keep from being overrun by the flames.

Damn you! Leave us alone!

Oh, how he hated them! With every glimpse of a
blue-clad body lying still in the snow, he hated them
more!

:Easy, Lan—:

He was beyond Kalira's cautions now; the flamelets
that had danced up and down his body flickered over
him in a frenzy, filling the air around him, and even
skimming over Kalira's back. She didn't seem to notice; there was a red glow of flame in the back of her
eyes, and every muscle was tense with strain.

What's that?

A roar from below—a hundred thousand voices
shouting in triumph and challenge—

They're here! There're here!

He had to let them know that he saw them—and
that he would still be fighting up here as long as he
could stand . . . and that he was about to drop the
barrier as ineffective.

POL tried calling again. *:Lan! Lan!:* Could the boy
see them? Did he even notice anything but the flames?

A flicker at the edges of the barrier warned him,
just on the periphery of Satiran's vision. It flickered
again, in a pat-tern of three—two—three. *Lan's using
that to catch our—my—attention.*

*:Yes, since there's no one with the boy to relay what
he's about to do,:* Satiran agreed. *:I think he wants to
drop the fire-curtain.:*

"The barrier is coming down!" Pol shouted, and
repeated the warning in Mindspeech.

:The fire-curtain's collapsing! Ware!:

"Archers, fall back! Form arcs!" the Lord Marshal

bellowed, and Pol and the trumpeters repeated that order as well.

Can Lan see this? he wondered desperately, and MindSent with all his strength. *:Lan, look down here! Give us time to get into position!:*

He could only watch and hope that Lan had heard him—or was already watching.

The archers moved farther up on the mountainsides, or dropped back behind the foot soldiers. The cavalry, light and heavy together, dropped away from harassing the Karsites and withdrew to the right and left flanks. The foot soldiers moved up, archers behind them, and made a solid, defensive line ten men deep, planting their pikes firmly in the churned-up snow to await the Karsite charge.

Abruptly, the flame-curtain flickered and died.

For a single, dumfounded moment, the Karsites stared at their enemies, with nothing between them. There was a moment of utter silence; not a man moved, as the two armies stared at one another.

Then one of the priests at the front of the group howled something, and the Karsites charged.

Screaming curses, the Karsite forces poured through the pass in a solid, black mass. *Why* had they chosen black as their color? Was it to contrast with Heraldic White? To stand out against the snow? To intimidate? It was working; Pol sensed the Valdemarans shrinking back a pace from the flood of blackness that threatened to wash over and drown them all.

There seemed to be no end to them; if the Valdemar forces hadn't already been at a fever pitch of excitement, the torrent of screaming men coming at them would have terrified even the hardiest. They surely outnumbered the Valdemarans by three or even four to one.

It terrified Pol. It took all of his willpower to sit calmly on Satiran and relay the Lord Marshal's orders.

They couldn't count on Lan. The boy was surely

exhausted by now, and unable to do anything but watch.

Before more than the first rank of Karsites had poured across the blackened line marking where the flame-curtain had been, fires flared *again*—but this time, in tall candles of fire that erupted violently out of the snow, then died to nothing, only to flare up somewhere else. They sprang up right in the path of the Karsites—they didn't do much damage, if anything, but they *did* break up the Karsite charge. Although a few fighters caught fire, rolling in the snow quickly put out their flaming clothing—but no man, having seen his fellow go up in flames, was quite as enthusiastic about running at the Valdemarans full-tilt, at the risk of plunging into one of those fire-fountains.

Then, as the push from behind forced the front ranks onward, Lan changed his tactics.

He brought up the curtain again, farther in toward the Valdemaran lines, but this time it was for a very different purpose.

He caught a full line of a hundred Karsites or more square in his fire-line, and *he held the flames on them.* Even over the din of battle, Pol heard the dying screams of those men as they tried to escape the inferno and failed, and his stomach lurched as the smell of burned flesh came to his nose.

"Oh, dear gods—" Pol breathed. Lan had not deliberately called fire down on Karsites and burned them until this moment. *What had made him do it now?*

The wall of flame died, leaving behind not only a blackened strip of land, but charred and twisted corpses lining it. The fire-curtain was gone, but this time the Karsites held back, despite the threats of their priests. They seemed to have figured out that if they were within the stretch where the curtain had already burned, they were safe.

For a moment, it looked as if the Karsites were at an impasse. They couldn't retreat, but they were not going to charge, either. Then a trumpet sounded an unfamiliar call, the priests screamed an order, and they started coming on again. But now, they charged forward in small groups of twenty or thirty, too many groups and too widely separated for Lan to stop with his flame-wall.

Lan wasn't going to give in. He sent up fire-fountains again, intercepting as many of the little groups as he could, and once again shrill and terrified screams rang out above the general mayhem. No one but Pol seemed disturbed by this change in Lan's tactics; in fact, from the Lord Marshal's muttered comments, and the shouts of encouragement out on the field, there were plenty who were cheering him on.

What's happening up there?

Satiran, prompted by Pol's unease, looked up to the place where Lan and Kalira perched. It was only the sense that something was wrong with *Lan* that prompted him to look up there, nothing more.

But he saw—or thought he saw—something.

He wasn't certain what it was—a movement among the rocks where nothing should have been, perhaps, a man-shaped shadow behind them. He might not have seen anything—he *did* have a touch of ForeSight along with everything else, and it might only have been that ForeSight that warned him.

All he knew was that suddenly his unease turned to horror, he *knew* that tragedy was a heartbeat away. Terror closed his throat, tasting bitter, and he tried, desperately, to project a warning into Lan's impervious mind.

:Lan! Lan! Hide! RUN!:

LAN was the dragon.

Driven by hunger that only increased with every new victim, he hunted the battlefield, pouncing on target after target, reveling in the screams of the hurt and dying, then going on to new prey. Flame filled his mind and soul, burning with unholy joy, insatiable rage. He had but one thought now—he would burn the world, if that was what it took, until the last of the enemy was ashes.

ALTHOUGH Satiran's eyes were fixed on the pair above, Pol wasn't the only Herald to *know*, suddenly, that catastrophe was about to strike.

The battlefield was disordered; now relative disorder became absolute chaos.

"The *hell!*" the Lord Marshal exclaimed.

All over the field, Valdemaran trumpeters called retreat, though no orders had been given for retreat. A dozen Mindspeakers bombarded Pol with panic-stricken calls to flee, then broadcast their warnings at full strength to anyone who could hear. Valdemaran fighters across the battlefield broke off their engagements and fled in no order at all, while beside Pol the Lord Marshal sputtered.

Pol stretched out his arm to Lan and Kalira, in a futile effort to stop what was coming.

A dark speck flitted across the distance from a shadow that might have been man-shaped, to the young Herald. Only a speck, insignificant—

—*WHAT?*

Something grabbed Lan and *shook* him. Distracted he glanced aside—

Just as a heavy crossbow bolt thudded into Kalira's chest.

All breath driven out of her, she could only gasp

and throw up her head in pain, but her mind screamed.

:LAN!:

Too late.

She flung her head around to stare at him as he scrambled to reach her.

Her eyes clouded with agony as she collapsed; but her gaze caught and held his. He reached frantically for her, but he couldn't hold her. A greater power than his wrenched her away from him.

He only heard her, fainter with each word, as her eyes closed for the last time.

:—I—love—you—:

Then she was gone.

UP on the mountainside, the tiny figure of the Companion crumpled, and fell with a single, heart-rending cry that Pol heard only in his mind, a cry cut off with the finality of death.

Up on the mountainside, Lan crumpled beside his lifeless Companion.

It was not Mindspeech as such, that cut across the brains of every living creature in and around the battlefield. It was a mental howl of anguish, of grief, of terror—it drove tears into unwilling eyes and sent some to their knees in the snow. It triggered the worst memories of every person on the field—Valdemaran and Karsite alike.

Pol clasped both hands to his head as the cry cut into his very soul. It went on, and on, a grief like a sword cutting him in a million pieces.

—and it was not sane.

Then—Fire, elemental, unstoppable, came to earth.

It exploded down out of the sky and drove down on the Karsites like the very hammer of the gods. It spewed up out of the snow to meet the down-rushing flames of the sky-fires. In a single moment, it transformed the entire side of the mountain to a furnace, an inferno, and it spread from there faster than a man could run.

—gods—

Now Pol knew why Heralds had seized trumpets to sound retreat, and mind-voices had sent the Valdemaran forces scattering for their lives. ForeSight had given them the warning that something apocalyptic was about to happen, but not what, nor in time to prevent it.

FIRE exploded down the mountain, an avalanche of flames.

Lan lay over Kalira's body, the dragon unleashed, unfettered, and free to ravage as it willed. All of his grief, rage, and hatred filled it and gave it a power beyond anyone's direst nightmare.

So long as it consumed him, he was beyond caring.

:Wait for me, beloved. I'm coming. But first, I will avenge you. . . .:

He closed his eyes, gave himself over to the dragon, and set the world, and himself with it, aflame.

KALIRA!: Satiran, lost in his own grief, shuddered once, then lifted his head to the sky and keened out his loss to the heavens.

Pol wanted to howl with him. Kalira was dead, struck down by a Karsite assassin's arrow. Lavan Firestorm had nothing to help him control his powers—and with the death of his lifebonded Companion, no reason to want to—no reason to live.

He needed no fuel for his fires now; he could burn

the rock of the mountains if he chose, burn the very air itself.

The fire had a voice—it howled like millions of damned souls. It had a mind, and the mind was mad. Karsite and Valdemaran alike scrambled to escape the battlefield before the fires caught them. From the ground to the mountaintop, there was nothing but flame. Fire churned and roiled, fire roared and shrieked, fire filled the sky. Vortices of flame twisted, hellish dancers with the grace of a streamer in the wind and the appetite of a demon—

Even as Pol watched through his Companion's eyes, Satiran's voice keening on and on in his mind and ears, those nearest the flames were suddenly sucked up by a wind or the firestorm itself inhaling, pulled off their feet, into the air, and then, screaming, into the maelstrom.

—gods—

The maelstrom pulsed once, like a spasming heart, and enlarged again. Bits of burning debris rained down around him, kicked out of the top of the vortex. Fiery twigs. Ashes. Coals and cinders. The bright, glowing skeletons of pinecones. Once, horribly, a burning, human arm that landed with a dreadful sizzle in the melted snow beside him.

Pol could only sit, and stare, numb with horror, paralyzed with grief. Satiran keened on, trembling, oblivious to anything else.

Something tugged at his arm, nearly pulling him from the saddle. "Come on, man!" the Lord Marshal's squire shouted in his ear when he didn't respond. "Come on! If you stay here, you'll cook!"

The heat from the inferno was incredible; the snow turned to steam before Satiran's eyes, the ends of the pine needles around him curled up. The firestorm pulsed again, spasming, and expanded once more.

"Come on!" the squire shouted again to Pol. Then, heroically, he seized Satiran's bridle and forced the Companion's head around. "Come *on,* you stupid

git!'' he screamed, kicking Satiran in the side.
"Move! *Move!*"

Neither of them could move on their own, but the
squire was not to be denied. He tied Satiran's reins
to his saddle, and his pony dragged Satiran behind
him by main force as they joined the flight to safety.

With a terrible moan, Satiran broke the connection
between himself and his Herald, leaving Pol in darkness, intolerable anguish, and bleakness of heart and
soul to match the dark behind his eyes.

He simply clung to the saddle, bent and broken,
weeping hoarsely, as he had not been able to weep
for himself, and it seemed to him that he would never
find his way out of the darkness and the grief. His
tears scalded his eyes, soaked through his bandage,
and still they fell; he tasted their salt on his lips, bitter
and harsh, but no more bitter than his heart. Satiran
trembled under his legs, shaking as if the Companion,
too, sobbed.

How long he sank in that hell of grief, he didn't
know; suddenly, there were hands on his arms and
voices urging him to dismount. The roar of the fire
was gone, and the air, cooler now, was scented with
scorched rock. He slid off Satiran's back into arms
waiting to catch him.

Ilea's arms.

He crumbled into her embrace, and gave himself
and his grief into her care.

Satiran collapsed beside him; Ilea helped him down
to the snow where he blindly groped for his Companion's neck and wrapped his arms around it as Ilea
cradled both of them, crooning wordlessly.

Out of the chaos of shouting and noises around him,
a single voice cut through his grief.

"Pol! Pol!"

He raised his head, responding to the frantic sound
of Tuck's voice.

"Pol!" The boy's hands were on his shoulders, pulling at his tunic, despite Ilea's attempts to stave him

off. "Pol, what happened to Lan? They dragged me away and won't let me go back—this Guard here won't let go of me! What's going on?"

He tried to answer, but could not get a word out of his throat.

But an answer came.

Pol had heard the Death Bell in the Grove toll before; he knew the sound of it as well as he knew the sound of his own name. But he had never before *heard* it with his heart—and never at such a distance from Haven.

Every Herald across the land must be hearing it—

It vibrated through him, somber, throbbing with unshed tears, and there was no doubt in his mind *who* it tolled for. Tuck collapsed beside him with a sob, and Ilea held them all while they wept until they could weep no more.

IT was four days before Pol could stand and walk again, four days before Satiran, surrounded by all the comfort the rest of the Companions could give, was able to act as his Herald's eyes again. Four days of sleep and grief, while the shattered army of Valdemar pulled itself back together, and put together the pieces of what had happened.

The only Karsite officer to survive the inferno had confessed that once the source of the hellfires had been identified, a handpicked set of marksmen had been sent up the mountain with orders to shoot, not the Herald, but the Companion. The priests wanted the secret of the fires, and they knew the quickest way to disable a Herald was to slay his demon-horse.

The firestorm raged for no more than a candlemark, but in that short time, it destroyed everything on the mountain and in the pass below it. Where there had been a pine forest, there was now a totally lifeless plain, with no sign of *anything* but ashes. No remains, no smoldering tree stumps, nothing. Everything from the ground up had been reduced to gray-white powder.

As Pol woke on the morning of the fifth day and struggled for the first time to sit up, Ilea told him all this in a few stark sentences.

"Elenor?" he ventured.

"We were in the rear, with the baggage," Ilea pointed out. "I don't think she had any idea what was happening until the firestorm—and I don't think she even realized *then* what had happened until she saw you and Satiran."

Pol fumbled for her hands, and found them clasped tightly together in Ilea's lap. He coaxed them apart. "And?" he prompted hoarsely, his voice ravaged by weeping.

"And—she's taking it hard." That, and the softening of Ilea's stiff pose, bringing her into his arms where she finally wept, told him all he needed to know.

"I know this doesn't help now—but she'll recover, though I doubt she thinks she can. We all will. . . ." He held her close, and let her cry herself out, she who so seldom wept, and more often for others than herself. He let her cry until *she* was exhausted, which took so little time that he knew she had been staying sleepless at his side until this moment. Then he made her curl up in his place, and stayed beside her until she slept.

:Satiran?: he called then, hesitantly, not certain that he would have an answer.

:Coming,: was the reply, lead-heavy with mourning, but at least it was a reply.

He heard plodding hoofbeats outside his tent, then, blessedly, vision returned, the view of his tent from Satiran's eyes. He stumbled to his feet, through the tent flaps, and flung both arms around Satiran's neck.

When they both emerged from a sea of mourning,

and took notice of the rest of the world again, Satiran rubbed his soft nose against Pol's cheek, tasting his tears. *:They want to send Fedor up the mountain this morning,:* Satiran said, hesitantly. *:To see what is there. Tuck wants to go, and Elenor, and the rest of the scouts. Ilea is going with Elenor. Do you?:*

He already knew that Satiran did, and he did not want his oldest and dearest friend to go alone. *:Of course I do,:* he said instantly.

The sad little cortege made its way up the side of the mountain, unimpeded by snow, ice, or trees. It was the most utterly lifeless place that Pol had ever seen; not a bird, not an animal, not even an insect. The total silence made the ears ring and made Pol shiver.

But when it came to time to climb the last bit of the trail, there was a problem; the heat of the fire had cracked the rocks and made the trail unstable, and too dangerous to try.

But Wulaf, the shepherd-turned-scout, stared at the trail with his jaw set. "Gi 'e me yon box," he told Fedor, who wordlessly brought over a beautifully carved box that had held the Lord Marshal's Seal until that morning, and handed it to him.

The boy stuffed the box into the front of his sheepskin jacket, dismounted from his pony and took his shoes off. Before anyone could move, he was scrambling over the rocks above the trail and out of sight.

He was back before Pol could start to worry.

" 'Tis same as th' pass; naught but ash," he said quietly, taking the time to put his sheepskin boots back on over his stockinged feet. Wordlessly, he handed Fedor the box.

Elenor sobbed into her mother's shoulder; Tuck's red cheeks were lined with tear-streaks.

He didn't open it, and no one asked him to. All eyes turned to Pol, who swallowed down his tears.

"Well," he said at last. "Let's take them home."

EPILOGUE

POL and Ilea picked their way along the goat trail to the place on the mountain where Lavan Firestorm and Kalira had died, with Satiran pacing alongside, though Pol no longer needed his eyes. Intensive work by the Healers had given him back the use of his own, although his vision would never be as good as it once had been. He never knew from what sources of strength Ilea found the way to Heal him, nor from where the Healers she recruited got the knowledge they needed to do so. But he could see again, however imperfectly.

It was the same procession that had gone up the mountain to be thwarted by the unstable trail, for the shepherds of this area under Wulaf's direction had worked all these months to make it safe for them to return. But there was a new addition, for Tuck had brought Lan's sister Macy, who rode pillion behind him.

Elenor had accepted no consolation whatever for about a month—but then, surprising even herself, she came to the end of her tears. Perhaps it was because it was difficult to sustain the illusion of an undying love on notes like, "Thank you for the headache potion, but can't you make it taste any better than *that?*"

Macy and Tuck helped her and each other, and Macy moved out of her parents' home and into the Palace as a member of the Queen's household—one of Queen Fyllis' personal embroiderers. It was a more comfortable place for her than her own home, and kept her near the people her brother had loved best.

When spring brought life back to Valdemar, and Wulaf sent word that the trail was safe, there was no question that they would all go. And now, once again, they rode single-file through the blasted pass. The ancient pine forest was completely destroyed, from the tallest tree to the earth itself, to a depth of the height of a man, as an experimental trench proved. Nothing would grow in the soil; perhaps nothing ever would again.

There had been no sign of Karsite activity anywhere along the Border. Then again, so much of the army and priesthood had been destroyed, it wasn't likely that *this* Son of the Sun would be able to hold his preeminence much longer.

The trail they rode now, although they had to go single-file, was far from the goat track Pol had first seen. This was a real trail, lovingly smoothed by hand and pick, that even an aged pony could follow. *The shepherd's memorial to the one who saved us,* Pol thought, with a painful lump in his throat. There might be more impressive memorials, but never one created with more sincerity and heart.

"Here," Wulaf said, pausing in a shallow, dishlike depression halfway up the side of the mountain. "This be the place."

Pol squinted, peering down at the pass, wondering what had happened up here. *Something* had happened to Lan even before Kalira's death. A touch of encroaching madness, perhaps? *If I had been here, could I have prevented that? And if I had been here, wouldn't Satiran and I have detected the marksmen, even cloaked by the Dark Servants?*

He, Tuck, and Satiran had pummeled themselves with might-have-beens for the past several months, with no answers to be found. It didn't look as if he would find any in this barren place either.

"Look!" exclaimed Ilea behind him.

He turned, to see her cupping something between her hands, down in the ash. He knelt down beside her.

It was a seedling, a tiny speck of green with two miniscule leaves.

"It's a firecone," Ilea said softly. "They're very rare, even here—it takes a fire to free the seeds from the cone, and even then, more seeds burn than ever sprout. It must have been here for years before—"

"Before it was freed," Pol finished for her, looking at the tiny thing with wonder. "But how it got here, of all places—"

Ilea shook her head. "There's no way of telling."

"Should we take it back with us?" Elenor asked, and a momentary thought of transplanting this bit of life and hope to the grave that held only ashes flickered through his mind.

"No," Ilea said. "It would never live. It needs ashes, mountain winds, and winter storms to thrive. Look—" she scraped the ashes away from the bare rock, to show how it was cracked and crazed. "This is what it needs; it can send its roots deep into the rock, and rise out of the ashes tall and strong." She patted the ashes around the seedling with a motion that was almost affectionate, then carefully dripped water into the mound of ashes from her water bottle. "It needs adversity to thrive."

He held out his hand to her, and she used it to get to her feet. "Something like Valdemar?"

She smiled, and if her smile held sorrow, it also held joy. "And—something like us. All of us."

:All,: Satiran confirmed. :All of us, together.:

For one last moment, they looked out over the mountains, wondering when adversity would cross them to find Valdemar again. *It won't be soon. Lan bought us that—peace, for a while.*

"And thanks to Lan, for a time we will have peace to grow," Tuck said, with unusual eloquence.

Pol nodded, and moved to put his arm around Tuck's shoulders. "Yes we will," he replied. "Just like this little tree. If it hadn't been for Lavan Firestorm, neither we nor the tree would still be here."

They stood together in the silence for a long time, each of them with his own thoughts. Wulaf was the first to move, collecting a handful of pebbles, and carefully ringing the seedling with a protective barrier.

Fedor did the same, then added the silver arrow-pin of a Royal messenger, burying it in the ash within the circle. One by one, they each built the wall of protection a little higher and thicker, some adding tiny keepsakes to the ashes. When Elenor's turn came, with only Pol and Ilea to go, she added a covering of paper torn into the tiniest of scraps, then wetted with water from her water bottle, to the top of the ashes to keep them from blowing away. Pol had a fairly good idea where the paper came from, for she had brought Lan's few notes with her, and he had noticed her shredding paper as the others made their offerings.

Ilea simply held her hands over the seedling, giving it the strength only a Healer could impart.

Then it was Pol's turn.

He slipped over the seedling a thin bracelet that Macy had made for him, braided of his hair and Satiran's together. He hadn't come here with the intention of leaving it, but—it seemed right.

He straightened up, and met the eyes of each of the others in silence. Now, he sensed that some deep wound in each of them had begun to heal. It was not closed yet—but in time, they would all be whole.

"Time to go," he said quietly, and they turned their faces home.

Mercedes Lackey

The Novels of Valdemar

MERCEDES LACKEY
& LARRY DIXON

The Novels of Valdemar

DARIAN'S TALE
☐ OWLFLIGHT   0-88677-804-2—$6.99
☐ OWLSIGHT   0-88677-803-4—$6.99
☐ OWLKNIGHT (Hardcover)   0-88677-916-2—$6.99

Two years after his parents' disappearance, Darian has sought refuge and training from the mysterious Hawkbrothers. Now he has opened his heart to a beautiful young healer. Finally Darian has found peace and acceptance in his life. Until he learns that his parents may still be alive—and trapped behind enemy borders . . .

THE MAGE WARS
☐ THE BLACK GRYPHON   0-88677-804-2—$6.99
☐ THE WHITE GRYPHON   0-88677-682-1—$6.99
☐ THE SILVER GRYPHON   0-88667-685-6—$6.99